CW00514973

The dedication of this book goes to the most radiant p
know, because you never stopped believing in me and
always a good friend.
Thank you, Catherine Morrissey, for everything.

Chapter 1

The Siege of Treforledge

Yellow Shade filled the sky projecting its warm rays of light onto the three islands of Treforledge. Islands that gave homage to the Blue Wizards. Creatures of magical intellect that represented the colour blue as their brand and name. The wizards who live and serve under the Lord of Treforledge were streaked in blue since the shade they were ripe. When they reached the end of their Ripeling stage they were permanently branded with the ancient colour. When the wizards of Treforledge were branded, blue would forever shine through that wizards' eyes and hair. Wizards in higher ranked positions such as generals or Seconds, were given moonlight feathers to show they were examples to be followed and part of the six sworn guards of the Lord of Treforledge.

The three islands the Blue Wizards lived on are joint and made up the Kingdom of Treforledge. The island to the west is Tree Island, that is populated with orchards of Drop Trees. The island north of Tree Island was Suala Island where training camps and shelters were stationed for young Ripe's to study the lore of crafts. And to the south of Suala Island stood the pinnacle of the three, Crafters Isle.

Crafters Isle was where the Lord of Treforledge lives along with the wizards of the Tree Bine Council. The Crafters who forge many objects from stones and rocks live among them, their unique qualities giving them the same privileges as the high ranked of the kingdom. The wide range of mountains on the coast of Suala Island offered the Crafters unlimited supplies for crafting and mining rocks to forge protective armour, shields, and gems and thanks to the wizard's own brand of magic enhance their fashionable objects with abilities that repelled anything.

Since the dawn of the wizards, it was always known that the Blue Wizards were best equipped out of their six coloured counterparts to mould and manipulate stone. When the Lands of Light were won and the domain of wizards ruled over all lands, the three islands of blue were given to the elder leader of the Blue Striped Army by King Dirm the Bronze for their services to the crown.

It didn't take the Blue Wizards long to have their workstations built and operational throughout the islands. But their desire for further extension pushed these curious wizards beyond their sanctuaries. Expanding their reach of the three islands, they discovered a tail? That trailed all the way to a large unoccupied mountain on the coast of Suala Island. Dwelling deeper into the heart of the mountain, the Blue Wizards unearthed hardened rocks and diamonds that had the capabilities to harness the cosmic energies of the Eight Shades of Sky.

The discovery of this mysterious mountain sparked the idea in the former Lord of the Blue Islands mind, Micja the Blue, that uniting the three islands and forming them into a United Kingdom was the best way forward in securing their legacy status. But Micja was the Chieftain of Crafters Isle and was powerless to persuade the other chiefs to pair their lands, but the thought of uniting the islands was so strong in his mind that Micja proposed the idea when he called a gathering between the three tribes.

During many gatherings after Micja's proposal the tribes of the Blue Islands and the three chieftains finally agreed that as a United Kingdom they could form their own council and untie themselves from the rulings of the Golden Kingdom. Agreements were made and unified under new liveable laws with all three chieftains agreeing and sealing their agreement by bonding their oaths within an unbreakable magical seal. For his brave attempts in forming this union and being a wise leader, Micja was crowned Lord of the United Islands of Blue. After Micja's coronation the bold lord invoked his first official command and ordered the Crafters of Crafters Isle to begin the structure of wooden roped bridges so that wizards could pass through each island on foot and cement their unification as a United Kingdom. The Crafters designed many roped bridges and magically enchanted them so that they wouldn't collapse due to overloading and laid them neatly across the coasts of every island, connecting them into a kingdom for the first shade in history.

The bridges were Micja's way of sustaining a professionalised peace between the clans of each island. Micja went on to name his newly fashioned kingdom and held a ceremony at the foot of the Twins. Announcing to all wizards that the union of the Blue Islands was to be celebrated for cycles of shades to come, and as lord it was his duty to elevate his followers, and that a stronghold such as theirs should have a name to be reckoned. Micja christened the three islands of blue, Treforledge. And to this shade the name has remained even after Micja perished from war wounds. Lorneid his disciple and close friend said after his own coronation that in Micja's memory, Treforledge will always be the name of the Blue Islands and sealed the name with a permanent enchantment that only he could unseal.

Five hundred cycles had passed since Treforledge's name shade and with it an increased growth in wizards which made evacuation that much harder as young Galli the Blue was finding out, as the sound of the annoying Sirens echoed throughout the Blue Islands. Their screeches spreading a panic Galli had been hoping to avoid. Having read, reread, and read again the history of Treforledge, Galli put the book back on the table she was leaning against and left the cave, hoping this evacuation didn't take as long as the last.

''Rac! make sure those straps are bound against the bridges borders or we'll be hurled side to side,'' called Galli after a young Ripeling. ''What is your staff for? You nitwit,'' she ushered, throwing an annoyed look at the Ripeling opposite Rac, who was using his hands instead of magic to tie thick lined bark to steady the rocking bridge.

The Ripe's carelessness added another strain to Galli's frustration due to her hatred for evacuation and the exhausting burden of having so many responsibilities on her shoulders. Gloom had injected itself into the chilly air flowing through the Blue Islands. As it normally did when the tides approached from the south. Workloads were doubled, Ripelings were forced to abandon their studies to lend a hand as crowds of cloaked wizards rushed in frantic panic to cross the roped bridges that would lead them to the high grounds of Crafters Isle.

The echoing sounds of the Sirens cry rang annoyingly in Galli's ears, making her face tense as she passed many groups of anxious looking wizards who were hooded and cloaked in heavy midnight blue garments, their fear visible even from under their long-shadowy hoods.

"Who could blame them especially after what happened the last shade when tidal waves paid Treforledge a visit," thought Galli, trying not to stare too long on each anxious face she passed.

It was indeed the reason so many wizards were making haste, to avoid been left behind to endure the coming tides. Crafters Isle was the only island among the three that had the abilities necessary to withstand the incoming tides. Thanks to the islands high grounds been over five hundred feet in length and width and having a rock shell coat able to withstand any wave lashed at it.

Galli remembered the last tilde wave which lasted two shades and left the population of Treforledge trapped within Crafters Isle with nothing to live on, but tree bark and water diluted with roots of the Tweedly Plants. In the wake of the storms passing many workstations and elderly Drop Trees had been destroyed beyond repair. Making living a discomfort for many, especially when food had to be rationed and Crafters Isle became swamped with sea sickness that required many wizards to distance themselves in fear that they might spread the infection further.

"It takes something bad to happen for the mind to grasp the reality of vulnerability," Galli remembered Lorneid telling her as he stared broken hearted at the last drowned body been recovered from the shores of the Twins. The death toll reached a thousand, with many survivors left contaminated with sea sickness. When normality was reinstated, it was decided among the Tree Bine Council that preservations needed to be in checked so that such a catastrophe would never happen again.

When the bodies of the dead were burned, and their ashes tossed among the cliffs, Lorneid travelled to the forests opposite the Charred Mountain to ask the Sirens for their services. The Sirens agreed to safeguard the Blue Islands but requested the protection of Treforledge from the Harpies. Lorneid granted their wish and allowed the Sirens to stay within the stores of the Charred Mountain. Galli had suggested the Sirens should be placed miles out to sea. But the council overruled her suggestion and voted that the Sirens should be positioned nearest the high peaks of the mountains opposite the Blue Islands. Though it pained Galli to admit, she was thankful the council overruled her lame attempt to get rid of the Sirens. Because the Sirens abilities to sense the change in weather was crucial to knowing when the tidal waves were drawing near.

No doubt just to rub it in the council voted that the lord's Second should watch over the Sirens to show the grace of their offerings were not going unnoticed by the wizards of Treforledge much to Galli's dismay she reluctantly accepted her task.

Crossing the rocky bridge, Galli brushed her loose hair behind her ears. Taking her steps two at a time, knowing it was pointless rushing, for Lorneid would know the reason she was absent and just laugh it off. Still, it was her duty to be present by her lord's side and disregarding her responsibilities was befitting of a lord's Second. Habits was what caused Galli's lateness. Fond habits and cravings for a new challenge to express her nesting skills. After an entire cycle of shade been constantly hand cuffed to Lorneid felt in Galli's opinion a waste of her talents. When Galli had arrived back to Treforledge to a hero's welcome, having led the Blue Striped Army to their first ever Ultimate Colour Crown. She expected after the novelty gradually disappeared; she would resume her position as general. But how wrong she was, the following shade after her return Lorneid paid her a visit in her quarters in Suala Island. It was there and then that he appointed Galli his Second. Galli neither grateful nor ungrateful felt forced into accepting this shocking promotion.

Galli found her new position a daunting one, because it meant she had to resign as general of the Blue Striped Army and move up to the Seconds quarters within Crafters Isle. So, when Galli was stationed upon the high peaks of Suala Island to oversee the remaining wizards across the crowded bridge. The temptation to visit her old training ground was too enticing to pass up. On her way back, Galli came across her successor, Irmkay the Blue, who was a young, handsome, and an intelligent wizard. Take away the fact he was just one cycle above Ripeling stage, Irmkay had proven he was equipped for the difficult position of General of Treforledge's army during the intense battles they fought alongside each other on their rise to becoming champions of the Ultimate Colour.

When Galli was appointed Lorneid's Second, it was Irmkay she voiced to the council to be her replacement. Having trained and fought alongside Irmkay, Galli knew his bravery and keen mind for battle were the key components needed to improve the Blue Striped Army's chances of reclaiming their Ultimate Coloured Crown.

Having not seen one another in shades they reminisced on past events while watching the Ripelings finish their last training session before evacuation. It felt to Galli, refreshing to be able to speak about something other than her lord's needs. Watching the young Ripe's little scrawny arms twirling twigs in their hands and shouting incantations that merely caused sparks to channel through their tame tutorial objects felt to Galli a more joyful way to spend her shades. But been the lords Second meant her qualities were needed elsewhere. And by elsewhere, been constantly by her lord's side. Deeming her irrelevant to the honing of Ripelings eager minds and a slave to Lorneid's every requirement.

''The downfall of my promotion,'' Galli randomly repeated to herself when she reminisced about the simplicities of life. Having survived the Ultimate Colour, Galli believed she could overcome anything that came her way. But one obstacle she was new to was forever stamping its authority on her. Judgement. A constant opponent that attacked her during council gatherings. This was because the Wizards of the Tree Bine Council did not approve of her been Lorneid's Second.

Galli was thankful that the councilmembers spent most of their shades within the confinements of their stores beneath Lorneids quarters so that she only heard their dislike for her during council meetings. This ill judgement was because the council seen Galli's appointment as an insult to their ways of ruling. Lorneid however did not take their views seriously and disregarded any complaint put toward him about his strange appointment. Feeling they could not force Lorneid to change his mind about Galli's appointment. The council instead made a mockery of Galli's ideas and used their dislike for her to overrule every proposition she believed would benefit the Blue Islands. It was Lorneid who silenced Galli's critics and reminded the council who was Lord of Treforledge. Lorneid announced to the Tree Bine Council that Galli's leadership and success in the Ultimate Colour were proven aspects to fill the absence of his deceased Second, Saladom the Blue. But even through the cries of Galli's inexperience to hold the position, Lorneid's mind would not be swayed.

And so, it was Galli who became the third Lord of Treforledge's Second. Following in the footsteps of Saladom the Blue who was old and frail when he died from an unknown sea illness. Stricken with grief, Lorneid had left the position vacant for an entire cycle of shade. Confiding in Galli when she questioned his decision to leave the vacancy unoccupied. Lorneid admitted gravely. "I couldn't find an appropriate wizard to fill the void left by Saladom."

Lorneid's words rung in Galli's ears as she passed more groups of anxious wizards walking the thin slope up Tree Island that led to the roped bridge. Catching sight of fully ripe wizards carrying their possessions rather than magically levitating them, Galli realized the strength in the wind which was strange because Yellow Shade had a warm climate not a windy one. But the force of the wind hurling down from the clouds no doubt erased the doubt from Galli's mind that it wasn't the shades effects causing the wind to lash against her but instead the force of the incoming tides. Making her understand why the wizards were choosing to carry their possessions instead of using magic, because the strong gales would challenge their concentration skills which was needed if a wizard was to maintain their hold over the object while using spells that defy gravity.

None of the wizards paid Galli homage when she offered them her services. Instead, they pretended she wasn't there, passing her by like she was not present making it difficult for her to remain pleasant as their sour expressions gawked at her while she overtook them on the road leading to the bridge. Seeing the long queue of anxious wizards crowding the border of the bridge, Galli decided she didn't need another thousand eyes piercing her with angry looks and turned from the crowd at the vined bridge and walked the long path toward the opposite bridge that Galli knew would be unoccupied. When she made it to the rocky bridge and crossed it, the Charred Mountain came into view as she entered the perimeter of Crafters Isle.

The Charred Mountain was a monstrous mountain that was layered in boulders around its base. Behind the front of the mountain were deep forests of Hawthorn trees that were used for staff making by the Crafters. It was a place the Blue Wizards only ventured, when necessary, due to the lands been swarmed by small creatures such as Cave Keepers and Sirens who were mystical creatures that lived remotely within the forest, but thanks to Lorneids alliance with the Harpies, most of the Cave Keepers moved away from the borders of Treforledge due to the Harpies appetite for sweeter meats. The Sirens stubbornly remained and were now protected from the winged vultures by the terms of their agreement made with Lorneid. Sparing them of the Harpies hunt which made Galli want to scream at the thought of having the creepy little mites so close to her home.

Galli headed for the Whaling Bridge, knowing Lorneid would be there watching over the Crafters before evacuation. Galli knew the gathered rocks would be kept in the centre of the island to keep the Crafters busy whilst in lockdown. For Crafters Isle was filled with caves and stores that could populate the entire population of Treforledge if necessary.

On the coast of Crafters Isle were cliffs and secret passageways in and out of the island. But after Lorneid allowed the Harpies to build their nests along the cliffs edge. The Crafters never ventured near the coasts anymore which was one of their many hiding spots when it came to evacuation. But even though all Blue Wizards were abided by the laws of Treforledge to have a good relationship with the Harpies, the Crafters refused to acknowledge any partnership with the winged beasts and their ancient beliefs due to the old trait that all wizards acknowledged the Blue Wizards for and that was their stubbornness. Lorneid however made use of the Harpies alliance. Using their skills of hunting, both Lorneid and the Harpies agreed that if the Blue Wizards armed them with strong forged armour and combat weapons, they in return would share their supply of foreign foods and remedies. With the Yellow Wizards of Dry Scales refusing to share their healing remedies, Lorneid was left with no choice but to agree with the Harpies terms. Since nothing grew apart from trees on the Blue Islands, this agreement was necessary for their survival due to the Orange Wizards of Tindisinge refusing to send food supplies since Treforledge defeated their army in the semi-finals of the Ultimate Colour.

When Galli was at the border of the bridge, she felt the temperature decrease rapidly making her wonder, 'How the temperature could drop so quickly in degrees during Yellow Shade?' Frigid air crept up the bottoms of her cloak causing her thighs and lower legs to rattle. Galli pulled her cloak around her body and began the short sweep through Crafters Isle. Galli felt something wet slide down her hand. Looking down at her numb hands she noticed thin layers of ice had grown along the white swirling lines stitched on the sleeves of her cloak. Gripping her collar Galli pulled the thick garment across her face, hoping by closing the gap from her neck to her chin, it would prevent the spawning ice crawl further up her body. Walking by the empty caves that were soon to be occupied, Galli felt the pressure of the wind ease, thus allowing her to walk freely and without fear of been stripped naked by the beating gusts. The short walk past the stores led Galli to the border of the Whaling Whining Bridge. Giving her a clear view of the Charred Mountain and the long shadow it casted over Treforledge. Narrowing her eyes, Galli made out a lone figure standing numbly at the end of the Whaling Bridge.

Unsurprisingly it was Lorneid standing alone and wrapped like Galli in heavy garments, watching from the peak of the mountain side while his Crafters chiselled and mined in silence. Crossing the Whaling Bridge, Galli noticed the stern expression on Lorneids face. A look Galli knew extremely well, it was the look of deep thinking. The same one Lorneid had worn the last shade the tides were drawing near. If Galli was a betting wizard, she would bet her staff the death toll of the last tidal wave was what caused the creasing lines on Lorneids facial skin. Remembering Lorneids loss of stability after the waves ceased and it was safe to explore the damage. He searched every aspect of Treforledge until every wizard missing was accounted for, but it did nothing to ease his guilt. Galli knew Lorneid blamed himself and as lord there was nothing, she, or anyone else could say to ease his guilt. All that was left to do was give the drowned wizards a decent passing into the realms of non-being. So, the Crafters built pyres and laid the dead among the dry wood and one by one they burned until nothing was left but ash that flowed along the sea breeze, drifting the dead toward the heavens.

When Galli crossed the bridge Lorneid stood in the same stature as he had that shade, with his staff held firmly in his right hand and wearing a cemented look that was unreadable. He was leaning on his tall oaken staff to steady himself against the strong gusts of wind coming from the coast. Studying the staff clenched inside his hands Galli recalled the stories she was told as a Ripeling about the battles Lorneids staff had fought in and won. It was streaked in blue and had latched together aqua leaves nesting still on its point. Unlike most common staffs Lorneids was branded with a name, Water Dancer. A name giving to it by Lorneids late father, Quiloc the Blue. Who was a noble warrior, remembered throughout the Lands of Light for his defeat of the mighty Sea Kraken, Arc the Flooder of Isles. From what Galli gathered about Quiloc, he was disinterested in politics or ruling and instead simply lived for the sole purpose of his family. Having died unexpectedly, Water Dancer, was the only heir loom left and Lorneid made sure his father's staff would live on to honour the legacy of his father's achievements.

"It was commanded usual routine was to be upheld within the islands of Treforledge," said Galli introducing herself with a curt bow.

"Ah, young Galli," said an amused Lorneid. "Pleasant of you to resume by my side, was another priority more important than your sworn duties?" Lorneid asked, the cold not adding any decrease to his humoured tone. "What would the Tree Bine Council say if word reached them that their lord and protector was left alone and unguarded beyond the boundaries of the Blue Islands?"

"The Council requested I should oversee evacuation," answered Galli with distaste, "I apologise for my lateness my lord; it will not become a habit," Galli promised trying her best to sound true.

"You worry too much," Lorneid said, disappointed by Galli's lack of enthusiasm. "As lord, I am permitted to do as I please and stationed inside my quarters isn't how I like to see out the shades."

"Tree Island and Suala Island are soon to be below a hundred feet of sea water before the turn of shade. The lord's absence has created unneeded uncertainty. May I ask why you have instructed the Crafters to mine when we are been stampeded with Ripelings and panicked wizards?" asked Galli.

"Apologies if I come off as rude, but when did security bother the bold Galli the Blue? Especially when she sneaks off from her duties to watch Ripelings train in the dirt pits," said Lorneid with a quick glance at Galli.

"My lord .... I ...,"

"Don't apologise," laughed Lorneid. "I know you still bare a passion for the teachings of young Ripelings. It is understandable you still yearn to see them fulfil their true potential," praised Lorneid.

"Your remarks are kind my Lord, but we are not on the same level when it comes down to sharing a passion for teaching," said Galli.

"Oh, really," said Lorneid, his smile faltering a little. "Don't you think I haven't been watching you closely since I appointed you my Second?"

"It wouldn't be hard since I'm by your side, every drop of every shade," Galli said a hint of boredom in her tone.

"Five shades have passed since your rise in position and what are your achievements?" asked Lorneid in a cool voice.

Galli remained silent with her head down and her eyes focused on the end of Lorneid's staff. Fearing she may have revealed too much of her ill feelings toward her position.

"Must I remind you of the benefits you have gained since your appointment to my ranks?" Lorneid asked remaining cool.

"I think the past can be resurfaced during a glass of heated Maul. If we manage to get through the crowds swarming our every route, we may get it while it is still ripe," suggested Galli, hoping Lorneid would take her offering as kind and not a getaway clause to escape the decreasing temperatures.

"Floods come and go. If you fear a repeat of the last one, rest assured Galli. Security is at its peak. Wizards patrol every bridge, Sirens are positioned and waiting for the first sign of any incoming tides," said Lorneid in an assured voice.

"I'm aware," Galli wanted to say. But decided against it. Instead, she allowed Lorneid believe he alone orchestrated the security provisions over Treforledge. When in fact it was, she who had instructed her lieutenants to keep the panic levels to a low, not wanting rushing stampedes swarming Crafters Isle and ruining Lorneids quarters.

The ear aching sounds of different voices along with gong sounds reverberated from the entrance of the Charred Mountain. Thin creatures with fragile gaunt features appeared through the crack of the mountain with their claw shaped hands raised over rocks much larger than themselves. Using their unique abilities, Crafters can easily uproot rocks and levitate them with ease. Observing from under the shadow of her hood Galli watched the Crafters simply rotate their wrists, using collective nonverbal spells to chip away the rough and sharp edges from the mountain rocks, using nothing but their eyes as chisels. Shaping the rocks into staff shaped rubies. The Crafters were tall with thin features. Their appearances identical as were their long feet and hands and long crooked noses with thin nostrils. Their bodies were layered in sheets of peach skin that covered over their fluid bones. Their shiny faces brightened their blue hair and eyes whilst the cloaks they wore were designed to be able to withstand any climate and were stained midnight blue with clear white lines swirling along the outside of their sleeves. The design resembling waves flowing along the sea.

Galli looked at Lorneid, who was studying the Crafters. Making Galli wonder was his light-hearted attitude a mask to hide the stress of the coming tidal waves.

Lorneid was a small bulky wizard with tense shoulders and a laid-back frame. Lines of grey were beginning to creep through his once shiny blue hair that lay straight and unmoved over his shoulders. Galli was like her lord in colour but nothing else. She was tall, slightly thinner, and had a shyness to her.

"The temperature in the shade has decreased rapidly my lord, may I suggest we draw back before we're frozen to the ground we stand on," tittered Galli, her teeth rattling inside her thin jaws.

"We cannot afford any delay," said Lorneid, his voice stiff and wispy due to standing in the cold for so long. "Requests from the Golden Kingdom have been flying in, with each passing shade," he added displeased.

"The king seems determined to have his halls filled with our rocks before the cycle of shade concludes," mocked Galli, her cold breath gushing through her gritted teeth.

"Regardless of the kings personal desires, we must keep his good will in our favour, if our lands are to remain legitimate to his ruling," Lorneid chittered, the cold beginning to unhinge his bubbly voice.

Galli knew Lorneid disliked his Crafters work been used as ornaments in a foreign kingdom but wasn't foolish to complain because if Treforledge refused the kings requests it could easily lead to war and every wizard alive knew that Treforledge did not have neither the strength nor numbers to win against the bulk of the Golden Kingdom.

Galli looked on as the Crafters left the chiselled rocks on the border of the bridge. For the younger stripped wizards, who were always eager to make an impression would scurry across and carry the rocks across the bridge and into the waiting arms of the Rock Grinders to magically mould the smoothed rocks into staff sized rubies.

"Don't be frightened young Ripeling," called Lorneid, "The spirits only answer to my voice, they will not hurt you," he laughed, the innocence of upcoming wizards fears of the non-existent seemed to warm his spirits.

Galli looked at the bridge annoyed at one of the freshly coloured wizards who stood nervously at the bridges border. It was obvious what frightened the coloured wizard. The Whaling Bridge was rumoured to have living spirits lurking within its wood and straps. The thought of living souls dwelling within the bridge was enough to frighten any young wizard. Lorneid and Galli watched the young wizard who was wearing a thin layered aqua cloak freeze to the spot by the shock of been addressed by the Lord of Treforledge. Whatever the young wizard was expecting to experience from its journey across the Whaling Bridge, one wasn't been spoken directly to by Lorneid. The nervous wizard approached the bridge cautiously wearing a look of fear that was clear even for a blind wizard to see. Galli who had seen such fear in her own reflection at the same stage of her own life knew that the young wizard was stunned by surprise. Except the difference between Galli's youth and the trembling wizard on the bridge were miles apart in hardship.

Something about the way Lorneid looked at the young wizard that seemed to kick started its senses. Because it had quickly regained its lost confidence and straightened itself to its full height, clicked his no longer trembling fingers and magically made the smoothed rocks levitate and swirl above his head. Looking at Galli then to Lorneid his eyes wearing a look of deep concentration the young wizard gave his superiors a smile before walking without fear along the Whaling Bridge, the rubies swirling like a lasso above his head.

"You see Galli, it's much easier to speak than to give orders," said Lorneid his face broadening into a beaming smile as he watched the young wizard cross the bridge.

"The young wizard fears the bridge. If so, why?" said Galli. "How am I to lead wizards if their minds are frightened by superstitions?"

"If the drop-in temperature bothers you so much by all means return to the warmth of my quarters. I daresay there will be a change to your attitude when I return," said Lorneid strongly.

Galli's expression soured. "It's just odd that in a warm shade the degrees suddenly drop so rapidly we barely notice......," But Galli broke off mid-sentence, taking a few steps toward the mountain entrance, to get a clearer view of the sky. Galli watched closely, noticing a ripple in the sky's colour.

"Shade draws to its end, how?" Galli asked, turning to see Lorneids reaction to the strange turn of shade.

Lorneids expression appeared blank, all colour drained from his dimming face, no doubt the sudden change in shade causing his glowing features to faulter. Lorneids silence only increased Galli's fears. Feeling a knot tighten in her stomach, Galli watched in horror as the sky became veined in fissures of wisped smoke of the darkest black.

"It can't be," gasped Lorneid, taking a few steps forward, his eyes now fixed on the changing sky.

"It's taking control of Yellow Shade and unhinging its effects," cried Galli in disbelief.

Twirling on the spot, Galli's eyes were widened with fear as her eyes met Lorneids. The realism struck both wizards at the exact same moment. Sharing the same fearful expressions, Lorneid snapped out of his tranced state the moment he caught sight of Galli's light blue eyes.

"Get to my quarters and do not dare leave!" Lorneid ordered marching toward Galli.

Before Galli could argue Lorneid had grabbed her firmly around the wrist and dragged her unwillingly across the mountainside. Lorneid's aggressive reaction shocked Galli to numbness for never had she seen him react in such an aggressive manner. When they were at the border of the bridge, Lorneid released Galli from his grasp to turn around and raise his staff at the mountain's peak, preparing himself for what was coming. Then out of the darkness streaks of green sizzling flames shot from behind the Charred Mountain. They soared over their heads and landed on the Waling Bridge. The flame's burst and coursed through the bridge's cords reducing them to ash that caused a cascade of flames to soar through the air and hit various parts of the three islands. The bridge collapsed into the Red Sea below, along with the unprepared wizards fleeing across to the other side. Galli who was a drop away from joining them was saved by Lorneid who had instantly pulled her away from the wreckage.

But as Galli regained her balance her heart had skipped a beat, watching helplessly as the bridges remains crashed into the Red Sea. There was one law to follow in Treforledge and all wizards obeyed it out of fear more than loyalty. That law was to never disturb the sea beneath their lands because if you did, certain death would follow. The moment the Red Sea was disturbed, it rose higher than all the lands combined, unleashing powerful waves that swept through Treforledge, drowning all the unprepared wizards. It had happened so quick and without a drop's warning that there was nothing the watching Galli or Lorneid could do. They were completely caught off guard by this well devised attack. Drenched in salt water and ears filled with wild screams Galli and Lorneid were stunned by the appearance of a black cloud that had risen from the Charred Mountain. The appearance of this freakishly overgrown cloud that was surrounded in a wisping charcoal grey aura froze the senses of Lorneid and Galli as it rose from the mountain's peak and swept over them, the sheer force of its presence was enough to knock both wizards off their feet.

The clouds intended target was Treforledge, and it swooped over all lands so fast that the wizards trying to escape were killed instantly. Galli quickly picked herself up and raised her hand aiming her index fingers at the soaring cloud that was circling around for another attack. But before she could summon her staff, she was hit hard across the head, so hard, she was knocked unconscious. Lorneid scooped her unconscious body up into his arms. Looking at her young peaceful face he said, ''I have a promise to keep,'' before disappearing with a twirl of his cloak.

There was no saving Treforledge or the thousands of wizards living within its perimeters. Once the cloud breached the Blue Islands it had spread a virus killing everything that grew. The Red Sea calmed and retreated to its settled state, but not before its destructive rage had claimed the lives of many innocent wizards and destroyed many homes and workstations. The death toll was beyond count, as all lands now lay under a black decaying ash. The few wizards who had managed to escape the onslaught used hidden passages to hide and wait out the siege, those less fortunate were brutally stripped, beaten, and bound by thorned stinging vines and hung on the highest peak of the Blue Islands. Their defilement used as a message as to what was to come to all wizards who stood against this new rising power. The source of that power was a well-known creature who had once ruled the Lands of Light before the rise of the wizards and was now hellbent on retrieving what was once his to the extent of madness. Feeling his way through the graveyard of wizards decaying under the self-absorbing ash. Lano the Lava Keeper stood watching the Blue Wizards of Treforledge hanging mutilated and wasted, their final breaths giving his appetite for vengeance a quenching longing for more.

Chapter 2

The Tail of the Storm

The chilling breeze swayed through the trees and clear streams. Peace combined with soothing silence could be felt everywhere, even the wind never troubled to hail against the peaceful state of Dulgerdeen the forest of many creatures. Trees tall, small, skinny, and wide filled the ancient forest with streams of many shapes and sizes flowing through beds of mountain rocks. Mass portions of the forest were divided between groups of creatures that obeyed the Kurlezzia's ways of ruling. The Kurlezzias knew by allowing other parties to build and safeguard strongholds within Dulgerdeen it would form a shield around the outer areas of the forest. Meaning less security on the Kurlezzia's part. But while the Kurlezzias protected the forest and patrolled its borders, other more fearsome creatures dwelled beneath sight and senses. One, was an elderly wizard who preferred solitude and abided by no laws only his own. That wizard was Carka the Static, a wizard who lived under the falls of the Streams of Clear that lay deep within the forest. No one knew where Carka came from, or why he chose to stay within the confinements of the forest. All that the creatures of the forest knew was he was very secretive about himself and avoided the forest creatures as best he could.

Carka settled deep within the forest. Building his surroundings to camouflage his cave under a flowing stream. The cave Carka chose was decorated with small comforts such as handmade cushions that contained many different feathers, he'd plucked from the dead bodies of elderly Varwels who had fallen to their deaths due to old age. Carka preferably kept to himself during his shades within the bowels of the forest, preferring his own company than socialise with the creatures of Dulgerdeen. Only appearing from his cave to stock up on needed supplies. The creatures of Dulgerdeen would avoid walking too near the Streams of Clear, with new rumours spreading every turn of shade about what dwelled beneath the falls.

Shadow Creeper and Death's Stalker were many nicknames branded on Carka which always cheered him up whenever he was strolling through the forest eavesdropping on the creatures for fresh gossip to digest. While it was the Kurlezzia herd who governed Dulgerdeen, it was Carka and his band of followers who the creatures of the forest feared above most and were continually looked for when their own remedies were ineffective against injuries and poisons.

Carka would trade his healing spells for objects he was unable to get without having to leave the perimeters of his sanctuary, his most sought-after objects been smoothed sea stones or foreign fruits. Beyond the point of trade, it comforted Carka knowing his attributes were doing some good for the creatures of the forest.

The ageing wizard sat in silence within the comforts of his cave enjoying the quiet for he had just finished repairing his water slope he had made from the bamboo sticks he'd rooted up along the out skirts of the forest and was now taking a hard-earned rest. Using magical gel on each end of the bamboos so that they held firm and strong when flowing water would flow directly through the bamboos and with a simple snap of his fingers the magic seal would lift from the end of the bamboo pipe and pour flowing water into his cave. It was an object Carka used regularly to wash and clean his fancy stone ornaments.

Ornaments were one of Carka's many prized possessions. Always hating depending on magical needs for a simple requirement, he managed to trap rare fireflies inside the sea stones he'd brought with him before leaving the Golden Kingdom. By Carka's command, the stones would vibrate recklessly, forcing the encased fireflies to ignite and glow and spread a radiant heat throughout his cave.

The sound of gasps and scurrying footsteps caught Carka's attention as he leaped from his chair and instantly twirled his fingers causing the lights shining from the sea stones to dim. Raising his right arm to shoulder height, the beams shining from the firefly stones soared like a comet and nested gently inside the clear white stones pierced in the centre of his palms. Concealed in darkness he stood against the caves wall ready to strike at the creature who dared trespass upon his cave.

''Carka,'' whispered a gasping voice.

Cautiously Carka stepped forward his hand aimed at the figure standing outside the waterfall shielding his cave. Waiting patiently, Carka slowly unbuttoned the straps of his cloak and brushed it from his shoulders. Felling its weight fall from him like a refreshing breeze in a dry heat, Carka scanned the shadow of the creature with his piercing gaze.

''Who dares trespass upon me at this drop?'' said Carka, moving cautiously nearer to the entrance with his arm outstretched ready to attack.

''Begging your pardon my lord,'' said a shaking voice with a gulping swallow. ''But I come with a warning,'' heaved the voice that began to sound familiar to Carka.

''Speak your warning and do so now or fall where you stand!'' thundered Carka, his voice echoing throughout the cave.

''If I may …. linger in your presence a drop….my lord, for what I have to say would be better presented by reignition instead of through a veil of water? I have come at significant risk my lord,'' squeaked the jittering voice behind the veil with many annoying pauses in its stuttering voice.

It was the tone of this frightened creatures voice that made Carka drop his guard. It would be foolish for any creature of the forest to try attack him while he stood in his sanctuary which was protected by many powerful unbreachable enchantments. Waving his hand at the waterfall, Carka forced it to split down the middle with a tame manipulation spell. Drawing the flowing water apart like a curtain, Carka created a measurable sized gap for the creature to walk through. Under the shadow of the waterfall, it stood no taller than four feet, its bronze fur drenched with the ends of each strand dripping of water the rattle of its teeth echoing like a vibrant bug in Carka's ears.

"Hinkelthorn," Carka said sharply, "What in all the shades are you doing so far down south?" he asked the little Rurrow creature who lived many miles north of Dulgerdeen.

Hinkelthorn didn't respond which made Carka wonder what had startled the usually jumpy little creature. Waving his hands smoothly across the cave, Carka's sea stones beamed with crimson light of white and ember. When Carka was satisfied with the temperature of the cave, he turned to face his unresponsive visitor. Hinkelthorns light blue eyes were flooded with tears, his thin lips were white and shaken. Carka noticed instantly that Hinkelthorn wasn't trembling from the water's dense temperature, but from Carka's experience a severe fright seemed to have had a traumatic effect on the little Rurrow.

"Gliders," quivered Hinkelthorn, "Gliders! They have invaded the pass from south to west and are killing at will. Those who refuse to join them are being slaughtered," said Hinkelthorn, his teeth chattering.

"Come near the warmth and be seated," gestured Carka, "Let's try to regain what senses you've lost on your travels," he said delicately.

"My senses are on tip form!" snapped Hinkelthorn, feeling that his warning wasn't been taken seriously. "I plead with you to listen my lord. Gliders in numbers far greater than ever are moving here to rid Dulgerdeen of you and your wizard counter parts," squealed Hinkelthorn, who had grabbed at the ends of Carka's robes and shook them in attempt to make him realise the seriousness of what was about to unfold.

Carka stared into the blue eyes that had a harsh line of anger behind their innocence. Having befriended Hinkelthorn and many of his Rurrow counterparts upon his arrival to this cave, Carka knew he would be a fool to disregard Hinkelthorns warning.

"Have you encountered them?" Carka asked trying not to sound concerned.

Hinkelthorns breathing came in heaves, causing tears to slide down his wet furry cheeks. The tiny Rurrow stood and wept in silence. Struggling to hold his emotions and keep level-headed, the strain was beginning to reveal itself through the little creature's whimpering.

"We'd only ended our hunt down by the moss-stained trees and suddenly the sky became shadowed, and the air turned cold, darkness consumed us and before I knew it my first and second born were laid dead at my paws," sobbed Hinkelthorn.

Hinkelthorn sobbed harder and let out many howls that reminded Carka of Rear Clars roars of triumph. Allowing Hinkelthorn a moment to grieve, Carka considered what he had said and how best to act on his warning. Hinkelthorn quickly regained himself and paused his sobbing. The loss of his heirs had stung him deeply, but Carka knew, that Hinkelthorn still had a large force to think of back home.

"They chased me through the forest, only stopping when I dived of the cliffs and into the streams. When I didn't resurface, they must have thought the fall had killed me," sniffed Hinkelthorn.

"Very brave of you to dive from such a fall under pursuit of Gliders, there powers are difficult to overthrow, you did well under the circumstances," Carka praised the teary eyed Hinkelthorn.

"I used the current to lead me here so I could warn you that they are searching every part of Dulgerdeen for you, it's partly the reason I'm still alive," squeaked Hinkelthorn with a hiccup.

"The entire population of the forest knows the Rurrows are friendly with me and my band of followers. You were an easy target. The real question is why a swarm of Gliders are searching for me?" Carka asked in wonder.

"Not a swarm my, a legion, large enough to eclipse the sky in darkness," said Hinkelthorn seriously, adding an extra strain of worry to Carka's mind.

A pulse of anger had begun to charge through Carka's knuckles, igniting a surge inside him that he hadn't felt in cycles. Unable to shake of the blind reason to why Gliders perused him. Carka had to ensure no further pain or death would be dealt upon the innocent creatures.

"You will come with me to the base of my follower's camp, there we will decide what methods to use to counter these Gliders and find out what they are after," Carka said with a strong surge to his words.

"I was hoping you would flee and travel to a haven beyond Dulgerdeen," said Hinkelthorn. "Because If Gliders are roaming through the forest freely, then I believe Gazzel, and his herd are either in league with them or too scared to stop them," said Hinkelthorn.

Carka had been so quick to act, he hadn't thought about the protectors of the forest. Hinkelthorn had hit the real source. Treason.

"Gazzel has opened his gates to the Gliders," Carka said sadly, feeling betrayed. "Knowing him as I do, the Kurlezzia's will see to trap me and my followers within the streams, and after we're slain, they'll use our bodies to destroy the enchantments I cast around my surroundings," Carka said hotly, the scenario playing out in his mind as he grasped how his demise would benefit Gazzel.

Carka knew with him out of the way, Gazzel would reclaim the Falls of Clear. It was common knowledge that the Kurlezzia herd hated wizards living within their forest, what was worse he couldn't do anything about it and if he tried many Kurlezzia's would perish. Though they had their differences it displeased Carka to learn Gazzel was so desperate to get rid of him that he would succumb as low as to join with the Gliders instead of trying to negotiate.

Carka always believed the Kurlezzia's despised wizards because they posed a threat to their ways of ruling and wielded powers they couldn't match, but Gazzel's betrayal was beyond a jealous grudge and Carka knew if actions weren't taken now, then many more innocents like the Rurrows would be slaughtered in the Gliders pursuit of him.

'Kill or be killed,' was an old motto Carka remembered been drummed into his mind by his former king, Dirm the Bronze, when he would prep his wizards for battle. It was in this precise shade that Carka dwindled on using his former kings' methods. Having never wanted a confrontation with the Kurlezzias nor any other creature for that matter, Carka sweated on his decision on what to do next. He smiled to himself, 'even after all my shades in exile trouble has yet again found me,' he thought with a smile.

"Perhaps I should flee, grab my companions and leave," Carka said, a grain of doubt beginning to swell his thoughts.

"You're sounding like you're giving up?" said Hinkelthorn shocked by Carka's unwillingness to fight.

Carka remained standing still, his fighting spirit decreasing, as the very thought of confronting a legion of Gliders made him wonder was, he still up for a fight or would it be safer to just leave? Considering his options, his weary grey eyes found themselves looking down upon Hinkelthorn. It was the hopeless look within Hinkelthorns eyes that showered away any doubt Carka had allowed consume his thoughts. Knowing that if it wasn't for Hinkelthorns bravery he would be defenceless against the Gliders. Carka smiled down upon the little Rurrow. Feeling that if such a small, helpless creature could find the courage to overcome a Glider pursuit having watched his kin been killed moments before then an ex-war general could show the same bravery and face these Gliders head on without fear or doubt.

"Quite the opposite!" said Carka strongly, a new surge of energy giving his old limbs a new lease of life. "Let us leave this cave before we are discovered," said Carka sternly.

Swishing his wrist, Carka levitated his cloak to rise from the stone floor and magically cover his body. About to leave Carka halted at the entrance of his cave, respectively waiting for Hinkelthorn who wasn't as quick a walker as he. When they were both outside the falls, Carka clicked his fingers sharply ensuring the protection surrounding his cave was lifted. With a lunge of his arm Carka rained a powerful swirling twister from the sky and forced it to strike his cave. The sheer force of the swirling wind reduced the cave beneath the falls to rubble and ruin.

"Why have you destroyed your home?" squeaked Hinkelthorn, who stood bamboozled by Carka's capabilities to single handily reduce boulders to rubble.

"Before this shade concludes, I will undoubtably be returning to Dulgerdeen," Carka said firmly. "It would be foolish to dwell on such an outcome been overturned since the creatures of the forest have turned against me," said Carka, feeling a twinge of sorrow as he took one last look at the place, he had made his home.

Carka led Hinkelthorn along the stone path he had designed many cycles of shades ago to help guide creatures of the forest safely cross the stream. The forest was quite with the addition of a flickering wind coursing through the fallen leaves scattered along the ground. Sniffing the air, Carka's eyes gawked the still trees in front of him as the elderly wizard prepared himself for an ambush.

"That smell," retched Hinkelthorn covering his nose with his arm, "What is it?"

Carka again sniffed the air and felt a wisp of smoke slither up his nostrils. "Burning flesh," he answered in a matter-of-fact tone.

Carefully and silently both creatures took themselves away from the path and made for the passageway leading north. When Carka and Hinkelthorn bypassed the outer layers surrounding the wizards camp, their vision was shrouded by thick smoke that slowly slithered through the thick leaves covering the light toned trees.

"Vanishio," whispered Carka flicking the air with a wave of his hand.

As the smoke split and flowed in different directions, what was left in its wake stung Carka like a knife in the back. Sighing deeply, Carka knew by the rustling of the trees surrounding him and Hinkelthorns whimpering that he had walked straight into a trap. Whispering sounds with cold rasping breaths filled the air as dark floating figures appeared from behind the shadows of every tree and bush, revealing dark hoovering creatures with soulless blank eyes and hung opened mouths, showing their forked moss-stained teeth.

Hinkelthorn cried softly in acceptance that his demise drew near, the poor creature clung to the ends of Carka's robe as if shielding his eyes would somehow stop the inevitable.

"The mighty Carka surrounded and alone in the deep dark forest," laughed a high pitch voice from behind the pack of Gliders.

"Rullin is that you?" called Carka unfazed by the Gliders. "My gosh! It's been cycles," said Carka in a false gesture.

The Glider general didn't seem fazed by Carka or show any indication that he remembered him from their previous encounter, Rullin merely tilted his head and considered Carka with a trancing gaze. The rest of the Gliders formed a thin gap in their ranks to create space for a winged creature who swerved and landed in a hail of wind and flowing leaves wearing a satisfied grin along its blue furred face.

"Dreaquirla," breathed Carka in a repulsive tone as his attention toward Rullin was quickly diverted to a creature Carka had last seen been sealed away for treason.

"Surprised to see me?" giggled Dreaquirla encasing her wings by her side. "I would be too had our fates been switched, but here I am alive and well," said Dreaquirla in a cold menacing voice causing dark shadows to arise under her narrowed eyes.

Carka's expression soured. In all his shades, he never expected to see the evil eyes of Lano's deadliest servant again. But Dreaquirlas reappearance did answer many of the gnawing questions niggling inside his head.

"Wondering am I alone?" teased Dreaquirla monitoring Carka's rotating eyes with joy.

Carka smiled at her confidence. Dreaquirla knew she was in complete control of the situation and relished in the prospect of having Carka exactly where she wanted him. Even though Carka was the captive, he couldn't hide his admiration for Dreaquirlas well devised plan. By waiting for him to leave his sanctuary and catch him in the open was well constructed and in the present moment, decisive.

The Gliders tightened their formation circling Carka and the trembling Hinkelthorn within a tight space. Determined and unwilling to bow down, Carka kept his gaze firmly on Dreaquirla, the pair now locked in a stare down with neither one willing to show the other the slightest sign of weakness.

"Can you feel the magic leave the forest?" mocked Dreaquirla. "Never have I smelt anything so sweet," she jeered inhaling the fumes with a satisfied embrace.

"I must admit my desire to test myself against a wizard is a longing thirst I have yet to quench, it would be a shame to pass up this opportunity when it has so pleasantly presented itself,'" said Dreaquirla readying herself for a lunge.

"Don't embarrass yourself by even thinking you have the capabilities to stand against me!" Carka said coldly throwing a look of disgust at Dreaquirla.

Dreaquirlas eyes tensed with anger, but her smile widened. "My master wanted you and your followers out of the way quickly, so you can see burning them alive seemed a less messy affair," cackled Dreaquirla madly.

Carka's knuckles tightened but through his heated anger there was no denying Dreaquirla was right. The stench was filled with odours of flesh and crisped salt, meaning his followers had indeed been murdered and burned to a crisp by handmade flames instead of enchanted ones, meaning their spirits would be unable to travel to the realms of nonbeing and instead be forced to live forever as trans spirits trapped between the realms of the living and the dead for eternity.

"They deserved better," Carka said his nostrils flaring in anger.

Dreaquirla laughed louder, her high pitch squeals strained Carka's ears, who could feel his fingernails pierce through the skin in his hands as the warm blood dripped down his hands and slid along his skin.

"So did my kin when they were clipped of their wings and used to the amusement of your filthy race. Was decency shown then?" shrieked Dreaquirla madly her eyes bulging.

"What about the Rurrows, did they commit any crimes? Unless hunting for food is illegal in your master's new regime?" Carka asked, patting Hinkelthorn on the head to assure him he was going to be all right.

"Your cowering friend failed to co-operate and received his just reward, a faith that will fall upon all who try deceiving me," said Dreaquirla.

"He has more spine than either of you," spat Carka darting the Gliders with looks of hate.

Before Dreaquirla could utter another hurtful line, Carka reacted aggressively by lifting his arm so rashly he caught her and the Gliders off guard. Flexing his ageing fingers to full length, Carka aimed his palms directly at Dreaquirlas smug face.

"Go ahead fool," dared Dreaquirla flapping her wings rapidly, "You'll die before uttering a single incantation," she threatened.

Patience was a strategy that needed a keen mind to operate when under pressure and Carka was a master under those circumstances. What Carka did not count on was Hinkelthorn to break the tension he had deliberately infected Dreaquirla and the Gliders with. Before Carka could give the slightest insight to his escape plan, Hinkelthorn had swallowed his fears and launched himself foolishly at Dreaquirla.

"NOOOOO!!!" screamed Carka.

Watching helplessly as the nearest Glider to Dreaquirla blocked Hinkelthorns futile attempt at an attack. Carka watched in slow motion as the Glider who came forward swiped opened its mouth and split Hinkelthorns body in half by the force of its wind wave technique. Dreaquirla burst into a fit of laughter as they all watched the little Rurrows body parts fall at Carka's feet. Dreaquirlas screeches forced their way through Carka's restraint barrier that he was finding unbearably difficult to keep at bay. He stared down at the two sides of Hinkelthorn, as his red blood soaked and stained his drenched furred coat. Hinkelthorns lifeless eyes caused a heavy lump to solidify and halt in Carka's throat. But raging out in anger wasn't Carka's style and though it pained him to remain passive he looked away from Hinkelthorns torn body.

Hinkelthorn had been brave, and it was because of his nobility that Carka was still among the living and not fuel to the wizard bonfire, and he wasn't going to toss that gratitude to the wind with a vicious outburst. Keeping count of the Gliders, Carka counted fourteen surrounding him and hundreds circling the trees and smoke. Resuming his gaze into Dreaquirlas mad twinkling eyes, he smiled cunningly, inflicting a flicker of doubt upon her furred features.

"Enjoy your reign my dear. I assure you it will not last long," warned Carka, with a curling smile that stretched his wrinkled face.

Winking at a disbelieving Dreaquirla, Carka pressed his hands into a tight fist. Screams filled the forest as a surging bolt of white lightning shot through the clouds and trees, striking Carka. The impact blew the Gliders aside, breaking their ranks, and knocking them against the trees and rocks. When the smoke was shooed away by Dreaquirlas flapping wings and the Gliders reformed, the winged creature instantly searched the place where the lightning had struck. But all that was left from where Carka had stood moments before was a deep black hole burnt into the ground with wisps of black smoke foaming from its mouth.

Chapter 3

A Promise Kept

Peach shade was growing stronger, making it difficult for the small crowd of weary wizards to walk without stumbling under the shades increasing heat. The Blue Wizards slow march up the thin slope was causing their pace to falter. Standing on top of the mountain slope, her tired eyes fixed on the dried volcano that sat on a plain island just a few miles out to sea was Galli. The volcano she was observing was one of the six volcanos stationed in the Lands of Light. Galli's fascination wasn't the volcano, but the cracks veined along its edges. ''Was her faith soon to be like this volcano?'' she thought, the skin on her face showing similar lines to the volcanos. The volcanos damaged state had been caused not long after the Mystical Creatures rebellion crumbled. The pine coned volcano was once Lano the Lava Keeper's Lair, and the base of his operations. Lorneid explained the history of the volcanos of Nocktar to Galli when she was appointed his Second and Galli knew the story off by heart.

It began when the King of the Golden Kingdom ordered the lords of all lands to crush the Lava Keepers base and extinguish all memory of Lano. Lorneid told Galli, when he and the other coloured lords got to Lanos volcano's they were forced to use crushing spells to unseal the defensive blocks shielding the entrances. What Lorneid and the other lords did not expect to find was that the lava flowing inside the volcanos had vanished without a trace. Leaving the volcanos dysfunctional. Lorneid told Galli that he believed the lavas disappearance was down to Lano never passing on his skills of lava manipulation, under his own superior belief that he would reign forever. But with Lano banished his six volcanos ran dry. Their powers and strength waning as their mystique slowly faded rendering them useless, so the king saw it fitting to leave them to rot and fade like their master.

When the weary survivors of Treforledge caught up to Galli, she broke free of her trance and turned away from Lanos volcano and moved onto level ground. Too tired to speak, she gave the weary faces staring up her a false smile before leading them into the mouth of a gorge. Upon entering the gorge, the temperatures cooled thanks to the shade sprayed down from the narrowed walls. Galli did feel selfish for not speaking words of comfort, but she wasn't equipped with the tools to give wizards hope or motivate them with charming words. Training Ripe's and commanding an army was easy compared to leading a crowd of scared and agitated wizards. A trait forced upon Galli due to Lorneids inability to walk.

When it was safe for Galli to think again, several questions began to wriggle through her mind. One question niggled at her the most, and it wasn't just the lump on the back of her head constantly reminding her of it. But because it made Galli feel angry and anxious at the same drop.

"Why had Lorneid prevented her aiding the defence of Treforledge?" was the question that frustrated Galli the most.

Giving Lorneid's condition, Galli couldn't ask him why, and it would look inappropriate on her behalf to go back and question him, since she was supposed to be leading the surviving pack. So instead of giving into temptation Galli studied the gorge to see was there a place they could rest without the fear of been exposed. The gorge's walls were narrow making the wizards-tired sighs echo along the passageway. Their groans of hunger and exhaustion caught Galli's attention, but she had nothing but words to offer and last she checked, words didn't fill empty bellies.

The small pack of young Ripelings whined to their confused elders who had no answers to their ongoing pleas. Running for their lives and consumed by fear had stabled the Blue Wizards need for supplements. But having spent a shade with nothing to do but think, had awoken their minds to its needs for functioning. Giving her own stomach a press with her fingertips, Galli shockingly became aware of how far her rib cage stuck out, even when she pressed firmly against her soft skin her stubborn bones refused to move back. There had been no drops to grab any food from Treforledge's stores. Having instructed the Ripelings to bring all substances to Lorneids quarters before the tides were due made Galli feel worse for her hurried procedures.

Looking back amongst the weary crowd Galli spotted Selpay. Selpay was one of the two wizards carrying Lorneid. One glance and Galli's frustration slipped away like a breeze; How could she be mad with Lorneid after what he had suffered to get them here? Too tired to focus, Galli recalled clearly how she had come to be alongside this pack of wizards, it played back in her mind like a wave and with nothing to distract her, Galli watched in her mind's eye the last drops she'd spent in Treforledge.

It was the commotion at the end of the tunnel Galli knew led to the bunker beneath the surface of Crafters Isle, which had woken her. Galli had found herself laying on a solid surface in a dazed state with a pulsing throb beating against her skull. The impact of the blow to her head had made Galli incapable of pronouncing a word without slurring, making casting light futile. So instead, she allowed the frantic noises echoing through the tunnel to be her guide. Following the hectic screams flashing lights burst into Galli's eyes and when she neared the tunnels end, she came face to face with a being, she knew would haunt her until her dying shade. Lorneid, brave as every lord should be, battled the growing shadow that was blocking the way out. Holding it back was a thick water shield conjured from Water Dancer. When Galli drew closer, she noticed the shadow was formed of dark wisping smoke that used shadow tentacles to puncture through Lorneids fading aqua shield. Never in her life had Galli been spine chilled by a creature's sheer aura. But the chilling vibe radiating from the cloud was power beyond imaginable, and what frightened Galli most of all were its scarlet eyes.

While Lorneid struggled to match the clouds immense strength. Galli knew there wasn't many drops left to act, finding her voice again Galli took command by using her leadership skills to instruct the frightened wizards huddled in fear beneath the entrance of the tunnel to get up and make for the tunnels entrance. It was her fear that fuelled the surge in her commanding voice, and it was enough to snap the frightened wizards to their senses. Barking orders while the elder wizards grabbed their young Ripe's she instructed them to make for the tunnels other end. When the darkness of the tunnel consumed the fleeing wizards, Galli turned her attention to helping Lorneid.

Attempting a Balasto curse without her staff decreased her strength and caused Galli to fall into a dazed state and wobbled her vision as the red jet intended for the cloud ricocheted and missed. When Lorneid became aware that it was Galli who was trying to fend off the cloud, he abandoned his defensive tactic and recklessly tried sealing the tunnel with an enlarging spell, but the drop it had taken him to complete the spell had weakened the solidness of his aqua shield. With his only defence faltered, the cloud seized the opportunity and used its long black tentacles to smash through Lorneids wall of water and lashed him across the chest with the side of its swinging tentacle.

The impact of the clouds attack flung Lorneid backwards into the air landing him on the other side of the tunnel. As the cloud tried to enter the cave, Lorneids enlargement spell activated and forced it back as an eruption of vines appeared from beneath the rocks and formed a wall of thorns which was strong enough to keep the cloud out. Rushing to Lorneids side, Galli could see the effect of the clouds strike take hold over his skin. A stretching wound that sizzled and bubbled was gashed across Lorneid's upper body. Refusing aid, Lorneid at once leapt to his feet and both him and Galli reinforced the caves protection before pursuing the fleeing pack. For an entire shade, Lorneid managed to keep up with the pack. But when they were beyond the boundaries of the Charred Mountain, his wound had begun to fester badly, as the poison coursed through his body made it difficult for him to walk. Wrenching and twisting in pain, Lorneids eyes bulged wildly causing him to react franticly and tear aggressively at his own flesh. Summoning his two remaining kin, Selpay and Leiva, the three wizards managed to restrain Lorneid before any permanent damage became visible. Galli enforced a sleeping spell upon him, its effects making him to fall into a comatose sleep, which allowed her to get a clearer look at his wound. After one inspection Galli knew the black gash spread all the way down to his hip was beyond her abilities to heal. But for Lorneids sake she tried every healing incantation she knew, but her attempts were in vain. Nothing Galli did would cleanse or stitch the wound. Thus, leaving Galli with no choice but to cover the wound from prying eyes and lead the surviving wizards to safety. Taking many routes Galli knew from memory, she led the frightened wizards to the high grounds heading east knowing the eastern paths would bring them closer to the misty mountains and beyond sight of any winged beast that may be searching the skies for survivors.

Deeper Galli sank into the gorge, the weary wizards trailing along behind her. With no assurance of an end just a continuation of a path befitting of walking on Galli spotted a bed of boulders with many cracked rocks laying alongside one another. Knowing it would be cruel to deny the weary wizards and Ripes a rest, Galli halted her stride and looked back to the last of her kin.

''Halt!'' called Galli, her voice crisp from lack of use. ''We will rest here for a short spell,'' she announced to the relief of the tired wizards.

The jaded wizards fell to their knees and backsides, the meaning of Galli's command like music to their ears. Galli who now stood away from her relaxing kin because she was too afraid to stare into their helpless eyes knowing she couldn't reassure them with hope that didn't exist. But in her solace an idea came to mind.

"Kikitil," called Galli to the crowd of wizards. Within mili drops Kikitil was at her side, wearing a look of exhaustion but still he managed a smile making Galli feel lousy for what she was about to ask of him.

"I need you to go ahead and see is there any food sources or anyone who can help us," Galli whispered in Kikitil's ear, not wanting the others to hear her desperation.

"These mountains are strange to me and the others. Where should I begin?" asked Kikitil looking at the top of the gorge's walls observantly.

"Above the gorge," answered Galli idly. "And make sure to stay out of sight. We cannot afford to draw attention to our position, whatever attacked Treforledge will surely have sent a scouting party to search for runaways," Galli warned keeping her voice low.

"I won't be seen," Kikitil assured her before taking his leave without further debate.

Galli respectively made a quick visit to every wizard to offer up her services and was glad that none needed any aid because it allowed her to visit Lorneid without delay. Leiva and Selpay the blue twins were knelt by Lorneids side when Galli reached their position. The twins were undeniably the reason Lorneid had returned to Treforledge. Galli knew how much he cared for them and understood completely why he would of went through what he did to ensure their safety. Appearing tough and unnerved, Galli saw right through the twin's best attempts of concealing that they were, behind their mask of toughness, exhausted. Having seen Lorneids state when they had made it past the Charred Mountain, both Leiva and Selpay refused to leave him behind, even when Lorneid pleaded with them to cast him aside and save themselves.

Upon Galli's coming both wizards' rose from their kneeling positions to make way for her to see Lorneid. Through the gap the twins formed, Galli got a clear sight of Lorneid sitting against a flat rock that leaned against the gorges dried wall still entranced by her spell. Leiva and Selpay bowed their heads to salute Galli, but she barely noticed, her eyes were only for Lorneid as she passed the twins with no intention of speaking. When she found herself standing over Lorneid he seemed unaware of her presence but before she could speak, she was distracted by a dry coughing noise.

"Begging your pardon, General Galli," came Selpays stern voice, "May I have a word…. in private?"

Looking away from Lorneids fading features, Galli could sense an eagerness in Selpays voice. Looking directly at both wizards through her tired eyes, Galli noticed how weary carrying Lorneid had affected them this past two shades. The twins were similar in so many ways, each had light blue hair that shone even in the dimmest of light. One of their few indifferences was that Selpay wore a stern look while Leiva had a kind ripe expression making him appear the weaker of the pair. Their eyes were bright and coloured like the blue shaded sky. The one other difference telling them apart was their hair styles. Leiva wore his hair long and free flowing while Selpays was braided into a long ponytail that lay platted down his backside.

"I have trained you for three cycles of shade and never have you spoken to me with such seriousness," said Galli looking at Selpay with severe interest.

Again, Galli had to battle her inner impulses, as much as she wanted to sit by Lorneid's side and ask him why he had chosen to keep her away from the fight. The responsibility of been the Lords Second was to listen to the generals, looking at Selpay, Galli spoke in a calm voice. "Lead the way," she sighed with a slight jerk of her head.

Walking side by side Selpay never uttered a sound, instead he led Galli down the same path she had previously led the surviving pack. Selpay came to a halt when he was sure they were out of earshot. Turning around, the young wizard looked beyond Galli to be certain they were a fair distance from the ears of the camp.

"What I am about to tell you must be kept between us!" said Selpay his voice firm.

Galli nodded, ensuring Selpay that what he was about to share with her would be kept in her confidence.

"I thought you or one of the others might have noticed, but having thought about it, I'm glad no one noticed my absence."

"Absence?" said Galli, a frown creasing her forehead. "But you've been carrying Lorneid since we left the tunnel."

"I was never in the tunnel," whispered Selpay, "I was stranded amongst the last fighters; we'd managed to get as far as the bridge only to find it destroyed."

"Which bridge?"

Selpay sighed before answering. "The Whaling Bridge."

At the mention of the Whaling Bridge a flash of memory projected itself right into Galli's waking eyes. Green sizzling fire burning through the bridge and killing every wizard who walked along its steps. "So that's why Lorneid used the tunnel to escape," Galli thought relieved to tick of one of the many questions she sought to have answered.

"How did you manage to escape if the bridge was destroyed and you were never in the tunnel?" asked Galli curiously, feeling annoyed that she didn't notice Selpays absence.

"What was left of my team hurried for the nests, hoping the Harpies would still be there, but they had fled leaving us with no choice but to return to Crafters Isle a......."

"How can you be sure the Harpies fled?" Galli asked cutting across Selpay.

"Their nests were untouched and there were no signs of a struggle among their midst," answered Selpay, "So we agreed to search for stragglers, until we were ambushed," said Selpay in a faint voice.

"By whom?" snapped Galli a little too aggressively.

Selpay looked over his shoulder, appearing anxious but answered when Galli let out a sigh of impatience. "Kcor and the trickster Tricklet," he answered.

Galli blinked in shock, taken a step back from Selpay she had gone from steeled nerve to jelly legged within drops. Regaining herself quickly, Galli just caught the rest of Selpays description.

"I managed to escape but when I noticed my team were not behind me, I retraced my steps to find they had fallen into Tricklets illusion."

"What did you do, please don't tell me you tried saving them on your own?" asked Galli, trying to remain passive.

"If I did, would you think we would be having this conversation?" said Selpay with an impatient tut of annoyance at how stupid Galli believed him to be. "No, I hid myself beneath the decaying bodies buried beneath the growing ash that now covers our lands until Kcor and Tricklet moved on."

"Kcor and Tricklet were banished by the king's rule, it has been two cycles of shades since then, are you sure it was them?" Galli asked unconvincedly.

"I saw what I saw," Selpay answered with a force behind his words, "But Kcor and Tricklet aren't our main concern, someone worse has returned." Selpay paused again to be certain there were no wizards nearby before continuing. "Which leads me to the reason I wanted to speak with you alone. When Kcor was passing he was telling Tricklet that the survivors were been rounded up and brought to his master, making me strongly believe Lano is behind the attack on Treforledge," whispered Selpay unblinking as he looked at Galli.

"Kcor the Viledirk has no master, he rules the Viledirkening armies and bows to no one," said Galli repeating the lines taught to her by Lorneid. "But if he has returned and speaks of master then Lano must be behind it, who else would have the power to gain Kcors allegiance?" said Galli feeling a knot tighten inside her stomach.

"Exactly!" agreed Selpay looking relieved that Galli was coming around. "The question is how do we prove it without getting ourselves killed?"

"We can't, and I will not lead what is left of us on a suicide mission, we have suffered enough without adding extinct to our titles," said Galli in a firm voice. "What I want to know is how you managed to slip into the pack unnoticed?"

"When the coast was clear I looped from the Twins and climbed the Charred Mountain. When I reached the top, I saw you and the rest of the Blue Wizards running past, it was at that moment that Lorneids legs gave in, so I slipped among the ranks when their eyes were fixed on Lorneid," answered Selpay.

"Well, you would go unnoticed when wizards are concerned more for their lord than what lurks in the shadows," said Galli bitterly, still aggrieved that she had missed Selpay slipping by her unnoticed.

Both wizards were so caught in the moment, they didn't hear Leiva approaching and both of them fell silent when he was a few yards away.

"What is it Leiva? You are supposed to be watching Lorneid," said Selpay.

"I apologise for my interruption," said Leiva apologetically, "But Lord Lorneid has woken up and has asked to see you."

Selpay made a move but was stopped by Leiva's hand gesture. "Lorneid wishes to speak with General Galli, alone," said Leiva, not meeting his brother's eyes but instead stared down at the floor.

Selpays cheeks reddened but his embarrassment did not halt his tongue. "Are you sure he said alone?" Selpay asked in a commanding voice.

"I'm certain," Leiva whispered, in a muffled voice that was just loud enough for Galli and Selpays ears to catch.

Selpay looked outraged and both Leiva and Galli knew why. Selpay was Lorneids eldest heir by a minimum of twenty drops. Being Lorneids next of kin, Selpay was heir to his titles once he died. Perhaps been side-lined for his Second had struck a nerve or Selpay was just annoyed with himself for behaving like an eager Ripeling. Whatever it was he turned to Galli, who was still digesting what Selpay had told her drops before Leiva had interrupted their conversation.

"Galli, didn't you hear Leiva? Lorneid has asked for you!" shouted Selpay, his frustration showing.

Galli's eyes shook, and like a flash, reality collapsed on her shoulders like a cold wave of water. Looking at Leiva then at Selpay she regained her senses. "I will send for you both when I have finished speaking with Lorneid," Galli assured the twins as she left their presence to finally get some closure.

Since Galli had last seen Lorneid, he was laid in a sitting position. Now, he was flat on his back under the shadow of the gorge's walls. Kneeling beside him, Galli carefully removed his ripped cloak from the upper part of his body. Clapping both hands over her mouth and nose, she turned her head in revulsion. But her attempts to block out the decaying smell was futile for the foul stench of dead flesh coursed up her nose, causing hot tears to flow from her reddened eyes and down her dry cheeks. Using her sleeve, Galli wiped away the line of tears sliding down her face. Swallowing hard she forced herself to look upon the festering flesh that now had purple ripples trickling along the edges of the long-blackened gash.

"Looks bad, eh?" coughed Lorneid, his breathing shallow.

Galli looked at her chief commander whose eyes were wide and faded, his once bright features were dimming, meaning death was a certainty. Swaying her fingernails just above the festering wound, a chilling feeling spurned Galli's fingernails that repulsed her hand away from the infected flesh.

"These injuries are unfamiliar to me, why?" Galli asked, a hard lump beginning to grow in her throat. "It seems whatever did this, carries venom as its weapon," she said examining Lorneids torn flesh with her eyes.

"No Galli," heaved Lorneid his breathing coming in puffs, "Dark magic did this," he gasped heavily, "Powerful dark magic casted by a shadow of immense power. What .... chance wo .... uld a wizard of light ha ...ve of rid...di...ng my body of such cursed enchantments?" choked Lorneid the requirements to speak causing him unmeasurable pain.

Black pus trickled down his lips and chin. Daring not to touch the gushy liquid, Galli magically waved away the flowing pus with a lazy swish of her hand.

"What must I do?" asked Galli desperately looking into Lorneid's fading eyes in hope that he knew of a remedy or spell that could reverse the curse that was quickly killing him.

"It's too late for me, Galli," gasped Lorneid, "surely a wizard of your expertise knows that" he gasped again. "What you must do as a favour to me is direct the survivors to Tip-Karps Mountain."

"The sphinx?" interjected Galli.

"Yes," gasped Lorneid his chest rising and falling.

"Tip-Karp will provide shelter, but you mustn't follow, I have a task that you must take alone, as a promise to me," heaved Lorneid his heavy breathing intensifying.

"Where will this favour take me?" Galli asked not taking her eyes away from Lorneid.

"Larmont," gasped Lorneid, his breathing beginning to quiver.

"Larmont?" Galli repeated slightly shocked. "Why Larmont, why not the Golden Kingdom?" she asked uncertain.

"An old friend of mine.... lives...... beyond... its coast, explain to him of our attack, what terrorises our lands and what destroyed our army," croaked Lorneid, who was using his remaining strength to get his message out clearly.

Galli waited for further instructions, but none came. The sound of Lorneids gasps ceased as the realism of his death struck Galli deeply causing soft flowing tears to slide down her cheeks and onto the blank peaceful face of Lorneid. Bowing her head, Galli kissed his forehead and gave him praise for the kindness he had shown toward her and thanked him for his sacrifice that saved so many Blue Wizards. When Leiva and Selpay returned the still body of Lorneid, and Galli's endless sobs was enough for them to know what had happened in their absence. The brothers fell to their knees, taking one of Lorneids hands and held it their grief beyond words.

Selpay murmured incantations that dressed Lorneid's wounds and wrapped him in sky blue silked threads, making his head the only visible part of his body. When word of Lorneid's passing reached the survivors of Treforledge they gathered around Lorneids corpse momentarily. Each Blue Wizard old and young gave thanks to Lorneid for his actions that saved their lives. Their words of thanks making Galli's guilt worsen as memories of Lorneid dropping his guard the moment he became aware of her being in the firing line made Galli question what might have been had she just gone with Blue Wizards and left Lorneid to fend off the cloud?

Watching the survivors standing in a ring around Lorneids body, Galli recalled the niggling question she had been longing to ask him and conceded as she stared at his lifeless corpse that the answer she craved had gone, just like Lorneid, to a place her voice could not be heard. Having carried Lorneid's staff with him the entire journey, Leiva broke rank and proudly strolled over to the pyre to lean forward and kiss Lorneid on the forehead before re-joining the circle of mourners. When respects were paid, Galli ignited sparks from her fingertips that lit the blue bands covering Lorneid in a blaze of glory.

When Lorneid's body was consumed in light gray smoke and blue flames, they all watched in silence as his remains were consumed by wisping white smoke that ascended to the shores of the Red Sea and high into the realms of non-being. As the smoke descended into the distance, Galli made a silent promise to herself, to avenge Lorneids and all the other Blue Wizards deaths. As the flames turned to ember Galli used the mourners silence to her advantage and announced to the weary wizards that she would be leaving to pursue a wizard that may help their situation. Seeing the effect Lorneids death had taken on Selpay and Leiva, Galli left Kikitil in charge of leading the survivors to Tip-Karps Mountain. There were no arguments from the pair because Galli was cunning enough to have pulled Leiva and Selpay aside before her announcement and explain that their grief would only delay the journey.

"I assure you; your safety will be guaranteed when inside Tip-Karps Mountain," Galli called over the radius out bursts and cries of abandonment. "Trust me all of you when my task is done, I will return. Trust me when I say I must do what Lorneid has asked of me," pleaded Galli, the sadness in the wizard's expression becoming too overwhelming for her to bear.

The one of many qualities Galli admired about Kikitil was his devotion to his duties. When the crowd's protests were becoming too much for Galli to withstand. Kikitil was the one who stepped up and slammed his staff firmly into the hard ground, causing tame fissures to erupt and knock the protesting wizards away from Galli.

"When does the stone question the tides? Never!" roared Kikitil. "It endures the waves with no question, and we are no different. Galli has given us a purpose now stop your whining and move it!" yelled an outraged Kikitil winking at Galli as he pointed the way with his outstretched staff.

One by one the survivors of Treforledge followed Kikitil's lead thus relieving Galli of her duties and giving her a bit of space to think clearly. Walking through the gorge a thin path leading up the mountains came into view. Kikitil having found it on his search for aid refused to share his discovery with Galli until Lorneids funeral was over. Leiva who was leading the group helped the weary wizards up the narrowed slope that led into a cave with a long tunnel where the rocks and pillars would provide the wizards with cover until they reached the mountain of the sphinxes.

Kikitil and Selpay stayed behind to speak to Galli before her departure. It was with a heavy heart Galli remained passive. Just staring at Selpay reminded her of Lorneids warm embrace and humour for his resemblance was uncanny to Lorneids.

"You all know where you are going?" asked Galli.

"I have visited the mountain of the sphinxes on many occasions. We will be fine," Kikitil assured Galli with a curt nod.

"Now I must ask you in return for directions, for I have never been to Larmont, nor do I know the way. I was hoping one of you may have some knowledge of its location," admitted Galli feeling it better to be honest now than later make a fool of herself trying to find a place she had never been before.

Kikitil walked to the edge of the mountain side and pointed to Galli's left. "See that green bed of grass sitting at the base of the mountain?" Galli peaked over the cliff and nodded to Kikitil. "That is a back passage that occupies many trails follow the eastern path and Larmont will reveal itself in due course."

"Thank you, my friend," Galli said graciously as they embraced in a tight hug before Kikitil left to join the others.

Selpay remained and waited for the coast to be clear before speaking. When Galli watched the last wizard enter the mountain, she was stunned to see Selpay holding Water Dancer out to her.

"What are you doing?" asked Galli.

"If you are going to be travelling alone then you're going to need this, I have a feeling Lorneid wanted you to have it," said Selpay.

"Water Dancer is a family heirloom, I can't take it Selpay, by right its yours," said Galli pushing it back toward Selpay.

"And I am choosing to give it to you, who knows what dangers you may face on your way to Larmont," Selpay said thrusting Water Dancer into her hands.

Galli looked at it with consideration and felt it was as light as a feather. "This staff is legendary and the last remaining heirloom of Treforledge, why are you giving it away?" Galli asked.

"Because you're the only wizard to bring honour to Treforledge since Quiloc, you earned the right to wield that staff the same way I haven't, you carried us and led the pack to safety, take it and honour Treforledge with future victories," said Selpay, respectively.

Lost for words Galli felt like she was carrying the weight of Treforledge in her hand. But a whelm of pride soothed her guilt and if she were going to make Lorneid proud then how better to do it than by using his own staff to help her, smiling Galli finally accepted the staff and as she did a radiant rush clamped her hand and staff together.

"When you return will it be to retake Treforledge?" Selpay asked with a keen look at Galli.

It was the least expected question Galli would have thought to be asked. Which was why her reply was so long coming. "We haven't the strength to launch a counterattack, the Blue Wizards are depleted, and you saw what happened to our armies, the wizards we've got left will not be enough to retake Treforledge," said Galli delicately, confused by Selpays sudden change in attitude.

"Treforledge must be defended! Or what would you have us become a band of refugees seeking aid from those who have looked down upon us our entire lives?" said Selpay, his eyes fierce.

"Help from foreign lords is the reason Lorneid asked me to travel to Larmont. We will not stand a chance of reclaiming our homelands if we do not swallow our pride and accept all the help we can get!" said Galli with a smoothness to her voice intending to not further rise Selpays thirst for vengeance.

"I will wait until our pack is able then with or without you, I will strike back at those who have humiliated us!" said Selpay in a final tone, before swishing his cloak and departing, leaving Galli to think about what will she do once her promise to Lorneid is done?

Chapter 4

The Ruins of Treforledge

Waves of strong currents lashed against the cracked rocks surrounding Treforledge. The beautiful Islands of blue once decorated with clear aqua stones now lay in a blanket of charcoal ash. Standing tall upon the peak of the Charred Mountain, looking down upon the desolation, was Bregit the Yellow, the Lord of Larmont. Concealed in his shabby brown stitched together cloak, Bregit felt secure standing still as a tree upon the mountain side. The lack in security around the Blue Islands made him anxious as he looked at the edges of every island and was surprised to see no one patrolling the islands perimeters.

What appeared to be snow falling and flowing down upon the three islands caught Bregit's attention. Plucking a handful of the specks from the air Bregit was amazed to discover that it wasn't snow floating along the breeze but hot grey ash that had latched itself over the rocks of the three islands, coating every inch of Treforledge in thick layers of decomposing ash. The only remains left of Treforledge that wasn't coated in ash were the identical pillars positioned to Bregit's left. Tall, strong, and facing opposite directions, these pillars were named the Twins. The Blue Wizards named them the Twins because of their identical shape and narrow length. But now, they stood covered in slimy wet seaweed giving their appearance the look of neglect. When the crushing waves erupted from the banks of Suala Island. They would beat against the immoveable Twin Pillars. Which made many wizards of Treforledge believe they too had the strength of the Pillars and would challenge their strength, by standing on top of the pillars and wait for the Red Sea's wrath to show face and decide their faith.

''To stand tall, proud and strong in the face of fear,'' were the words every Blue Wizard recited before facing the incoming waves. Because if that wizard, without using their magical powers was still standing after the waves settled, that wizard would be given a place among the ranks of the Blue Striped Army. When Lorneid was made Lord of Treforledge he made this daring challenge one to be passed if a wizard wished to join his army. Sualas Whirl was the name Lorneid baptised the powerful sea waves, because of the waves swirling unpredictability and due to the waves only erupting from the banks of Suala Island. But Bregit wasn't gazing upon the Twins for that obvious reason, he was instead searching for a stairway, and he found it with a second glance at the left-hand side of the right pillar. Spiral and curved the stair was carved into the pillars by the Crafters who designed the stair to shorten the journey from the Charred Mountain to Crafters Isle.

Sniffing the air, Bregit sensed it was foul with decay. Ash, black with specks of grey continued to flow motionlessly through the air like snow, the sea breeze was doing its upmost to increase the speed of the ever-growing ash falling upon Treforledge. Walking at a slow pace, Bregit moved cautiously to the top of the mountain's peak. When there, he was embraced by a fouler more sickening odour that caused his nose to wrinkle.

"What power could have done this kind of damage?" he breathed below a whisper.

The sight of the Treforledge's state saddened Bregit deeply because he knew the kingdom was of purity with no ill bearings to anyone, yet here it stood, in ruin and despair. This persuaded Bregit not use the spiral stair in fear he may walk into a hidden trap. Staying invisible was his only safeguard now, and he was not about to blow his cover by walking straight into a laid-out trap.

Using his sharp toenails, Bregit dug them deep into the mountain's hardened rocks, which allowed him to slide slowly and quietly down the mountain side with no trailing dust left in his wake. Twisting his ankles at the base of the Charred Mountain, Bregit came to a halt just before his feet hit the sand base of the mountain's peak.

Piles of crafted rocks laid sunken in the sand, making Bregit wonder, 'How many innocents, unprepared wizards had flung those rocks away in desperation to escape the onslaught?' Turning away quickly, not wanting to dwell too long in the sweeping view, Bregit made out the border of the ancient Waling Whining Bridge a few yards away from where he stood. Looking down on the soft sand he noticed an unusual, shaped mark carved deliberately into the sand. Edging closer with a keener eye to the ground, Bregit recognised the prints did not belong to any creature he'd come across before. For wizards always left their nail marks when hurried. Sighing with annoyance at himself, he knew he had fallen into a puzzle laid out by someone jesting him to take part into solving. Squatting as low as his aching legs could, Bregit rolled back his damp sleeves, revealing his thin arm that had not yet recovered from the long climb up the mountains. Swaying his hand above the stomp mark, he placed his fingertips an inch above the footprint.

"Let's see who you belong to," Bregit said softly, with a look of deep concentration.

A white aura flowed along Bregit's hand. Feeling the electrical current grow in strength, it slithered along his wrists and up to his outstretched fingers, giving warmth to his shaking limbs. When he was confident enough energy was generated, he flexed his fingers sharply, forcing the electrical surge to shoot from his fingertips and smoother the print in the sand.

"What the……," cried Bregit retracting his hand as a prickling pain had surged through his entire arm. Due to the force of his own spell rebounding and causing the skin on Bregit's hand and lower arm to sizzle and smoke appearing as if he had come into direct contact with acid flames.

"Remarkable," gasped Bregit, studying his burnt hand with fascination. "It's as if this creature foreseen a moment in future shades when a wizard would find their prints and concealed its identity with a back-firing charm," he said shockingly, the sense of his own statement increasing the growing fear within his mind.

Never in his long life, had Bregit come across a creature with the skills to repel magic. Magic was the only weapon wizards owned that frightened the mystical creatures and if they have found a device or weapon capable of repelling magical abilities, then Bregit had to investigate the matter further. Looking with deep worry at the ash stained Treforledge, Bregit knew the answers he craved were somewhere beneath or above the blackened ash-stained rocks. Considering his options, he knew the quickest route into Treforledge was to cross The Waling Whining Bridge. So quietly, he brushed his fingernails over his injures muttering an old healing incantation he had learned as a Ripeling. After the third sweep of his fingers Bregit's burnt flesh began regenerating at a rapid pace, when satisfied his spell had done the trick, he lowered his sleeve and made for the bridges border.

The lack in security troubled Bregit when truth be told he should be gracious. Remembering his last visit to the Blue Islands, he recalled the joy filled atmosphere flowing through the islands like air, now it was reeked with death and misery. Lorneid was the one who greeted Bregit on the shade of his arrival and walked him through the three islands as an honoured guest which gave Bregit a feel for the place. Lorneid introduced him to every particle of his beloved home. But it was the bridge that caught Bregit's attention the most. Truth be told, he cared little for crafts and rocks having learned many of those skills as a Ripeling.

"Our Crafters built that bridge," Lorneid told Bregit proudly. "I remember our late king paid our islands a visit and asked was it handmade. It was indeed your grace I replied," Bregit recalled as echoes of Lorneid's bumpily voice floated into his thinking.

Lorneid went on to tell Bregit that the king admired the Crafters work so much he said he should station his Lutiz's to work within Blue Islands.

"They might learn something besides watching my every move," he remembered Lorneid telling him with a pride.

The friendly Lord of Treforledge always took a huge amount of pride from the kings only visit to Treforledge. Bregit didn't posse neither the nerve or heart to tell Lorneid, that the king had indeed mistook a wrong turn for Larmont and stumbled upon the Blue Islands by pure chance.

The Whaling Whinging Bridge was built to aid the Rock Grinders, who spent many drops carrying rocks and stone from the Charred Mountain all the way to Crafters Isle. Lorneid explained his Crafters would have to walk for miles back and forth tirelessly. Until the three islands united and joined their lands by roped bridges. There was only a slight catch to the positioning of one bridge and that was because it was laid directly above the home of the whaling spirits that dwelled deep within the Charred Mountain. These whaling spirits would occasionally come out to float above the Red Sea, doing everything in their power to stall the bridge from been built. Using amusing tactics such as burning every tree for miles, disrupting the Crafters, and terrorising the already scared Ripelings to the verge of fearing entering the mountain. It was heavily rumoured, that the Lord of Treforledge captured the whaling spirits that haunted the cliffs of the Charred Mountain and trapped the mindless trans spirits deep within the oaken wood the Crafters used to make the bridge. When Bregit came across the bridge, he questioned Lorneid about its inhabitants. But the enthusiastic lord denied such claims and simply put the rumours down to foreign superstition much to Bregit's dismay, for he longed to know did magic exist that could bridge the gap between the living and the dead?

Edging closer to the bridges border, Bregit felt his heart sink to the bottom of his stomach. The bridge was nowhere to be seen. Jogging closer the realisation became clearer to a horrified Bregit as he looked down upon the Red Sea to see the remains of the ancient bridge floating at the bottom of the cliffs, between the rocks and pillars of Crafters Isle. Keenly peering at the gushing waves beneath him, Bregit made out other objects floating alongside the bridges remains. Bodies, soggy with iced blue hands along with dead black skin trailing along their legs drifted motionlessly above the strong currents. The blank empty eyed expressions worn by the dozens of dead wizards were frightening, for each one wore the same frightened expression.

Observing the dead bodies and the brutality their bodies have been forced to endure made Bregit's insides swell with pity. He tried to imagine they had died before falling into the water, but he knew in his soul that these wizards suffered until their dying breath. Resisting the temptation to pull them free from the fierce Red Sea was hard to keep at bay. Under the circumstances Bregit knew any attempt to use his powers so near the coursing waves was a death sentence. Leaving the dead wizards floating and repeatedly beaten against the rising tides was all he could do, because if he pulled them out, he wouldn't be just giving away his location but would in turn anger the Red Sea.

''What class of being would dare destroy a unique monument of Treforledge?'' said Bregit with disgust, as he watched a couple of wizard corpses hit against one another as they swirled along the sea waves.

He forced himself to look away, knowing if he stared any longer at the innocent eyes that reflected his furious expression, he would no doubt give into his anger and retaliate with foolish actions. Peering once more over the cliff, Bregit restrained himself from looking at the floating corpses and instead turned his attention to the bridges remaining parts. Examining the broken wood with a sharper glance, he noticed most of the bark that floated above the waves had dark marks licked along its edges.

''Scorch marks,'' breathed Bregit.

Judging by the scorch marks stained over the bark, a conjurer of fire no doubt brought the Whaling Bridge tumbling down and must also be the one responsible for the ash spawned across Treforledge. Steading himself, Bregit moved his eyes away from the horrific images of decomposing flesh, his mind had detected a strange energy signal, one with a dark flow of radiant power that seemed to be coming from within Treforledge. The question was where?

Whatever this energy was it caused Bregit to doubt his sole pursuit. Because never had he sensed such raw power before. He knew if it were a wizard a magical trace would lead him directly to it. But this power was blocking his senses and caused his head to hurt whenever he tried locking onto its location.

''This power I'm sensing is beyond anything I've ever felt before,'' Bregit said with uncertainty.

His instincts niggled at him, recommending that he should track back and get reinforcements. But a stronger more determined voice broke through the barriers of his cautious thinking. Reminding him that if he allowed whoever dwelled within

Treforledge to grow in power or worse, leave and destroy other unprepared lands, he would forever carry the guilt for stepping aside and allowing this being to cause more chaos. This very thought swung Bregit's mind toward pursuing this source. Taking the only route, he was sure to be untouched, he made his way west of the mountain side. Passing by many tall pillars that stretched as far along the mountainside as the eye could see.

"Not as young as I once was," gasped Bregit slowing his stride a few miles from the bridges border, due to the cramps in his legs causing his muscles to cramp.

Leaning against the mountainside panting, he wiped away drips of sweat sliding down his forehead by using the long sleeves of his cloak. Bregit dabbed the filthy brown cloth gently against his face and neck. Exhausted, he still refused to summon his staff, knowing full well, if he could sense this unknown creature's power then the opposing creature would no doubt sense his, the moment he casted a spell. Ignoring his cramping pains, Bregit walked on, the mountains shadow concealing him from any onlookers. But when the mountain's shadow waned, Bregit approached with caution making sure to avoid tripping over the detached rocks that had fallen from the mountain side. Once out of the mountain's shadow it didn't take him long to find what he was looking for. Anonymous and camouflaged by vines and dead roots that once belonging to a Drop Tree which had grown beyond its use to produce drops.

What lay beneath the vines and dead roots was a secret passageway that would lead Bregit straight into Crafters Isle. When the passage was discovered by Lorneid, he kept it between himself and a few trusted friends, Bregit, among those Lorneid considered a close friend was shown the tunnels location on his tour of the Blue Islands. Lorneid told Bregit that by using magic to conceal the entrance it would be easily detected. So, he decided to instead plant a Drop Tree above the tunnels entrance. And to avoid questions as to why he planted a Drop Tree so far from the Drop Tree Orchard, Lorneid casted a virus on the Drop Tree, to shorten its lifespan.

The Drop Tree died a shade after Lorneid cursed it. Rotting, the tree trunk quickly faded, leaving only its thick roots in its remembrance. This tactic proved even beyond Lorneid's expectations. The Blue Wizards even made jokes and laughed at their lord's foolish attempts to try grow Drop Trees beneath sand. Lorneid always one to have a laugh joyed in their amusement saying he felt he needed to try and solemnly admitted he had gone beyond his depth and had reaped his reward. And to this shade no one has ever detected that Lorneids foolish attempt was actually a cover up. A trick to fool the fools who believed him the fool was indeed a master stroke on Lorneid's part, and it was a story that always made Bregit laugh when the innocence of Lorneid's actions would repeat in his mind.

Bending on one knee, Bregit examined the covered entrance with his palms. A wave, cold and repulsing gusted through his fingertips numbing his hand. Sighing with relief, Bregit smiled knowing the entrance was safe to open. Concentrating his eyes flashed, summoning a bright white beam to rise from the depths of his focused gaze. The vines covering the tunnel sprung into life, once they became aware of Bregit's presence, they launched themselves at him.

"Dovstilreez," whispered Bregit softly.

His freezing spell combined with his white beams grinded at the thick green leafed vines. Once their movements were frozen from the inside. Bregit's surging beams wrestled with the stubborn plants. Stronger willed than he had predicted forced Bregit to generate more energy than he'd intended to overpower the vines stubborn stance. Eventually it paid off, as the beams split the roots and vines in half. Effortlessly Bregit removed the broken roots and smoked leaves with a wave of his arm. In the vine's absence lay a small wizard size hole, dug so deep beneath the sand even the Red Sea could not reach it.

''I hate tunnels,'' sighed Bregit. The memories of his last trip down the secret tunnel were nowhere near pleasant on Bregit's part. Placing his legs inside the hole, he sighed heavily preparing himself for an unpleasant experience.

''Pallas,'' said Bregit, closing his eyes as a bone cracking sound split through his ears as the hole magically widened, swallowing him deep into a pit of darkness that Bregit knew would lead him closer to who was behind all this chaos.

Chapter 5

The Road to Larmont

Galli was so preoccupied examining Water Dancer that she didn't notice Green Shade had eclipsed Peace Shade. Meaning the temperatures would decrease making her thankful for her heavy cloak. Lime rays creeped through the clouds spraying their effects of doubt across the lands laid ahead. Fortunate for Galli she was initiated since the shade she was ripe. Rendering the shades effects useless against her, and with a long journey ahead she was thrilled to not have the shades effects added to her ongoing worries. The lands of grass were not difficult to find. Seaweed green and twice Galli's height the grass stood out like a flame in the night. Tiptoeing quietly through the soft grass, Galli repeatedly skidded on the slippery mud every few steps. Had Galli not been in possession of Water Dancer, she may have found herself face first in the thick, slippery mud that refused to allow her any rhythm in keeping her balance. But her frustration soon began to irritate her bones, breathing deeply and calmly Galli flushed out her burning desires to burn every blade of grass to ash. 'That would rid my problem,' she thought, the images of grass burning to ash filling her mind with satisfaction.

''Stupid idea,'' she breathed, nodding her head in disapproval.

To wield her powers in the open would draw attention and jeopardise her journey to Larmont. Pulling herself together Galli calmly hopped over the slippery patches and after a couple of miles of falling and crawling through mud holes. The grass decreased in height, giving Galli a clear view of what lay ahead. Two pathways, one leading east the other southeast.

''Oh no!'' Galli said her heart sinking.

Studying one pathway to the other, Galli couldn't make heads or tails which path she was supposed to follow. The annoying journey through the mud fields had pushed away Kikitil's directions from her memory. Knowing she had a fifty-fifty chance of taking the right path and a fifty-fifty chance of taking the wrong one, Galli considered doing something she would never have suggested if Lorneid was present. But the daunting thought that what would happen if she took the wrong pathway played through her already doubting mind. And Galli needed to get this meeting over with so she could stall Selpays attempts to go on a suicide mission to reclaim Treforledge, the very thought putting an extending strain on Galli's decision making. Considering her options; knowing there was only one way to get out of this pickle, Galli tightened her grip on Water Dancer. Knowing full well what she was about to do was forbidden to practice in the open, Galli went against her better judgement. Continuing before her conscience got the better of her, Galli tipped Water Dancer against her forehead and said firmly. ''VisnibPeldey.''

Suddenly long, thick, and glowing threads of beaming purple rays appeared, slithering around Galli's forehead like a serpent. Embracing the threads warm aura Galli allowed them to take full control of her instincts. The feeling was blissed to embrace, even if the effects were short, it felt comforting for Galli to escape reality and dwell in peaceful solace. With no doubt or hesitation, Galli's legs under the influence of her threads turned and walked the southeast pathway. Having walked half a mile confidently, a pinching feeling broke through Galli's peaceful state, niggling at her to lift the enchantment. How she longed to stay in this state of feeling carefree and unburdened, but in doing so she would be leaving herself vulnerable to inception. Closing her eyes, she snapped herself back to reality by dreamily saying. ''Leaknog.''

Galli retraced the actions of the past shade, when she was fully convinced, she was in full control of her body Galli continued walking on the southeast pathway hoping her magical instincts served her well. Thick trees with long branches sprouting thin twigs stood in rows along the stone path. The trees long shadow dimming Galli's vision. When the darkness came too strong to depend on sight alone, Galli whispered softly to the latched together leaves on top of Water Dancer. ''Nelope.'' The leaves detached, revealing an egg size blue Malas stone carved in the shape of a star. ''Tillareasilob,'' Galli whispered softly.

Raising Water Dancer above her head, a radiant beam of brightest white shone from the stones tip spreading light all along the pathway and diminishing the darkness. With Galli's radiant light giving her clear sight of the path ahead, she walked freely at an increased pace. When the line of trees ended Galli about managed to break through a tight gap of thorned ditches, only to find herself staring at two hills with a trench splitting the hills apart.

''Whoa,'' Galli gasped, staring at the wonderful beauty laid out in front of her.

'All flowers of colour must grow here,' she questioned with fascination.

Stretching out her hand, about to touch the pink and purple polka a dot flower with green and yellow petals, it began to rustle, spraying a haze of sparkling powder from its centre core. When Galli shooed away the haze, a tiny, winged creature familiar to Galli appeared out of the flowers core. The winged creature now staring at her with wonder was a Pixie Lott. A mystical creature who likes to dwell within high fragranced flowers. The tiny pixie considered Galli for a short spell, annoyingly buzzing around her head, and staring curiously at her with its wide black eyes that had a glim white pupil in its centre that Galli was aware narrowed when it was in the company of strangers. Following its every movement, Galli couldn't help but smile as the tiny creature zoomed from one side of her head to the other. Its skin was pink, but its wings were a mixture of yellow and blue which was strange to Galli but overall, she found it cute.

''My apologies Wizard of Blue if my scenting disturbs you. It is not my intention to be crude,'' squeaked the pixie.

''Scent away. I cannot say the scent you are looking for resides within me,'' Galli said defensively.

''It's not every shade a foreign wizard stumbles among my domain,'' said the pixie, who had stopped swirling around Galli to nest on her nose and stare curiously into her blue eyes.

''You've nothing to apologise for,'' Galli said kindly regretting her ignorant tone. ''Perhaps you could help me, my knowledge of these lands is slim at most.''

''I'm not sure I can trust you yet, for many have wandered through my gardens with sweet voices and kind faces only to betray my kindnesses with acts of defilement and cruelty,'' said the pixie its voice no longer squeaky.

"I am no bringer of darkness," Galli assured the pixie seeing the grim look appearing on its face.

"Darkness cannot travel on foot, it lingers within, that is why I needed to scent all of you," explained the pixie.

"And was my inspection clarified?" asked Galli.

The pixie's small lips raised into a broad smile. "The light shines bright within you and upon you meaning you are pure, but it doesn't sway the question," squeaked the pixie.

"What question?" asked Galli.

"Why is a wizard cloaked in blue travelling to Larmont if unfamiliar with its lands, brandishing light carefree if uncertain?" questioned the pixie.

"I am here on the agreed terms of my deceased lord, I promised him I would find an old friend of his," Galli stated with an innocent smile.

The little pixie's eyes widened even more, the white pupil in its centre growing in length as did the satisfied grin on its tiny face.

"Bregit," squeaked the pixie making its wings buzz annoyingly, "You seek Bregit?"

'So that's the wizard's name,' Galli thought, feeling a smile stretching her cheeks.

"I have come to Larmont to meet with this Bregit. Is there a possibility of gaining your aid, my only lead is to follow every east path that comes my way?" pleaded Galli.

"I cannot lead you to Bregit's tower. If I were to leave my gardens, who would keep watch over the Flower Covered Mountain?" squeaked the pixie.

"Flower Covered Mountain, where?" questioned Galli frowning.

The pixie pointed its tiny finger at the flowers stretched along the green grass and when Galli looked up the answer to her question revealed itself. Blankets of flowers coloured differently and shaped in opposite shapes and sizes, blended perfectly to camouflage an entire mountain from sight.

"It's beautiful," Galli said dreamily, entranced by the sight she was bearing witness to.

The mountain was beautifully decorated in such colourful flowers and plants that it sprayed a rainbow over its peak. Vines thick and strong hung from every entrance to allow creatures to climb safely up and down the flowered covered rocks.

"Me and my kin have guarded the Flowered Mountain since the banishment of the Gliders, and are duty bound to never leave," squeaked the pixie.

"Gliders were banished, how?" Galli asked frowning.

"Bregit, is how," answered the pixie. "Cycles of Shades ago a swarm of Gliders resided within the mountain opposite the Flower Covered Mountain," squeaked the pixie pointing its thin arm away from the beaming mountain to point its tiny fist at a more horrifying sight.

"Oh my!" gasped Galli horrified.

The scene was appalling to look at. The mountain opposite the colourful Flower Mountain was blackened with scorch marks stained on every rock. Nothing seemed to grow even the rain considered it unworthy to spill its drops upon its disfigured state. Chunks from Galli's view had been ripped from the mountain's sides, but what creature had the power to do such damage?

"What did this?" Galli asked, imagining sea serpents or fire creatures. The only creatures Galli believed capable of inflicting this kind of destruction.

"Gliders who once lived within The Dark Mountain," answered the pixie. "Their cruelty drove away all goodness surrounding Larmont and drove creatures of light away from our lands."

"Were you the only creature brave enough to stay?" asked Galli finding it weird that she hadn't come up against other creatures.

"The Slithers remained alongside the pixies, even after they were uprooted from their mountain's depth and slaughtered. Arb the head Slither managed to escape with six of his kin," squeaked the pixie.

"Escape where?" Galli asked entranced by the pixie's story.

"To the shores. That was where Arb met Bregit who was building his tower at that shade. After explaining what the Gliders were doing Bregit sympathised Arb's sufferings. We watched from afar as the wizard of yellow walked without fear into the Dark Mountain with only his staff for company. No one knows what happened once Bregit came face to face with the Glider pack or how he managed to do it, but one by one, the swarm of Gliders who had killed and terrorised so many creatures fled their caves and scattered, never to return. Bregit walked out unharmed and since that shade he has been known to all living in Larmont as lord," the pixie said with approbation.

As fascinating as this story was it still didn't convince Galli who had seen the capabilities of Gliders when she was competing in the Ultimate Colour and found it hard to believe a single wizard could defeat a swarm of creatures who were believed to be the most powerful mystical beings to roam Nocktar.

"Gliders are the most powerful mystical creatures to live in the Lands of Light. This Bregit is either an extremely gifted wizard or a fraud," Galli said unconvincingly.

"Regardless of how he done it. Bregit the Yellow has been since his arrival a friend to all. Without him Larmont would have been reduced to nothing but a land of darkness," the Pixie squeaked fiercely, not liking Galli's disbelief of Bregit's actions.

The pixies mention of her lands covered in darkness brought Galli back to her own agenda for been here and swept away her curiosity instantly.

"If you cannot lead me to Bregit, I am sure a creature of your stature can at least point me in the right direction," Galli said with a hint of flattery hoping it was enough to sway the pixie's mind.

The pixie smiled at Galli's praising words. Zooming over her head it stretched out its tiny arm and pointed its finger at the gap separating the two mountains.

"Go through that laneway splitting the mountains. When you find yourself outside of the it a Malas stone path will be waiting that leads to many different destinations, the one you need to follow is east, only east! Stray from the eastern path and you will find yourself lured by the enchanted bed of vines that will prove hard to defeat if they are woken before their hibernation is up," warned the pixie.

"You have my sincere gratitude pixie Lott for your much-needed help and kindness. I am sorry I cannot linger and discover more of Lamont's beauty, but I urgently must meet with Bregit," Galli admitted regretting the urgency in her words.

Galli gave the pixie a kind smile and walked carefully by the colourful flowers being extra careful not to stand on any. When she reached the thin gap separating the two mountains, Galli turned to admire the beauty of the flowers once more.

Observing more closely, Galli's insides began to tighten with nerves, besides her nerves, home sickness was beginning to creep into her mind. It had only now dawned on her how much she wished she were home living the life she hated just to regain a speck of feeling needed again. The only thing keeping her moving forward instead of back was her promise to Lorneid. It was his dying wish that fuelled Galli now as she upright entered the gap between the mountains without fear.

If the Dark Mountain looked damaged from the front it compared little to its side. Mould, slime, and dried dirt hung down the cliffs, slowly decaying the stones it latched to. What was worse was the dead smell that contaminated the passageway which forced Galli to stick to the side of the lane that was less foul.

''Yuck,'' wretched Galli, covering her mouth and nose with the collar of her cloak to ensure she didn't inhale the foul odours flowing from the mountain.

Having made it through the laneway between the mountains. A grey stoned path with thin straps of tree bark at its sides lay at the end of the gap separating the two mountains. North, South, and East were the paths layout. Galli presuming no one bothered to make a west path because it was obvious where it led. Before taking her first step upon the path leading east, unable to resist she turned around to take one last glance at the beautiful mountain she had taken close to her heart.

''Strange, both mountains resemble the two sides of wizards in an uncanny way. Some are dark and consumed with darkness, and some are filled with light and purity that shines throughout us all,'' Galli said lightly to herself, as she looked away to begin her journey to Bregit's tower.

''Well phrased, young Ripeling,'' came a chilling voice from behind Galli that caused her to scream aloud with fright as a hooded figure appeared from out of the shadow of the mountain

Chapter 6

The Council of Shadows

Sliding side to side at such intensity there was nothing for it but to hold on and hope his stomach wouldn't come up his throat and splatter out his mouth. Thankfully for Bregit, the ride was short lived. Unable to control his landing, he was flung from the tunnels mouth and spat onto the wet surface of the tunnels hard ground. The aftershock was difficult to overcome, laying in what seemed a puddle, Bregit struggled to regain his stance. Taking him several attempts until he could stand without his surroundings spinning around him. The weight of his drowned cloak taking half the blame for his imbalance.

''Damn Lorneid and his sarcastic ideas!'' cursed Bregit, leaning against the tunnels hardened walls that offered no comfort only bone chilling cold.

Closing his eyes Bregit waited for the nausea to cease knowing walking now would only cause him to stagger and fall again. Placing both of his shaking hands on each side of his thumping skull, he pressed his fingernails against his temple massaging them in attempt to soothe the dizziness he was been forced to endure. When the spinning eased, Bregit scooped up a handful of water from the poodle on the floor and slowly rubbed it against his swollen lips. The muddy water offered some comfort, but it did nothing to extinguish the elevated temperatures that were causing Bregit's skin to bubble rapidly. Feeling both sides of his face, stinging pinches shuddered his body. Watching in complete shock Bregit couldn't explain the hardened lumps pumping up from the tip of his wrists, arms, and body. Reacting instinctively, he scooped handful after handful of muddy water from the puddle and splashed it all over himself.

Still, it wasn't enough to quench the lumps growing thirst. Rashly Bregit licked the dirty water from his fingers, but it still wasn't enough, the thirst was still spreading throughout his body forcing him to tear off his damp cloak and dive into the muddy puddle. Repeatedly he rolled back and forth, allowing the water to touch every particle of his bubbling body. Though the muddy water halted the bubbling it was when the water was absorbed the bubbling would resume. Gasping, Bregit fluently weaved his shaking hands and casted a powerful shrivelling jinx on himself that coated his body in a silver aura.

''Ah,'' Bregit sighed in blissful relief as he lay spread eagled in the puddle. When he looked again the bubbling lumps were frozen and had shrunken into small warts filled with yellow pus due to the effects of his shrivelling jinx. Squeezing each wart with gritted teeth the gooey liquid burst onto Bregit's trembling fingers. Wiping the drooling pus from his skin, Bregit noticed his body was now covered in reddish pimples that didn't fade away after his shrivelling jinx's aura lifted.

After many drops huddled in the middle of his flesh, Bregit realised he was no longer quivering. Getting to his feet he gave himself a shake and though he was no longer shook it still it required many drops before his senses returned. In his wait for his mind to settle, Bregit wondered could the tunnel be enchanted to keep wizards from using it as a short cut Because if his suspicion was correct then he wasn't going any further defenceless. Unconcerned about the risks of his actions Bregit outstretched his hand and summoned a thin white stick streaked in yellow stripes into his waiting hand. This streaked stick was Bregit's staff and unlike common staffs his had three curved twigs on its top, each twig framing a triangular shaped Malas stone dyed in a sunset yellow.

"Give light to my lack of sight," Bregit said softly, tipping the point of his staff gently against the tunnels wall.

When Bregit withdrew his staff, two lines of clear blue flame crawled with pace up the walls and slithered down the tunnel giving him a clear view of the tunnels path. "Much better," said Bregit beginning his walk down the tunnel.

Like most underground tunnels, they were long, dull, and boring. With nothing to think of except of when it would end. Bregit strolled cautiously, now guided by his enchanted blue flames, he became aware of heavy drops falling on the bald patch on top of his head.

"Rain has decided to rest above Treforledge this shade," said Bregit in a faint voice while holding out his palm to feel the dripping water fall gently into his palm.

The sound of the rain would drown out any noise made underneath the surface which was why Bregit now wore a relieved smile on his face. "Perhaps luck has sprinkled its dust on me, this shade," he said sarcastically unable to hide his joy, as he continued the daunting walk down the tunnel.

Forgetting that protective enchantments were casted inside the tunnel. Bregit walked blindly into an invisible solid object that rejected him passage. Flying backwards a surging pain shot through Bregit's backside as he collided with the tunnels hard ground that caused him unbearable pain. The impact winded him, causing Bregit to heave repeatedly as he lay with his face in the dirt clutching his mid-section. Stubbornly he forced himself not to cry out as he waited with nerves of steel for the pain to pass.

"How could I have been so careless!" Bregit growled aggressively.

Furious with himself for his lack of wisdom and the pain of his collision pushed Bregit's annoyance to breaking point. Steading himself, his knees still buckled from the collision, he raised his staff and aimed it at the magically enchanted area as blood red beams pulsed within the three Malas stones contained in his staff. "BALASTO!!" bellowed Bregit, his voice echoing throughout the tunnel.

Bregit's curse caused the three Malas stones at the top of his staff to glow a darker shade of scarlet. Combining their charges, the beams formed into a triangular formation that shot instantly at the invisible barrier and shattered it into a thousand sharded pieces that flowed motionlessly in mid-air.

"Vanishio," said Bregit sternly, waving his hand at the scattered specks, causing them all to disappear in the blink of an eye.

Heavy drops began to pebble dashed from the cracks at the top of the tunnel. Spilling down all sides of its walls and clearing away Bregit's enchanted flames. The extinguishing of his flames wasn't the concern, the thick grey smoke rising in the flame's absence did however cause Bregit concern. The combination of his Balasto curse and the invisible barrier no doubt was the reason behind the walls collapse. Unwilling to dwell in the shrouding smoke, Bregit moved swiftly from the scene, wanting nothing more than to put as much distance between himself and the scene of the explosion. When the smoke became an irritation Bregit wove his hands repeating the Vanishio spell to rid the path of the blinding smoke. The smoke cleared giving him a dimmed view of the tunnel. When near the end of the tunnel his senses began to tingle causing his eyes to blink furiously. This niggling in his head was Bregit's magical intelligence sensing another possessor of magic nearby. Focusing hard he tried finding the power signal, but he was too late, for the source had vanished as quickly as it had appeared. Comparing the power surge Bregit had sensed a moment ago to the one he had felt on the island's border, failed in comparison. But his concern was swept away by the sight of the exit. But before Bregit could touch it, a foul stench of stale sweat filled the air and swept up his nostrils. The smell seemed to be coming from a small bundle of dirt-stained robes that Bregit had unknowingly walked on.

''Who are you?'' came a disembodied voice from under the pile of robes.

Alarmed Bregit cast a white beam from the tip of his staff, shining it over the pile of dirt-stained robes. But found nobody hiding underneath the filthy garments and looked around the tunnel for the creature. 'Could this be one of the whaling spirits haunting Treforledge?' thought Bregit half heartily.

When the voice never resurfaced Bregit didn't dare move, fearing if he did or made any attempt to leave, he might be attacked or fall victim to another hidden trap. Playing it safe Bregit felt it best to just answer and get an insight into the being that stalked him.

''I am Bregit the Yellow, Lord of Larmont and friend of Lorneid the Blue,'' Bregit replied lightly, feeling he had nothing to hide.

''Bregit,'' gasped a rasping voice making him spin around.

Feeling a light breeze sweeping past his ankles Bregit was almost blinded by a beaming blue light that appeared from under the pile of robes. When the beam died, Bregit found himself staring at a skinny stick shaped wizard covered in dirt and dust. Its long blue detached hair hung loosely over its face. It only took one glance at its fragile body to convince Bregit that this wizard had not eaten or drank anything in shades. But before he could speak a rasping, dry voice uttered something from the thin gap in its cracked lips.

''Thank the stars you've come,'' said the stick figure, its voice hoarse and dry, ''I had begun to give up hope, fearing I might have to rot inside this tunnel,'' it said in a grateful tone.

And then without warning the stick figured wizard approached Bregit, who gave no sign of restraint and instead allowed the stick wizard to feel his robe and arms with its scratched hands and blackened fingers. Knowing if he were in the same position, he too would act in the same manner to confirm the figure was in fact real and not a mad illusion.

''Why are you here? Don't you realise your homelands lay under ash?' asked Bregit, swiping his cloak away from the wizard's clutches to examine the crinkled and torn robes laying at his feet.

Pressing his foot down on the torn cloths, Bregit kicked one aside only to be embraced by a powerful smell of rotted flesh. The wicked stench coursed through Bregit's opened mouth and nose causing him to spit out in disgust.

''I should've warned you, but I thought you wouldn't believe me,'' whimpered the stick wizard his voice fearful.

Retreating, Bregit studied the dry liquid stains on the tunnel's walls. It smelled worse than death. Twirling his eyes, he looked with wonder at the gushy blue faded eyes staring at him with the same fearful expression.

"Who are you?" Bregit asked in a commanding voice that startled the scared wizard.

The force of Bregit's voice caused the fragile wizard to shake terribly. Once the stick wizard became aware that Bregit's staff was waving warningly in his face the stick wizard swallowed hard before answering.

"I am Irmkay the Blue," he mumbled, "Before Treforledge was decimated I was a member of the elite squad sworn to protect the three islands of Treforledge."

"And why have you remained hidden while your kin perished defending their lands?" Bregit asked firmly.

Irmkays breathing quickened under the force of Bregit's demands. Bregit could tell the pressure of his questioning was making it difficult for Irmkay to recollect his memories. Sympathising Irmkays sufferings Bregit did, however he still needed to know why there were blood stains covering the robes in front of him.

"I was stationed to safeguard the Bridges," Irmkay began in a dried stiff voice, "I did as I was instructed, me and my two companions Lim and Burwilt kept watch of the Bridges. Then Lim heard movements coming from the edge of the Charred Mountain and alerted Burwilt who alerted me."

Irmkay took a moment's pause to clear his throat and while he did Bregit moved closer to the wall opposite him to see the marks on the walls were indeed scratch marks, but they were too deep to be wizard's markings which meant Irmkay wasn't alone.

"We debated for a brief spell about who should see what was causing the unsettlement. Lim and Burwilt decided to go together leaving me in charge to watch over the bridges. When they did not return, I remained at my station and when I was finishing my rounds along the narrow slip to the coast, I saw flames soaring through the sky and landing on the bridges. The flames burned through the bridges cords and released all the whaling spirits contained within the bridges oaken wood."

Bregit chuckled to himself and nodded his head with a grin, 'so there were spirits latched within the bridges core' he thought admiring Lorneid's loyalty to safeguarding his kingdoms traditions.

"Whoever attacked Treforledge had inside information about its defences and how to penetrate them," Interrupted Bregit turning to Irmkay with a look of suspicion.

"How?" asked Irmkay appearing shocked., "Only Lorneid and his Second would know how to unlock the defensive enchantments surrounding Treforledge. I was there and seen it collapse, believe me no wizard shot those flames," voiced Irmkay, his eyes wide making it easier for Bregit to know he was telling the truth.

"Then explain your version of events, why does Treforledge lay in ruin?" Bregit asked frowning.

"The first flame caught me of guard, the second I managed to get back to the bridge's border before it landed. Green flames, shaped in the form of a serpent soared from the peaks behind the Twins. Before I could do anything to protect the bridge a surging cloud rose from the depths of the left twin. Charging so fast and without hesitation all I could do to avoid been killed in its rampage was jump into the rising Red Sea."

"You jumped into the Red Sea and survived?" Bregit asked unconvinced.

"Yes," said Irmkay simply. "The waves beat me back and forth, but I managed to pull myself up by climbing the cliffs. When I caught my breath on a bed of rocks, I glimpsed sizzling flames coming from Crafters Isle," said Irmkay.

"Acid flames," breathed Bregit; who was sure he'd heard of that technique before, the question was where? "My apologies Irmkay please continue. I have a feeling our meeting is reaching its conclusion," said Bregit delicately feeling rude for interruption Irmkay.

"I watched as the whaling spirits were set free of their bondage. Once free they wreaked havoc on the Blue Islands. Destroying our workstations and homes."

"What became of you, how did you come to be trapped in this tunnel?" asked Bregit.

"Unable to stand I lay flat on my stomach hoping not to be seen or heard. As I lay drowned and exhausted, I heard voices nearby," said Irmkay.

"What did the voices say?" Bregit asked, his interest growing.

"It was speech unknown to me, slurry and deep with ice chilling gongs to its every word was its tone," answered Irmkay. "But that's not all, I may not know what the voice was saying, but one voice was familiar to me. I'd heard it my whole life when waves crashed against the cliffs and rocked the Whaling Bridge so viciously, they would screech ear popping wheals loud enough to shatter Malas stones to dust. It was the speech of the spirits and from the manner of the bone chilling voice it was no doubt commanding them."

"Commanding!" Bregit shouted, too sharply as his aggressive reaction caused Irmkay to jump back with fright. Recovering quickly though Irmkay continued.

"Drops after the conversation died the Whaling Spirits began wreaking havoc along the pathways leading to the Twins, no doubt they were asked to search each tunnel for hideaways having lived in these parts longer than living memory," said Irmkay.

"What did you do when the coast was clear?" asked Bregit.

"I ran as fast as my legs could carry me to alert the Harpies who lived on the outskirts of the Blue Islands. But in my rush, I unknowingly stumbled into a bed of hidden vines that held me captive. Hundreds of them bound and strapped me and when I tried to break free, they pierced my skin with their sharp thorns and injected me with paralysing toxins."

"Wait!" Bregit interrupted, showing a hand to stop Irmkay, "You escaped the Red Sea an onslaught and moved undetected by Whaling spirits. Now you're trying to convince me that you somehow escaped from the clutches of vines who managed to paralyse you?" said Bregit trying to decide was Irmkay a good liar or just lucky.

"I never escaped the vines, had it not been for the pack of Harpies flying by I would indeed have died. The Harpies saved me after they themselves had fled their nests before the fighting reached their hill. I just happened to be the lucky one to be noticed in their search for the tunnel's entry," said Irmkay in a dejected tone.

"This unknown speech you heard is a mystery, no creature to my knowledge has a slur in its voice or can speak to spirits," said Bregit puzzled by this unimaginable skill.

Choosing to believe Irmkay even though the pressure he was under at that moment could've caused his hearing to go astray. Bregit considered every aspect of Irmkays tale. The only thing he couldn't get his head around was no wizard had the ability to persuade spirits to obey their command, the lure to that craft was indeed a secret yet to be unearthed.

"My thoughts exactly," agreed Irmkay.

"Spirits are dead with loyalty to no one; wizards have the power to protect themselves from them but being able to control them is a power many would give their staffs to possess," said Bregit, a frown creasing his forehead as he again looked at the pile of shabby robes beneath his feet.

"This unknown has other unique capabilities. I'm guessing those robes don't belong to you?" said Bregit indicating Irmkay to unveil more of his story with a piercing look.

"No," answered Irmkay, looking at the pile of robes with a fearful glance.

"The stain on those robes makes me wonder how your still here if the wearers of these robes perished. Because you said yourself, you were strapped and pumped full of toxins that disabled your body," said Bregit, raising an eyebrow in wonder.

Irmkays lip began to tremble, his hands twitching uncontrollably. Though Bregit felt under little threat, he cautiously tightened his grip on the bark handle of his staff for precaution.

"I didn't kill them, if that's what you're implying," said Irmkay, his voice on the brink of breaking.

"I want to believe that, truly I do. So, tell me Irmkay, how is it that you're still alive while the others who shared this tunnel with you have perished?"

"Luck is why I am alive. The fog that killed so many wizards should've killed me too. I'm not entirely sure how I survived but I've a mad idea that may explain why," said Irmkay his words shaky.

"Go on," urged Bregit as Irmkay hesitated.

"A few drops after we settled, screams came from outside the tunnel. Even in the distance we could hear the cries of screaming wizards. And I won't pretend I enjoyed been part of the Harpies company for I dislike their beliefs. But I could tell from the Harpies anxious stares they too feared what lurked outside the cave. So, we sat in silence, each one of us who still drew breath hoping the chaos outside would stop. Then out of nowhere it began, first their skin began breaking out in bubbles that surged from beneath their skin. The confused Harpies desperately cried out for water. When I went in search for water, I found puddles about half a mile away. But when I tried to retrieve the water, I was knocked back by an invisible barrier that wouldn't let me pass."

Bregit's mouth hung open and dry, he had completely forgotten about Lorneid's forcefield and how difficult he himself had found it to overthrow. Still the question lingered.

"This tunnel is buried beneath the Red Sea; water surrounds it and you're telling me none of you could find a water source?"

"None could be found; we only had a marginal space to walk thanks to the energy shield blocking the tunnel. Due to lack of water the Harpies eventually gave in to their mad desires and clawed madly at themselves not caring what self-harm they caused so long as they eased their sufferings," said Irmkay. "I tried stopping them but when I approached, they attacked me. After they had torn away their feathers and skin they curled up and started muttering to themselves. But that's not all when they would toss and turn, I seen a purple glint shining from the centre of their eyes," said Irmkay shuddering at the relapse of reliving the past.

"The mark of dark magic," muttered Bregit swaying his fingertips along the wall and felt the bareness of the cold hardened clay chill the warmth of his hand. Deep claw marks scratched along the walls were squiggled and scribed into the wall but there was no sign of a message or symbol to say what was causing their unheard-of symptoms. "Those poor souls" he uttered, feeling a swell in his chest, "What happened once they lost control of their senses?"

"Two shades passed before the screaming stopped. It was then that I dared to approach again, in hope the Harpies had regained sense, but my hope shattered like wood against iron, for all I found when I returned were eight ripped apart bodies naked and stripped of all dignity," whimpered Irmkay, the memories of the Harpies torment still a sore subject for him to recall.

"What became of them?" Bregit asked stiffly, picturing in his own mind the suffering those creatures must have endured before their bodies crippled.

"I burned them," answered Irmkay. "One by one I piled them on top of another, rapidly filling the tunnel with light grey smoke."

"That was a foolish thing to do," Bregit snapped irritably, "Smoke from dead corpses would arise suspicion and give away your location," he said annoyed.

"I was scared and alone with creatures that wanted to destroy themselves. I feared they may come back as reanimated mindless creatures," said Irmkay, his voice trembling.

"Fair point," Bregit agreed, "but you've avoided the question I asked," he reminded Irmkay his voice becoming stern as he looked at the trembling wizard suspiciously.

'I've not avoided your question. I can only give you my theory and not a descriptive answer, because I can't explain how I didn't follow in the same faith as the Harpies. But when I became aware that I didn't need to rip the flesh from my body, I wondered had the toxins from the vines that trapped me saved me from the effects of the poisonous fog?" said Irmkay hesitantly.

Having never learned the effects of toxins and spores of different lands apart his own, which were partly different from the roots of the Blue Islands, Bregit was unsure whether what Irmkay was saying to be true which was his reasoning for not arguing the prospect further.

"My knowledge of foreign vines and their toxins are slim. Only those that dwell in the forests of Dulgerdeen could answer your theory correctly. However, you've been fortunate to survive. It would be foolish to deny luck has indeed smiled upon you," Bregit said lightly, a hint of sarcasm in his tone.

"It's a shame I couldn't have figured it out sooner, I could've saved more lives," whimpered Irmkay, dapping at the flowing tears trickling down his cheek.

"Don't be so hard on yourself, be grateful you have lived. If you did not, I would have no clue to what I am up against," said Bregit calmly.

"I've no idea who's behind this destruction," Irmkay said in earnest. "All I can remember before I was swallowed into a pit of plants was a pair of scarlet eyes forged of flame, scorching through everything its gaze fell upon."

"That makes no sense," said Bregit, feeling frustrated and shaking his head in disbelief. "No creature could do this single handily; It would take an army of highly trained wizards to cover so many lands in such a small number of drops.... Unless.... Red eyes scorching everything it gazed upon. Acid flames," said Bregit trying to recall why these felt familiar to him.

Images of flames flashed through Bregit's mind awakening a loud high pitch cackle. A cackle Bregit knew would stay latched inside his mind until his dying shade. "Lano," he gasped, in a fearful voice.

"Lano," repeated Irmkay in a curious voice.

The drained wizard stared at Bregit for a contradiction that never came. Bregit stood still with his back pressed against the tunnels cold wall. The evidence he'd gathered so far pointed in Lanos direction. Still, even Lano didn't posse the power to murder thousands of wizards or lay siege to three remote islands.

"It can't be him," said Irmkay, shaking his head in disbelief. "Lano the Lava Keeper was defeated in the last alliance and banished to the waste lands of Nocktar," Irmkay reminded Bregit.

"Correct. Lano was defeated. I was there, fighting alongside the king when Lano surrendered and begged for his life to be spared. To the disapproval of the coven and lords of lands the king granted Lano and his lieutenants mercy," said Bregit.

"Even if we both convince each other Lano has somehow broken the bonds of his imprisonment and fled the waste lands, we would need hard evidence to convince others," said Irmkay firmly.

"That is why I have travelled here, alone and concealed," Bregit said plainly.

"Are you saying you're going to enter Treforledge?"

It was Bregit's unresponsive tone that answered Irmkays question.

"That's suicide you know that?" cried Irmkay loudly.

"I am equipped with knowledge and powers that will aid me in my pursuit, forgive me Irmkay but my mind is set and nothing you say or do will sway me from my cause," said Bregit sternly.

"All I'm saying is. We would fare better with the Seven-Coloured Army behind us. Surely you know what will happen once you leave this tunnel?" pleaded Irmkay.

"I respect your concern, Irmkay. But if I were to turn back now, I will have wasted a shade travelling here for nought. Alerting the Golden Kingdom would take two shades to get there and another shade persuading the king and the coven to join our cause and many more shades gathering their forces and flying back here. While that is occurring, Lano, or whoever is behind this destruction will have moved on to another defenceless land," Bregit explained in a restrained voice.

"But to face whatever destroyed Treforledge alone won't do you any good neither. Listen, what happens if you die? There will be nobody to explain to the king what has happened here. Don't you see what I'm trying to say. You don't have to do this alone!"

Bregit carefully stepped over the dead Harpies' robes. Quickly moving toward the entrance, raising his hand about to unseal its defensive camouflage, Irmkay spoke breaking his concentration.

"I'll come with you," Irmkay offered, trying with all he could muster to sound brave.

Standing up straight, his face stern with a focused look did nothing to hide Irmkays worn eyes and the stretching lines of exhaustion trailing along his tired expression. Bregit sighed deeply keeping his back turned to Irmkay. Dismissing the willingness of young wizards was never easy, especially when that wizard had a concrete reason to risk its life avenging its lost ones. Bregit expected Irmkays proposal the moment he'd argued against his mission to go into Treforledge alone and had made his decision at that precise moment. Truly because he couldn't carry the burden of protecting Irmkay with him.

''You will leave this tunnel the same way I entered. Follow until you see a round hole in the centre of the wall, climb it. It will guide you to the foot of the Twins and with luck away from prying eyes,'' Bregit instructed calmly.

''What then? I have no place to go,'' said Irmkay.

''Make for Tip-Karps Mountain. Tell him I sent you, he will provide you with shelter. Go now before I leave, so I will know once I've gone there'll be no possibility you can follow me,'' Bregit commanded in a firm tone.

It wasn't an order or been unpleasant and Irmkay took it as so, he bowed his head to show his gratitude before leaving Bregit's side.

''Cunlat,'' Bregit whispered, waving his hand with little effort across the sealed entrance. A clicking sound told him his spell had worked. As the blanket of invisibility coating the tunnels main entrance was erased.

'I wonder what awaits me once I make it through here' he thought hoping for a less painful journey than his earlier one. Stepping slowly through the thin gap between the lines of pine grass, Bregit felt a soft sea breeze blissfully brushed against his sweat covered face. Once out of the tunnels thick and stuffy air, he turned and directed his index fingers at the entrance of the tunnel. Swirling his wrist, he sheeted the entrance in its blanket of invisibility. Heavy rain lashed from the dark clouds above, drowning Bregit top to bottom within a few drops after leaving the tunnel. With no trees or caves nearby to seek shelter, Bregit was forced to wither the pelting rain as he entered the Rock Grinder's workstations. Well, what was left of them. The black ash had smothered the stone paths and homes belonging to hundreds of Blue Wizards their dead bodies now left on display surely for the amusement of this sick minded creature.

''Not even a decent passing,'' sighed Bregit sadly, shaking his head in sadness.

The remains of hundreds of dead wizards came into view, all of them still wearing their thin sheets of bark to show they were Crafters of stone and rock. Walking along the graveyard of wizards buried under the thick blackened ash, Bregit came across a hill decorated in nests. This was exactly what he'd been hoping to find. For these nests belonged to the Harpies. Their nests were handmade and designed to be long and wide enough to fit two Harpies. The nests were made up of dead twigs and multi coloured leaves to give them colour coordinate appearances which made them easy to burn and be used as beacons to signal approaching danger. A wooden stairway was nailed into the hills outer wall as a way for wizards to take a short cut to Lorneids quarters. When Bregit reached the foot of the hill he began his climb up the wooden ladder. More out of hope than expectancy he poked his head in every nest he passed; not wanting another Irmkay situation on his hands. Halfway up the ladder the rain calmed as Bregit slowly made his way up the hill. When he was high enough to see the top, a rustling sound caught his attention. Daring, Bregit leaped into the nearest nest and quickly poked a small peep hole using his fingers to see what was moving beneath him.

''Seems all clear,'' came a firm voice.

When Bregit looked down he was stunned to see slithering slimy coils moving above the wizard's corpses, its mad yellow eyes scanned its surroundings while the rest of its great lengthy green coloured coils was wrapped tightly around a nearby rock while its feathered wings lay calmly at each side of his back. This creature was Jaed the Winged Serpent who was one of Lanos generals who commanded a huge army that lived in the depths of the Red Sea.

"Could've bet my wings I sensed a presence," hissed Jaed angrily, his eyes like rays of sunlight excelling through his cold pupils.

"Don't gamble things I already have my eyes on," said the giddy voice of another mystical creature that was familiar to Bregit.

Tricklet the Kric had appeared, his white face clear to see even in the darkness. Bregit couldn't believe what he was seeing. Two creatures deep in Lano's council stood talking below him. There was no doubt about it now, Lano was behind the assault on Treforledge. Peering through the peep hole, Bregit stalked Tricklet, his sneering grin always tipped him to the verge of murder. Tricklet was a creature with remarkable powers of deception and an expert illusionist. Standing at four feet with thin lime coloured hair, his face broad due to him grinning consistently. But the fascination about Tricklet wasn't his sleezy appearance, but his eyes. Tricklets eyes always made Bregit wonder, did the little illusionist get lost in his own mind game? Because never had he seen a pair of eyes that had no focus only a never-ending twirling line of red which he used to hypnotise his prey before eating them. Standing amazed inside the nest. Bregit watched Jaed and Tricklet talking among themselves with not the slightest care of been overheard.

"Why would you need a pair of wings, when all you have to do is click your fingers and you'll vanish on the spot?" hissed Jaed, his head moving closer to a smiling Tricklet who stood rotating small pebbles around his head to amuse himself.

"Perhaps, I would like to fly instead of disappearing it's always good to try new things," laughed Tricklet, vanishing before he'd finished and reappearing above Jaed while blowing puffs of dust from his mouth into the winged serpents face making Jaed cough and spit venom from his slit nostrils.

"Fool!" hissed Jaed viciously. Loosening his coils from the rock they rested on and rising to his full height Jaed spread his wings wide and dived with his mouth spread open to show his sharp spiked teeth drooling with yellowish venom. Before Jaeds mouth got within inches of a gleeful Tricklet. The great serpent was grabbed around the throat by a large paw with long black claws that pierced through his scales, keeping the serpent at bay.

"Aren't you two ever going to play nicely," growled the strong voice of Kcor the Viledirk.

Using his brute strength, Kcor flung Jaed across the ground with ease. The Viledirkening Chief wore a look of annoyance that added to his cold expression. Tall muscled and covered in bronze hair. Kcor was one of the toughest opponents the wizards ever faced. His skin is thick making it difficult to kill him in combat. He had long brown hair that covered each side of his face and stretched all down his backside. Most creatures mistake the hairline for a tail, which for some reason offended Kcor, who isn't famous for his sense of humour. Kcor didn't have any powers, but his brute strength and impenetrable skin allowed him to withstand almost anything.

"Why aren't you two stationed in the locations you were told to watch?" growled Kcor, his golden eyes piercing Tricklet with a look of annoyance.

"Keep your hair on Kcor," said Tricklet smiling. "Me and Jaed here thought we sensed a wizard poking around these parts, thought we'd check it out," said Tricklet.

"Strange, I thought I sensed the same power but when I got here the trail went cold," Kcor said coolly while watching Jaed lift himself from the ground.

"You don't think a wizard has seen this place and gone to get help?" asked Jaed looking at Kcor to Tricklet with a worried look.

"Don't jump to ridiculous conclusions," growled Kcor. "There are no wizards living within a hundred miles of here and Alacoma reported no survivors made it five miles from the Charred Mountain."

"Then why are you here? Shouldn't you not be grooming the master's shoulders telling him how pretty he looks in silk," jeered Tricklet, his voice sweet.

A grim look appeared on Kcors face that created a dim shadow under his eyes. "I'll allow your remark to pass this once since I'm in a good mood," said Kcor sternly, his eyes narrowing, "The answer to your question should be obvious to a mind manipulator. I too sensed a presence, whether it belonged to a wizard I am uncertain. Nether the less, our master must be informed," said Kcor in a strong voice.

Bending his muscular legs Kcor pounced up the hill of nests unaware a wizard lay hidden nearby. Jaed slithered up the hill, his long fluid body taking an age to make its way up the hill of nests. Tricklet sat on a rock until Jaed was out of sight before clicking his fingers and vanishing in a puff of aqua coloured smoke. Anticipating there need to alert their master, Bregit summoned a thread of cloud from a nearby cloud. The moment he touched the thread he instantly became invisible to the naked eye. The thread of cloud lifted Bregit high above the hill of nests, giving him a bird's eye view of Crafters Isle. Watching from a high distance while Kcor led the way while Jaed slithered behind not wanting to join in the Viledirks company. Kcor occasionally sniffed the air, by his unmoved expression the Viledirk was unaware of Bregit's presence.

"Come on!" growled Kcor jumping down from the top of the cliff and landing easily on sand filled lands that were covered in smoothed blue stones.

Catching up Tricklet, Jaed and Kcor entered what Bregit knew to be Lorneids quarters. A long stone table with nine small fires placed instead of chairs sat in the centre of the sand filled ground. The smoke rising from the small fires was entranced to not flow away but instead stay positioned above the flames and form into a dark grey cushion in the shape of a cloud. Bregit looked at the top seat, where a hooded figure sat. Skinless was its body, cloaked in black with skeletal features. Lines of grey hair brushed neatly back sheeting over its forehead. Pitiless black was the colour of its eyes that narrowed into thin slits at the sight of three approaching creatures. A loud hiss left his toothless mouth. Its annoyance creasing its features. The Lava Keeper slowly rose from his seat placing his bony hands against the table inflicting fear into Jaed and Kcor who approached their master with caution.

"My lord," they both said together, bowing to their master.

"Rise," hissed Lano, sounding exhausted, "And explain to me why you two are here," said Lano in a low hissing voice.

"Three," squealed Tricklet, who appeared by Kcors side.

Lano pierced Tricklet with a look of annoyance. Sitting back down he looked at them in turn, waiting for one of them to explain why they were not following his orders. Kcor stepped forward, kneeling at the foot of the stone table.

"My lord. Forgive our interruption, but myself, Jaed, and Tricklet believe we sensed the presence of a wizard just outside the Crafters workstations. When we got there Jaed and Tricklet had lost the scent," Kcor explained in a faint voice.

"We agreed my lord, that we should go to you with this at once," hissed Jaed.

"When you discovered there was no wizard, couldn't the three of you half-wits decide between yourselves to let one of you come and tell me while the other two went back to performing your duties?" hissed Lano coldly.

The three creatures lowered their heads in shame, not knowing what to reply in fear of angering Lano further so instead they remained silent.

"Did it ever occur to any of you fools, that this presence you all seemed to sense was a trick to lure you all away from your positions," spat Lano, slamming his skinless fist on the stone table.

Kcor, Jaed, and Tricklet never uttered a sound. The anger expressed by Lano sending vibrant waves of fear through the creatures.

"Which would allow foreign wizards to easily climb up and sabotage what we've worked so hard to gain," spat Lano, in a furious growl that made his black eyes grow a darker shade of black.

"Tricklet!" hissed Lano angrily.

Lanos vicious reaction caught Tricklet off guard. Frightened, the little illusionists body automatically burst into smoke. Forcing Tricklet to disappear on the spot. He reappeared in an instant, looking flushed from his lapse in control. Pretending not to have noticed, Lano spoke in a vicious tone.

"I want you to gather the others right now! If one wizard has entered Treforledge and sent for reinforcements, we will not have the numbers to counter."

"Why? My lord," asked Jaed, hasn't Dreaquirla returned from Dulgerdeen?'

'Oh no,' thought Bregit feeling a wave of dread come over him.

Dulgerdeen was full of mythical and mystical creatures. Only Carka, an old friend of his lived there. If Dreaquirla gained an alliance with the Kurlezzias they would surely tell her Carka lived in Dulgerdeen. Which would make Carka an easy target for an ambush. But a wave of calm came over Bregit who knew Carka to be an intelligent wizard with extraordinary skills, he may yet be alive Bregit told himself as he listened closely to what answer Lano gave to Jaeds' question.

"Word has yet to reach me of Dreaquirlas attempts to gain the mythical creature's aid. I am positive she will convince the creatures of Dulgerdeen to rally to our cause. Unlike some, Dreaquirla has yet to fail me," hissed Lano, piercing his generals with a sharp look.

Tricklet took Lanos insult as his excuse to leave his master's side and do what he had been commanded. Leaving a trail of glittering smoke in his leave.

"Sit both of you," ordered Lano, pointing at their seats.

Kcor and Jaed obeyed without question. Kcor been second to Lano, sat at the top of the table while Jaed a general, sat a row down from Kcor. Lano resumed his seat at the end of Lorneid's table. Placing his fingertips together and closing his eyes, appearing to be deep in concentration, or meditating Bregit couldn't tell from his view. Kcor sat with his furry arms folded, wearing his usual grim look while Jaed lay his head on the table appearing bored. Tricklet returned quicker than expected and was joined by three mystical creatures. Creatures Bregit had no trouble naming.

~ 53 ~

Alacoma the Winged Lord of the Skies. Ockrupver the shamed sea creature and Molem who was Lanos servant who must have done something great if he has gained a seat on Lanos council.

"Welcome my, Generals," greeted Lano his eyes still closed, "By the look of surprise on your faces, you are wondering why I've summoned you here? When our last gathering was a shade back. Well, I have a special treat for you all," hissed Lano, standing up from his chair and smiling menacingly at his council.

Bregit leaned over the cloud he hoovered upon waiting anxiously for Lano to present his treat. Gripping the handle of his staff he readied himself for whatever Lano was planning to show his Generals. Lano silkily walked around the table embracing the curious looks he received from his council members. When he reached the end of the table all eyes were upon him. Slowly Lano stretched out his arm and directed his index finger to the cloud Bregit gazed down from.

"Council of Shadows. May I introduce you all to Bregit the Yellow."

Chapter 7

Carka the Static

"It's extremely dangerous to approach a wizard without them knowing I could've reacted a lot more aggressively," said a furious Galli, her breathing coming in puffs due to the fright she'd received by the sudden appearance of this hooded figure.

In her frightened state, Galli accidently shot streaks of red from the tip of her staff. But the hooded stranger lazily waved Galli's unopposed attack away with a swish movement of its wrist. Eyeing the tall figure who was concealed in a damp grey cloak that looked like it had been made from creature's skin and knitted together with flower vines, made it impossible for Galli to get a clear view of what lurked beneath its overly large hood.

"Apologies young Ripeling, it wasn't my intention to startle you," came a gruff voice from beneath the long hood. The cloaked stranger moved a few steps closer to Galli, carrying with it, the stench of dampness. "My drops here have been short and less spent communing with pixies," it mocked with a dry cough.

"You've been following me?" said Galli, raising Water Dancer threateningly and turning it to face the hooded stranger.

"Following no, watching yes," replied the stranger defensively. "I was curious to see a wizard from Treforledge walking through the lands of Larmont, so I watched from afar as you shared words with the pixie," contradicted the stranger in a raspy voice.

"You're well informed of where I've travelled from," Galli fired back, feeling a little unnerved. "For a wizard who has just arrived here."

Clearing its throat, the hooded stranger spit out a vile green slime that stuck to the malas path, watching the slime slide and solidify, turned Galli's insides.

"Every wizard with common sense knows the wizards who live in Treforledge are stained and coloured in blue," sniffed the stranger, "and drop your guard!" said the stranger sounding vexed.

"Who says my guard is up, how do you know this isn't how I appear when I speak to prowlers that lurk in the shadows?" Galli said in a warning tone.

A laugh followed by many hoarse coughs broke through the stranger's hood. "Ah…," it sighed, "a Ripeling with a smart mouth," cackled the stranger with various dry coughing. "I have no intentions of quarrelling, especially with a Ripeling. My magical intelligence alone makes you an unworthy opponent," the stranger said with a false laugh added to its sneer.

'Unworthy?' thought Galli, feeling her fingernails begin to sink into the leather grip of Water Dancer.

"Who are you?" asked Galli impatiently, feeling she'd been fed enough of this lurchers taunts.

Skeletal hands slithered from beneath the holes in its sleeves, revealing thin grey arms with long claw shaped fingers. With a loud click of its fingers, it created a whirling gust of wind that swirled along its body cutting away every bit of fabric it could find. When the wind consumed the strangers body whole, its cloak vanished, giving Galli full view of what hid underneath. Tall, thin, and hunched backed with light grey skin and wearing lines of ageing all over, it looked at Galli with stern white narrowed eyes. Unfazed by its appearance and nakedness, Galli was however, surprised by the colour of its hair. White was uncommon and to Galli unheard of. Having watched wizards die of old age and many from sea sicknesses, she was certain its colour wasn't down to illness or age.

"My name is Carka, Carka the Static," said the stranger, his voice deep and croaked, "And I come from the forests of Dulgerdeen."

"Dulgerdeen?" repeated Galli. "Then why are you so far from home?"

"Why am I here you ask?" Carka laughed hoarsely, "The answer to your question may startle you more than my appearance," he laughed again.

"Can't you not just simply answer?" said Galli getting annoyed by Carka's jibing. "You're wasting drops leaving this unnecessary conversation open," Galli said coldly.

Carka who was examining his hands didn't seem the least bit offended, he merely jerked his head and began to walk down the pathway leading east. "For now, we shall walk together to Bregit's tower, with much haste," said Carka, without looking back at Galli.

Leading the way Carka snapped his fingers, again! Causing a sharp echoing sound to reverberate through Galli's ear drums. Causing pain to sheer through her head and force her to put her hands over her ears to ease the throbbing ricocheting throughout her thumping skull.

"Cut it out!" yelled Galli, unable to withstand any more as she fell to her knees due to Carka's unbearable shockwaves crushing her senses.

The echo reverberating throughout Galli's skull stopped at once. Teary eyed and frustrated, Galli looked up to see Carka was no longer naked but covered in a heavy, cleaner cloak of silver silk that had long sleeves and a light hood.

"Shockwaves of the wind, little ripe. Add enough concentration and you can mould even the air itself into solid objects of one's desire," said Carka smirking, "Didn't want my reunion with Bregit to be awkward with me showing up naked now did I?" he laughed hoarsely.

Carka's laughing irritated Galli who thought his humour was outdated and unkind but his skills with magic did appear to be advanced compared to her own because Galli had never seen a wizard use the air to create solid objects. Again, Carka didn't wait for Galli's response. Instead, he began his journey down the malas stoned pathway, the shine from his silver robes blending with his flowing white hair. Following him, Galli deliberately hung back, not wanting to join in Carka's company. Instead, she observed him, wondering what kind of wizard he was? Unsure of some things Galli was positive of one; Carka was extremely old. His hunch back and grey skin tone made that obvious. Galli assumed Carka's skin was in such bad shape because he spent most shades in different temperatures? His belittling remark about his magical intelligence been superior arose suspicion, if so powerful, then why hasn't she heard of him? Lorneid always spoke about the creatures of Dulgerdeen, and never did he mention a wizard living among them, nor did Gazelle the Herd Lord of the Kurlezzias who traded with the Blue Wizards on occasions.

"You know, when asked to introduce yourself, it's common to have the same curtsey applied in return," said Carka, his neck turning slightly to see what effect his words had on Galli.

Galli's expression soured, she knew what Carka was doing, and she wasn't going to allow herself to be minimised by his sneering any longer, even if it was only a joke to Carka, Galli didn't find his manner amusing.

"I am Galli the Blue, commander of the Blue Striped Army of Treforledge and Second to Lorneid the Blue….," she began but was silenced by Carka.

"Whist," he whistled. "Your name was all I needed. To explain yourself openly walking along a pathway full of Leaf Leapers is suicide. We do not know which side those annoying mites are on," warned Carka, his voice below a whisper.

A spell of silence fell upon the pair. Carka continued leading the way while Galli purposely trailed behind. Every turn east Carka followed without hesitation and with every new turn they encountered new batches of rare flowers with sprouted leaves that sprayed their scented odours into their air waves.

'The Backstabbing Attempt,' Galli remembered Lorneid telling her when he demonstrated the same technique in their private sessions, the luring techniques of rare flowers that lived in the wild. 'They will seduce you with fragrances capable of ensnaring the senses, then when your guard is down SMACK! You find yourself coiled and trapped in their thorned vines that paralyse you the moment they sink into your flesh,' were the cautious words of Lorneid.

Carka didn't give the flowers a drop's notice. In Galli's situation it felt better to watch them, she may have knowledge of their luring abilities, but she had never seen the extent of their powers up close. Which was why she was keeping a firm grip on Water Dancer just in case the moment presented itself. Having held her staff for so long in one hand, the grip had become drenched in sweat, which took Galli back to the last shade she had to hold on to her staff for such a lengthy period. It was during her final challenge of the Ultimate Colour Tournament. When her army overcame the odds and claimed their first ever Ultimate Colour crown, by defeating the undefeatable Black Striped Army.

Having given Leon, the commander of the Black Striped Army, the opportunity to surrender Galli remembered holding her staff into the face of the prince for so long it felt like an age before he surrendered to her. When Galli swapped hands and held her staff in her left hand she noticed when looking at Carka's two free hands what she had missed during her observation of him.

"Where is your staff?" Galli asked curiously.

Carka scoffed. "Very perceptive aren't you, for a Ripeling," said Carka with praise. "I abandoned my needs of a staff many cycles of shades ago. I prefer to use these," said Carka turning both wrists and showing two square shaped malas stones pierced deep into his palms.

"It's much easier to travel when you're not burdened with a staff. A simple spell can hide my identity and make many creatures believe whatever I tell them, but if I am seen carrying a staff or relying on one to channel my powers then my lies are deceived, and my identity revealed."

"It's wizarding law that wizards channel their powers though an object chosen by a wizard's tutor. If a wizard chooses to not use their chosen object to wield their powers......"

"Wizard's rule, ha," laughed Carka aloud. "You and Bregit will no doubt find each other interesting. Wizard's rules are to be followed by the blind and to be believed by those too cowardly of seeking strength. I fashioned myself a new rule that few wizards have the nerve to speak of."

"Which is?" asked Galli feeling she already knew the answer.

"Freedom," answered Carka simply. "To no longer abide to rules, which blind us to the truth."

"Oh my," gasped Galli, "You're an exile, which explains why you've come from Dulgerdeen."

"Well studied," praised Carka, his tone unmoved from its mockery. "Let us speak no more of it and just say for your piece of mind, that I left my colour behind when I realised, I could become more than what they wanted me to be," Carka finished.

"Lords of lands and members of the coven are the only wizards capable of changing their objects to wield magic. So, either you were a high ranked wizard in your youth or a thief of knowledge," said Galli eager to know was Carka indeed a wizard of privilege.

"I am aware of the rules written by those who dwell above us. If I want them explained again, I'll remember a know it all only lurks behind me!" snapped Carka, sounding annoyed by the amount of questions Galli was throwing at him.

Galli could feel her face burn with heated anger, but held back her tongue, knowing it would be foolish to pick a fight with Carka. Especially when he was leading her directly to Bregit's Tower.

"We walk the same path, to a wizard we both need to see. That does not mean we are friends, now kindly keep your lips sealed if it's not so difficult for you to restrain yourself until we get to Bregit's tower," Carka stated firmly throwing Galli a look of annoyance.

When Carka turned around, he swished aside his long grey hair with a twist of his neck. And in that split drop Carka was blinded to his surroundings. It happened in slow motion, before Carka's hair could rest on the side of his head, a thick vine had risen from the sand beneath their feet and struck him hard across the face. They had unknowingly walked into a sand pit that had woken due to both wizards unknowingly trespassing on their beds. The vine that struck Carka had knocked him aside with one swipe. The force of its strike was so strong Carka was powerless to prevent himself colliding face first with a nearby tree.

Watching his body crash and fall motionless into the bed of vines froze Galli's instincts and numbed her senses as more vines, thicker and longer appeared from the sand pits, surrounding Galli in a tight formation that had no gaps and in her mind no escape. As a large vine dived at her Galli snapped out of her paralyzing state and wove Water Dancer fluently crying. ''Rislawier!''

A protective wall of clear aqua water folded and formed into a sphere shape shield that cocooned Galli inside its protective layers. The strength of her aqua shield withstood against the vine's vicious attack, repelling it due to the sheer force of her shield. But the vines continued pounding Galli's water shield making it difficult for her to keep her concentration, as every strike unhinged the shields strength. The weight of the vines pounding caused splashes of water to spurt against her eyes and break her concentration.

Hundreds of vines now surrounded Galli making her wonder did they have some tactical intellect because they changed their approach by attacking in dozens, no doubt to increase the impact of their strikes. The strain of keeping her aqua shield intact was taking its toll on Galli's body. Falling to one knee under the increasing burden, Galli refused to give in and surrender. As the thoughts of letting Lorneid down filled her with emotion Galli got back to her feet wearing a look of cold fury on her face. Preparing herself for a final stand, a thundering voice echoed through the sand pit. The ground quaked violently, unhinging the vines wall, forcing them to separate. And through the cracks in the vines detached wall Galli saw him, standing at full height with his arms wide and glowing in a radiant beam of pure starlight. Wearing a look of hate that stretched his ageing features.

Carka was back on his feet. His reappearance catching the vines attention and drew them on to his position. Showing no signs of restraint, the ageing wizard shot bolts of white lightning from the tips of his fingers. The sheer power of his attack shattering the incoming vines to dust as Galli stood in disbelief to what she had just seen. Walking unnerved, the aura surrounding Carka reduced the twigs and roots he passed to dust, sending a crackling sound throughout the bed of vines.

''TEAN-TAY-TOL!!!'' bellowed Carka, waving both arms to the sky.

Bursts of blinding white beams erupted from the square mala's stones nested in the palms of his hands. Swirling high into the sky they formed into thin bolts of lightning, which swooped down from the sky like a shooting star. Expecting an explosion Galli backed away. But when the lightning bolts landed upon the bed of vines, Galli was left surprised by the unexpected outcome of Carka's manoeuvre. Instead of destroying the vines and their base, Carka swirled his wrists and entangled the vines with the bolts, taming the vines fluidity. Clenching his fists tight, Carka's lightning bolts tightened their grip around every vine and with a deafening snap every vine was reduced to specks of dust that hung immobilised in mid-air. With the sand pits clear, Carka swept away what remained of the vines with a wave of his hand. As Galli crossed the pit to congratulate Carka the glowing light shining from his body faded along with his murderous expression.

''Let's get moving before anything else decides to surprise us,'' Carka said in a stiff tone.

He passed Galli and resumed his strut down the eastern path leaving her to feel the shame of her foolishness. Galli remained standing over the remains of the vines too consumed with the embarrassment her eagerness for knowledge had almost cost them. Apologising wasn't Galli's forte, but the weight of guilt seemed to have drowned out her stubbornness. Considering her approach on how to rectify herself, Galli looked up to see that Carka was gone. Too afraid to call out his name in fear of drawing more attention their way, Galli paced the malas path until it hit a dead end. Ditches thick with sunset yellow petals stood in Galli's way. The sound of rustling caught her attention. There in the centre of the row of ditches was a gap, big enough for Galli to squeeze through. Reaching the gap, she peaked her head inside, only to be met with darkness. Biting her tongue, she passed through the ditches and entered what she considered to be a forest as the loud crackling sound of dead leaves been stood on filled her ears with every step she took. Guessing, Galli presumed the leaves were some sort of signal to alert nearby creatures of approaching creatures. She had to admit, it was a well taught out siren. The hedges surrounding the forest formed a protective layer around its inhabitants. The trees Galli instantly noticed had red and green berries growing out of its branches. The very sight of the juicy berries made Galli's stomach-ache with hunger. But these delicious looking berries were unknown to her, and she wasn't going to be remembered in cycles to come as the wizard who died because she couldn't fight temptation and gave into a little hunger pain. Moving by the hedges, Galli focused her senses, and hoped she would be able to sense Carka's energy. But the only thing her senses caught were the crunching sounds of the dead leaves she had blindly stepped on. Crackling, the leaves detached and sent echoing sounds throughout the forest, frightening away all the nearby Leaf Leapers who were nesting at the tops of the thin trees.

''Could you make any more noise?'' came Carka's voice, from out of the shadows.

He stood a few trees away concealed in the shadow of the trees, but from the dim rays of light that had managed to break through the thick leaves blocking the sky's light entering the forest revealed the gash where the vine had struck him. Remembering Lorneids injury Galli quickly offered to heal it, but Carka shrugged her offer with a low grunt and walked silently through the forest. When Galli finally caught up and was walking alongside Carka, she found her voice.

''It's my fault you were attacked, if it wasn't for my questioning, you would have anticipated the vines attacks…, I'm sorry,'' Galli said her shame visible in her apologetic tone.

Carka did not turn his eyes but kept them firmly straight while Galli didn't dare press her apology and decided to remain silent as a whisper while Carka wrestled with his response.

''I taught Ripelings for most of my life. Curiosity is an unbearable thing to have bottled up inside,'' said Carka his voice less stern.

This appeased Galli's low spirits. She could tell this kind of emotion was as much unsuited to Carka as it were to her.

''It's like an annoying itch that just will not go away, but what I've learnt throughout my own youth is, without questions knowledge cannot be gained,'' Carka said, like a wizard who had just woken from a daydream and was now ready to take life seriously again.

"Perhaps the duel with the enchanted vines was in fact beneficial," thought Galli feeling her own stress levels reducing.

"My long shades in solitude have made me less aware of a young Ripelings eagerness for information, so save your apology. There isn't a need for it, now let's move on, these woods are a fair distance and I want my face recognisable when I greet Bregit," said Carka giving Galli a faint smile.

The woods went on forever. Every tree they passed was covered in thin tan, brown bark that were neatly lined in rows that narrowed together making it difficult for Galli and Carka to move at their usual pace. On most occasions Galli and Carka were both forced to slip through the gaps in the rows of tress to get deeper into the forest. The shifting and changing position quickly rubbed away Carka's change in mood. He continued to grunt every drop his hair would get caught between sticky branches or thorned twigs. Galli on the other hand didn't mind and found it amusing hearing Carka curse aloud while he picked all sorts of twigs from his straight and perfect hair.

"Bregit and his plants," cursed Carka who had accidently stepped on a bunch of Tweedly Plants and caught his foot in an empty nest that had fallen from the treetops. "A wizard of his stature should be among the clouds not rotting away alone in Larmont, enchanting its inhabitants" spat Carka bitterly kicking away the nest in frustration.

Carka's mood swinging made Galli believe Carka had split personalities, she didn't dare ask him in case he took it as an insult, but the signs were there to see.

"You know Bregit?" asked Galli.

"Yes!" replied Carka. "He was once a pupil of mine. Amazing capabilities he has, it was a shock to all wizards who knew him when he left the Golden Kingdom to live a life in exile," said Carka.

Carka looked at Galli, to see would Bregit receive the same disappointed look he had when she'd learned he was an exile and was shocked to see no reaction to her calm expression.

"If Bregit is an exiled wizard, then how is he lord of one of a coloured land?" questioned Galli.

"The creatures of Larmont gave Bregit that title not the king," stated Carka, "he left his position as Depth Head General to live a life in solitude."

"Why?" asked Galli who couldn't picture any wizard giving up that position unless there is a good reason to do so.

"No one knows," Carka answered with a sigh. "One shade he was Depth Head General training the stripped wizards amongst the clouds, next shade he was gone without a word to anyone."

"Didn't the king not look for him after he left?"

Carka laughed. "Wizards like Bregit are smart and cunning, not to mention patient. Bregit no doubt would as I believe, have devised a safe and secure way to leave the Golden Kingdom without arousing suspicion. Remember he is the Lord of

Larmont meaning he is not particularly hiding,'' said Carka, giving Galli a nudging hint to think about.

''Secrets,'' breathed Galli, ''He knows something that may dethrone the king, or a scandal that may lead to a civil war?''

''We may never know. I doubt Bregit would throw away his only safeguard that keeps him safe from the services of the king just to appease someone's appetite for knowledge,'' Carka said seriously.

''But surely, it must be close to the subject being discussed? Why else would he be allowed leave without a bounty on his head?''

''When I first met Bregit. I had chosen a life away from the teachings of Ripelings and settled deep within the forests of Dulgerdeen.''

''Why Dulgerdeen?'' asked Galli wondering why any wizard would want to live among creatures who despised wizards.

''It is populated with creatures that hate wizards. It was the perfect sanctuary for a wizard to be punished for his abandonment,'' laughed Carka. ''Bregit, a curious wizard sought me out and pledged himself to my teachings. After our first lesson I knew he was bright enough to learn all I had to offer by his own means. So, the question lingered, and it didn't take me long to figure out why Bregit had travelled so far to seek me out. He wanted to learn the ways of manipulating, creating, and controlling the weather. But throughout all our lessons he never once gave away the slightest reason as to why he'd left his position in the Golden Kingdom. When I finally asked, Bregit had mastered the ways of controlling the weather and needed no further lessons. Bregit left Dulgerdeen and never returned. I could've blackmailed him, but my senses had already told me Bregit was too powerful to be easily unhinged, the only way I could've extracted the information would've been to by force,'' said Carka.

''Why didn't you extract the information without Bregit knowing?'' said Galli testing the water a little by challenging was Carka superior to Bregit.

''Had I reason to attack Bregit I would not have held back, however my reasons would've been for my own selfish desire and that is despicable. I allowed Bregit to leave my sanctuary warning him to keep his learnings from me a secret, that it would be foolish to brag about techniques that were now forbidden.''

''Isn't it against the laws of wizards to change the course of the weather?'' asked Galli. ''Last I checked, all rituals were wiped from the memories of all who knew about them by the former king Dirm the Bronze. Lorneid himself was cleansed of his memories so how come your memory didn't get wiped clean?'' Galli asked while pulling sticky twigs from the ends of her sleeves.

Carka looked at Galli his eyes piercing her with an x-rayed gaze that made her cheeks burn scarlet. Resuming his strut, Carka walked along considering this young wizard and how advanced her power and knowledge were compared to his at that age.

''You've done a lot of research on the subject,'' said Carka in an impressive tone. ''But yes, you are correct, the memories of all Depth Heads were extracted of all knowledge related to weather control. I sought solace far from the king's ruling and abandoned my duties to him and secretly left the Golden Kingdom before the laws banishing the weather rituals were enforced.''

"So, you're the last wizard in possession of the knowledge of how to bend the will of the weather?" asked Galli.

Fascinated with Carka's story Galli had forgotten about the thin gaps between each tree and caught the ends of her cloak within a small hedge that had long sharp spikes sticking out from the ends of its twigs. Tugging it hard Galli managed to release her cloak from the spikes but tore the bottom ends off her cloak much to Carka's amusement, who stood smiling at Galli's sulked expression at the long gaps torn off her cloak.

"I'm sure Bregit has a spare cloak somewhere inside his tower, now can we press on before an entire shade is wasted walking through this forest," said Carka rolling his eyes at Galli's Ripeling antics.

Galli slid through rows of trees making sure to be careful not to step on any flowers. When she was by Carka's side she repeated the question, she had asked him before her cloak got caught in the spikes.

"Well, are you?" Galli repeated, not caring one bit about been pushy.

Carka smiled at Galli's unwillingness not to be disregarded, he liked wizards who refused to be ignored and by the determination shown by Galli made him dwell on the thought that she hadn't gained her position as Lorneids Second for been a good Crafter.

"I was the only wizard left who owned the knowledge to manipulate and control the weather, but now there are two who possess the ancient knowledge. If you had of been paying attention, you would already know the answer to your question," answered Carka.

It was if a light had switched on in Galli's brain, how could she be so thick to have missed it when Carka had clearly giving her the answer.

"Bregit," squealed Galli with excitement, "He is the other Storm Brewer, isn't he?"

Carka didn't reply but sighed deeply with relief as a thin slit within a long row of spiked hedges came into his view at what looked to be the end of the forest.

"Finally," breathed Carka looking to the sky with relief.

"What's beyond those spiked hedges?" Galli asked in a discomforting tone that had dawned over her excitement like a dark cloud.

"Bregit's tower that's what," answered Carka walking through the gap with no precautious steps taken.

Galli pushed her way through the narrow gap with the addition of the odd prick digging into her hair. When through the gap she was instantly blinded by bright lights. Raising her hand above her forehead to block the light, Galli glimpsed what was casting the blinding beams. It was a statue of a wizard standing tall upon a round water fountain, it was positioned in the middle of a Malas courtyard that was filled with multi-coloured sands. The rays of light reflecting off the statue shone brightly for anyone visiting to see.

"This Galli is the homeland of Bregit and that statue you're staring at is Nette the Yellow, Bregit's late father who died in the war against the mystical creatures. The fountain he stands over is filled with star sprinkled water that rumour has it, if drunk, grants the drinker a glimpse into the future,'' said Carka, who was waiting for Galli on a thin footpath made of stone.

From the unconvincing tone Carka spoke when detailing Bregit's fountain gave Galli enough of a nudge to know he wasn't a big supporter of superstition.

''It's unbelievable,'' breathed Galli who stood fascinated by Bregit's amazing craftwork.

Bregit's mixture of colours overwhelmed Galli so much she was entranced by the glittering water swirling through the staff in Nette's hand and bursting through the diamond and the three-drop tree leaves at its top which sprinkled onto the stone base Nette was placed upon.

''Fascinating,'' said Carka dully rolling his eyes and moving along without another look at the fountain.

Not wanting to pass up the opportunity to see first-hand the rare beauty of crystallised water. Galli peaked her head over the fountain, as she looked down at the water, it was exactly as Carka had described, clear and sparkling, the rays of light reflecting off Nette made the water appear to have a rainbow shining over it. The temptation to sip the clear water was itching at Galli, but if it was true what Carka had said about its powers granting the drinker a brief glimpse into the future, was enough to stall Galli's desires. Resisting her temptations, Galli looked at her reflection instead, apart from the dirty hair and tired lines from under her eyes from a lack of sleep she appeared quite herself which surprised Galli, having so narrowly avoided death she would have expected her image to have changed by traumatic stress. But Galli's examination went no further thanks to Carka's loud tuts of annoyance that forced her to remember why she had come all the way to Larmont. Turning her attention away from the fountain Galli walked the narrow path, looking up to see Carka was standing under the shadow of Bregit's tower.

The tower stood at least a hundred feet, and appeared to be built using long thick trees, stripped of their roots and bark, and held tightly together with straps of thick vines that were lined, rowed, and piled on top of each other. What covered over the trees and vines were thin sheets of black, that Galli had no knowledge of, but they looked effective because there were no signs of the tower collapsing or ageing.

''Probably some kind of melted rocks,'' Galli thought not wanting to dwell any further on Bregit's mysterious overcoat as she reached a crossed face Carka who stood with his arms folded.

''Nice of you to catch up, I'm sure you travelled all the way to Larmont just to gaze romantically at Bregit's tower,'' Carka said in a cross voice.

Galli didn't argue, but instead straightened her head and focused her eyes on a flowing waterfall that had no start or end but hung between a tall frame latched to the oaken doors of Bregit's tower.

''What's that?'' asked Galli staring curiously at the flowing water.

''That's the barrier keeping us out here looking so grim,'' answered Carka bitterly.

''How,'' asked Galli.

''Only the caster can pull back the sprinkled curtain of clear water,'' Carka replied with dislike.

And he proved it by waving his right arm over the waterfall which was effortlessly pushed back a few paces by Bregit's obedient spell.

"Of course," laughed Galli. "It's a defensive coat to protect the tower from been infiltrated."

Carka smiled despite his annoyance. "Correct again," he said in an impressed tone.

Galli peered at the flowing curtain. Knowing not to touch it, she waved her palm inches across the flowing water and felt an invisible force pushing her hand back.

"What happens if anyone tries to force their way through it?" Galli asked, as a cold sensation flowed through her fingertips, making her quickly withdraw her hand.

"Why don't you try it and find out for yourself?" said Carka sitting on a reddish-orange cloud that had appeared out of nowhere.

"How are we to alert Bregit to us been here if we cannot even go through his door?" said Galli angrily kicking the sand beneath her feet in frustration.

"The curtains only close when Bregit has left the towers perimeter, he is after all, the Lord of Larmont," said Carka in a relaxed voice. "It is Bregit's responsibility to safeguard his lands. He hasn't the luxury of having thousands of Lutiz's standing watch while he sits lazily within his tower," said Carka laying back on his comfy cloud.

"Strange don't you think that a wizard with advanced skills and power doesn't have slaves to do his security?" said Galli.

"Bregit if you should know is against slavery in all shapes and forms, for that reason and a many more is why he left his position as Depth Head General. Now enough small talk for one shade, be seated. Bregit will be a long before the turn of shade," said Carka in a confident tone as he closed his eyes.

An identical cloud to the one Carka lay on appeared beside Galli. Feeling there was nothing more she could do but wait she too sank into the reddish orange cloud. Instantly she was consumed by a warm blissful feeling that erupted all through her body relieving Galli of all tense and soreness she had endured from walking so far on so many different surfaces.

"Bregit has good welcoming skills I'll grant him that," said Galli dreamingly before drifting into a deep sleep.

Carka on the other hand remained wide awake. His sharp white eyes catching every sound and movement. He refused to allow sleep to consume him, preferring to sit quietly watching the enchanted water barrier, wondering where his old friend had gone, and why wasn't he in Larmont?

Chapter 8

A Watchful Shadow

The saying goes there comes a stage in life when all you can do is sit and do nothing. Well, that was precisely Bregit's alternative. The shock of been discovered had stunned him. causing Bregit to lose focus at the wrong moment and in that moment of uncertainty, had allowed Lano to seize him. The Lava Keepers conjured snake like fiery whips somehow burned through Bregit's concealment spell, unveiling him to the Council of Shadows. Pulled from the air Bregit was stripped of his staff and bound against the hard-stone tablet that sat across Lorneids stone table.

Swirling his wrist, Lano made his fiery whips tighten around Bregit's wrists and ankles making any attempts of escape inevitable. Wearing a look of unmeasurable pleasure, Lano pressed his skull hard against the point of Bregit's nose, giving him a clear insight of the endless depths of the Lava Keepers pit-less eyes. Lano now wore a smug look of satisfaction that stretched his skinless features, making the scars on his face stretch, giving the Lava Keeper a more menacing look.

"Never," breathed Lano, taking a short pause to allow the realism of Bregit's capture digest. "In my wildest dreams did I imagine, I would be the one to single handily capture Bregit, Lord of Larmont, and banisher of Gliders," jeered the Lava Keeper.

"Titles earned not taken by murder and deceit," said Bregit coldly.

Kcor moved toward Bregit letting out a low growl as the Viledirk retracted his claws and pulled back his muscular arms and just as his strike was about to make contact Lano intervened by slamming Kcor aside with a wave of his arm.

"No!" hissed Lano smirking at Bregit, "This will be treated with care, I have come too far to be thwarted by one wizard," hissed Lano his nostrils flaring.

The council all looked at Lano, wondering why he had chosen to stop Kcor killing Bregit. Sighing, the Lava Keeper looked at the calm unmoved yellow eyes belonging to Bregit which showed less importance in Lano and more of his surroundings.

"For my many fallen comrades I witnessed you slaughter, I should end your legacy now and demean you in ways that would erase shades of torment," hissed Lano, swiping the air with his arm.

A howl of pain echoed throughout Lorneids quarters, as Bregit slid down the stone tablet, hanging loosely having felt the full force of Lano's rod of multi flames been dug into his mid-section.

"But I know killing you now will no doubt activate that statue of yours to signal more to your location, so for now you will remain our humble guest, and learn the true purpose of demeaned," hissed Lano.

"You demean yourself," heaved Bregit, the pain of Lano's blow adding stern to his voice, "By claiming victory when there was none to be won, by using deception and illusions as weapons to win. Has your shades in the wastelands made you lose what little dignity you once had?" spat Bregit, his eyes bulging with rage as the thumping pain beat against his ribs.

Lano chuckled but everyone in Lorneids quarters knew by his smug expression that Bregit had crossed the line when he had mocked the ways Lano constructed his battle tactics.

"Were the Sages shown decency when Dirm the Bronze invited them into the Golden Kingdom as guests and slaughtered them within the halls of his former kings? I put it to you Bregit, what decency was shown to my comrades when they surrendered to you and your kind? Death was their submission! So, do not lecture me about necessities in war when your kind have pushed us to the brink of desperation," hissed Lano coldly.

"Still the narcissists," Bregit said with disgust, "and still unwilling to accept you were wrong, and by doing so have forced you to use methods your elders would deem unworthy," said Bregit.

Lano gawked at Bregit with cold fury but just as the Lava Keeper was about to counter Bregit's belittling remark a frothed voice cut across him.

"The wizard seems unfazed," voiced the sea creature Ockrupver, not caring that he had just interrupted his master.

"What is it Ockrupver?" hissed Lano with venom in his tone.

Past experiences had taught Ockrupver some painful lessons in the terms of keeping opinions left unsaid. Rotating slowly from his clouded seat, the sea creature rose to his full height and cleared his throat, gurgling a rough sound that sounded like there was water clogging his windpipes. Lano's neck cricked, his dark eyes bored on Ockrupver and threw his general a look of annoyance. Eying the slimy green creature with ripples along most of its fluid body. Ockrupver no doubt resembled a slug, apart from been extremely longer and fatter. What Bregit found hardest about Ockrupver was where the pinpoint of his voice came from? The reason behind that inability was because Ockrupver had no face, only a wide black hole in the centre of his top that had oval shaped swollen lips latched around its mouth. Having fought against Ockrupver in the earlier war, Bregit knew having seen first-hand that whatever got sucked into Ockrupvers mouth, never seen the light of another shade again.

"How would a creature with no eyes even know how a wizard looks?" said the winged beast Alacoma smugly.

Alacomas little taunt infected the council with a snigger, even the grimace Lano could not resist broadening his cheeks slightly. But Ockrupver pressed on, ignoring Alacomas sarcastic remark.

"His calm breath and frail attempts to deceive capture should be enough reason to arouse suspicion," said Ockrupver silencing the councils cynical sniggering.

"The wizard does seem pleased," said Alacoma abandoning his mocking voice and returning to his usual sharp pitch tone.

"Perhaps he has spies ready to strike when we least expect," suggested Molem, his eyes darting at each nearby cloud.

The council followed the rock creatures' intentions fearing Molem's theory to be true. But Lano nodded his head in disappointment as he watched his council behave in an improper manner befitting of their rank.

"The only thing pleasing Bregit, is the doubt he has spread throughout your weak minds," hissed Lano in a tone that wasn't aggressive but did have a chilling vibe added to it which inflicted fear throughout the council. "If the Lord of Larmont had support, wouldn't you think as generals yourselves that his sworn protectors would have come to his aid by now?"

The council fell silent and judging by Lanos disappointment in his council Bregit could tell by the heat radiating from the Lava Keepers body that he was about to lash out, but to his surprise Lano remained calm.

"But to be sure," hissed Lano a curling smile stretched across his face, "Let's unhinge that calm mind and see has our new companion brought his coloured friends along," hissed Lano looking at Bregit with a look of pleasure.

"Tricklet!" called Lano.

The little trickster appeared beside his master instantly looking unsure as to why he out of the others was being chosen.

"I will gift you the sole honour of breaching the wizard's mind. But be cautious, infiltrating a wizard's restraints can be difficult," warned Lano moving away from Bregit.

"My lord," came the firm voice of Kcor, "If we are going to penetrate the wizards mind, shouldn't we demonstrate the seriousness of our cause and remove everything he knows and send his empty shell to the king as a message to how serious our cause is," suggested Kcor piercing Bregit with a deep look of hatred.

"Leave the wizard with nothing," hissed Lano, smiling at the depth of Kcors suggestion, "All right," he agreed without taking a single drop to consider. "But I want his body unharmed," added Lano firmly, his instructions gaining him a rare smile from Kcor.

Tricklet appeared thrilled by his added charge. Rubbing his hands together, the little trickster placed his fingertips over Bregit's hardened face, blinding him to what was going on around him.

"I've waited an eternity for the chance to test my powers against a wizard," laughed Tricklet madly. "When I'm through with you wizard, you won't know the meaning of the word magic."

"Just get on with it!" hissed Lano impatiently.

Tricklet cracked both sides of his neck, making his eyes rotate round and round until a tiny red dot took shape in the core of his eyes. The council watched with wonder, while Lano paced up and down the stone table his mysterious eyes carefully monitoring Tricklet.

Bregit could feel Tricklets trance beginning to gain momentum, feeling a sensation arousing his senses he knew he had mili drops to react or his mind would be lost in limbo forever. Before Tricklets illusion took hold over his mind, a blinding white flash erupted from the depths of Bregit's eyes causing fissures of sweeping dust to erupt from the sand floor beneath their feet at such momentum, the entire council were lifted into the air. Screams and cries echoed across Crafters Isle as Bregit's spell caused the Council of Shadows to smash against the rocks and stones scattered across Lorneid's quarters. Reacting swiftly, he freed himself of Lano's fiery bonds and retrieved his staff by orchestrating his fingers to summon it back to his welcoming hand. But before he could make his getaway, Lano appeared through the haze of sand his rod aimed at Bregit.

"Off so soon," asked a heaving Lano, "Where are your manners lord Bregit, you seem to have forgotten that when one trespasses upon another's territory its only right the trespasser serves their punishment," hissed Lano.

Before Bregit could comply. Lano deviously exhaled and spat from his mouth spheres of malting lava. Reacting, just on que Bregit swung his staff aggressively, parring Lano's destructive technique away toward the clouds, lighting the sky in a glow of murderous red.

"I should have known you were acting; the excitement of your capture overcame my reason. A mistake I will not allow happen again," panted Lano, the energy it had taken to conjure his technique had zapped him of most his strength.

Circling one another, black eyes staring coldly into the focused yellow they both waited, with their weapons gripped firmly within their grasp, both Lano and Bregit aware that one mistake could be fatal.

"Failure has become the story of your life, again you wish to carry out a rift between wizards and creatures believing yourself a saviour. When in fact all you are is a power-hungry fool who cares nothing for the sufferings of others, just so long as you get what you want!" said Bregit fiercely.

Tensely waiting, Bregit expected another sneak attack from Lano, but the Lava Keeper's patience had grown in his solitude. Making Bregit uncertain to what was coming next. A bold plan was quickly beginning to form inside his mind, one that may ensure his safety but in turn could seriously damage any hope he had of escape if he miscalculated even a speck of the spell. On a scale Bregit could easily fight it out with Lano, with his council members laying on their backs entranced by his sleeping spell Lano was vulnerable. Still Bregit resisted and in doing so was giving Lano the upper hand and an increase in morale.

"Magically gifted you are Bregit," Lano conceded with a low hiss, "But even you must admit you are no match against the combined strength of my council," hissed Lano, nodding his head toward his sleeping council.

Bregit glanced out of the corner of his eye, through the sand floating around him and Lano he caught sight of movements. "How?" he gasped in sheer disbelief.

The effects of his sleeping spell had somehow worn off the council. The blinding beams of light hovering above their eyes had dissolved, giving all six council members back their sight. As one by one they woke, rubbing the white dust from their eyes. Their anger radiating strong vibes that caused the hairs on Bregit's neck to stand up. Kcor and Jaed reacted aggressively by flinging themselves at Bregit. But their charge came to a quick halt at the commands of Lano who cast a wall of molten fire between his council members and Bregit, denying the proud creatures their vengeance.

"We gave you the chance of surrender, now Bregit, you will suffer the same faith as those who have opposed us," hissed Lano, walking through his wall of fire.

"Underestimating your opponent will always be your downfall," said Bregit the fire dancing in his eyes as called aloud. "Ella Slown!"

"Where is he?" Screeched Lano, rubbing his eyes and blinking furiously. "He was here just now!" he hissed looking around Lorneids quarters in search of Bregit.

Lano shot a sharp look toward the clouds nodding at Alacoma who understood his intentions. The winged beast spread its large brown and gray wings, which lifted his feet above the sand and with a rapid swirl, a hurl of wind lifted Alacoma through the clouds leaving a gust of wind in his wake. Alacoma returned moments later, having searched the entire perimeter. The winged beast shook his head in disbelief. Indicating there was no trace of Bregit among the sky.

"The back passage," gasped Tricklet, his voice ice cold.

"How do you know?" barked Kcor, kneeling beside Tricklet and looking at the little trickster only to notice his eyes were blank and unseeing. "Something is wrong with him!" voiced Kcor unconcerned as he waved his paws across Tricklets blank face, "he's not stirring at all," said the Viledirk looking at Lano.

But Lano seemed to not want to look at Tricklet and instead stared at the hills as a tense nerve tightened in his jaw as he debated on what to do. Not taking long Lano quickly snapped back to his senses.

"Never mind how he knows, get to the back passage at once before Bregit escapes!" hissed Lano viciously swiping the air with his hands.

Lime-coloured flames lashed from Lanos rod and swished toward the hill. A sizzling blaze erupted the moment the surging flames licked against the nests of the Harpies.

"Shouldn't be too difficult for you to find." "NOW GO!" Bellowed Lano.

Without question the council obeyed, all but one. Tricklet. The trickster continued sitting in a folded position, his eyes spiralling out of control all the while twiddling his thumbs. Refusing to look at him Lano left Lorneids quarters to search the lower grounds of Crafters Isle.

Unfortunately for Bregit, he had not managed to make it all the way to the back passage. The incantation he had used to escape Lorneids quarters was a shade stopper magical seal, which was overly complex to learn and harder to control. But when performed to perfection the magical seal allows the conjurer to cease the shades and freeze all that moves. The effects of controlling such magic does have its limitations for it drains the conjurer of energy at an accelerated rate.

Already drained from his journey to Treforledge. Bregit in his desperate attempt to escape almost zapped himself of energy. Weakened to the brink of collapse he'd barely made it down the hill of nests. But his lack of strength did have its upside because it allowed Bregit to overhear Lano's orders and now he knew where the council believed him to be going. Abandoning the attempt to enter the back passage he now lay under a pile of deceased wizards trying with all his might not to breathe aloud. For Alacoma the sky creature was sitting above him, unaware that his prey was buried beneath the decaying bodies he sat on. Peeking through the gap in a dead wizard's arm Bregit could see Alacomas sharp eyes scanning the area. The light from the burning nests nearby giving the sharp-eyed beast a clear view of the Rock Grinder's workplace.

Alacoma was a disciple of Iraz the Grey Falcon. It is unknown if they were related but judging by Alacomas light brown talons and his agile speed combined with the gift of manipulating wind did nothing to hide the similarities both beasts shared. When Iraz died during the Battle of the Skies, Alacoma took charge of the winged creatures that dwelled in Wivirid, the lands of hills that are far away to the west of Nocktar. In Wivirid Iraz built himself an army of winged beasts that rumour had it can eclipse the sky. But Bregit knew why Alacoma sat safely above the corpses. Because even dead, a wizard's body is enchanted to only be handled by another wizard. If Lano or any other creature made any attempt to move a wizard's lifeless body a painful death would quickly follow. But this small comfort did nothing to make Bregit feel secure due to Lano's ability to recognise him when concealed by his own enchantments.

''What other powers had his old foe learned in his exile?'' Bregit wondered as he stalked the ever-aware Alacoma. Lano was trained by the evillest fire creature to exist in Nocktar. Elan the Flamed Phoenix. 'Perhaps the Lava Keeper was the creature who killed the wizards of Treforledge,' thought Bregit his curiosity causing his concerns to grow deeper.

''Alacoma,'' came a roughed voice not too far away, ''Have your keen eyes seen anything of worth?'' called Kcor.

Drops of water dripped down onto the dead corpses and slid against Bregit's cracked lips. ''Sea Water,'' Bregit thought, feeling the saltwater slide along his face meaning only one thing, that Kcor had been searching the Red Sea for Bregit.

''Only the ashes moved by the swift breeze,'' came Alacomas dreamy voice.

''Well, if you see anything, don't hesitate to alert us,'' said Kcor, moving on quickly desperate to escape Alacomas company.

''Doesn't it bother you?'' asked Alacoma, his stern voice returning.

About to pounce up the ash-stained hill, Kcor turned his neck to look at Alacoma with dislike. ''If you explained what you're talking about then perhaps I would give an answer to your question,'' growled Kcor.

''I would have thought been Lano's sworn protector, you would have noticed something odd, but some aren't blessed with brains and brawn,'' laughed Alacoma, causing his beak to make an irritating snapping sound.

There were few things that bothered Kcor but laughing got under his skin like a hot flame against flesh. Swiftly the Viledirkening lord leapt into the air and before Alacoma could even flap his wings, the lord of the skies neck was wrapped tight within the grasp of Kcors clenched paws. From where Bregit lay, he could see the black sharp nails of Kcors paws slowly pierce the thin neck of Alacoma who flapped his wings aggressively in attempt to loosen Kcors hold over his neck.

''You better start making sense, or I'll roast your futile body in the flames and feast on what hides under those feathers!'' growled Kcor, barring his teeth at the bulged eyed Alacoma.

''I.... ca..n..tt... annsssseeerrr,'' choked Alacoma, his eyes watering from lack of oxygen.

Kcor released his grip, dumping Alacoma on the ash-stained rocks inches away from where Bregit lay. Alacoma gave himself a shake. Kcor looked down upon the winged beast with a look of loathing. When Alacoma raised his head, their eyes locked on one another with hate.

"If you haven't noticed by now brute," choked Alacoma, "Then I'll open that narrowed mind for you," said Alacoma coldly. Pausing the winged lord massaged his neck with the point of his wing, when he was convinced, no long-term damage was caused, he continued. "You must be aware of Lano's recent behaviour, especially the paranoia he's developed."

"Paranoia?" repeated Kcor, "What in the eight shades are you talking about?"

"I am talking about his recent change in behaviour. The snapping at anyone who disturbs him. Behaviour which has given me reason to believe our lord is hiding something," admitted Alacoma, his tooth at the front of his beak snapping at a nearby twig.

"If Lano decides to withhold information from us, then it is for our benefit. May I remind you who formed this alliance and shone light on us all when we had given up hope?" said Kcor sounding like he had rehearsed those lines in his sleep.

"Oh, please! I've endured enough of your speeches and praises of affection for our lord to last me an eternity," mocked Alacoma.

"Lano is the one who gave us hope that we could take back the lands that were stolen from us. Questioning his motives will get you in deep trouble," warned Kcor.

"My allegiance to Lano stands firm," said Alacoma truthfully. "However, even you can't deny his change in behaviour."

"Lano is our lord and master, whatever his mood, we are his trusted lieutenants sworn to serve him and be faithful," stated Kcor.

"Trust operates on both sides," contradicted Alacoma. "And I'm certain trust grants equality, especially since we are all risking our lives for the same thing," retorted Alacoma.

"You have had your chance on many occasions to speak openly about these ridiculous concerns of yours!" growled Kcor losing his patience. "Now have you any other suggestions to add?"

Alacoma gave Kcor a shake of his head to show he had nothing further to add to his suspicions.

"Then continue your search and stop wasting drops by adding fuel to a dead thought," growled Kcor flexing his muscles as he prepared to leap up the hill of nests.

But before he could pounce Alacomas voice whispered in his ears.

"Our master is under orders from a higher power," said Alacoma quietly, but just loud enough for Kcor to hear.

"The shades in the sky have addled your mind," said Kcor taken back by Alacomas dangerous presumptions. "Lano serves no one, there isn't a creature alive who would dare challenge his authority," said Kcor.

"Then why did he go frigid when Tricklet spoke of where Bregit was heading?" questioned Alacoma.

Kcor remained tight lipped appearing to be considering Alacomas theory. By the satisfied grin stretching Alacomas face was convincing enough for him to know that Kcor was tracking back to the moment Tricklets voice had deepened and turned cold.

"Finally beginning to sink into that stubborn head?" said Alacoma.

"If, Lano were under orders from a higher power wouldn't we have sensed or seen this phantom?" asked Kcor sarcastically. "Lano has not left our sides since we reformed the council, maybe he's stressed," suggested Kcor. "The pressures of ruling an army, claiming Treforledge and now the Lord of Larmont has discovered us, that's enough to make anyone abandon their senses," growled Kcor.

"We'll just have to be patient and see who is right and who is wrong, won't we?" Alacoma said smoothly flapping his wings. "I'm going to scan the skies, since there's nothing but dead corpses lying on the surface," and with that Alacoma soared swiftly into the clouds.

Kcor watched him drift away a look of distrust appearing along the lines of his furry face. He sniffed the air, before peering closely to the ground, but no scent did he find, so he left leaving Bregit alone beneath the corpses to work some method of escape.

When his mind was blank to any idea of escaping a chilling vibe blended with the air and spread through Bregit's body like a virus, numbing his senses. Looking up through the gaps between the bodies Bregit watched in fascination as a whirling black thread of smoke twisted and folded in mid-air until forming into a red eyed cloud that radiated power on a scale Bregit had never felt before. With just enough will power to resist looking into the cloud's eyes Bregit pulled himself up from the corpses he was using to conceal himself and ran as fast as he could. But he did not get far as a piercing pain lashed across the back of his legs causing him to fall to his knees.

Feeling the cloud drawing closer Bregit attempted to raise his staff in hope to heal his wound, but it was whisked from his grasp by a streak of silver light. Watching hopelessly as his last defence twirled in mid-air and beyond his reach, Bregit looked to the ground in defeat. Kneeling in pain, he looked in search of his disarmer. But no matter where the cloud was it had succeeded in its purpose of slowing him down. Feeling its presence lurking around him, Bregit tried to get a lock on its location but strangely every attempt he made was effortless because it was moving at such speed it was impossible to know where it lurked.

"Come forth … reveal yourself'…. creature of darkness," called Bregit.

A glimmer of scarlet red sparkled in the darkness as smoke began to spin rapidly, forming into a levitating cloud shaded in a dim grey with thin slits at its top and a wider slit spread along its centre where from Bregit's view appeared to be a mouth.

"Was this the source of the power he'd sensed upon his arrival to Treforledge?" thought Bregit.

''It's you I've been sensing this entire shade?'' said Bregit, his voice tense due to the throbbing pain in his lower legs.

The cloud never answered but Bregit could have sworn the slit where he believed its mouth was curled a little. Bregit took the clouds reaction as a yes. Leaning his hand on his left knee he struggled to rise further than a crouched position.

''NO!'' growled Bregit feeling his anger pulsing his insides.

Using what strength, he had left. Bregit stubbornly rose to his feet to face the cloud. Not to challenge it or try to reason with it but to face death up right and brave and not kneeling and pleading. The cloud seemed to acknowledge Bregit's actions, because one moment it was yards away the next it was hovering above his head. The rays of its scarlet eyes growing in power as they shone over Bregit like a ray of sunshine. Embracing death, Bregit spread his arms out wide and welcomed the killer blow that he predicted was drops away from been delivered. It happened so fast Bregit dared not believe it true, as a winged creature shrouded in darkness swooped from the clouds with gusts of surging winds at its back. Taken completely by surprise the cloud was hurled away by the force of the creature's aerial attack. The burning rays that shone over Bregit left his eyelids heavy from staring into them for so long leaving him in a hypnotised state. All the while a duel had begun and from what Bregit could make out through his blurred vision was that the cloud was gliding through the winged creatures' attacks and was using its own sprouted tentacles to slash away the gusts been hurled down upon it.

Sensing the cloud was winning the battle of wits Bregit knew it was only a matter of drops until it overpowered the attacks been hailed down on it by the unknown winged creature. Knowing the risk, Bregit outstretched his palms, flexed his thin fingers, and focused all his energy on a spell he hoped would finally end this cloud for good. For Bregit now feared this cloud was the higher power Alacoma was warning Kcor about.

''Deltro,'' whispered Bregit mustering all his will. He watched as tiny orange bulbs appeared in the centre of his palms. Absorbing what remained of his strength, Bregit urged the glowing bulbs to stretch and fold. Layer after layer the bulbs grew stronger before forming into a tiny pocket size ball that Bregit allowed to flow through his fingertips.

''Do what you were made for,'' he gasped fighting to remain conscious.

Taking flight, Bregit used his eyes to guide the glowing bulb, making sure to keep it away from the eyes of the cloud. Watching the cloud overcome the gusts whooshed down from the clouds Bregit knew he had mere drops before the cloud was victorious. Steadying his hands, he injected his last ounce of strength to enhance the bulbs momentum. The bulb at once glided past the notice of the cloud, and before it knew what was happening it had had sunk deep into the core of its wisping body. Channelling the last of his energy, Bregit snapped his fingers.

BOOOOOOOOOOMMMMMMMMMMM!!!!!

The explosion was so intense, it shook the foundations of Crafters Isle. Causing rocks to crack and slide from the cliffs and fall recklessly on the defenceless lands beneath. The shockwaves shot through Bregit's body, blasting the fatigued wizard away from the scene as the sky lit up in streaks of yellow. Bregit now lay spread eagled on his back layered in rubble, staring at the black clouded sky with not a care or worry to crease his drained face. With his body paralysed from the shock waves of the explosion, all he could do was lay waiting for deaths hold to claim him. He only hoped he would die long before Lano or his council found him. It was an unpleasant thing to dread in his situation but the thoughts of his life dimming under the punishable acts inflicted by Lano was one way he didn't want to go as the feeling of been lifted gently from his body eased Bregit's worries, for now he was certain death had claimed him. With such a warm embrace relaxing his soul. Bregit allowed himself to be drifted along the waves of clear air until darkness shut his sight and the exhaustion of battle locked him in the blissful arms of everlasting sleep.

Chapter 9

The Ancient Mountain of the Sphinxes

The annoying whispers of creaking wind brushed against Bregit's face as he had woken to find himself laying on a smoothed rock surface. As the confused wizard lay curled up on the hard ground, he tried piecing his juggled mind together. Even presuming was this where wizards went when they died? But whenever a fragment of memory would materialise, Bregit's mind would sear him with a sharp pain, making it difficult to concentrate on memories. Which eased his concerns because if he was feeling pain then he surely was alive but in hindsight he still wasn't sure whether that was an advantageous position to be in right now. His encounter with the Council of Shadows had taken its toll on Bregit's body. Because every attempt he made to rise from his unsuited position he would be forced back down by unbearable pain that had infected his entire body.

''Where am I?'' he asked moving his eyes up down and side to side.

Searching for the tiniest piece of clue to where he was his attempts were pointless, because his eyes couldn't make out his surroundings due to his inability to move. But Bregit's dwelling was short lived due to the sound of beating thumps coming from afar. Knowing the consequences Bregit forced his way through the pain and twisted his neck sideways, causing him to cry out in agony. The pain was like nothing Bregit had ever experienced and that was saying something. Sinking his teeth, he bit down hard on his lips gnawing so wildly he could taste the warmth of his own blood drool down his gums. But strangely the taste of his own blood defrosted the numbness inside his mouth and slowly gave him back the use of his mouth. Through the stinging tears of pain, he was able to make out his surroundings and was annoyed to find he was entombed in a cave no bigger than a cell. Flashing blue flames forced his eyes to squint, from what Bregit could make out logs were placed in brackets along the caves walls with blue flames flowing along their tips, giving the bare cave some recognition.

The thumping sounds drew closer and with-it rampant stomps that rattled the ground. Staring at the round entrance to the bare cave, Bregit watched on as a shadow stretched over the archway, shrouding it in complete darkness. The thin blue flames flowing above the logs dimmed to a narrow, increasing Bregit's fear. Waiting, his every nerve tense, Bregit accepted that this meeting with Lano was going to be a painful and humiliating one. But through the shadows appeared an enormous figure that equalled the doorway in height and width. A speck of silver sparkled in the darkness as its enormous figure moved into the cave its heavy breath coming out of its nostrils in puffs that whistled in the darkness, giving off the taste of mint scented leaves.

Squinting his eyes to focus, Bregit could make out the approaching creature that stood on all fours. Halting when within marginal distance from where Bregit lay, he finally got a glimpse of a face he never thought he would ever see again. Wearing a tense facial expression, the creature was covered in golden-brown fur stretching all along its back and trailing down its muscular legs. Bregit sighed with enormous relief as beams of starlight shone from the creatures flat well-groomed wings that were coated in white razor-sharp talons that were trained to follow their master's command. A wave of radiant power flowed throughout the enormous creature whose very presence spoke for itself, powerful and intimidating. Its sharp silver eyes looked down upon Bregit with a serious expression.

"I'm glad to see you again …. old friend," coughed Bregit, his spirits elevated.

The creature's mouth broadened into a pleasing smile, causing its silver eyes to widen. With a twirl of its front paw the dimmed blue flames burst of midnight blue flame, spreading much needed light along the bare cave.

"You've had quite an ordeal young Bregit," said the commanding voice of Tip-Karp the Sphinx. "To walk away or in your case, fly unscathed from the belly of the Council of Shadows is a triumph."

"It was you who brought me here?" said Bregit his brow tense, trying to remember meeting Tip-Karp in Treforledge.

It certainly wouldn't have been difficult, but every attempt Bregit made to recollect his past deeds, his mind would shut him out and send stinging surges directly to the core of his brain forcing him to retreat to spare himself further agony.

"Yes, it was I. But what stirs me to concern is why you were in Treforledge alone?" asked Tip-Karp, in his usual long, dull, and boring voice that still held a commanding tone within his words.

"I travelled alone to Treforledge based on rumour. I never expected to stumble upon Lano and his council and a graveyard of my own kind," answered Bregit.

This sentiment made Tip-Karp drop his unforgiving attitude and with one of his paws lifted Bregit up and positioned him against the caves wall, allowing him to look at Tip-Karp without straining himself.

"Easy old friend," recommended Tip-Karp. "The journey here has given you a little of your strength back but not enough to be hasty. Relax now and allow your beaten body to heal before trying any further movements."

"I'm getting old," breathed Bregit half-heartedly, finding a small comfort in his more fitting position.

"Your sense of humour hasn't," said Tip-Karp. "From the injuries I have tended to, you are extremely fortunate to be alive. All I can advise now is plenty of undisturbed rest."

"Undisturbed rest," Bregit repeated, laughing hoarsely, "As if such a thing exists in Nocktar," he added hoarsely.

But Bregit's joy quickly faded due to the sharp pain in his ribs, the unexpected stab of pain causing him to groan in agony. Breathing in and out to ease the cringing pain, Bregit looked up at Tip-Karp trying to appear unconcerned.

"I take it I am in one of your stores beneath the rocks of your mountain?" but before Tip-Karp could respond Bregit went on. "Allow me to ask a simple question in return old friend?"

Not a creature to be cut across on the point of speech, Tip-Karps eyes narrowed at Bregit's insolence, his respect however was gracious enough to allow the weary wizard to continue without further argument.

"How did I get here? For some reason, my memory has deserted me. Leaving me in a state of confusion that has no desire of lifting," Bregit confessed.

"You were fighting a creature with no shape or form ……," Tip-Karp began but was again interrupted by Bregit.

"Yes. I remember now," gasped Bregit as a wave of shock washed over him. "A cloud with red eyes appeared as I was hiding from Lano and his council," said Bregit, feeling a cold shudder crawl up his spine.

"I knew confronting this cloud head on, I would be certain to fall to the same faith I'd found you in, so instead I used one of my many unique gifts," said Tip-Karp.

"The Sleeted Gales," said Bregit, not needing his memory to be sure of what technique Tip-Karp used to attract the cloud to his coming.

"Correct. I managed to draw the clouds focus away from you, but sadly I underestimated its strength. Had it not been for your spell forcing the cloud to explode, I doubt any of us would be here to recollect on past events. Whatever that being is, it has abilities beyond anything I have ever encountered," said Tip-Karp with a seriousness added to his cautious words.

"The Exploding Lantern," breathed Bregit the scent of the spell flowing from his fingertips. "But If I caught it with that spell then surely the cloud perished?" he said more to himself than Tip-Karp.

"For our sakes I hope so, I dread to think what damage such a creature could do if allowed roam freely throughout the Lands of Light," said Tip-Karp.

Bregit placed his right hand on his head and closed his eyes, focusing hard, he tried with all his might to recollect the events that occurred within Treforledge. But the last unblurred memory he could find was of himself hiding under a bed of dead wizards and looking up to see a cloud with red eyes staring back at him. Whatever occurred after that moment seemed determined not to resurface?

"Seems my mind doesn't want me to remember my duel with this shapeless malice," Bregit said opening his eyes, feeling irritated.

"Memories come and go my friend," whispered Tip-Karp his fierce gaze looking at Bregit with empathy. "The memories we wish to disregard latch to us like sticky pox, while the ones we hope to keep and cherish always seem to slip away. I am sure if it is important to you your mind will reveal them in due course," Tip-Karp said smoothly.

"I'm glad to see your good will has not changed since our last meeting old friend. The shades passed has benefited you well," said Bregit hoarsely forcing a weak smile.

"Forgive me if rudeness is shown, but I would like to know something," Tip-Karp said seriously.

Bregit looked at Tip-Karp and was reminded why he was one of the most feared creatures among Nocktar. Bound by his own laws to safeguard the Lands of Light, Tip-Karp also yearned to know the dealings of all who dwell in his mountain. A small price to pay Bregit was aware to have an alliance with a sphinx.

"Why were you present in Treforledge. Seems a bit far for the Lord of Larmont to go on a mid-shade stroll?"

Before Bregit responded he heaved aloud, his eyes bulging with shock by an unexpected cough ball of sand that had erupted up his throat and charged uncontrollably out of his mouth like a herd of Kurlezzias hunting its prey, it was such a sight that it made Tip-Karp turn away in disgust.

"Your manner is vile," said Tip-Karp, watching with dislike as Bregit vomited over his smoothed cave.

Looking a bit taken back by Tip-Karps reaction, Bregit choked up a large amount of sand and spat it on the floor which helped clear his throat and give him back the use of his normal voice.

"I was informed that Treforledge had been attacked and that Lorneid the Blue had fallen. I had to see for myself was it true, so I journeyed on foot to the Blue Islands only to discover it was Lano and his council behind the siege," answered Bregit.

"Yet, you managed to escape. How?" asked Tip-Karp frowning.

"I was forced to use a quick shade stopper seal. Which allowed me to get away but not far. Due to my lack of food and water, I barely made it to the Harpies nests. I dragged myself beneath the decomposing bodies of the deceased wizards before the council were aware of my escape," answered Bregit.

"If a Ripeling attempted to do what you did, I would turn a blind eye in the belief of inexperience. But a wizard with your knowledge should know better than to perform such a complex spell!" barked Tip-Karp aggressively, spitting saliva on his groomed mane.

"I had no other choice," said Bregit defensively, his own temper rising.

"Shade stopping is one of the most dangerous branches of magic. Had a glitch of your spell gone wrong many innocent creatures would have suffered because of your ignorance," said a furious Tip-Karp, not even trying to hide the disappointment in his voice.

The atmosphere changed drastically between Bregit and Tip-Karp. Both creatures stared at the other finding it difficult to agree on the terms of Bregit's actions. But Tip-Karp was too eager to remain frustrated for long and continued where he had left off.

"I too heard whispers of an uprising brewing within Treforledge and like your foolish self, I went to investigate. But I unlike you, aimed to see and flee not follow and fight," said Tip-Karp, dragging every word, supressing his better judgement over Bregit's own failings. "Upon my arrival I was fortunate to catch a glimpse of Lano accompanied with a floating cloud that looked a lot like the one we battled. The cloud lingered alongside Lano while he strolled through the battlements, but I was unable to hear the conversation they were engaged in due to the distance between us."

"I bet he enjoyed his little stroll, killing wizards seems an eternal thirst for that fiend," said Bregit with boiling anger as he imagined the sick smirk Lano wore as he gazed down upon the defeated wizards of Treforledge.

"Not as pleased as you think. On the contrary Lano seemed strange, quivering he was when I got close enough to hear him speak. Something Lano said before I settled into my hiding place must have angered the cloud in some way."

"Lano always had a way with words, no doubt he came out the victor of his little sparring match," interjected Bregit his anger still prickling his senses.

"I've no doubt he would have if the cloud didn't wrap him within black shrouded whips and punish him severely," said Tip-Karp. "Through his pleading cries, Lano uttered words such as source and near the cliffs. When the cloud released him Lano began sniffing the air, claiming to sense a familiar presence. Fearful it was my own scent I fled for fear of exposure. I travelled on foot to the Charred Mountain and used its weakened state to cause a tame avalanche that may have distracted the watchers from hearing me take off. I returned to my mountain with great speed. My priority was to send envoys to Larmont seeking your aid."

"Seems your messenger returned to sender with your message undelivered," said Bregit smiling.

"I never found out from my messenger that you had abandoned your post and travelled to Treforledge," said Tip-Karp, not finding Bregit's tone amusing.

"Then how did you know of my plans?" asked Bregit.

"It was the wizard you released from the back passage," answered Tip-Karp. "It was he who told me about your one wizard mission and knowing what danger you were in, I left at great speed for Treforledge in hope that you weren't discovered, and lucky for you Bregit that I did, because that cloud was within drops of finishing you for good! Had I been any later we would not be having this discussion," said Tip-Karp firmly.

"I give you my thanks for saving my life, but now I must regain my lost strength and much more quickly than I intended. For there are many lands to be journeyed and little drops to do it," Bregit said flexing his tired fingers.

Tip-Karp looked at Bregit, bedazzled in wonder as to how he was going to travel anywhere in his condition. The sphinx watched while Bregit wove both his hands gently over his thinned legs, muttering incantations that roused a soft breeze from the tips of his fingers. Whistling lowly Bregit commanded the air rotating around his hands to fold and cover his lower body.

"What are you doing?" asked Tip-Karp confused by Bregit's antics.

When Bregit finished muttering, silence fell over the cave and was shattered by a deafening cry of pain that reverberated throughout the cave and along the halls. Bregit shook uncontrollably making him fall on his side as bubbling lumps creeped up his neck and lower body creating wavey ripples along his skin. Tip-Karp stood watching, horrified by what he was seeing. Laying unmoved on the floor Bregit's long blonde hair hung loosely hiding his dimmed face. The bubbling lumps slowly sunk back into the depths of his body easing his discomfort.

"Bregit," Tip-Karp whispered trying not to startle him. "Bregit," he called again raising his voice slightly, "Are you ok?"

Resuscitated, deep coughs charged from Bregit's throat that blew his hair back and forth. With a great heave, he lay his hands flat against the floor and pressed his fingertips hard into the flat smoothed surface.

"Allow me," began an astonished Tip-Karp but the sphinx stopped halfway as Bregit raised his hand to stop him coming any closer.

Standing upward and straight, Bregit placed his left hand against the caves cold wall for support as he heaved heavily, the effects of mending his body magically showing its reasoning that it should not be tried lightly. Feeling his old strength flow through him again Bregit praised his old friend Carka for teaching him such a useful spell.

"Unbelievable," gasped Tip-Karp, his eyes blinking furiously in disbelief at Bregit's repaired body. "I've never heard of magic capable of healing wounds like that, how did you do that?" breathed Tip-Karp.

"Magic," said Bregit, not looking at Tip-Karp but around the cave. "Where is my staff?" he asked in a stern voice.

"In my quarters," answered Tip-Karp still standing unsure as to how Bregit was standing fully healed in front of him. "It suffered heavy damage when you cast your last spell, but rest assured old friend, it is fully mended," assured Tip-Karp.

"Good," said Bregit untroubled by anything Tip-Karp had said. "I'll need it for my journey," he said in a more assured voice as he walked by Tip-Karp and toward the caves entrance.

"Wait, Halt!" called Tip-Karp, in a strong voice causing the cave to shake. "Where are you going?"

Bregit stopped when he had reached the entrance, turning his head slightly he looked at Tip-Karp from out of the corner of his eye.

"I must alert the Golden Kingdom to what I've just seen take fold in Treforledge," Bregit answered in a serious voice.

Tip-Karp took a step back, shocked by Bregit's intentions. "They will not help," said Tip-Karp, nodding his head strongly. "The King of the Golden Kingdom only cares for those who live among the clouds, not the affairs of those beneath him, you above all of them know this too well," Tip-Karp said sternly.

"What would you have me do, pretend it never happened and allow Lano a free pass to destroy more lands?" said Bregit, turning his neck and looking directly at Tip-Karp.

"There are other wizards that can help, send envoys to Saradice and Dry Scales or Tindisinge," advised Tip-Karp. "Lorneid had many supporters that would rally their forces to avenge his death, don't go to the Golden Kingdom and be rejected when several lords of lands are within a shade's journey away," said Tip-Karp.

"You forget old friend; every lord of land is sworn to do the kings bidding. If I were to travel to every lord and persuade them to gather their armies and fight for me without the consent of the king. He would see that as treason and execute the one responsible for assembling the armies of Nocktar and leading them into a war without his concession," said Bregit, hoping Tip-Karp understood his predicament.

Sighing deeply Tip-Karp nodded his head in disagreement. "I have known you for many cycles, and what I have learned in those shades of friendship is the stubbornness that fuels you. I cannot force you not to go, but I wish my words broke through that wall you call pride,'' said Tip-Karp sounding annoyed.

''I must do what I believe to be right. If the king decides to be blind to the destruction of Treforledge, then I genuinely believe Nocktar will again be Lano's to rule. Will you travel to the Cloud Stair with me old friend?'' Bregit asked hopefully.

''Long has it been since I climbed that stair, to keep it so, I will not travel alongside you, old friend,'' said Tip-Karp deliberately making his voice sound kind.

''After all we've suffered together you still remain intolerant to the king. Why?''

''I have little tolerance for the wizards who live in that kingdom,'' said Tip-Karp tensing his jaws. ''They are greedy and believe themselves superior to us all and besides, I must await my envoy, he has yet to return from Larmont. If he is not back by the end of blue shade, I must go looking for him.''

''Perhaps your envoy has been captured by spies of Lano,'' Bregit suggested. ''It wouldn't surprise me if that fiend had one or two sneaking around this mountain. I doubt even this majestic mountain will repel Lano's forces once he has gathered his old strength.''

Before Tip-Karp could argue, heavy breaths filled the tunnel leading into the cave. The sound of footsteps followed by heavy breaths echoed along the halls. Something or someone was slowly nearing the cave with little care of been heard. Bregit prepared himself as did Tip-Karp. Both creatures eagerly waited, ready to pounce the moment anything appeared. Bregit who stood nearest to the entrance spotted a creeping shadow growing along the wall. Aiming his hand at the cloaked figure now standing in the frame of the caves entrance, the figure halted before slowly lowering its hood. The hood fell and rested on its shoulders, revealing a white-haired hunched back wizard. Feeling his cheek bones lift Bregit lowered his guard at the sight of his old mentor.

''Carka,'' breathed Bregit with relief. ''What brings you to the ancient mountain of the sphinxes?'' he asked.

''I will explain all when I am re-joined with my companion,'' answered Carka, heaving heavily and sounding like he had travelled for shades without rest.

''Companion?'' barked Tip-Karp, who looked furious at the sight of Carka. ''How many have you brought to the mountain of my elders?'' he demanded to know at once, stepping toward Carka who pierced the sphinx with a look of dislike.

''Easy,'' Bregit protested, looking from Carka to Tip-Karp. ''I'm sure there's an explanation to why Carka is here, with unknown company,'' said Bregit lightly.

''Calm yourself sphinx,'' growled Carka, his breathing easing, his gaze on the other hand showed no sign of soothing. ''Your little messenger led us here, ranting on about dangers in Treforledge. Galli and I were waiting for Bregit outside his tower when your messenger appeared, and after hearing what he had to say we agreed to go to the sphinx's mountain hoping to find Bregit there,'' Carka explained in a cold manner.

''Why? May I ask were you awaiting my return to Lar………,'' Screeched Bregit; his last word was drowned out because of the pain that had unexpectedly soared through his head forcing him to lean his hand against the caves wall to prevent himself falling.

It happened in a flash, so fast Bregit had no way of preparing himself. All he could do was watch as flash after flash of his own memories swam across his waking eyes. When Bregit's final memory diminished, he fell to one knee trying hard to control his breathing, the shock causing him to shake uncontrollably. Carka held his hand up to Bregit's face, the stone pierced in his palm glowed white as Tip-Karp stood back not wanting to be the target of a misdirected spell as Carka soothingly put Bregit to sleep.

"How did I get here?" gasped Bregit springing up to his feet only to feel the ground spinning around him.

Bregit had woken in a cave completely different to the one he had previously woken in. He knew the difference right away because this cave had a glow, he had seen many of cycles of shades past. "The Pool of Clear," he whispered, remembering the pool when he had last entered the ancient mountain of the sphinxes.

"Right, you are, Bregit," came Tip-Karps dulled voice.

Turning his gaze from the pool, Bregit found the large sphinx laying on a bed of white feathers licking his enormous paws.

"The Pool of Clear can inhabit any water and cleanse it, making it pure so that the creatures of this mountain can use it to drink and strengthen what energy they lost on their travels. My elders believed in purity so much, they decided to leave the Lands of Light knowing that as long as indifference stood in the way of wizards and creatures' purity would never be found again within the Lands of Light," Tip-Karp stated dully.

"Pssst," spat Carka, who had appeared out of the shadows of the cave with his arms folded and a look of impatience in his lined expression.

Tip-Karp who lay licking his wet paws looked at Carka with his sharp silver eyes, both creatures trading loathing glares as Carka came further into the light.

"Your elders deserted Nocktar because they knew wizards were the new dominant specie of this planet and fled because admitting they were second to us would mean giving up their hold over this mountain. So, save your little speeches of purity for the next unfortunate visitor to come to this rotted place," snapped Carka harshly, his worn voice still having a sting to his words.

Tip-Karp rose from his bed, his muscles tensing due to Carka's sneering remarks, and just as both creatures prepared themselves a spark ignited in Carka's palms. Fearing a fight may break out Bregit came between the pair.

"Let's leave our thoughts about the sphinxes leaving and their reasons for doing so to ourselves Carka," said Bregit briskly.

"Yes, lets," agreed Tip-Karp, a flush of anger reddening his furry face as he turned his attention to Bregit.

"You asked how you managed to get here, that is easily explainable. The spell you used to heal yourself and attach your broken limbs must have weakened your mind causing it to collapse under the stress of past events. Carka and I felt it better for you to rest within my chamber, so he put you asleep and carried you here, because we are awaiting your friend's companion who has not yet revealed itself'," explained Tip-Karp laying back on his feathered bed.

"I thank you again my old friend, your kindness is welcome. The reason for my collapse was the flood of my own memories charging like a tidal wave from the core of my mind to my eyes. Though I cannot say the experience was eventful, I cannot deny I am overjoyed by its rewards."

"Perhaps now, we can work together with the information we have gathered and find a solution to ridding us all of the same problem," said Carka coldly, piercing Bregit with a look of annoyance.

"The memories of my journey through Treforledge have returned giving me more reason to worry," said Bregit, looking at Carka. "There is only one solution," he added.

Tip-Karp and Carka remained silent, not even asking Bregit what his intentions were. Instead, Tip-Karp resumed licking his paws while Bregit and Carka stared into the others fearless expressions.

"It's true then? Dulgerdeen has fallen into the hands of Lano?" asked Bregit.

Carka remained tight lipped his answer however revealed itself in the weary eyes of his old mentor who turned his back to face the darkness of the chambers wall.

'Carka looked deeply troubled but why? Had he too encountered the cloud?' Thought Bregit.

"It's true," sighed Carka deeply after a few drops of consideration. "The forests of Dulgerdeen belong to Lano and his council."

"Another land of Nocktar has fallen to Lano and no counter strike from the king!' growled Tip-Karp. "Doesn't the king's lack of action, not prove that he doesn't care?" he appealed to Bregit.

Bregit continued to stare at Carka's back wondering what Carka had suffered that he had to turn to him for help. "How many survived besides you?" Bregit asked, ignoring Tip-Karp.

Carka swallowed hard before answering, "None."

The knowledge of Carka's followers demise created a silence that stretched throughout the chamber. No one could tell how long this silence lasted but all three were thankful that it was broken by a young wizard cloaked in blue. The wizard came hurrying through the sealed entrance of Tip-Karps cave looking flushed by her awkward introduction.

"Oh my," gasped a mortified Galli clapping her hands over her mouth, "My apologies for my rude welcome," she said breathing fast. "I had no idea where the sphinx's chamber was, so I've been wandering around this maze of a mountain looking in every cave for creatures to get directions from," Galli explained not taking her eyes away from Tip-Karp's floor.

"Is this the companion we've been patiently waiting to arrive?" asked Tip-Karp, an amusing smile creeping up his furry face at the innocence of Galli's embarrassing introduction.

"Yes, this is my companion," answered Carka stiffly. "May I introduce Galli the Blue, Second to Lorneid the Blue of Treforledge."

"Treforledge," repeated Bregit hotly. Bregit looked at Galli more closely, noticing how similar her appearance was to the other wizards who lived in Treforledge. "So, there were survivors other than Irmkay," he said, "But how did you get away without been detected by the council?"

"Give the Ripeling a chance to catch her breath!" barked Carka, throwing Bregit a furious glare.

Taken back by the manner of Carka's fierce demand, Bregit became aware of how exhausted Galli appeared. Her blue hair hung loosely and diluted in stains of mud and neglect. Lines of exhaustion and unrest along with the appearance of grief dimmed her glow to leave the young wizard a shadow of her former self. Bregit's obscurement of Galli forced his curiosity to the back of his mind, what filled his racing mind now was shame. Approaching Galli, he put an arm around her shoulder and lead her to the wooden bed he had recently indulged in himself.

"Sit and rest," he offered. "Whatever tale you have to tell can wait until you 're ready. Please forgive my rudeness, my eagerness for answers blinded me to not see how drained you were," said Bregit in an apologetic tone.

Galli accepted Bregit's offer and sat herself comfily within the oaken bed. Turning his attention to Carka, Bregit spoke to his former mentor in a measured voice.

"What happened to Dulgerdeen and the wizards who lived within that forest?" he asked, leaving Galli's side, and stepping closer to his old mentor.

Carka stared at the ground and then at the gloomy green walls, considering where to start. Twice Carka clicked his tongue against his cheek, with a swirl of his head he began to speak.

"I was approached by a creature of the forest known as Hinkelthorn....,"

"The Rurrow?" interjected Tip-Karp.

"Yes," answered Carka shooting the sphinx a look of wonder as to how he would know what creature Hinkelthorn was?

"What happened next?" asked Bregit his eagerness resurfacing.

"Hinkelthorn seemed deeply troubled, then next moment he was speaking rather hurriedly."

"What did he tell you?" asked Bregit, his eagerness making him appear hasty.

"He told me that Gliders had invaded the forest and killed his eldest kin," answered Carka.

"Gliders?" said the trio together as they exchanged looks of surprise.

Carka rolled his eyes, continuing without given them the slightest of notice.

"Having narrowly escaped a Glider pursuit Hinkelthorn sought me out and when he came to my cave, told me that Dulgerdeen was now infested by an army of Gliders. Through his voice I sensed no lie, it was at that moment that I digested the truth and pieced together that the Kurlezzias had betrayed me."

"What proof do you have to prove Gazzel betrayed you?" asked Tip-Karp who found the thought of Gazzel betraying him absurd.

"Call it intuition, but my instincts serve me well and I would bet my eyes Gazzel wasn't hard pushed to allowing the Gliders access into Dulgerdeen if it resulted in my downfall," said Carka sternly.

"I would measure your instincts to be nothing more than ill news toward creatures you dislike, Gazzel has been protector of Dulgerdeen for cycles of shades and has dedicated his life to safeguarding the creatures living within that forest," said Tip-Karp, not buying Carka's presumption to be fact.

Before Carka could argue the matter further Bregit took it upon himself to cut across the two creatures before their argument reached an endless cycle.

"Regardless of the Kurlezzia's hand in this, let us draw back to Carka version of events," said Bregit frustratingly.

"Concealed in the shadows they anonymously stalked me. It had been a trap all along as swarms of Gliders surrounded us." Carka felt a twinge of sorrow as he drew closer to recalling his encounter with Dreaquirla and Hinkelthorns death, a moment he wished he could live again so that he could alternate the outcome.

"How did you escape?" asked Galli.

"By been patient. But I was thwarted in my plan by Hinkelthorn. The loss of his kin had maddened him beyond reason and in his lapse, he surrendered to his impulses and tried killing Dreaquirla, but his actions shattered my plan of both of us escaping....," Carka paused to take a deep breath trying his upmost to conceal the pain Hinkelthorns death had inflicted on him. "Hinkelthorn was split in two by the wind waves of Rullin," sighed Carka, the death of his friend no doubt the reason the strong voice behind his disciplined mouth had swelled.

"Excuse my interruption, but with Hinkelthorn gone you could have fled without hesitation, why did you stay?" asked Bregit.

"The same reason you went to Treforledge, curiosity. I wanted to see with my own eyes who had sparked the chaos," answered Carka. "When it was made clear that Lano was behind the attack, I showed my storm brewing skills by conjuring a powerful bolt of lightning from a nearby cloud that lifted my body from Dulgerdeen and safely above the clouds. When it was safe to land, I travelled on foot disguised as a traveller through many lands hoping to warn the inhabitants of what loomed nearby. But I found no creatures or wizards on my journey to Larmont," finished Carka.

Silence consumed the inhabitants of Tip-Karps cave once more as Carka's tale had shocked them to the core. Carka resumed his back facing them while Galli looked lost in the presence of creatures, she felt were too important to speak her worries to. Bregit appeared unnerved but was still refusing to leave while Tip-Karp watched the trio of wizards knowing he had to be the one to refresh their memories before they went their separate ways.

"Dulgerdeen and Treforledge are now under the control of Lano, it is now up to you three to decide what steps must be taken to prevent Lano gaining control of other lands," said Tip-Karp.

"I don't believe Lano desires any more lands, think about it" said Bregit urgently. "He doesn't have the numbers to protect all Lands of Light and knows he needs to keep his army intact," Bregit reminded the sphinx.

"You're forgetting the one being who can tip the balance in Lanos favour, and I am astonished two out of the three of you have yet to mention it," said Tip-Karp firmly.

"The cloud," breathed Galli.

"What are you talking about?" asked Carka turning around sharply and looking from Tip-Karp to Galli with a firm look.

"None of us can tell you what the cloud is, because we've never seen anything like it before, what we can tell you is that its powers are as strange to us as its appearance," said Bregit.

"So Lano has fostered another creature into his council, perhaps this one may exceed even the Lava Keepers expectations," said Carka who relished in the challenge this new adversary offered.

"Let's not allow worry to cloud our senses, this cloud maybe powerful, but let's remember Nocktar is full of creatures capable of defeating this new tyrant. It isn't the first to rise from the darkness and seek to destroy the wizarding race," Bregit reminded them.

"Says the wizard who couldn't defeat it," sneered Carka. "After all I taught you and you couldn't even handle a cloud, I'm disappointed Bregit, solitude seems to have made you soft!"

"I have no answer to my failings, but from my experience duelling this enemy I can assure you the four of us combined wouldn't slow this cloud in its destructive rampage," said Bregit.

"I too have seen this cloud and witnessed its powers, and I've never seen Lorneid pushed to his limits before and even his skills were nothing in comparison to this cloud," said Galli backing up Bregit's theory.

"Does this demonstration not give you enough clarity to the fact that we alone cannot triumph against Lano and his reformed council? We must set our sights on the Golden Kingdom and persuade the king to counter Lano before he eliminates the rest of the kingdoms!" Bregit shouted to Carka with urgency in his voice.

"So, the faith of our specie rests on the decision of one wizard?" asked Galli.

"That one wizard rules the entire planet," stated Bregit firmly, "His ruling and decisions are final."

"More's the pity," murmured Carka.

"It may seem simple to one who does not know what it's like to be in that position," Bregit inhaled deeply to balance his patience. "But the king is the law enforcer and we as abiders, must serve his rule even if it displeases us."

"Sounds like you respect the king and his position?" said Carka.

"And what gives you that impression?" Bregit fired back.

"Ah, let me think," mocked Carka in a teasing tone. "Maybe your defence of a king unfit to rule and the hint of appreciation to the difficulties of his position," said Carka in a mocking squeaky tone.

"Your feeble taunts don't affect me Carka; I will say this before I take my leave, it's no coincidence we four are here at the same moment."

"Now you believe faith has paired us together," laughed Carka enthusiastically. "Spare me the lecture Bregit and go toddle along to the king," said Carka coldly.

Bregit shot Carka with a look of annoyance. "What do you propose we do?" he asked.

"I will act as I see fit to stop Lano, but I will not waste drops going to the king to be rejected when there are other methods to be considered," answered Carka.

"This squabbling is getting us nowhere," said Tip-Karp, "but as much as it pains me to admit, Carka is right. The king will not empty his kingdom and retaliate unless there is solid proof to back up your claims, and unfortunately the words of a deserter will not persuade many."

"My priority is the safety of the innocent and if I've to come across as a helpless fool, then so be it. Sacrificing my dignity would be a small price to pay in attempt to persuade the king to summon the Seven Coloured Army and rid Nocktar of Lano," Bregit said impatiently.

"Then we say goodbye for the present and maybe for good," said Carka unmoved by Bregit's speech.

Refusing to look at the trio. Bregit brushed by Carka who gave him a nod of disapproval as Bregit pulled back the curtain and vanished into the hallway.

Chapter 10

The Plate Pathway

"Nilope," said Bregit sharply pointing his staff at the boulder in front of him. His spell pushed aside the round boulder, by doing so, forced it against its will to roll over to his left-hand side. In the boulder's absence was a cracked hole carved into the wall that took the shape of a lightning bolt. Walking through it the refreshing feeling of clean air flowed through his nostrils, as Bregit walked out into the open breeze of the mountain side to find himself standing on the doorstep of Tip-Karps Mountain. A rumbling sound frightened Bregit that he instantly spun around with his staff raised and eyes focused. But when nothing leaped out from behind the rocks, a calmness soothed his anxiety. As he watched with a smirk, while the enchanted boulder automatically rolled back to its preferred position of shielding the entrance of the mountain.

'Clever,' thought Bregit admiring the sphinx's way of arming their sacred mountain with admiration. "If there's no way of seeing the entrance then there's no possibility of penetrating its defence," Bregit recalled Tip-Karp telling him on his first visit to his mountain.

Turning away from the concealed entrance, Bregit walked a few paces to find a twirling slope of narrowed steps forged from the rocks of the sphinx's mountain. Walking down the thin steps, Bregit noticed each one he stepped over was crystal clean, no doubt Tip-Karp handled this. The sphinx did take immense pride been lord of his elder's mountain. When the steps ended at the bay of the mountain that was sheeted with clear glittering orange sand which stretched out for miles, giving any passer by the feeling of walking on air. Bregit, however, refused to indulge in this desire and took precautionary steps to ensure he left no trail of his footprints behind. Using his abilities to control the air around him Bregit levitated above the sand and glided swiftly across the bay.

Clicking his fingers, he slowly lowered himself down on to the soft grass just inches away from the sea. Withdrawing his staff from the inside of his robe, he stared at a white circular object floating beneath the still water. Grasping at the air Bregit spoke in a deep voice that caused surges of wind to spiral around his hands.

"Great sea of old hear my cry, reveal to me what I plead to see, for trouble brews beyond the eye of the wizard I pray will not deny."

The wind instantly ceased. The echoes of his voice rung out in the distance as Bregit stood as still as the mountains behind him, praying the sea answered his call. Then as if remotely controlled the plates rose from the water and one by one, they formed into the legendary Plate Pathway, which was one of many clever creations made by Dirm the Bronze. Who used his unique talents to line rows of plates three centimetres apart from the other until they formed a long path that would lead any travelling wizard to any land within the boundaries of the Lands of Light!

''Thank you, great sea,'' Bregit murmured in gratitude.

Placing his right foot forward, Bregit touched the first plate. But before his other foot moved onto the plate, he caught a whiff he had sensed before. Twirling on the spot Bregit seen a cloaked figure walking over to him from across the bay. It was the blue wizard Galli, who walked right up to Bregit looking at him with interest as she halted her stride metres from where Bregit stood to tuck a small bunch of Tweedly Plants inside her robes.

''I know, I should've come forward sooner and revealed my intentions, but you seemed determined to go to the Golden Kingdom alone, but before Lorneid died he wished for me to meet with you,'' said Galli not once taking her tired gaze from Bregit.

''Why would Lorneid want us to meet?'' Bregit questioned Galli, frowning.

''He wanted you to know what happened to Treforledge and what killed him,'' answered Galli.

''I have been to the ruins of Treforledge and faced the creature responsible for its destruction, which is why I am going to the Golden Kingdom because I know as you do that whatever that creature is cannot be defeated unless we have support,'' said Bregit.

''Well, I've upheld my promise to Lorneid which allows me to return to my kin, unburdened,'' said Galli sounding disappointed by Bregit's lack of understanding Lorneids dying wish. She turned away in anger and walked back toward Tip-Karps Mountain.

Bregit was a bit shocked by Galli's rudeness and even laughed at her while watching her walk across the bay. He wasn't sure why Lorneid would send her to him, surely there was a deeper meaning but what was the question? 'Perhaps Galli would be the perfect wizard to describe what attacked Treforledge she was there when it happened and who better to have on your side than an eyewitness,' were Bregit's thoughts as he quickly made up his mind.

''You may travel alongside me if you wish,'' Bregit called out, ''maybe there is a reason Lorneid wanted our paths to cross, but your version of events would be vital if we are to persuade the king to join us.''

Galli thought about it for a moment and glanced back at Tip-Karps Mountain before answering. ''Lorneid believed in you so much he fought against death to instruct me to find you, this brief meeting was not what he wanted? Nevertheless, I will go with you but if it goes wrong my promise to Lorneid ends and I will find my own means of avenging my kin,'' Galli said looking at Bregit seriously.

''Deal,'' said Bregit smiling.

Both wizards stepped on the pathway with Bregit a plate ahead of Galli. Moving with haste, they were out of eyeshot of Tip-Karps Mountain momentarily.

''Is this your first experience walking on the plates?'' Bregit asked Galli in a calm voice.

''Yes,'' Galli replied sincerely. ''Lorneid forbid us to never wander along the plates. If you do not know the way, lost you will find yourself,'' said Galli, in a voice that came across as well rehearsed.

'Lies,' Bregit said to himself. Knowing full well that Lorneid sent many envoys to other lands when he would trade his rock made weapons for finer silks and organic foods that grew leagues away from Treforledge.

''He was right to recommend such caution, there are no maps written or directions given. The wizard who wishes a destination and needs to walk the plates to get there, must ask the sea for its permission, the pathway is only designed for wizards no creature can enter and if they tried the protective spells Dirm casted to shield the pathway would kill them instantly,'' said Bregit.

''Is that why you spoke to the sea to show you were a wizard and not some creature under false pretences?'' asked Galli.

''Well observed,'' said Bregit surprised. ''Yes, the sea will only allow wizards in great need to use the plates and wizards who need the path for selfish needs are turned away. However, if the plates reveal themselves the same way they did for me, it means that wizard has previously walked on the plates. Seems you too are welcome, the sea did not reject you, perhaps you too were destined to see the Golden Kingdom,'' said Bregit.

''I don't believe in destiny,'' said Galli in a stern tone. ''Destiny makes one's mind think too much about things that haven't yet occurred.''

The wisdom of one so young speaking out about her beliefs turned Bregit's neck slightly in curiosity. Looking at Galli, out of the corner of his eye. Bregit studied her, because never had he heard one so young speak so maturely, especially in the company of a superior wizard.

''Dismissing the unknown is like walking without sight, many have wasted their lives believing in what you disregard,'' Bregit contradicted. ''Destiny is for all, even doubters believe they have some part in the universe or why else were we giving power?'' said Bregit in a silky voice.

''We were given intelligence not power,'' Galli contradicted back in a confident tone. ''Intelligence made wizards realise they had power destiny played no part in wizards rising from nothing to become the dominant species of this planet.''

''I refuse to believe for a single drop that you are a doubter. Frightened maybe? Unintelligent no!'' said Bregit sharply. ''However, what we see with our own eyes is much more understanding than words passed down from the ages, and what mine have seen have convinced me that our powers invite unnecessary conflicts.''

''Such as?'' asked Galli sounding interested again.

''Take Lano for example, he used our powers as a rallying cry to call the mystical and mythical creatures to his cause, without a shred of proof to back up his ludicrous assumptions. But his influence did inflict fear in many minds, so much, it spread like a virus, until the entire population of Nocktar were on the wizard's doorstep baying for their blood. And all because one creature believed it was his destiny to end the line of wizards. I put it to you, what would you do in Lanos situation?''

Bregit's voice was firm with a sharpness added to it, making Galli's shoulders shrink. It was a deliberate attempt by Bregit to inflict a grain of fear in Galli's mind and to remind her who was the superior of the two.

"I would stand for what I believed to be right and by right, protect the lives I swore to protect. Even if it were my destiny to cleanse Nocktar of mystical creatures, I would ignore it because by acting on my destiny I would be causing unnecessary wars and countless casualties, for my own personal gain rather than the safety of Nocktar," answered Galli.

Bregit gave Galli a look of approval but said nothing further on the subject. They walked for miles without speaking. No doubt this was down to Bregit's little speech unhinging Galli's wall of denial. When they came up to a crossing of plates leading opposite directions. Bregit simply continued walking straight with Galli on his heel. Mile after mile, plate after plate they walked, the scene never changing. The determination Bregit was showing to reach the Golden Kingdom seemed to inject Galli with the push she needed to not whinge like a Ripeling but swallow her pride and get on with it.

"You brought Tweedly Plants from Tip-Karps Mountain?" Bregit asked his voice wispy.

"Yes," replied Galli, her jaws jittering from the drop in degrees.

"I would advise you to slowly nibble on the roots, we are about to pass through a large patch of sea where the cold temperatures will make it difficult to think," Bregit cautioned strongly.

"And the Tweedly roots will do what exactly?" Galli asked, her breath coming in puffs.

"They will warm your senses and clear your mind, which in turn allows you to keep focus. Remember, the sea has a mind of its own and can play many tricks if allowed enter your mind," warned Bregit with a firm tone. "I take it Tip-Karp recommended you bring the roots along with you?"

"Actually, it was Carka," Galli answered rummaging in her pocket, "He also instructed me not to allow you dictate me," Galli added examining the Tweedly roots.

Bregit scoffed. "Carka always had his ways with wizards, he must think you worthy if he is already gifting advice and sharing knowledge without first proving yourself."

"If Carka believed me worthy, he never showed it," jittered Galli the drop-in temperature causing her voice to rattle.

"He never does," said Bregit. "Carka always taught what he knew, for knowledge is nothing if not shared," Bregit growled, imitating Carka's tough voice.

"Why isn't he a member of the coven if he is so highly recommended among wizards?" Galli asked, before swallowing a handful of roots.

"Pass me a root," gestured Bregit, putting his hand behind his back.

Receiving a root that wriggled in his hand Bregit chewed it quickly and swallowed it whole not wishing to taste the roots foul flavour. As both wizards digested the roots, warmth flowed through them like water down a slope, erasing the numbness beginning to creep under their skin and filled their bodies with a blazing heat that radiated through every fibre of their bodies.

"He was cycles of shades ago when I was a Ripeling," Bregit answered his tone warm again thanks to the effects of the Tweedly roots.

"Why did he leave his position?" asked Galli.

"Carka disagreed with the former kings ruling and decided instead of rebelling against him, he would instead, disappear, and so he did," answered Bregit.

"Where did he go?" Galli asked the Tweedly Plants melting away the coldness in her voice.

"Carka found sanctuary deep within the forests of Dulgerdeen and in his solitude built a stronghold that refuged foreign wizards and out casts considered unworthy to serve in the Golden Kingdom or any land for that matter. It was where I went when I left the Golden Kingdom and learned the magical arts from Carka, his teachings made me the wizard I am now," said Bregit with praise.

"Surely, he wasn't the only wizard who disagreed with the king's ruling?"

"He wasn't," said Bregit plainly. "As I recall from Carka's own words, several wizards wanted the kings ruling ended, unfortunately those wizards weren't blessed in mind or power as Carka was," said Bregit.

"They were afraid, afraid to lose their positions because they didn't think they could triumph," said Galli, feeling disappointed at the lack of courage of these so-called superior wizards.

"Treason to the crown serves the penalty of death which would have undoubtedly been any wizard's faith had they challenged Dirm's authority. The combined strength of the coven wouldn't have been a match against the brute strength of Dirm, and knowing Carka as I do, he would never have allowed any wizard to die for his cause," said Bregit.

"Didn't the king send his Lutizs to search for Carka? I read that none without the authorisation of the king can leave the Golden Kingdom," said Galli.

"Wizards such as Carka can hide themselves completely from sight by using branches of magic beyond the skills of mere Lutiz's," Bregit answered, raising his brow slightly.

"Aren't those spells considered illegal?" Galli asked, feeling sure she'd heard the phrase been mentioned before.

Bregit laughed. "The laws of the Golden Kingdom are bound to those who have lived and learned above the clouds, how does a wizard from Treforledge know of its laws?" asked Bregit.

"Lorneid told me the way wizards above the clouds live, their manner of speech and their advanced magical knowledge. As Lorneids Second, he taught me everything he knew about the laws wizards follow among the clouds," Galli answered defensively.

"What are your thoughts about their ways, would you leave the life you now to be part of that society?" Bregit asked silkily.

"My upbringing wasn't easy," Galli admitted in a tense voice. "I struggled adapting when I was learning how to control my magical powers and was teased because my skills were far advanced than other Ripes," she said bitterly.

"The curse of been a genius," Bregit said smiling.

"You can relate what it feels to be out casted?" asked Galli looking up at Bregit.

"I was born and raised in the Golden Kingdom," Bregit reminded Galli. "Remember all who live there are believed to be intelligent."

"Lorneid kept a close eye on me when my powers got the best of my emotions, which got me given the nickname, Lorneids Pet, even the council members casted their jibes when I was appointed his Second."

"An uncommon position for one so young, even you can't deny it does come across as favouritism," Bregit said smoothly.

"Before I was appointed Lorneids Second, I led the Yellow Striped Army to its first ever victory in the Ultimate Colour," said Galli in attempt to make Bregit see she wasn't chosen just on the basis that Lorneid liked her.

"A remarkable feat," praised Bregit. "Still, been a good warrior doesn't make one a good ruler, I daresay that quote was mentioned more than once during your council sessions," said Bregit kindly not wanting to spark an argument.

"Oh yes," Galli agreed. "But in response to your question I will tell you this, I have been the subject of the Golden Kingdoms ignorance and I would never shame myself by leaving the life I love to become a spineless serpent like them," answered Galli, the memories of her past experiences in the Ultimate Colour heating herself a steam.

"Not all wizards who live inside the Golden Kingdom are spiteful. But power corrupts the good in all and prays on its glory hunters," said Bregit lightly.

"You're admitting wizards are easily seduced by the offerings of power?" questioned Galli.

"I would be a hypocrite if I said no," answered Bregit. "I daresay the king himself would openly admit his kingdom is full of power-hungry wizards, why do you think the Ultimate Colour was organized?"

"To keep the armies of the Lands of Light competitive," answered Galli.

Bregit scoffed. "That is exactly what Dirm wanted everyone to believe. But Carka and I saw through his wall of deceit and that is why we left the Golden Kingdom."

"But why, the Ultimate Colour is only beneficial to the coloured army that wins, how can it be deceitful?" asked Galli.

"After the war against the Aqua Guardians, Dirm and the coven sought a way to quench wizards' thirst for power and prevent future uprisings. They devised a less death toll way of securing their positions and keeping the lords of lands at bay. Dirm summoned all lords to the Golden Kingdom and put his idea of the Ultimate Colour to the vote. All lords agreed to Dirm's terms without second guessing his motives."

"Why, surely, they sensed a scheme taking shape in the background?"

"Nope," said Bregit shaking his head. "And you know why, because Dirm knew after the war was won the wizards who had fought alongside him had gotten a taste for battle and would jump at the chance to continue fighting. Only now it was over coated by crowns and immortal statuses, how blind we all were to the schemes of a king who would stoop to the lowest pit to keep hold of his power,'' said Bregit feeling his anger rising.

"But with Dirm dead why didn't Nzer put a stop to the Ultimate Colour?''

"Dirm was too cunning and bound the Ultimate Colour within the magical foundations of the Golden Kingdom, making it tie in with the deep magic invoked by the first wizards, meaning if a new king decided to erase the tournament, he would in turn be destroying a part of wizarding history and that is a violation against the agreed terms on which the Golden Kingdom were made,'' Bregit told Galli.

"How do you know all this?'' asked Galli.

"I was Depth Head General and was taught about the flow that keeps the Golden Kingdom safe,'' answered Bregit.

"So Nzer allows this to continue knowing full well it's wrong, and you're putting our faiths in his hands?'' said Galli, "How is he any better than his father?''

"It's like what I said before, power corrupts the mind and Nzer became another victim to its offerings,'' said Bregit his voice wispy.

"This occurred when he was crowned king, right?''

"Yes,'' answered Bregit. "The pressure became too much for Nzer at such an early age, to handle. Having to restore peace with many lords and kill those who refused to bow to his will not to mention having the coven constantly looking over him like a shadow made him act rashly to please those constantly in his ear. Those burdens were the reasons Nzer left the Golden Kingdom without telling anyone.''

"Did you ever find out where he went?'' asked Galli.

"No. And I never asked. Nzer returned two shades later with a look I had not seen him wearing since the eve he was crowned king.''

"What look was that?'' asked Galli.

"A broad unforced smile, which glowed through him like a beacon. Shortly after his return, Nzer announced he had found a companion named Hails the Blue, the keeper of knowledge from the southern lands. They ripped two sons of distinct colour. Then when all seemed bright in his life, gloom quickly sprinkled its dust upon the king's happiness,'' said Bregit gravely.

"What happened?'' asked Galli feeling that nothing good was going to be threaded along Bregit's response.

"Hails was killed in the war against the Aqua Guardians,'' replied Bregit softly. "Nzer forever blamed himself and I would bet my staff if he hadn't his sons to carry on Hail's memory, he too would have journeyed to the realms of nonbeing to be alongside her,'' said Bregit honestly.

"Do you think that's the reason he changed? Because he had learned what it was like to feel a pain that would never heal?'' asked Galli.

"His feelings for Hails were strong enough to erase his needs for greed and cruelty. Nzer had learned by watching her kindness toward their sons that he did not want the life he had experienced under his father to portray over his sons.''

"He seems like a spoilt Ripe who needed a lesson in the ways of life,'' said Galli. "From what you've described about him, he blames things beyond his control to excuse his misdeeds in life.''

"Sadly, that experience is what stirs most wills to be righteous," sighed Bregit.

"Don't think my meaning unkind, but let's not forget he killed many wizards before Hails came into his life and in the process ripped wizards away from the ones they were closets too," said Galli coldly.

"That's a fair point," Bregit muttered in agreement.

"You said the king had two sons; Leon the Black I know from the Ultimate Colour. Who is the other?" asked Galli.

"That would be Lucifer the Red, who is second in line for the throne behind Leon his older brother," Bregit answered smoothly.

"I never heard of him," Galli admitted while trying to remember had she read about the red prince somewhere before.

"Nzer kept his sons very well protected when they were Ripe's, he barely let them out of his sight and when they were old enough to move to the Depth Mountain to begin their training Nzer wouldn't allow it and instead taught his sons the magical arts himself."

"Seems overprotective, who would dare harm the king's sons?" said Galli.

"Suffering makes us weaker or stronger depending on how we deal with the situation, however in Nzers position I would agree with what you said. Nzer was dealt both sides of light and dark and overcame them, his reward two sons and an overgrown paranoia to losing everything he held dear."

"You're referring to his sons, right?" Galli asked unsure.

"Had you asked me that question when I was a Depth Head General I would have answered yes without hesitation? Unfortunately, I cannot give that answer, for grief plays a monopoly with the mind and can lead wizards to places that have no end. Nzer gave up caring for his sons shortly after they became coloured, believing he had fulfilled his promised to Hails. When the princes were branded their colours, they were given titles, armies, and strong holds to hold and live…."

Bregit stopped talking and watched in fear as a dark fog appeared out of nowhere. Watching it surround him he looked round to find Galli gone. The fog had somehow creeped along the pathway, for a moment Bregit feared Lano had somehow infiltrated the paths defences. Rooted to the spot he felt a vibrant wave in the air. Trusting his gut feeling Bregit followed the sound waves.

Experiencing the same Galli watched as a dark fog shrouded her vision making it impossible for her to see anything besides the plate she stood on. "Bregit!" cried Galli, in a panicked voice. "Where have you gone?" she called aloud but no response came.

Galli remained on the plate too frightened to move. Raising Water Dancer, she looked constantly around, searching for any sign of a sneak attack. Using the point of Water Dancer, she stretched it into the shrouded fog until she felt it contact with a solid object. Convinced it was the next plate, she leaped onto it and the next and next until it was clear Bregit had somehow vanished. When she was about to turn and head back Galli was blocked off by a long black serpent with thin wings that hissed viciously at her with a barred mouth held together by its long sharp teeth.

"Get back creature of the sea!" warned Galli. "I will not ask again," she threatened aggressively aiming her staff at the serpents hungry, mad gleaming eyes that Galli knew belonged to a Black Tail.

A deep-sea creature that dwells in the pits of darkness, and usually travels in packs to protect themselves from bigger and more powerful sea creatures. 'If it were alone, how did it manage to get by the protective enchantments Bregit claimed to be impenetrable?' thought Galli.

But it was not alone for long, even through the fog the Black Tail's blackened skin was visible. Swarms of slithering tails slid through the fog, their wings outstretched, blocking every gap and cocooning Galli inside their dome of darkness.

"Who dares cross my domain? Give voice to your coming or be treated like the rest who cross me," came a chilling cracked voice that lurked in the shadows.

"Threats will not sway me Black Tail," said Galli aiming Water Dancer at the Black Tails. "Be gone before I rid this place of your existence," she threatened unfazed by this charade.

"Black Tail?" said the chilling voice. "How insulting, you speak to no creature of the deep young wizard," said the chilling voice.

Galli looked around and became aware that none of the Black Tails mouths had moved, they were still firmly shut, their eyes focused entirely on her. "Then to whom do I speak?" Galli asked looking around for the slightest movement of one of the Black Tails mouths.

"I am known to many and wronged by all, follow me at will or forever remain still," laughed the voice.

"Might I give a wild guess and answer that riddle with one of my own. What lurks in darkness seeking the weak to use as spies while he lays hidden within his mist?" came the commanding voice of Bregit.

He had appeared behind Galli with his staff raised and wearing a determined look upon his face. Galli could sense from Bregit's look that whatever lurked in the shadows behind the Black Tails frightened him for Galli had never seen him look so serious. The Black Tails hissed viciously at Bregit's appearance. There long tongues breaking through their barred teeth that dripped thick drops of venom onto the plates below them. Galli had to dodge several drops by jumping fluently to the nearest plate.

"Bregit where have you been? And what is causing this fog?" Squealed Galli.

A chilling laughter echoed through the fog that caused the plates to shake and rattle causing Galli to slide to the edge of her plate.

"Be still," came Bregit's voice as he grabbed Galli's shoulder to steady her.

"What is causing the plates to react this way?" Galli asked watching the plate she stood on vibrate uncontrollably.

"A creature who joys in creating uncertainty, let us not be folly to its game," said Bregit strongly his eyes darting to every Black Tail.

"Black Tails bring me the yellow one, kill his companion," ordered the voice.

Before any Black Tail considered their approach Bregit with an aggressive swing of his staff, conjured wind waves so powerful they easily ripped through the

Black Tails shield which forced them to detach, weakening the strength of their barrier.

"LOOK OUT!" bellowed Galli, but her warning came too late, as a long claw with sharp nails erupted from under the plate Bregit and Galli stood on.

Completely caught off guard Bregit was lifted from his plate and clamped tight within the claws grasp enabling him to move. "Finally, I get to claim the life that cursed me to live as a parasite," roared the voice in triumph.

Galli aimed her staff at the claw but hesitated because Bregit was too close and if the claw decided to use him as a shield to block her attack, then she may hurt Bregit. Watching unsure what to do as the claw sunk into the Red Sea with a wriggling Bregit its firm grip.

"No!" cried Galli. Watching on as the last strand of hair belonging to Bregit vanished beneath the Red Sea, Galli aimed Water Dancer at the spot where Bregit had vanished and cleared her throat before calling, "RUPFOT!"

White streaks shot out from the point of Water Dancer, spinning in mid-air they circled her awaiting her command. Pointing at the Red Sea, Galli watched as her swirling streaks dived and sank into the plinths of the red water. Waiting nervously hoping she hadn't acted too late, Galli watched her every nerve tense. Then when she was about to give up Water Dancer began to vibrate as an electrical charge pricked her fingers.

"RALPHBINE!" she cried aloud lifting Water Dancer above her head and to her relief hooked Bregit out of the Red Sea and lowered him onto the plate beside her.

Choking and retching Bregit got to his feet, as drops of sea water dripped down his hair and face. Somehow, he had managed to keep hold of his staff and aggressively he directed it at the Black Tails with a look of cold fury fuelling his power Bregit roared, "BALASTO!!"

Bregit's curse was so immense it reduced the Black Tails to tiny specks of dust that hung motionless around the plates. Waving his hands Bregit swept the specks away as he investigated the sea.

"The fog, it's gone, but why?" piped Galli watching in wonder as the dark fog diminished before her eyes.

"Like all cowards, they only fight when they have a crowd, reduce the attacking line and hide they shall," breathed Bregit clutching his chest as the effects of nearly drowning began taking its toll on his body.

"Are you all, right?" Galli asked unsure how to approach Bregit.

"Quite all right, and may I say how grateful I am to have asked you join me on this journey," praised Bregit with a smile of gratitude.

Touched Galli's features glowed brighter, but her hunger for knowledge gnawed at her. "What was that thing that attacked you?"

"Duxpice," answered Bregit, his breathing resuming its normal rhythm. "A soul leacher that haunts the sea and its inhabitants and specialises in twisting the mind of creatures to do his sick bidding," said Bregit sorely.

"He said you cursed him, why would you put a curse on him?"

Bregit pretended not to have heard the question and tried avoiding Galli by dabbing his sapphire against his wet robes and hair. ''Ah that's splendid,'' he sighed with relief as his robes and hair steamed as if they had been laid out in front of a blistering fire.

''Forgive my rudeness but didn't you hear me? I was wondering was there any truth to what Duxpice said about you cursing him?'' asked Galli.

Bregit sighed before answering. ''That is a tale to be told another shade, let it slip from thought for now, we have more important matters to attend to, now let us be gone from here before Duxpice comes back with stronger reinforcements,'' cautioned Bregit beginning his walk along the plates.

''You said this pathway could not be breached by mystical creatures or was that just a lie to keep me quiet?''

''I must admit, you have much bite for one so young,'' joked Bregit, who was using his fingers to comb back his dry hair. When he seen the worry on Galli's anxious face his benign smile faltered. ''Joking aside, I too was coming to that possibility until I was pulled under the sea, my only belief and this is more a guess than fact. The fog and Black Tails manoeuvre to erase the light must enhance Duxpice's powers, it was said many shades ago only a great mind could breach any magical enchantment and it seems old Duxpice has found a way to overcome that barrier,'' said Bregit hiding his concerns to spare Galli adding more strain to her own.

The weariness of the quarrel with Duxpice had drained both wizards of strength, fortunate for Bregit and Galli they still had a small portion of Tweedly roots to keep their grumbling hunger pains at bay. They walked with hastened pace keeping their eyes and ears opened for any sign of trouble.

''I was impressed by how quick your reactions were, most wizards would've coward in fear in your situation,'' said Bregit, feeling he had to praise Galli for her quick thinking in the face of danger.

''I thought I was too late and that I would have to add your name to the list of wizards I failed,'' said Galli bitterly.

''Had I fallen to Duxpice the fault would not have been yours,'' said Bregit firmly. ''Do you feel responsible for the deaths of Lorneid and your fellow Blue Wizards?''

Galli kept her head low to hide the shame on her face. It only took a glance from the corner of his eye for Bregit to realise Galli held herself accountable for the deaths of her kin.

''There was nothing you could've done to save them,'' said Bregit kindly. ''You feel foolish and ashamed while wishing you could exchange places with those you feel you let down?'' said Bregit.

''Yes,'' Galli said sadly looking up at Bregit in wonder to how he knew how she was feeling.

''What you feel is a pain no magic can heal, survivors who have been forced to watch those they care for die usually develop different emotions, take it from someone with experience.''

''How do you cope when the images become so clear?'' Galli asked eager to know was there an end to this pain.

"I learned to accept what was and be wise to not dwell on past events," answered Bregit. "I knew Lorneid well, he would have given his life to save any wizard for he was a rare fish in a pool of sharks, who didn't judge for wealth or power but for the good in one and I must admit he found a good one in you Galli," said Bregit, turning his head to give her a praising grin.

"Thank you, your words are a great comfort," said Galli wiping away the lines of tears that had slid down her cheeks with the sleeve of her cloak.

"The spells you used to draw me from Duxpice's clutches were not basic taught. I can only assume you learned such spells from your superiors?" said Bregit.

"The Ripe's born in Treforledge learn faster than those of worth, Blue Wizards are taught magic that will benefit them for crafts and manipulating stone, but when I was appointed Lorneids Second I was given access to all books that taught me magic deemed unnecessary by our tutors, because all they cared about was turning Ripe's into Crafters."

"I can only imagine the joy your new position brought to the Blue Wizards seeking higher rankings," said Bregit.

"Many believed it a rouse, the dim-witted ones thought I'd somehow bewitched Lorneid," sniffed Galli a rare grin appearing on her saddened face.

"You must have made a good impression to have gained Lorneids favour. He was after all good willed but not one to be deceived by imitations or flattery," said Bregit.

"A thought that tickled my senses also, but when I pressed the subject Lorneid assured me he chose me for reasons only others would see," said Galli.

"A fair statement, a heavy burden also to put upon one so young, how did you cope with such strains?"

"It's like what I said, we Blue Wizards adapt quicker than most," Galli replied sternly making Bregit laugh by her unwillingness to gloat.

They continued their high paced walk along the Plate Pathway, every sound of a leaping sea creature or passing by winged beast made them shoot blue and yellow streaks in their direction, diverting the passing by creatures' miles from their position. Bregit assured Galli it was necessary in case they were spies of Lano, after Galli refused to send creatures away from needed off springs. But needy off springs were the least of Bregit's worries for Purple Shade was drawing nearer and with it an effect that even the Plate Pathway couldn't shield them from.

"The Cloud Stair isn't far from here, let's speed up our pace before Purple Shade is upon us," Bregit called over his shoulder.

"So, the rumours are true, the eight shades of sky do enhance the abilities of creatures?" asked Galli. "Because Purple Shade is when sea creatures can come up from the sea," said Galli.

"Wizards long gone into non-being have searched endlessly for answers about the mysteries of the shades that fill the sky. What scraps of information our ancestors rooted out was beneficial, for without their discoveries and research wizards would be forced to hibernate?" said Bregit.

"But it is true then, the shades of the sky have their own powers that can enhance capabilities?" asked Galli in a hurried voice.

"I'm afraid it would be unfair to fill your head with false ideas, for I haven't the right answer to give to your question, only my beliefs which could go as far astray from the correct answer as a Leaf Leeper carrying false information," replied Bregit honestly.

"What if we are destined to never discover their meaning, but are cursed to linger on our beliefs, maybe that's the shades true effect?" said Galli.

"You would do wise not to dwell on what ifs, but focus on what could be, they may seem similar but are miles apart in comparison," said Bregit seriously.

"I meant no disrespect," said Galli looking worried.

"The shades began, meaning some form of creature created them and in doing so made them unpredictable, why you may ask, I however, believe the shades are merely tests."

"Tests?" Galli repeated, unsure whether Bregit was serious or not.

"Yes, the test of strength," answered Bregit.

"I don't quite understand," said Galli feeling confused.

"Strength is what wizards lack, when our elders rose from the Red Sea, they were forced to hide from the shades effects until our great founder Dillitron the Silver created the Glints ritual, which is a combination of dark and light fused together to repel the shades effects."

"How does that ritual work?"

"The Glints spell, well, it's common knowledge now, since Dillitron shared his invention with his fellow wizards," said Bregit.

"He shared his invention, didn't Dillitron fear his spell may be used as a weapon?" asked Galli.

"Dillitron was not like most wizards, he believed that no wizard should endure the shades effects, so he travelled to all lands occupied by wizards and shared the knowledge of how to repel the shades effects. Within a cycle of shades all wizards young and old were casted with the Glints spell. Weren't you ever curious to why your face has a shiny glow beaming from it?"

Galli looked at Bregit her eyes narrowed, she hated been made fell like a mere Ripeling even if it were in the presence of a lord, but Bregit's question was too tempting to avoid by been stubborn.

"I thought all wizards were born with glowing faces," answered Galli.

"As one in your position is supposed to believe, you see the cleverness of it. To cast the Glints spell when the Ripelings are young and unknowing."

"But why all the secrecy?" asked Galli.

"To erase the question, knowledge is valuable to those in position of power," said Bregit sternly. "There are creatures who would give their fortune to be allowed walk through the shades effects unharmed."

"That's plain selfish," said Galli outraged. "Creatures deserve the same rights as us," she said a sting to her tone.

"Unfortunately, that's how dealings are done all over Nocktar," sighed Bregit. "Wizards trade their spells for portions of lands or valuables depending on the wizard but are by law forbidden to aid or interfere with mythical or mystical creatures.''

When Galli opened her mouth to speak Bregit hushed her with a whiff of his breath. ''Let us leave it there for now Galli,'' said Bregit raising his staff nonverbally telling Galli to be quiet.

''Why have we stopped?'' whispered Galli.

''We are here,'' answered Bregit, his voice full of relief.

Galli looked around, seeing nothing at first. Then looking up to the clouds, she saw it. Wide steps formed of clear white cloud materializing at their feet and leading high toward the white clouds in the sky.

''Welcome Galli to the Cloud Stair,'' said Bregit to a brazen Galli.

Chapter 11

The Collector of Twigs

The climate had changed drastically since Carka's departure from the sphinx's mountain. Purple Shade had broken through green shade, eclipsing the lime-coloured grass in a violet colour spraying the lands of grass and its inhabitants with its powerful heatwaves, making the air warm and gentle as it brushed against Carka's tense skin, but his surroundings made him feel on edge. The dampening part about the Grass Lands was that it exposed anyone and anything for miles making his journey awkward because there wasn't a shadow or tree in sight to shield his identity. Knowing that a creature with a half decent shot could easily shoot him down while he walked alone in the wide-open field, prickled Carka's anxiety. Under the sleeves of his shabby cloak, he swirled his wrist clockwise and non-verbally casted a simple protective layer of pressured air that solidified into an invisible shield which swirled around his body covering him head to foot. The security of his wind shield steadied his nerves as he walked with his head high through the Grass Lands.

Footprints of different shape and size were easy to recognize since they were stamped firmly into the cracked earth beneath the shortened grass. But the prints didn't give Carka any indication as to what kind of creatures dwelled anonymously within the Grass Lands? Because during the rise of the Aqua Guardians, Dirm the Bronze had sent envoys to the Grass Lands for reinforcements and permission to camp his approaching armies so they could rest before heading to defend Treforledge from the sea creature's attack. Sadly, for Dirm he received no reply or aid. Which in turn aroused suspicion among the coven silver chair holders. But with a war brewing they were unable to investigate the matter further, and with the Aqua Guardians seizing control of several islands ashore of the Grass Lands there were little drops to abandon war preparations.

The Aqua Guardians to Carka's knowledge made no attempt to seize the Grass Lands, which always gave him reason to wonder why. There were rumours from Gazzel and other creatures of Dulgerdeen that spirits powerful enough to control creature's minds lived beneath the grass and enjoyed using their powers of deception to toy with their victims before luring them to their deaths.

These mysterious activities were not unheard of and reminded Carka of a skilled illusionist who had equal skills to these phantom theories. That creature was a general of Lano's known as Tricklet, a skilled creature in mind lure and its dark arts. It was a small comfort to know Tricklet was the last of his kind and Carka should know, having led a squad of Lutizs to the deepest caves of Soldarc and inside the festering pits where no light shone, and illusion contaminated the very air itself. Carka remembered the young Krics been ripped apart limb by limb under his surveillance.

It wasn't a battle to be told in gatherings or brought up in civil conversation because in Carka's opinion it wasn't a battle but in hindsight an onslaught.

How far the Grass Lands extended didn't bother Carka but surely a water source or different patch of land had to be close by? He had walked for miles without the slightest change in scenery, all the while ignoring the aches in the bottom of his legs. The grass was so short now, Carka was seeing clearer prints left in the surface. Serpents no doubt, the lengthy line trailing in opposite directions explained as much. When he tried touching the ground, Carka was pelted by a surging breeze that pushed hard against his flaring cheeks. The invisible wind shield he was cautious enough to cast around himself made sure he wasn't knocked back by the force of the unexpected gusts. Nonetheless he was still caught unaware, what took Carka mostly by surprise was the magical trace generating within the howling wind. Feeling the aura of powerful magic tickle his senses, indicated he was indeed heading in the right direction and furthermore its caster knew he was looming. The feeling of been watched changed Carka's mood drastically, shifting his burning cheeks into a cunning smile. He knew by coming here it may cost him a lot more than he hoped to gain, but he needed to gain the Harpy's alliance to counter Lano's aerial advantage over the wizards.

Carka's cycles in exile had snapped his senses back together and the drops he'd spent within the mountain of the sphinxes made him realise how vulnerable he had left his fellow counterparts. Guilt also played a part, but Carka had no drops to dwell on such emotions. It didn't matter now, all that did was finding the Harpy alpha and convincing him to call his army and fight for the wizards. Carka felt he owed it to the wizards he had failed and by bringing the Harpies into the fold may redeem his abandonment and ease the guilt nested within his conscience.

Walking along the dry grass, Carka reflected on the Lava Keeper's triumphs. With Dulgerdeen in Lano's clutches, and Treforledge destroyed Lano now ruled two powerful strongholds. If he turned his attentions north toward Larmont all that would stand in Lanos way were enchantments casted by Bregit. And with Bregit thousands of miles away, there would be no wizard to reinforce the protective spells. And if Lano manages to breach Bregit's defences Larmont would be completely defenceless. The very thought caused Carka to fear for those unable to sustain the mystical creature's attack. Knowing Lano as Carka did he would move silent as night and sting like a serpent's venom poisoning every land he passed. What stretched Carka's concern was Lano's new weapon? Was it as powerful as Bregit had described it irked Carka that Bregit admitted to been bested so easily? Especially since it was Carka who had taught him how to fight. Knowing his own luck Carka was sure he would eventually cross paths with this cloud and when that moment presented itself, he would see for himself just how powerful this cloud was? Thinking of Bregit, Carka wondered had his old friend made it to the Golden Kingdom and did he have the sense to bring Galli with him? If Bregit is successful and gains the king's trust. The balance of power will shift, and Lano will no doubt be defeated in open battle. However, Nzer the Purple wasn't like his father who was cruel and hard-headed but was cautious to never underestimate a threat. Nzer on the other hand was more a diplomatic ruler who believed war was the last choice to be considered. Carka accepted that Bregit was only doing what he believed to be just, but deep down he knew Bregit's attempts would be in vain. No king in wizarding history has ever sent their army so far south with no assurances or proof to what they were fighting. The only way to bring the king and his army to the fold would be to bring Lano's head and sit it at the king's feet or one of his council members alive to torture into telling what the Lava Keeper has planned. Without a shred of proof, Carka was certain there would be no counter strike and Lano's power and numbers will continue to rise while the king and his coven ignore his return. Which gave Carka an ounce of sympathy toward Bregit, who was a good wizard but lacked the qualities to believe that some wizards cannot be swayed by words alone.

Traces of magical energy poked Carka's senses as he walked by tree trunks rooted deep within the earth. Every few drops Carka's eyes would cringe with the pulsing energy he was feeling swirling his senses. Following the waves of magical signals, Carka continued walking left when he was sure the magical current surrounding him was urging him to walk right.

''Misleading'', thought Carka, amused with the daring of this hoodwinker.

The pull of weight now forcing its way into Carka's mind was difficult to repel but he kept it at bay just long enough to sneak his own mind into the flow of energy trying to infiltrate his thoughts. Continuing to follow the magical signals Carka allowed whatever presence trying to deceive him believe he was their puppet and that they were pulling the strings. Carka felt the caster was either weak or unable to keep up the intensity of its spell for its false mirage was badly casted by a dabbler no doubt in the arts of ritual casting. Amusing Carka further, he began forcing his mind to creep slowly through this second-rate caster's tame attempts at ritual casting. Staring at the grass that was level with not a blade out of shape or place Carka chuckled.

''How long can you keep this up?'' he called out whilst halting his stride.

With a swerve of his arm Carka's palm erupted of crimson flames that he lassoed above his head. Waving his free arm, he spread the flames across the grass, moulding them into a protective cocoon that shielded him completely. Fierce and ferocious were Carka's flames, so fierce they erased the hoodwinker's illusion to reveal frail figures circling his ring of fire, appearing as if curious to what had unmasked their concealment.

''Show yourself false and I will grant you no mercy, conceal and the wrath of the skies will fall upon you!'' thundered Carka, his voice powerful and strong.

The wind had turned ferocious and unstable. The sky had lit up in a sparkling glow that gave Carka glimpses of what was trying to hoodwink him. The drumming sounds of thunder shook the sky as the hoovering figures that were white as snow and as dead as night came closer. The flames danced in Carka's eyes as the squabbling pale figures drifted closer. His threat had no bearing on them nor did his flames have the fearful effect he had anticipated. The pale imitations simply eased through his swirling vortex of flames. Then when Carka was about to summon the full might of the sky a deep voice whispered in his ears that numbed his senses and paralyzed his body. The voice wriggled through Carka's ears causing him to drop his guard and fall to his knees. The fear of a simple breath inside his ear had scared him like he'd never been scared before, a look of complete shock etched his features as fear took over his mind making Carka feel as fragile as flame against flesh. Then came a high pitch deafening scream that shot right through Carka like thunder in the night. Unable to lift himself by the pressure been applied down upon him, Carka could do nothing but endure shrieking pain that caused him to scream his lungs out in agony. The force of the whaling screams dissolved Carka's wind shield, leaving him utterly defenceless. Accepting defeat Carka fell to his knees with his head down looking at the scorched grass as the screaming stopped. When he peered his head, he was met by hoovering frail ghosts with empty eye sockets and hung open mouths. Six he counted, circling him as they pressed against his face, the ice chill aerating from their presence causing his skin to crawl.

"It seeks our council," came a deep gong voice, but Carka couldn't tell which hoovering figure the voice had come from. It seemed the voice had passed through them all.

The light breeze and purple shaded sky returned but the resumed shade and temperature did nothing to conceal their frail figures which meant they owned camouflage abilities. Their white hair hung loose and detached; their torn see-through rags concealed what was left of their dignity. It seemed an age that Carka spent on his knees waiting for these spirits to deal out his execution.

"What are you waiting for? I'm defenceless and worn to the bone or is my punishment to be bored to death?" shouted Carka annoyed by this silent torment.

"Come, wizard of silver, your journey has been long with little rest. We are what you seek and what you seek is not far from here," said the same gong voice hat reverberated in Carka's ears.

Amazed, Carka almost jumped to his feet. Fixing his cloak and wiping the ash from his hands he asked, "What are you?"

"Follow us Carka the Silver, and we shall tell you all you need to know," said the cracked voice and again it seemed to slither through all six frail figures.

Following the band of pale figures, the scenery stayed the same until the trunk of a dead tree sitting in the centre of the short grass came into view. When at the base of the trunk a hole wide enough for a wizard to fit through became noticeable.

"Follow," said the shaky voice. When Carka looked up to try catch who of the six had spoken all he got was six fingers pointing at the entrance. "The answers you crave rests at the bottom."

Not one to be lured Carka stood firm. "You lead," he said coldly. But the see-through figures ignored his request and waited like statues for him to enter the tunnel. "Fine," huffed Carka sinking into the pit.

When inside the clammy tunnel, he found it was filled with the roots and stems of trees that were no longer above the surface. The spirits waited for Carka to enter their domain and when he did, they huddled together murmuring slurry groans that made no sense at all to Carka, but he felt that this must be their methods of communication. When low enough and beyond the light of the entrance, it became so dark the white glow of the spirits left Carka's sight. After several knocks against the tunnel's wall Carka's frustration got the better of him, when about to ignite a spark, he felt a cold chilling hand grasp his arm firmly.

"Light shrinks the dark," hissed the spirit viciously. "If you are to commune with me and my fallen kings then you would do well to leave the light behind," warned the figure it's voice deep with breath as cold as ice.

Carka moved slowly his hands out front, he could no longer see the white floating figures but felt they weren't too far away. "Fallen Kings?" thought Carka, unable to rub off the cold chill left on his arm. What did that mean, was he about to find out the identity of the creatures that refused to come to Dirm's aid during the war?

The tunnel came to a quick end. Carka slowly tipped his way forward entering the base of a tree, whose roots had spread throughout a gloomed thick layered base. Dead leaves filled the dry earth with the walls veined in twigs and dead roots belonging no doubt to cut down and withered trees. The white figures hoovered in the centre of the circular base, all waiting for Carka to enter. Doing exactly that, Carka cautiously with his hand at the ready to ignite every root and stem the moment the frail figures tried to seize him.

"The Lair of Twigs," came a drowned voice, but from where Carka could not tell.

Carka's eyes narrowed, he looked at the levitating figures that now shone as bright as the sun with eyes darker than the longest night. 'Their sanctuary no doubt,' Carka thought.

"What are you, how do you come to be here?" asked Carka looking at the hoovering figures in turn.

Sniggers leaped from one end of the lair to the other, echoing through Carka's ears and ricocheting back again, bouncing from one end of the lair to the other before vanishing, leaving a long silence in its wake.

"We are what becomes of those burdened to rule. We are those who have been stripped of power and body to rot beneath the fallen trees and watch the lives of others from a distance," answered the chilling voice that treated with Carka before he had entered the tunnel.

"Forced to rule what?" said Carka sharply. "I doubt my kind has ever seen this place or any of you before," said Carka honestly.

"In life we called ourselves wizards alike to you, but now having crossed the path beyond the veil of seeing we have learned the truth and live here for the shame of our existence," said a gong voice that passed through each spirit.

Carka's expression tilted. "You're the spirits of dead wizards?" he said scoffing at the prospect.

"Yes. We were once kings, blessed with power and wealth, now we are spirits neither living nor dead, but cursed to dwell in this pit for eternity," said a different voice, a voice neither cold nor broken but stern.

"Dirm?" gasped Carka.

As Carka's words faded, one of the pale figures broke from the huddled group and glided toward him. Through the dark holes where its eyes once were and the toothless mouth and the faded features Carka could see some resemblance to his former king.

"You see me thoroughly now my old friend, clean of sin and power. Perhaps it is redemption for my foolishness to believe I could stamp out all my rivals without suffering the consequences," said Dirm dully, but his mouth never twitched making Carka nervous as to where his voice was coming from.

It seemed from Carka's point of view that the voice had somehow echoed through the pale imitation of his former king. But the source of the voice was nothing in comparison to the shock Carka felt at this precise moment. He couldn't believe what he was seeing with his own two eyes. He had journeyed to the Grass Lands in a half-hearted attempt of seducing the Harpy's to the wizard's cause. To find the spirits of the former kings was a thing Carka believed unimaginable.

"The five spirits you see behind me were once the kings of Nocktar, my own father resides there, but he is too far gone to realise who or what I am," came Dirm's echoing voice.

"Gone! Gone where?" asked Carka wondering where a dead spirit could possibly go.

"Lost in the powers of the curse placed upon every king to sit on the throne, our bodies are first to fade then our minds will slowly decay until we become creatures who dwell in the dark and fester on all sources of life," answered Dirm.

It didn't take long for Carka to discover what Dirm was referring. "You become Gliders, are you saying every Glider is a former king of Nocktar?"

'Possibly I am unsure of the origins of Gliders, what I am sure of is soon he will have numbers far greater than yours and will rise to swallow the Lands of Light in his web of deceit."

Carka moved closer the temperature decreasing slightly but he did not care. "Who do you speak of?"

"The elder Glider. He is the one who waits patiently beyond the Lands of Light and far from sight until the storm has passed and the last king has fallen," answered Dirm in a faint tone.

"That makes no sense, if one king falls another will rise in its place," Carka reminded Dirm.

"Unless Lano reclaims his title. Then the line of kings will end and the darkness beyond the Lands of Light will press forward and spawn their mists to reclaim back what we took, and no creature or wizard will stand against them," said the echoing voice of Dirm.

"Are you telling me, Gliders will rise and challenge us?" asked Carka unconvinced.

"They wait for us; we are the watchers of the Lands of Light. Our master waits for the war between creatures and wizards to conclude and when the dust settles my master will come in numbers beyond count to build a new from structure from the ashes of his enemies."

Carka couldn't take it in, an army of Gliders lurking beyond sight was preposterous. But as he considered the possibility of a Glider army ridiculous an old memory came back to him, one that still haunted him regardless of it occurring in his youth. The Glider he had met in the depths of Dulgerdeen had beaten him and quite easily and could've finished him there and then but decided against it and instead glided away. Could that same Glider be the one Dirm was referring to?

"We are the last to linger within this lair, when we leave and become whole, the Gliders will rise from their pits and darken the skies in despair."

"If what you say is true then why does your master wait, why not come now and finish us all? I'll tell you why, because he doesn't exist and whatever you are is a just for what you were in life. Don't try play me Dirm! I have seen through you in life, and I can see through you now, a wretch and a fool," spat Carka.

"We have one power, and that power allows us to watch the lives of you and every creature alive until the shade comes when we become a part of the Glider army and rise to kill those we once swore to protect," came the echoes of Dirms voice.

"You forget Dirm, wizards have abilities beyond the skills of any Glider and with every Drop Season we grow in the thousands while you've been dead for numerous cycles of shades and still you linger. By the shade, your master decides to attack, wizards will outnumber you ten to one," Carka said in a confident tone.

"The Twig Collectors are blind to the outcome because our master keeps his thoughts separate and tells none his secrets in fear that one of his Twig Collectors turning tail to warn the wizards. But rest assured my old friend, the battle will be glorious, it is a pity you will not be there to see it," said Dirm, his old cruel sense of humour resurfacing.

Carka blinked, his head in clinched slightly. "Do you plan to kill me now or will my faith be decided not long from now?"

"It grieves me old friend to admit, but yes you will not see the end of this war brewing between creatures and wizards. But do not feel aggrieved, your spirit will go forward unlike mine."

"Then I will get to the point to why I came here," snapped Carka the precise moment of his death the least of his worries.

"I already know why you are here. Since Lano escaped his banishment, I began following your journey through the roots of every tree and stem since you were forced to leave your home under the waterfalls in the forests of Dulgerdeen."

"There were no trees along my journey here," said Carka coldly his eyes narrowed in anger to how detailed Dirm was about his former lodgings.

"Trees of ash, oak and weir once covered the grounds we found you wandering along, their roots grow deep and strong enough to survive even when it's head has been cut off giving us Twig Collectors unlimited access to your movements."

"Because their roots remain strong beneath the surface and out of sight," jeered Carka who knew full well the strength of trees and their roots.

"Exactly. The twigs and roots allow trans spirits such as me and my fellow kings to see past, present, and future events."

A moment of silence passed and, in that moment, Carka knew his identity was no longer a secret. If Dirm's abilities allowed him to see the events of the past, then the former king had learned why he had fought so hard to become his personal advisor and knew Carka's reasons for abandoning his duties.

"I spent many shades wondering why a wizard of your stature left my service when you had fought so hard to claim the position. Now death has allowed me to see and understand the reason behind your choice. You were sent to spy on me and safeguard the rest of your kind."

"All for nought in the end seen as my kin perished under your rule," said Carka in a final tone, not wanting to dwell on the subject.

"So why was it one of my generals who killed me instead of you, out of all my followers and advisors you were by far the best, even I sought no quarrel with you out of fear that you may defeat me?" admitted Dirm.

Carka looked at Dirm's pale empty features with a look of suspicion. 'General?' he thought wondering was Dirm trying to trick him?

"Death has awoken me to the realism of life and shredded the illusion I spent living under. Power and titles mean nothing when life fades and all that is left of you are memories soon to fade," said Dirm, his echoing voice had lost all effects and was reduced to a whimpering whine that almost made Carka feel sorry for his spirit.

"Death may have woken you to the reality of how justice should be served but not me. I knew when you plotted against my kind what madness drove you. Power corrupted you and made you blind," said Carka coldly. "I wished while I laboured in exile that you would meet your demise and when the news was brought to me, I felt a swell of pity, not for you but for me. Because I was too proud to do it myself. Had my honour not outshone my lust for vengeance I would have died in the name of my fallen kin," Carka said coldly.

"Your words are hurtful, but they are wasted, for I have no body to feel old friend. I have played back my life on many occasions and have not felt an ounce of regret. I will, before joining my fellow kings divulge to you your deepest desire."

"And what is my deepest desire?" asked Carka sarcastically.

"You have searched the Lands of Light for any scrap of knowledge remaining of any living descendants left to your line," answered Dirm.

Before Carka could argue Dirm's echoing voice contaminated the lair cutting across Carka's attempt at an argument.

"I can tell you there is one who still lives, hidden and changed in many ways that it has never known it's true self," echoed Dirm.

"Who?" asked Carka, a little too eagerly.

"I cannot say, the Twig Collectors are forbidden to tip the balance of the present with knowledge that may change the future. I have already seen what you hope to achieve, perhaps you have too you are a clever wizard after all," acclaimed the echoing voice of Dirm.

"Peace is what I desire nothing more," retorted Carka.

"You cannot deceive me with lies Carka. I have seen your desires and peace is one in a lengthy line of pursuits you crave to achieve," said Dirm coolly.

"Perhaps, still my priority at this precise moment is the present war not ones that haven't occurred yet," snapped Carka, hating the fact Dirm was calmly contradicting him.

Carka could feel his patience wearing thin, he had the answer he'd been looking for, but Dirm was deliberately withholding vital parts just to antagonise him.

"Do I know this descendant or where to find he or she?" Carka asked forcing himself to stay calm.

"You have corresponded as you have with many wizards since your leave of exile," teased Dirm.

"You refuse to lead me further?"

"That is correct. As a servant of the Glider lord, I am forbidden to advise his enemies with information that may lead to the wizard's victory," answered Dirm plainly.

"Then we have nothing more to discuss," Carka said in an unforgiving tone while turning his back on Dirm and beginning his journey back to the surface.

"Leave you shall and journey far you will but in vain," came Dirms echoing voice that reverberated along the walls of the lair. "As darkness descends the light shortens and soon old friend me and my Twig Collector counterparts will be released of bondage to join our true master," warned Dirm his voice deep and grave.

Carka was at the entrance, the chilling draught creeped through his cloak causing his skin to tighten and his bones to shake. It was then that Dirm appeared in front of him and spoke with a strong voice that almost echoed the one he used in life.

"Our existence has remained a secret, if you endanger our privacy with an utter to your wizard friends, I can honestly say the consequences will be served in ways that are in my experience unimaginable," warned Dirm.

Carka scoffed as he strolled by Dirm's spirit and out of the Twig Collectors lair, wanting nothing more than to get as far away as possible for a fresh spark had ignited a once dead hope, one that may indeed tip the balance of this war.

Chapter 12

An Alliance with a Sphinx

Waiting alone in his silent cave Tip-Karp watched the stream of clear from his bedsit knowing the moment was at hand. Clearing his mind, the sphinx couldn't sway his previous conversation with Bregit and Carka away so easy, for it was one that proved decisive in directing him toward the decision he knew he now must take to secure his safety. While he dwelled, a chill swept through the halls of his mountain, coming to an immediate halt when a tall, hooded figure appeared through the entrance to his cave. The figures skinless hand broke through the long thick curtains of his gloomy cave. Tip-Karp rose to his full height, tucking his wings neatly against his sides before bowing his head as Lano the Lava Keeper entered his cave.

"You received my request?" asked Tip-Karp unmoved by Lano's arrival.

Lano lowered his heavy hood, revealing his gaunt features as his blackened eyes studied Tip-Karps cave with a venomous stare as they pinpointed to where the voice had spoken from.

"From the information my advisors gathered, I quickly discovered it was you who prevented the death of Lord Bregit," hissed Lano.

Before Tip-Karp could answer, Lano had without the sphinx's notice slithered as if he were the serpent his tongue professed him to be, along the sand and settled himself on the base of his fountain.

"I am honoured you came," said Tip-Karp in a welcoming manner. "Under the circumstances I believed my request may have missed you before you departed Treforledge," said Tip-Karp smoothly.

Lano tutted with annoyance. "Do not pretend you were unaware of my current location, you of all creatures are too acute to think flattery can weaken my mind," Lano hissed in a warning tone. "But I won't deny your message took me by surprise, it's just I wasn't completely sure I could trust a wizard lover," hissed Lano mockingly.

Tip-Karp remained level-headed, pausing for a moment to allow a calmness to sheet over the tension. "I travelled to Treforledge to seek some truth about what caused its downfall," said Tip-Karp.

"And how far did your curiosity get you? Couldn't have been far if I didn't sense your presence," hissed Lano.

Tip-Karp slipped off his bed and moved further away from Lano's aura and leaned over his pool of clear to gaze upon the lines of rippling water that trickled coolly through the many different passages spread throughout the mountain.

"During my search of Treforledge I came across a duel been fought by a shadow and Lord Bregit…" Tip-Karp began but was interrupted by Lano.

"And you felt the need to save him, but in turn are expecting me to trust you when you have just admitted to saving the very beings I aim to destroy?"

"I owed Bregit the Yellow a debt," Tip-Karp said strongly.

"It must have been quite a debt for you to leave your cave and travel all the way to Treforledge?" jested Lano.

"When the war of the Red Sea ended the purple king despite my involvement in the truce, wanted me executed and my mountain used to shelter a new breed of Pin-Fars. Bregit the Yellow stepped forward and reminded the purple king of my worth to build a better stability for the benefit of all lands and its creatures," said Tip-Karp.

"To prevent further uprisings no doubt," hissed Lano, sounding unconcerned about Tip-Karps past predicaments.

"Bregit may be a wizard but his gratitude that shade saved me along with my mountain. I have been waiting cycles of shades to repay my debt and now that it has, I am ready to serve a true cause," declared Tip-Karp, with a strong surge behind his words.

"That is why you saved him?" asked Lano his brow raised as he examined the sphinx for a sign of uncertainty.

"That is why I saved him," repeated Tip-Karp his voice firm.

Lano smirked seeming satisfied with Tip-Karps explanation. The Lava Keeper strolled along and seated himself on Tip-Karps feathered bed. "I am here for one thing, if we cannot agree on my terms then you will be branded a traitor to my cause do you understand?" hissed Lano.

Tip-Karp nodded his head to show he understood Lanos terms and waited patiently for him to explain what his role will be under his charges.

"My numbers have doubled in the past shade. Dulgerdeen has joined with me, and it won't be long until Selavroc is among my supporters. With you among my advisors we could finally dethrone that power-hungry king and resume Nocktar to its original state," hissed Lano.

"And who's command will I be following? Yours, or the shadow you hide from your other advisors?" Tip-Karp questioned, smirking at wiping the smugness from Lanos face.

Lano's expression soured. "I am head of the Council of Shadows; my word is law and no others," he hissed aggressively.

"If you say so," said Tip-Karp unconvinced. "I have decided to abandon my ties with the wizards and cleanse the Lands of Light of their rule. My ancestors fled knowing war would be upon them if they refused to obey the wizards, it would be dishonourable of me not to fight alongside those I have sworn to protect,"

"All ties?" asked Lano. "I was under the impression you shelter the survivors of Treforledge and keep them beneath the rocks of this very mountain," hissed Lano, a deep sting behind his hissing.

"You have keen eyed spies, so good perhaps, they somehow gained knowledge to what goes on in my mountain," praised Tip-Karp.

"Not quite," hissed Lano. "I can tell a wizard's stench a mile away and the odours creeping up my nostrils tell me at least a dozen refuge beneath me," hissed Lano with disgust.

"May I remind you that while I live my duties as a guardian to all life sources still holds bearing, even to wizards. Do not enter my mountain and dictate about the services I provide," said Tip-Karp sternly.

Lano had not flinched or reacted in any way toward Tip-Karp's aggravated reaction. Instead, the Lava Keeper continued sitting with his fingertips pressed together, wearing a grimace look of cunning on his scarred face.

"I have asked you to travel here so that we can reach a fair agreement and end the unbalance between us. We must join and fight if the Lands of Light are to be restored to the way they once were," protested Tip-Karp.

Lano considered for a while, sitting on Tip-Karps feathered bed with his eyes closed and his thoughts locked within a concentrated trance.

"The terms will be agreed when I have proof of your loyalty," hissed Lano after a long spell of consideration.

"How can I prove I am trustworthy?" asked Tip-Karp his silver eyes unnerved as he looked at Lano who was still sitting with his eyes shut tight.

As Tip-Karps question loomed in the caves gloomy air waves, Lano's eye lids flickered open. Grinning his usual evil grin made the hairs on Tip-Karps neck stand up as the black daunting eyes of Lano gawked the sphinx with a logical stare.

"Use that ancient mind of yours and find the answer," hissed Lano smiling menacingly.

"Wouldn't they be more valuable to our cause alive? Tamed, they are the best crafters of rock among the Lands of Light," suggested Tip-Karp careful not to sound concerned.

Lano's face tightened, a wicked hiss escaped through his gritted teeth. Getting up from Tip-Karps feathered bed he silkily strolled over to the clear water and dipped the tips of his fleshless fingers into the still pool causing ripples to crease the flow. Making Lanos reflection difficult to make out as heated steam began rising from the pool as the Lava Keepers anger began to bubble and radiate through him.

"If I wanted hostages and bargaining chips, I would have kept the Blue Wizards I slaughtered in Treforledge alive. Either follow my commands Tip-Karp or the deals off and this mountain will fall into the ownership of the Gliders," Lano threatened, his hissing intensifying.

"If, I am to advise you, then why am I been threatened for doing what my lord has titled me to do?" asked Tip-Karp calmly not allowing Lanos frustration to unhinge his manner.

"Because your lord wants every race and line of wizard dead, so that in a thousand shades from now, creatures will never know the age of wizards ever existed," hissed Lano with content in his voice.

"So, your plan is to erase the knowledge of all wizards, dear me, there was me thinking it was just your old lands you craved. But like most who have tried understanding your ways, they always end up taking a wrong turn when it comes to piecing your plans together."

Lano grinned, impressed by Tip-Karps admiration.

"If you do win this war, how do you expect to wipe out knowledge, legacies even the powers of the most advanced specie of our age? Or do you not recall your last attempt to thwart the king."

"My memory is as good as it was the moment my rebellion failed," hissed Lano smoothly. "I endured the waste lands. Scraped a living out of rocks, watching and waiting for my defeated comrades to waste away under the scorching sun," Lano hissed bitterly.

"I voiced my concerns on the matter to the king during my own trial. Advising Nzer that creatures of your stature deserved a noble death not a pro-longed one, but as you well know, the king was determined to use your defeat as an exception to what happens when you oppose the might of the Golden Kingdom," said Tip-Karp.

Lano either pretended to not have heard Tip-Karp or he just didn't care what he had to say on the subject. Lano seemed to be looking at the wall, but Tip-Karp could tell he was remembering the hardships he'd suffered in his banishment and the humiliation he knew would never weaver in the minds of those who once respected him.

"Each shade I forced myself not to die, not to give up so that one shade, I would reclaim back the lands I ruled and destroy the race of wizards for good," hissed Lano his voice deepened.

"I admire your strength and courage, however if your depleted army was decreasing by the passing shades, how did you obtain such a formidable force in such a small number of shades? Unless you've acquired the power to raise the dead," added Tip-Karp with a raised eyebrow.

"I wish," hissed Lano with a false laugh. "The rise of my new power is my story to tell and perhaps when you have proven yourself trustworthy, I may share such remarkable tales with you," teased Lano.

"My loyalty will not be turned; I will do as you bid to rid our lands of our enemies," promised Tip-Karp.

"Then rid this mountain of the scum beneath our feet and be quick about it. I will not have my army and council waiting ashore on the account of filth," spat Lano.

Without question Tip-Karp stretched his powerful wings as wide as he could, darkening the cave and eclipsing both creatures in their shadow. His razor-sharp talons detached from the curved point at the top of his wings and levitated by their master's side. With a jerk of his head each feather soared out through the entrance of the cave.

"They won't be long," Tip-Karp assured Lano. "While we wait, I want to know a little bit more about what I'm signing myself up for," said Tip-Karp folding his large wings neatly against his sides.

"Once the south is firmly within my grasp, I will gather my full strength and lead my army to the Cloud Stair and force that idiotic king to march his army against mine," Lano hissed calmly.

"That's your grand plan, a full-on assault against superior numbers and trained killers?" asked Tip-Karp in disbelief.

"You disapprove of my intentions?" questioned Lano his eyes tensing.

"I believed you a tactician of war," Tip-Karp said sounding annoyed.

"One of the best living," hissed Lano smirking.

"The waste lands have addled your mind. The Lano known throughout Nocktar would not lead the best chance of defeating the wizards into open battle with little to no chance of victory. Forgive my manner but your plan only has one outcome," said Tip-Karp honestly.

"You underestimate me, yet you still want to join my cause, you're quickly beginning to sink sphinx!" Lano hissed coldly, waving a threatening finger in Tip-Karps face.

"I do not doubt the army nor its leader," said Tip-Karp smoothly. "But attacking the base of the wizards is suicide, not only is it impossible to enter the Golden Kingdom but they will have the high ground, giving the Seven Coloured Army every opportunity to avalanche spells from the safety of the clouds," Tip-Karp said sagely.

"I have an army of Viledirks in my front line and an army of Varwels so large they block out the shades. The Red Sea beneath the clouds cannot be touched by none other than a sea creature and I have two at my command and a creature who can sense movements a mile away," Lano reminded Tip-Karp.

"Tactics I feel have yet to be tested in open battle," said Tip-Karp with every intention of making Lano realise how ludicrous his plan was. "Forgive me, but if that were the case you would have returned shades ago. Your council were torn asunder by the Seven Coloured Army, no special aptitudes will over-turn the same out-come as before."

"Every member of my council will play a part in my great plan. If their part is performed the way I intend, then we will shower the sea with the bodies of all opposing wizards," hissed Lano firmly. "So, save your concern. I have devised this plan for two cycles of shade. I know the mind of the king; he will push aside my return and protest I died like the rest of my kind," Lano hissed impatiently.

"The king may be none the wiser to your plans, but Bregit and Carka are not. Their influence could rally a great host," Tip-Karp pointed out.

"Well, if we fall under their challenge the blame will be yours for saving one of their lives, had you not interfered Bregit the Yellow would be a distant memory," hissed Lano.

"An innocent mistake, but my error did have its benefit."

Lano raised his head for Tip-Karp had paused to make sure he had his full attention.

"Bregit travels with Lorneids Second Galli the Blue and intends to inform the king of your return by using the Plate Pathway as his safe route," said Tip-Karp.

"I know!" Lano hissed annoyed. "Duxpice has reported Bregit's movements and cried about how he let him slip from his grasp. What of it, Bregit will rally nothing, he has no proof of my return, all he has are whispers and visions, two components I daresay will sway the king from his throne. It's like what I said, I know the king's mind, he will not leave his kingdom in pursuit of me based on hearsay," hissed Lano in a confident tone.

"Duxpice?" said Tip-Karp shocked. "You allow that traitor into your camp. He cannot be trusted. If let loose upon the Lands of Light Duxpice will kill thousands of innocent creatures," voiced Tip-Karp.

"Spare me your self-righteous," hissed Lano. "Duxpice will patrol the seas and out skirts of all lands. Have you forgotten he is cursed to never walk the Lands of Light again."

"A creature of Duxpice's intelligence will find a way around his curse and twist it to his advantage. You know what experiments he practices and still you trust such an unbalanced creature to be loyal to you?" asked Tip-Karp astonished by the depths Lano has succumbed.

"I do," answered Lano simply.

"You do not care then… about the innocent creatures Duxpice will kill in his rampage?" asked Tip-Karp.

"Did the same innocent creatures defend me when my army were stripped, beaten, and dragged through every acre of land. Where was such mercy shown then I ask you?" hissed Lano with a sizzling hiss to his words.

"Perhaps you are right, but you must also know that as a sworn guardian I will be forced to take matters into my own hands if Duxpice reforms his old ways?" said Tip-Karp firmly.

"I would not dare come between the laws of your kind, I have ample respect for the sphinxes as you well know, but until Duxpice commits any crimes he will do my bidding," hissed Lano.

"There is something else I want to know Lano, why are you on the verge of revealing yourself when hiding within the shadows has benefited you greatly in numbers and victories," said Tip-Karp.

"A faceless shadow can only conceal itself for so long. I will not explain my intentions; my actions will speak clearer than my words ever will, I assure you."

"And what part of your great plan will befit me, or will I sit on the side-lines watching you orchestrate your grand plan?" asked Tip-Karp.

Lano's smile curled into a wicked smirk. "You will strike from behind while I lead from the front, following a path only you can follow because it was you and your ancestors that designed it all those cycles of shades ago," hissed Lano softly to a stunned Tip-Karp.

Tip-Karp remained passive on the outside, but his insides had frozen. The great sphinx stared at the smug eyes of Lano and dreaded to think what the Lava Keeper was going to do with this piece of information.

"Who did you have killed for that information?" asked Tip-Karp careful not to sound shocked.

"The total wasn't a great deal I assure you," answered Lano who now relished in the discomfort he was spreading throughout the cave.

"I cannot follow such a dangerous path alone, you know that?" protested Tip-Karp.

"My Gliders have bred during my exile, you will be given command over them, in return you will do your duties or die trying."

"Guards to watch me or in hindsight kill me if I betray you," whispered Tip-Karp.

"Precaution is vital in war Tip-Karp," breathed Lano. "I will send Kcor by the turn of shade. The protection your mountain provides will help my army with needed provisions. It is a long march to the Cloud Stair and having my army well prepared is vital if I am to prevail."

Swishing noises echoed along the halls of the mountain; the curtain pulled itself aside giving way for the sharp talons that entered the cave and lay in a row on Tip-Karps bed. Lano walked across the cave and looked down on the black stained feathers a look of unmeasurable pleasure appearing on his skinless face as the evidence of more wizards dying gave the Lava Keeper immense joy.

"The stains of a wizard's insides, a fine way to prove yourself," hissed Lano sounding impressed. "Now that your mountain is clean of filth allow us to speak openly for a short spell."

"I was under the impression we were been honest with one another?" said Tip-Karp frowning.

Lano chuckled. "Find me a creature who's honest and I'll show you a creature of no worth," he laughed again. "Honesty," spat Lano as an unexpected cold vibe reverberated through him that made the hairs on Tip-Karps legs stand up at the sudden change in Lanos attitude. "A fool's beliefs that are preyed upon by power seekers and the desperate."

"We sphinxes believe in honour and trust; it is what sets us away from the darkness," voiced Tip-Karp using his own brand of skills to erase the chilling vibe Lano was casting along his cave.

"And look where they are now, gone! Leaving us to fight for the lands they swore to protect," hissed Lano aggressively.

"The Sphinxes left the Lands of Light believing you would protect their lands and not jump into battle at the first sign of an opposer. Had your hot temper even considered negotiating with the wizards. The war would have been avoided and not to mention the many death tole and the extinction of many creatures who aided you because they believed in you!" growled Tip-Karp aggressively.

Lano's face tensed, it was perfectly clear he was not used to been spoken to in this manner, but Tip-Karp having endured Carka's snipes about his ancestors had had enough. Lano stood up to his fullest height, his soulless eyes fixed on Tip-Karp who did not back away.

"Had your precious ancestors not cowered and fled, the war would have been won and the wizards would be extinct. Do not lay blame on my head because I acted to protect my lands instead of fleeing across the Red Sea," hissed Lano dangerously.

"This sparring match is getting us nowhere," said Tip-Karp calmly, trying to soothe the tension.

Lano retreated to the pool leaning against the soft rocks his smile cunning. "The past is the past it cannot be altered," hissed Lano.

"At least we agree on something," said Tip-Karp his voice having lost most of its bark.

Lano swept his skinless fingers along the calm pool, staring at his tired expression. ''The reason I have lingered longer than I intended is because you have information I do not.''

''What information, I thought you knew all there was to know?'' said Tip-Karp in a reserved tone.

''I need you to open your mind and draw out the entire map of Nocktar and I mean all of it, remember sphinx I always know when I am been lied to, so no tricks,'' warned Lano, eyeing the sphinx with a dangerous look.

''What good will a map do you?'' asked Tip-Karp taken back by Lano's unusual demand.

''Everything,'' hissed Lano, enjoying his provocative.

Tip-Karp looked at Lano unsure, wondering was the Lava Keeper simply making fun of him? ''My knowledge of Nocktars lands only stretch to the Lands of Light even I don't know what dwells beyond the Red Sea,'' Tip-Karp admitted truthfully.

''The Lands of Light are my sole concern, what lives beyond and under them is of little meaning to me. The map I need from you has many passages long gone from memory. It is my right to know of these secret passages and as your lord it is now your sworn duty to obey my commands.''

Tip-Karp felt the tension swirl around his cave. Finally, Lano had shown his venom and knew he was in full control of Tip-Karps loyalty. Because Lano knew if Tip-Karp refused to share his knowledge, he would no doubt have him killed and his mountain would be wiped away or worse given to the Gliders.

''The maps of all lands are stored deep in the bowls of my keeps, beneath the rocks and under the sea,'' said Tip-Karp feeling robbed.

''Good, lead me to these keeps and be warned your ancient skills won't shield you from my powers,'' threatened Lano.

''Follow me, my lord,'' gestured Tip-Karp flexing his left wing, he lifted the curtain hanging above the entrance of his cave. When Lano was outside Tip-Karp took one last glance at his chamber before letting loose the curtain to lead Lano down the halls of his mountain.

Chapter 13

The Stair Guard

"It's amazing," breathed Galli while gazing at the Cloud Stair with fascination.

"It's a beauty to behold," Bregit agreed, but something in his voice didn't sound excited at all. "But let's not be tempted and instead await our guide," he said smoothly as he grabbed a hold of Galli's sleeve to prevent her touching the cloud step.

"Guide, why do we need a guide?" asked Galli, a flush of embarrassment reddening her cheeks due to her excitement getting the better of her judgement.

"The Cloud Stair has always been safe guarded, since before you or I were ripe from our drops," Bregit explained in a tamed manner. "No creature can step on the stair without the approval of the Stair Guard."

"And what guards the stair?" asked Galli who was imaging an army of enslaved Pin-Fars patrolling the skies.

"Wizards of course," Bregit replied simply. "Who else would the king trust with the safety of his kingdom? However, powerful spells, rituals, and impenetrable enchantments casted down through the cycles are in place to prevent outsiders infiltrating the stair," Bregit explained plainly.

"Oh!" piped Galli. "I had no idea there were so many precautions placed upon the stair," Galli admitted feeling more relaxed now that she knew why Bregit had prevented her stepping on the stair.

"Without permission from the Stair Guard access into the Golden Kingdom is denied," said Bregit, his eyes now rigidly fixed on the stair. "So be warned Galli that smart remarks and back cheek will be unnecessary in our attempts to gain the Stair Guards favour," cautioned Bregit.

Galli smiled and knew that Bregit was challenging her to keep her mouth shut and allow him to do the talking. Which suited her fine. Looking around; Galli's view of the plates she was standing on were gone. Stunned, she pressed her toes and felt the solidness of the plate but the bright glow shining from the Cloud Stair veiled her sight completely.

"Have you any idea who the Stair Guard is?" asked Galli.

"Before I left my position as Depth Head General the Stair Guard was an old friend of mine," said Bregit. "Jicimash the Black was his name but that was cycles passed and Jicimash was getting on by that shade so I would presume by now he has stepped down to allow more younger roots to occupy the position," answered Bregit.

"What becomes of Stair Guards, once they pass on their position?" asked Galli, picturing elderly wizards talking among one another, the burdens of work never again to dampen their spirits.

"They resume their place beneath the king's ruling or die," answered Bregit seriously.

Galli's jaw dropped and when there was no sign or hint of sarcasm in Bregit's expression, the reality of his words sunk like a stone in water in Galli's stomach giving her a queasy feeling. "Seems unfair don't you think?"

"As valuable as a wizard's life is, the king sees a wizard of no use, or a waste. If a wizard has gone beyond the capability of performing its duties for its kingdom, a waste it is believed, and death is its penalty."

Looking at Galli's shocked reaction through the corner of his eye Bregit patted her shoulder with his hand, smiling kindly at Galli with a faint movement of his cheeks. Feeling it better to explain the difference in circumstances between Treforledge and the Golden Kingdom now, before she had to see first-hand later.

"You may think it unfair but ask yourself what is a wizard to do when the shackles of work have been lifted? Having spent your entire life living, breathing, doing the same thing shade after shade until it consumes you and becomes you. And then when old age takes hold over you and you're stripped of the position you hold dear, ponder what becomes of you then? Many wizards choose death in spite to sitting upon a chair for their remaining shades beckoning to the wizard who stripped them of their life's worth."

"Killing because one wizard considers another wizard unworthy is horrible. Treforledge would never execute an elderly wizard, our laws forbid the killing of one another," said Galli with a deep malice to her words.

"The laws of Treforledge and the Golden Kingdom are vastly different. I know because I have seen the law enforcers of the Golden Kingdom with my own eyes. They see kindness as a weakness, and I am telling you now Galli to hold your tongue to whatever you may hear about the rulings amongst the clouds, arguments against the kings ruling could land you an instant death sentence," Bregit warned with a firmed voice.

Galli nodded her head to show she agreed to Bregit's terms. But knew the killing of weakened elderly wizards would be one term she would never agree to.

"The king is a tolerant wizard who takes discipline and rules seriously, be extra careful not to entice him," advised Bregit, looking at Galli with a stern expression.

Before Galli could ask what kind of manner she needed to show before the king, a flicker of black caught her attention. Lifting her head to see what was causing the twinkle in her vision, Galli looked up to find a tall figure with long stringy black hair identical in colour to its wide narrowed eyes, strolling down the Cloud Stair, holding a tall thin wooden staff streaked in lines of black between its thin fingers. As the Black Wizard came closer into view, Galli could make out the broadness in its upper body, that reminded her of a wizard with similar features.

Bregit stood as still as a Drop Tree against a hurling wind, where's Galli couldn't keep her eyes off the approaching wizard, her gut feeling telling her something wasn't as plain as this wizard appeared. The Black Wizard was wearing a light see through cloak revealing a light armoured breast plate with a symbol of a crown carved into its centre. A crest Galli instantly recognised because the symbol was the crown of the Ultimate Colour, the crown she had won in the previous tournament. Everything about this wizard came across as royalty from its clean features to the smirking grin that made Galli suddenly want to sink her fingernails deep into its face. And it was that maddening feeling that confirmed where she had seen that emotionless face before.

"I know who that is," Galli whispered to Bregit. "That's the wizard I beat in the Ultimate Colour a cycle of shade past!"

"Are you sure?" Bregit asked with a look of uncertainty.

"I'm sure," replied Galli her voice now below a whisper. How could she forget the face of the one who had made her victory a misery instead of a triumph? After the victor was announced the leading commander of the Black Army snapped his staff in half in frustration, flinging its remains at his dead comrades before storming out of the arena.

Bregit looked from Galli to the approaching wizard. "Then how is he here? oh…. unless he suffered the humiliation of giving up before been killed," said Bregit smirking.

When Galli nodded confirming Bregit's theory to be true a curling smile that Galli knew to be a joyous etched across Bregit's face.

"I can't imagine the embarrassment the king must've felt witnessing one of his own forfeiting at the hands of a wizard from Treforledge," said Bregit with a satisfied grin on his face.

But Galli did not find Bregit's remarks amusing at all. "You're degrading my comrades and me by saying such a thing," she said coldly, the quick change in her tone causing Bregit to look slightly offended.

"Degrading?" said Bregit who looked taken back by the seriousness on Galli's face.

"You heard me," said Galli folding her arms and turning away from Bregit.

"Do explain," said Bregit frowning.

"Why do you act surprised when informed that one of the king's wizards was defeated and forced into the shameful act of submission by a wizard of Treforledge?" Galli asked pouting.

"I merely sneered, but it wasn't directed at your victory or in any way belittling the wizards of Treforledge. No, I found satisfaction at the thought of the king's expression at seeing his own son beaten to what the king and all who serve him believe to be an unworthy opponent!" said Bregit as honest as he could.

"Son?" gasped Galli looking again at the Black Wizard coming down the steps.

'Perhaps this was the punishment for losing his Ultimate Colour crown,' thought Galli.

But from the expression the Black Wizard was wearing, he didn't appear like he'd been cut of any losses. Standing on the last step of the Cloud Stair looking at them both with a loathing glare, his black eyes as cold as snow that looked down on

Bregit and Galli's haggard appearances with a sneer. When he took a step away from the Cloud Stair a wall of cloud parted him from Galli and Bregit.

"Its all-right Galli, it's simply a precaution just in case we're imposters," Bregit assured Galli, who had instantly gripped Water Dancer with both hands in fear of attack.

"Bregit the Yellow," said the Black Wizard in a sweet, charmed voice bowing his head to Bregit. "And I see you've brought a slave along with you to keep you company," he said in a piteous tone.

"Leon the Black, son of Nzer, prince of Nocktar," said Bregit bowing his head. "The wizard you believe to be my slave is in fact my companion, Galli the Blue of Treforledge."

Galli did not bow or show any sign of welcome towards Leon, but merely stared at him with narrowed eyes, devising cruel words inside her head that could unhinge that blood boiling smirking face.

"Why, have you come all the way from Larmont without sending any word of your coming? My father does not take kindly to surprise visits as you well know," Leon said smoothly, his dark eyes boring into Bregit's.

"I had no means of sending word to your father," answered Bregit. "But I must speak with him urgently. Will you allow me passage, or shall we discuss more meaningless topics?" asked Bregit his tone slightly unceasing.

Leon stood looking at Bregit his broad grin stretching. "It would be my pleasure to guide you to my father's chamber," said Leon in his casual voice. "However, your slave must stay put until you return," said Leon smirking at Galli.

Galli opened her mouth to argue but she was cut across by Bregit's firm voice that caused Leon's eyes to widen with shock.

"Step aside or fall by my stroke!" bellowed Bregit who had raised his staff and somehow managed to break it through the cloud barrier.

"Have you lost your mind?" snarled Leon who had not flinched at Bregit's aggressive reaction but merely grinned at how easy it'd been for him to lose his cool.

"I will not stand here and be told what to do by a wizard undeserving of the colour he wears!" thundered Bregit the anger he had restrained from erupting had finally gotten the best of his good will. "Decide and be quick about it," Bregit threatened fiercely, his staff edging closer to Leon's face.

Leon remained smiling, saying nothing, and instead glared at Bregit his eyes slightly narrowing. Leon knew he was no match against Bregit in a duel and was not stupid enough to seek a quarrel with him, still it was he not Bregit in the position of power in this moment.

"Lower your staff and passage I'll grant," said Leon after a short spell of consideration. "And let it be noted, a threat on the king's son will not be easily forgotten," Leon said coldly.

Bregit at once lowered his staff but the anger he had allowed escape refused to wither giving him a hardened look that seemed determined to stay on the face Galli had come accustomed to seeing kind and benign.

Leon waved his hand uttering the words of passage. ''I Leon the Black, Stair Guard of the Cloud Stair grant passage to Bregit the Yellow and his companion Galli the Blue,'' he muttered bitterly.

The white glow of the clouds shrunk meaning passage was granted. Bregit allowed Leon to walk up the stairs first. When they were all standing on the soft cushiony step Leon snapped his fingers sharply. The stairs began to vibrate, magically elevating them toward the high clouds above. Having never set foot on the Cloud Stair, Galli found it a master stroke to be allowed rest instead of having to walk all the way up.

''This is sublime,'' said Galli excitingly.

''The Ripeling grows excited, I wouldn't blame her, if I'd been raised grinding rocks and training ill witted Ripes, I'd be glad to escape to see how decent wizards live,'' said Leon coolly.

Galli's grip on Water Dancer tightened, but one glance at Bregit quickly ceased her tongue. Remembering her promise, she felt it would be wise to do what he had instructed and remain quiet.

''You should relish this moment Galli, very few foreigners get the privilege to walk the Cloud Stair. I daresay its effects have mystified even your curious mind,'' said Bregit giving Galli a warming smile.

''Let us hope my father finds what you've to tell him of worth, or your threats will be judged before the coven,'' said Leon with his back facing them, his words sending a shudder through Galli's short-lived joy.

''You are old enough Leon and much wiser to know not to be arrogant to a superior wizard. All the same you tried and failed. And like all in position of power you will run cowering to another higher ranked wizard to finish what you could not,'' Bregit said calmly as if he were speaking to a Ripeling.

''You'd do well not to speak to my father in that manner, he isn't one to be bullied by the threat of force,'' said Leon grudgingly.

''If your father remains the same wizard that I last spoke with then he will understand the reason for my actions and forgive any fear I may have inflicted upon his son,'' said Bregit.

Leon did not reply and Bregit either through tiredness or not wanting further conversation with Leon said nothing more. The three wizards stood still allowing the stair to lift them higher and higher until they were so high the Red Sea was no longer visible through the white clouds.

''How high up is the Golden Kingdom?'' asked Galli looking to her left- and right-hand side seeing only mountains of pure white cloud.

''It's extremely high above the surface, so high that the lands of Nocktar appear as tiny pieces above a red pool,'' Bregit replied smiling.

''The Ripeling that stands beside you, please enlighten me as to why she feels the need to be here? I seem to recall Treforledge and Larmont been separated by many lands. Why are two wizards from different lands journeying together to see the king?'' asked Leon in a deliberate slow voice.

"The reasons to why Galli travels alongside me is a matter between myself and her and has little to none concern to a Stair Guard," answered Bregit with a commanding force behind his response.

"If I were a suspicious wizard, I would think something else has dragged ye from your pits something that may be too great for the worthless of Treforledge to best and the great Bregit to defeat," said Leon laughing.

"I will say this before I meet with your father," Bregit said at once in a calm manner. "Do not under value the less fortunate than yourself. I would have believed having lost your Ultimate Colour crown to a wizard from Treforledge you would have learned not to disrespect foreign wizards."

"Pssst," spat Leon. "The wizard who stole my crown will beg me to let her die come the next Tournament," Leon said in a sour tone.

"I stole nothing!" hissed Galli fiercely abandoning her promise to Bregit. "The wizards of Treforledge won the Ultimate Colour by a combination of teamwork and out thinking our opponents," said Galli in a firm tone.

Leon turned on his step, staring into Galli's light blue eyes, as flashes of his first defeat played back through his dark eyes. Until the face of the wizard who had dethroned him upon the sands in front of the entire wizard population projected from his eyes and found shape in the face of the wizard standing beneath him. The wicked grin Bregit had wiped away returned to Leon with a lot more menace to it.

"So, the wizard who stripped me of my title stands a mere step away, should I seek my revenge now, or will I wait?" breathed Leon his black eyes now looking at Galli with a desire for vengeance.

Galli tightened her fingers around Water Dancer awaiting Leon's strike, but it never came. Leon regained himself and turned on his heel resuming his position of having his back turned to Galli and Bregit.

"It would be dishonourable of a prince to strike down a weary opponent, perhaps when you are rested, we can organise a rematch?" Leon suggested with a grimace.

Galli neither accepted or rejected Leon's challenge, right now at this current moment, all that mattered to her was how to make the king believe her without getting hot headed or impolite. Judging from Leon's attitude Galli's victory in the Ultimate Colour has made her more enemies than friends within the Golden Kingdom.

"Let's not allow the outcome of the competition create a line of hate between two worthy competitors, to have dethroned a wizard of stature must have taken great skill in mind and combat, wouldn't you agree at least to that?" said Bregit his tone appeasing.

"Perhaps," muttered Leon in dislike. "However, it was my blindness that caused my downfall, I never believed it possible that a pack of filthy wizards from Treforledge would even compare against the elite of my lieutenants," said Leon.

"Wizards of Treforledge are far from filth!" shouted Galli aggressively. "We are the ones who make the armour you wear in battle, shape stones and staffs to your suiting, all the while you sit upon stairs with beaming smiles while having a luxurious lifestyle," cried Galli her voice shaking with anger.

These words had an enormous impact on Leon, he like all other high ranked wizards were not accustomed to been answered back to by those they believed themselves superior to. But Leon's belittling remark about Galli's fellow wizards had caused her to let go of her restraints and snap.

"You have much to learn in manners Galli of Treforledge," said Leon in an amused tone. "I would advise that your superior wizard teach you in the ways of disobedience before meeting with my father. But between you and me little Galli, I refer your victory over me a fluke and nothing more," Leon said slyly.

"Can we put this feud aside for a brief. There are more pressing concerns at hand as you well know Galli," said Bregit in an impatient voice.

"What's got the calm Bregit so startled, I wonder? Concerns at hand, what concerns do you speak of?" asked Leon, his smug grin broadening.

Bregit kept his eyes firmly on the end of his staff, knowing he had foolishly let slip a vital detail to why himself and Galli had travelled to the Golden Kingdom, knowing Leon would detect a lie, Bregit knew he had no choice but to reveal his true intentions.

"Right, you are Leon. We have come seeking the king's counsel. Our reason is far greater than you think, great perils have come forth from the bowls of darkness that now threatens to establish itself upon us again," said Bregit seriously.

"Darkness is rising again you say, well if you're going to ask my father to gather his forces and deploy the Seven Coloured Army on a two-shade journey to Larmont or Treforledge you might as well turn back now," laughed Leon.

"It is the Golden Kingdoms sworn duty to protect all lands of Nocktar when the lord of that land needs reinforcements," said Galli.

"Spoken like a true Second," sneered Leon. "The Lands of Light are occupied by wizards who have been taught and trained in the magical arts are they not?" asked Leon arrogantly.

"Yes," answered Galli hating Leon.

"Lords of lands oversee the protection of their lands not the Golden Kingdoms armies! We are not petty Orpels, we do not rush out to every pleading wizard that comes crying at our door," said Leon proudly.

"With you as Stair Guard, I find it hard to believe these pleading wizards ever made it to the king's door," Galli said coldly.

"The king rules the Lands of Light and it will be his decision not yours as to where his armies will travel," Bregit reminded Leon.

Leon scoffed at Bregit's dig at reminding him who was indeed in charge. "Much has changed since your departure, but I'll let you see that for yourself," said Leon smiling as the stair came to a firm halt.

They were so busy agreeing and disagreeing with one another that both Bregit and Galli hadn't noticed an oaken door appear at the end of the steps. It stood between eighteen to twenty feet in height and twice its width, with leathered straps spread across the door keeping it sealed.

"This is where I leave you," came Leon's charmed voice. "My duties as Stair Guard doesn't end until next shade. Pity, I would love to be there to witness the extinguishing look of hope drain from your faces when my father declines both your pleas,'' laughed Leon aloud as he waved his hand at the oaken door causing the straps to unlatch from the door.

Leon descended into the shrouding clouds leaving Galli and Bregit alone and glad to see the last of his grinning face. A sound like snapped twigs caught both wizard's attention as a white line broke through the thick bark that trailed all the way from the doors top to bottom, and as the light grew brighter the realism became clearer.

''One door that breaks into two,'' said Galli watching as the oaken door split, and slowly spread apart making enough space for Bregit and Galli to slip through.

''One of many powerful shields that defend this kingdom. It would take great skill to unseal this doors defences. Only those who are in the king's inner circle know the spell to unhinge its many defences,'' said Bregit.

''Is it safe? To go through I mean,'' Galli asked Bregit feeling unsure.

''Quite all right,'' Bregit assured her. ''Leon has removed its straps; it will take a full shade until they fall back into place.''

While he said it Bregit walked with ease toward the door. Galli quickly followed him and together they walked through the split doors and into the beaming lights of the Golden Kingdom.

Chapter 14

The Scorched Hills of Wivirid

Carka walked hooded and cloaked under the shade of the hills, hiding under the tall trees due to a swarm of Varwels passing by. The Varwels were heading east making Carka unsure of their destination but was glad they were in a rush because he didn't want to encounter them so close to the Twig Collectors lair. When the coast was clear he resumed his walk but even with the appearance of the Varwels he was unable to divert from his mind what the spirit of Dirm had told him. Still rattled from his encounter with the Twig Collectors, Carka constantly looked over his shoulder to be sure they weren't on his trail.

The Twig Collectors existence had split opened Carkas mind completely, because never would he have believed such creatures existed, but having seen them with his own eyes he could no longer live-in denial. Carka knew the power of necromancy existed due to the tales told to him about Sar the White the good wizard gone bad who dabbled in black magic. Sar was one of the first wizards who disbanded from the group of the first wizards and set his sights further than wallowing among the clouds. Sar sought to seize control over the creatures of Nocktar. In his quest he revived many dark spirits and used them to kill numerous creatures and consumed many lands in his stand against Lanos ruling to deny wizards homelands among the Lands of Light. But Sar never got the chance to challenge Lano because the elders acted quickly to Sar's disastrous plans. It required the full might of the six elder wizards to kill Sar in the end, knowing it was the only way to return the revived spirits to the realms of nonbeing.

But Sar was cunning enough to leave the incantations he had used to perform such dark magic written in an indestructible book that he named, Demonic. When the elders placed the book within the vaults of the Golden Kingdom, they were shocked to find it gone once they relinquished their hold over it. The dark book of spells where abouts to this shade are unknown and it worried Carka to think that this Glider lord may have found Sar's book and was using it to build himself an army of resurrected spirits.

It would explain how the Twig Collectors exist but with little knowledge of the dark arts Carka remained puzzled, because if there was a dark wizard disguised as a Glider out there raising the dead for its own personal desires the damage could be catastrophic.

Dirm's information about a Glider lord hiding in the shadows planning to seize control of the Lands of Light for itself somehow frightened Carka greater than the threat of Lano. Perhaps it was how ineffective his greatest attacks were against the Twig Collectors that made him weary to this threat because in comparison Lano was killable and these newfound foes were on a higher more dangerous level.

If these Glider servants were this formidable then Carka dreaded to think about how powerful this Glider lord could be? Especially if his theory was correct and it was indeed a wizard using Demonic to perform magic, he deemed unnatural to disguise itself as a wizard?

Panting Carka kept looking over his shoulder fearful the ghost of Dirm may have followed him from its lair. He had taken the east path that led to high hills coated in grass. For this was the path he intended on taking before he was found by the Twig Collectors. Having heard rumors that the alpha Harpy Grith resided among the hills and had built hundreds of nests to keep the female Harpies close by for repopulation, Carka knew he wouldn't be too hard to find.

Carka knew the Alpha Harpy who was named Grith, because he had helped him out in a situation between a vicious Rear Clar many cycles of shades ago and due to Carka saving him from a gruesome faith the Alpha Harpy granted Carka his services, but back then he was young and stubborn minded and having heard about Grith's methods to maintain his position Carka told the Alpha Harpy he would one shade come to claim his reward.

The grass hills stood like pillars in a wide scale of land that was used by winged creatures to build strong nests and live peacefully, due to Alacoma and Dirren been loyal to Lano, Carka was sure he could convince Grith and the Harpies occupying the hills to fight for the wizards. For Harpies were loyal to no one and fought no wars, but Carka was hoping to change that and bring a balance to Lanos ariel advantage.

''The Hills of Wivirid,'' breathed Carka, now standing on top of a grass covered hill.

But it was not the scenery Carka had anticipated, there was no green grass coating the hills or any sign of a Harpy. The only thing that was clear to Carka was the thick smoke, black and fused with grey ash covered the hills leaving Carka in a state of shock as to who was behind this destruction. About to abandon his mission Carka's attention was swayed by the sudden echo of a painful cry that sounded like someone was being tortured. Listening, Carka heard the cry again and decided to take a closer look. Climbing up a steep hill, he dragged himself up along the ashes. When he got closer the top of the hill, Carka could make out voices and the crackling of breaking twigs on a hot fire. Pulling himself to the top of the hill he lay on his stomach and raised his head barely over the burnt grass to look down on the surface.

What Carka seen as he lowered his eyes sickened him. Bodies ripped and torn apart were spread along the edge of a large bonfire, where a pack of Viledirks sat chewing roasted meat and talking triumphal amongst themselves. Carka recognized the Viledirk sitting away from the fire and cheerful Viledirks, it was Kcor the Viledirkening lord and Lanos most trusted advisor.

''Keep that feathered slug quiet or I'll rip out its intestines,'' said one of the Viledirks while it licked the juice from a long bone that no doubt was a leg once belonged to a deceased Harpy.

Looking away from the pack of savaging Viledirks, Carka found the source of where the painful cries had come from. About ten yards away from the fire hung a frail body hanging loosely on a wooden cross, its wings were spread to breaking point and its palms had thick Harpy claws nailed through its wrists and feet to keep it hanging in an agonizing position.

''Grith?'' breathed Carka.

The Alpha Harpy was so consumed in pain and despair he kept his head down as more of his kin were tossed into the blazing flames as fuel to keep the fire blazing.

''We can't kill him'' growled Kcor viciously to his pack. ''Have you not listened to a word I said! This filth pinned to the cross is the only male Harpy and without him the race will die out!''

"With all the feathered brats his maids breed surely one would be male," said another Viledirk who sat closer to Kcor.

"There are many male Harpies born under the full moon of purple shade, but Grith here chooses to kill them before they are strong enough to challenge him, so don't look so disheartened to see your kin being slaughtered Harpy, you do it for a living," growled Kcor to the weary Grith.

Kcor's information about how Grith remained in his position seemed to sicken the other Viledirks, who in their own perspective were savages themselves but to kill their own young was something the Viledirks were strongly against.

"So why is he to be kept alive?" asked the Viledirk after licking the juice from a long bone.

"It's said Harpies the male ones especially, can trace the movements of the ones they have imprinted with and seeing as this filth has imprinted with every female Harpy in Nocktar, he will have no trouble leading us to them," answered Kcor with a cunning smile that revealed the sharp ends of his front teeth.

Watching from above Carka made out thirteen strong Viledirks as a daring plan took form inside his head. And just as Carka was preparing to make his move something chilly brushed against his face. Fearing the Twig Collectors had followed him he rolled over onto his back and raised himself up to find himself face to face with a swarm of Gliders. Cold dread numbed Carka to the spot as Rullin and his fellow Gliders closed in on the stricken wizard. But Carka wasn't one to go out without a fight and it was his fighting spirit that sparked a surge in his rise from the ground. Unwilling to give the Gliders an inch Carka quickly summoned the Flames of Elan to his side with a ferocious wave of his arms. Flames surged from the depths of his hands and formed a protective barrier between himself and the Gliders.

Feeling the flames warmth Carka twirled his arms and unleashed the cursed flames upon the hills to the shock of the unprepared Viledirks. Rullin and his pack scattered to the safety of the clouds as Carka leaped from the hill side. Landing in front of Grith he easily withdrew the spears hinging the Harpy to the cross. Grith collapsed to the ground a groan of pain left his mouth as he struggled to remain conscious.

Two Viledirks pounced from the hill in attempt to catch Carka off guard, but they were picked away by the ever-aware Flames of Elan that parried the Viledirks away easily. Carka magically levitated Grith into the air and was about to summon a bolt of lightning to get them away from the burning hills when a swift strike caught the wizard unaware and caused Carka to fall to one knee in pain as his own blood gushed down his face and dripped down his chin.

"An honorable lord would have the decency to greet their opponent before attacking, I see your shades in the desert has erased what dignity you once had," spat Carka brushing his cheek gently with the tips of his fingers, making his deep gashes heal instantly.

"Victory is the result I require, how I get it isn't necessary," growled the deep voice of Kcor as he stood unfazed by the flames surrounding him.

"Lano must want a clean sweep if he has risked sending you all the way here, or perhaps he has found himself a new lacky to do his dirty work," laughed Carka.

Kcors eyes narrowed so low his brows were almost joined, but besides his anger Kcor had not lost one speck of his sharpness as his feline instincts were emerging through his hardened skin. Carka fired a Balasto curse, but Kcor reacted sharply and leapt out of the way using the smoke from the fires to hide himself from Carka's attacks. Carka stood still listening, knowing if he extinguished the flames, he would cover the hills in a thick smoke that would take drops to erase, and that wasn't available to him at this moment. Because one mishap and Kcor would pounce, and no doubt rip him to pieces. It wasn't hard for Carka to detect Kcors movements but due to him moving so fast he was finding it difficult to get a lock on him making it extremely difficult for Carka to strike him down.

''The Bolts of Iraz,'' gasped Grith through gritted teeth.

Carka smiled at the Alpha Harpy, as a wind rider Grith would know better than anyone that ground-based creatures like Kcor were weak when it came to aerial attacks. Smiling as he raised his hands Carka wove them fluently in the air feeling instantly the force in the air begin to intensify as flames, ash, grass, and earth were swallowed and fused into Carka's swirling vortex until Kcor was revealed clutching his claws deep into the ground trying with all his might to evade been drawn to Carka. But Kcors stance was futile, and it didn't last long, for none usually did when up against the power of the sky. With a roar of defeat Kcor unwillingly soared toward Carka who conjured straps from his fingertips that bound the wrenching Viledirk head to toe in mid-air.

''Kill him Carka,'' gasped Grith pleading with all his might. Grith tried getting up but found the effort to great to overcome due to his wings been clipped and having piercing holes pierced deep into his feet.

''He's more beneficial to us alive,'' said Carka making Kcor rotate in mid-air.

''Carka don't make me beg,'' growled Grith. ''Him and his filthy race murdered an entirety of my pack, kill him or heal me and I will do the deed myself,'' begged Grith his battered body shaking in anger.

Carka knew by denying Grith his vengeance he would never live it down but on the other hand Grith was in no condition to try force the issue so Carka levitated Kcor to his side and with a low flick of his finger the Viledirk became still. Carka grabbed the threads containing Kcor and placed him onto his shoulder and looked at Grith with sorrow.

''I hope one shade you will forgive my decision old friend; I assure it is for the best,'' said Carka in an apologetic voice.

Just as Carka was preparing to leave he was shrouded in a dome of black smoke. When the smoke shriveled a cloud hoovering in mid-air had a limb Grith hooked on the sharp end of a sprouted tentacle. Carka felt a wave of raw power hit his senses so fiercely it caused sweat to drip down the back of his neck.

Disposing of Grith by tossing him into the ashes of his kin a pair of scarlet eyes sparkled from the depths of the cloud as it slowly advanced on Carka who knew just by his own instincts that he was no match against this creature. As he stared into its blazing gaze Carka remained rooted to the spot. Wishing he could put his skills to practice against the creature who bested Bregit. But he knew he would be a fool to engage, especially now that he held the only source of persuading the king that Lano had returned on his shoulder. Carka smiled to himself surprised by his own maturity. Focusing like he'd never done before his eyes turned white and just as the cloud figured out what was going to happen it had already happened and Carka was gone in a burst of white lightning that lit up the hill of nests and left the cloud looking coldly at Carka's fading glow dimmer in the sky

Chapter 15

The Golden Kingdom

"Wow!" breathed Galli; her eyes widening with utter amazement by the wave of shining lights filling her eyes. "I've never seen so many bright colours," she confessed dreamily.

"The view is something to behold I'll admit," said Bregit in a flat tone.

Galli inhaled the clean refreshing air, tickling her so refreshingly, she could feel it undulling her senses and clearing her weary mind. But her joy was short lived as a firm hand gripped her shoulder, causing a cold shiver of reality to crush Galli's dream state. Gasping as if she had just been woken too early from a pleasant dream, Galli breathed furiously, using her knuckles to rub her eyes she instantly realised, they were no longer filled with beaming lights. Turning to Bregit with a blank expression she was annoyed to find him amused by her state of shock.

"What you have just experienced were the effects of a luring illusion, a simple trick to miss when it is concealed by bright beams," Bregit explained at a slow pace. "The idea behind the illusion is to open the minds of those fascinated by their beams. While the victim is indulged by the beams they are unknowingly been entranced by the undetectable spell and lured into a dream state so powerful it dulls the senses and makes your living body a tool for the ritual caster," said Bregit indifferently.

Galli clenched Water Dancer firmly, the burning feeling of humiliation irritated her bones, as she was yet again made feel a fool by the ideas of the wizards from the Golden Kingdom.

"Don't be angered by how easily seduced you were, all wizards who have visited the Golden Kingdom have fallen victim to the same trap," Bregit said in hope to soothe Galli's frustration. "When I was Depth Head General, many visitors fell under the same illusion and woke up hanging by their thumbs in the cloud chamber's."

Galli knew Bregit was only saying this in attempt to spare her blushes, but the thoughts of other wizards falling under the same spell did ease her frustration a little. The embarrassing thoughts of waking in a dungeon surrounded by taunting Ripelings shooting sparks at her rear end did make Galli appreciate having Bregit by her side.

"Thank you," she said in a bittersweet tone.

Bregit nodded his head, a smile of praise widened his cheeks as he stared ahead to view the surroundings more acutely. When Galli looked toward the same direction her eyes were filled with images of temples coloured in sky blue. Galli at once recognised the light blue rocks the moment she laid eyes on them, simply because they were forged in Treforledge, by a professional Crafter. Galli knew this because only a Crafter was capable of manipulating rocks to not leave a single crack after been chiselled. Galli could also tell by the smoothness of each square rock that a soothing spell had been casted over the outer layers by the Crafters, with the addition of flamed melted copper to permanently seal the sea rocks on top of one another. The Crafters branded them Shore Rocks, because that was where they found them, washed up on nearby shores on islands near the out skirts of Treforledge.

Swaying her eyes a few yards from the blue temples, Galli's vision was now consumed by glows of beaming rays of scarlet red. Boulders twice the size of any wizard were lined in rows behind one another. Each boulder trailed along a curved pathway that led to a green seaweed coloured mountain far out into the distance.

"Why do all coloured paths lead to that mountain?" Galli asked, eyeing the moss-covered mountain through her squinted eyes.

"The temples of blue to your left are home to the Blue Striped Wizards," answered Bregit with a deep sigh. "The red boulders to the blue temples left are home to the Red Striped Wizards. The Yellow Petals to the south, which appear to be overly grown flowers are home to the Yellow Striped Wizards. The pumpkin stalk to the north shelters the Orange Striped Wizards, and lastly the black hoovering clouds above us are the resting places for the Black Striped Wizards," finished Bregit nodding his head upward to show the location of the Black Wizards base.

Galli's neck hurt from having to twist and turn so much, but she did not complain. Aching neck muscles were little to complain about when getting a first-hand insight of the Golden Kingdom. Seeing the different homes of the Striped Wizards was fascinating. The Blue Temples were built using the rocks Galli's kin had reshaped which gave her a swell of pride that she couldn't measure with words. The red boulders were also made by the Crafters of Treforledge. The reason for them been red was because they were plucked from the wastelands and harnessed in blazing forges. The Crafters designed them to withstand any climate and to radiate warmth from beneath the ground. Lorneid named the reddish rocks, Flares. Seeing these familiar stones made Galli remember Lorneids quarters, they too were seeded with Flares beneath the rocks of Crafters Isle. A cautionary act implied by Lorneid in preparation for the cold shades.

The enlarged flowers Bregit had said were yellow weren't entirely yellow, they also had a sunset orange fused within their roots that were veined along the petals and ended at the soft bulbs that nested neatly in the centre of the wonky petals. Not far south of the yellow flowers was a beanstalk with strong roots and thick vines twirled and fused together that stood around a hundred feet tall. Its long vines had detached and now looked like branches that had round shaped pumpkins dangling from the ends of each vine with a roped ladder hanging from a square door in the centre of the pumpkin.

"How did a beanstalk grow on clouds? I thought stalks needed to grow beneath the earth to extend this high?" Galli inquired, remembering Lorneid telling her that all roots need soft soil and unlimited supplies of clear water to grow strong.

"That beanstalk was fully grown when it was brought to the Golden Kingdom," answered Bregit. "It was a meant as a gift from the deceased Lord of Selavroc, Orakil the Silver. But after Orakil took lordship over the fogged lands, he quickly discovered that the fog consuming the lands was permanent and not so easily moved. In attempt to save the dying plants and rare herbs, Orakil sent many plants and roots across the Red Sea with flocks of Varwels in a final attempt to safeguard the rare plants from going extinct."

"A flock of Varwels carried this all the way here," interrupted Galli, thinking even the entire population of winged beasts would find it difficult carrying this enormous stalk thousands of leagues from Selavroc.

"Allow me to finish!" said Bregit annoyed at Galli's interruption. "Orakils gifts were graciously accepted, by all whom he intrusted their wellbeing to but while the ever-caring wizard was caring for everything else he had forgotten to take care of himself."

"That was a noble thing to do, under the circumstances. Orakil could have easily left them to rot," said Galli, feeling a rush of pride for the act of kindness shown by the dead wizard she never knew.

"Orakils actions were decent but in his sole mission to save what he could from the fog he disregarded its abilities," Bregit pointed out.

"I've never heard of the fogs of Selavroc," Galli admitted feeling she was missing the point.

"Really?" asked Bregit appearing shocked. "References to the fogs of Selavroc are used as commonly as magic, didn't you ever hear the phrase as immovable as the fogs of Selavroc?"

"No," replied Galli, shaking her head.

Bregit looked at Galli in wonder finding it strange that she was unknowing about such common knowledge, but he drew back to his story before Galli became aware of his gawking.

"I noticed when Orakil lumbered before the king in the coven's chamber, that he was barely stable and fretting over sounds in the distance that no one else could hear. I expressed my concerns to the king that Orakil should remain within the Golden Kingdom until he was in the right frame of mind to travel," said Bregit, in a flat tone.

"So, no one bothered to investigate why Orakil had suddenly become deranged?"

"The king didn't take my concerns seriously nor did he take Orakils gift with gratitude. He decided to cast the stalk away from his halls and be used to shelter the Orange Striped Wizards," said Bregit.

"It's a pity Orakil didn't offer the stalk to Lorneid, he would have gracefully accepted this fine gift," said Galli, knowing how beneficial a stalk would be to the wizards of Treforledge.

"All the same the stalk was safe from rotting and decaying into memory and that was all that mattered to Orakil, he left the Golden Kingdom at once and was never seen alive again," said Bregit.

"You said Orakil died; how?" asked Galli.

"When I was a cycle of shade into my lordship of Larmont, my Cave Keeper friend Arb came to my tower and told me he had been informed by the Varwels of Selavroc that Orakils body had been found close to a Gliders mist. The Varwels couldn't give a full description of Orakils death but confirmed his mind had died many shades before his body," answered Bregit.

"That's terrible!" cried Galli her voice becoming brittle.

"Quite right," Bregit agreed. "The beanstalk along with many plants that blossom throughout Nocktar pay tribute to Orakils kindness and will do so until all memory of him has diminished within those who had the pleasure of his company," said Bregit with praise for his old friend.

Feeling she needed to divert the subject away from Orakil, Galli found a fresh unspoken category to question Bregit further about.

"I just can't imagine wizards living under these circumstances, I thought they would live within the confinements of the Golden Kingdom, not like this," said Galli, staring unimpressed at the small confinements the striped wizards had to live in.

"Just because you are born among the wizards of the Golden Kingdom that does not mean you automatically become their equal. Harsh training regimes are put in place to see do wizards have what it takes mentally and physically to be regarded a coloured wizard. And even if that wizard survives those exhausting regimes, they are then tested in front of the king to meet his expectations and if that wizard doesn't meet the standards set then they fail and are considered second class and unworthy of a brand," said Bregit.

"Treforledge may be all about crafting rocks but at least we weren't forced to live like slaves," said Galli with gratitude.

"Thankfully, wizards of other lands think differently to those who dwell amongst the clouds so when next you yearn to be somewhere else because you deem your life unfulfilled remember this scenery and be grateful for what you have," said Bregit.

This struck a chord in Galli's mind and reminded her about how she detested been Lorneids Second, looking back now she wished she could scream at herself for behaving so ungratefully and for thinking what she had was beneath her. Bregit was right you don't know what you have until its gone and Galli was living proof of that statement.

"I would have thought someone would've been sent by now," said Bregit in a shrill voice.

"Why can't you lead the way?" asked Galli.

"I no longer have the authority to walk freely among the clouds, after I left my position as Depth Head General and became Lord of Larmont, I was and always will be treated like all foreigners and must await passage to be granted to me," Bregit answered smoothly, his decrease in standard not fazing him at all.

They continued to wait, Bregit was calm but alert to every sound while Galli took the long silence as the perfect opportunity to take a more observant look at the black striped wizard's inhabitants. The black clouds could fit at least four wizards on them with enough space to fit a drop tree.

"Why does the Black Striped wizards live above the rest?" asked Galli looking at Bregit in wonder.

"You just answered your own question," said Bregit smiling. "The Black Striped Wizards live so high and far away from the other Ripelings because they believe themselves superior to those beneath themselves."

"Having fought against them, I have no disagreement with their skills in combat, but I would've thought living and surrounded by one another they'd show a professional respect to one another," said Galli.

"It's not that simple," said Bregit steely. "Each band of wizards is trained in different arts in attempt to become better than the other. The intensity of their training develops into fear of losing to the opposing colour and that fear of loss expands into bitterness, that can if allowed, stretch into hate," Bregit explained, making it clear for Galli that conscience and choice are removed when the Ripelings of the Golden Kingdom are ripe.

"So, this all leads back to fear, fear of failure has turned these wizards to dislike the other just because of the indifference in colour. The laws of this kingdom are dumb, so dumb I am amazed wizards allow themselves to serve such a leader," said Galli.

"Fear takes on many shapes inside every mind, allow it to latch inside you long enough and it grows until it is all you know. Not all wizards were fortunate to be born away from the king's rule, which is why you shouldn't judge them so harshly! These wizards had all the courage and fight zapped from them before they even knew they had it," said Bregit calmly.

"That's a fair point" Galli admitted after a moment's consideration.

"The paths you wanted to know about, they all lead to the doors of the Depth Mountain," said Bregit, pointing his finger to the far distance.

"Is that where you taught all the Ripelings?"

"Yes. The Depth Mountain has many entrances. Each doorway welcomes a different coloured hallway filled with chambers. Within those chambers are the Depth Heads who teach their branded Ripelings the ways of the magical arts, healing rituals, the differences between plants and roots and the history of our elders along with the studies of Mystical and Mythical creatures."

"They really take it seriously up here," said Galli.

"It's what separates them from everyone else, their methods of one hundred percent are there for all to see and it is why the Seven Coloured Army are the most feared army among the Lands of Light," said Bregit. "Perfection is one of many things the wizards of the Golden Kingdom admire, anything less and the consequences will be far greater than a whipped arm," said Bregit sternly.

"The Ultimate Colour was designed for wizards from foreign lands to come forward and express themselves, and if the coven believes a wizard worthy, they will be given the chance to join the Seven Coloured Army......,"

Bregit's eyes widened with shock. A sly smile curled his dry lips as he turned his head to look at Galli who could feel his yellow curious eyes bore on her; Galli could feel his racing mind finally piece together the secret she had kept hidden from her closest friends.

"I misjudged you," Bregit said smiling with a tilt of his head. "So, tell me what reason made you decline the coven's offering?" asked Bregit.

"It wasn't the coven who offered me a place among the Seven Coloured Army," said Galli trying not to sound ungrateful. "It was the king," she answered slowly, each word making her realise what her life may have been like had she not refused.

"Really!" piped Bregit who wasn't used to been shocked twice. "You must have made an impression to have gained the kings favour."

"Perhaps!" said Galli insecurely. "When the king summoned me to the deserted arena, I felt like a young Ripeling again. Overwhelmed and lost in my own personal desires." Galli sighed deeply before continuing. "I had forgotten in my triumph that it wasn't just mine but Treforledge's and that I was its servant and representative not a glory hunter seeking to advance my position. The moment I stepped back into the arena where I had experienced my moment of triumph was when I felt the harsh reality wash over me. I wasn't going to abandon my comrades after we'd worked so hard to rise above the heel we'd been placed under for so long," said Galli with fierce pride.

"Admirable," said Bregit softly. "How did the king take your refusal?"

"He told me my place belonged with the elite and if I wanted, the position of commander would be mine if I left Treforledge and gave my services to The Golden Kingdom."

"You made a brave decision that shade, many would have given their staffs to be offered that position," praised Bregit.

"Yes! Well, I had no intentions of commanding the wizards who had made my victory feel so little, my place was in Treforledge. I told the king I had sworn my own oath and that was to protect the Lord of the Treforledge until his or my dying shade."

"Wise words to use when refusing a king's offer, he above all would value the sacred oaths of lord protectors," said Bregit.

"He admired my loyalty and gifted me this," Galli said softly.

Figuring if Bregit was going to meet with the king, he may recognise Galli and ask had she unlocked the secrets of his emerald shield. Galli felt it was better to tell Bregit now rather than see the look of distrust appear on his face when they met with the king. Galli pulled from under her cloak the shield she was given from the king. Bregit lifted his thin arm, touching the base of the shield gently.

"This was indeed the king's shield; its name is Mirror," said Bregit weaving his hand around the shield with a gentle sway of his arm.

"Mirror?" said Galli, in wonder.

"Yes, Mirror, named for its reflective powers," said Bregit, removing his fingers from the emerald shield.

"I didn't know it had a name," said Galli as she wove the shield around her arm.

"Given by myself during the battle against the Aqua Guardians," Bregit said turning his gaze from the shield and looking at Galli.

"You owned this shield, then how did the king come to possess it?" Galli asked with interest.

"We were in the heat of battle, striking for survival against creatures with unnatural strength. When I saw the king lose his staff in the commotion, I flung mirror in his direction as a wave of spears sank from the sky hoping he read my intentions."

"And did he?" asked Galli.

"Of course. But not before he was slit by two arrows that had been dipped in powerful poisons before been loosed. The poison coursed through the king's face making him appear lazy eyed on one side of his face."

"But the Aqua Guardians don't use archers," Galli recalled.

"No, they do not," said Bregit smiling. "But I never said the arrow was shot by an Aqua Guardian," contradicted Bregit. "Other creatures took up arms against the wizards and when peace was agreed many of those creatures begged for forgiveness, pleading they were forced and black mailed into fighting for the Aqua Guardians."

Galli scoffed, even Bregit showed signs of humour in his tone while speaking of the creature's pleas of deception because they both knew it was far from fear that ignited the mythical and mystical creatures into aiding the Aqua Guardians.

"The king's appearance may have suffered and made one side of his face disfigured, but he fought valiantly through the pain. Catching Mirror, he repelled the next wave of incoming spears and sent them back from whence they came with enhanced speed, giving the archers no chance to avoid their reflected attack.

Listening to Bregit's description, Galli grasped the handle of her shield. It was so light yet able to withstand anything thrown at it. But she hated having to depend on it, because it made her feel in debt to the king whenever she was forced to use it. What was worse she had the shield in her possession when Treforledge was attacked, had Lorneid not knocked her out then maybe she could have prevented more casualties.

"Are you feeling all right?" Bregit asked noticing Galli's saddened expression.

"Yes," lied Galli.

"While in the presence of high ranked wizards don't allow your emotions to control your actions, many have lost their lives for less," said Bregit his voice sharp.

"And where do these high ranked wizards live? I can't imagine they live with the striped wizards?"

"The high ranked wizards stay in the king's temple with a direct passage from their quarters to the coven chambers. It would be an exceedingly rare sight to see a high ranked wizard strolling through the Golden Kingdom," answered Bregit.

"Then how do they communicate with one another, get food for example? I doubt they have a direct route to everlasting food stores," said Galli.

Bregit huffed aloud. "The coloured wizards of The Golden Kingdom have Orpels to do their needed requirements," he said in a faint voice.

"Orpels? I've never heard of them before what are those?" Galli asked curiously.

"Shush," whispered Bregit, "very few have. They are wizards, just less fortunate."

"Less fortunate?" said Galli her face blank in wonder.

"Orpels are second class wizards who live in the Golden Kingdom. They once trained and fought for a position among the Seven Coloured Army, but when it came to proving their learnings in front of the king, they failed the test and were shamed by the king for their lack of wit."

"Shamed in what way?" asked Galli.

"A life sentence of enslavement. If you think the Ripelings accommodations are unaccustomed, then I dare say your eyes would roll back at the sight of an Orpels lodgings."

"I never knew that if you fail the kings test, you would be disgraced. I presumed a wizard would've been allowed resit the test once they were ready," said Galli.

"You have a lot to learn about the regimes of the Golden Kingdom," said Bregit keeping his voice muffled. "The only reward for a failed wizard is to be wiped clean of everything they are and shamed forever," stated Bregit.

"Degraded more like," Galli said feeling her jaws tensing. The thought maddened Galli. To be told wizards like herself where been used as slaves for not living up to a wizard's standard made her want to whip up her staff and lash out at those who see it befitting to treat their own kind in such a disgraceful manner.

"In other wizards view maybe. But an Orpel will be forever beneath the heels of a coloured and stripped wizard and forced to serve until bonds of slavery are broken or death takes them," said Bregit his tone appeasing.

"Why hasn't anyone done something to overrule this law? Surely there are those who disagree with this form of cruelty?"

"Do not allow your own judgement to eclipse your senses," warned Bregit. "To speak openly as you just have within the Golden Kingdom is treason, so keep your voice down!" ushered Bregit.

"Slavery is a prelude to war in many lands, wasn't that the reason the Aqua Guardians rose from the Red Sea and quarrelled with the Purple King?" asked Galli.

"It was one of many reasons they disagreed," replied Bregit. "Fortunate for us we had Tip-Karp to negotiate the terms and save both species from the burdens of further desolation."

"But weren't the agreed terms meant to stamp out slavery?" asked Galli a little too quickly because she had unintendingly cut across Bregit, but he allowed her question to finish before continuing.

"The slaves of all lands were freed of bondage. Slavery was dismissed and forbidden in every land of Nocktar. The accords were signed by each lord of land, the king, and Tarlbok the Aqua Chief. But the laws of the peace terms only….,"

"Applies to the lands and not what dwells over or beneath them," finished Galli the realism finally becoming clearer in her head.

"Very quick off the mark," said Bregit smiling at Galli's sharpness. "The king even gave his slaves a nickname. Orpels. Which is a made-up word used to mask slavery and evade the conflicts of war between opposing creature's," said Bregit his voice now below a whisper.

But before Galli could extend the conversation Bregit nudged her in the ribs and nodded his head upwards to show they were no longer alone. Looking up Galli's eyes were met by a beefy figure who was standing feet away, wearing a stern unnerved expression. Its body was covered in a tight fitted shiny golden armour making it appear brawny. Its silver hair lay neatly combed and wet, making the bright rays of light reflect off its silver strands. In its right hand it held a long bronze staff that reached to the tip of its chin. Two silvers leaves lay on the staffs top with a bronze ruby shaped sphere nested between the silver leaves. Bregit stepped in front of Galli to greet the armoured wizard.

''You must be the king's guard?'' asked Bregit politely moving a few steps toward the stern-faced wizard.

The armoured wizard didn't reply. Instead, it looked Bregit and Galli up and down before making a grizzling grunt sound once its silver eyes stopped their examination of them. Its breathing was heavy and rough. Galli wondered if it was incapable of speaking under the influence of some enchantment casted by its master.

Bregit ignored the king's guard's impolite manner and continued speaking in a polite voice. ''I am Bregit the Yellow lord of Larmont and behind me is Galli the Blue from the Blue Islands of Treforledge, we have travelled the Plate Pathway to seek an audience with your king,'' announced Bregit.

Still the king's guard did not reply, but Bregit continued speaking unwilling to allow the insolence behaviour shown by king's guard to affect his moral.

''Are you here to merely stand and stare at us all shade?'' said a more determined looking Bregit.

The kind lines had vanished from his face, to be replaced by harsh ones of frustration that creased Bregit's ancient features. Tilting its head slightly. The king's guard gawked at Bregit. Its silver eyes narrowed as both wizards exchanged looks. Then with a low grunt, the towering kings guard straightened its neck, turned swiftly, and walked along the path, his golden cloak trailing behind.

''Let us walk before we stumble upon unwanted company,'' whispered Bregit loud enough for Galli to hear.

Bregit stepped off the clouds and onto the leaf covered path doing the same Galli took her first step away from the clouds. The moment her feet touched the leaves she was momentarily reminded of home. The relaxing feeling of soft comfort flowed through her body, erasing all thoughts of aching and tiredness.

''Where is he taking us?'' asked Galli loud enough for the king's guard to hear.

''To the temple of the king,'' answered Bregit.

''How'd you know that?''

''The king's guard only leaves his king's side when he has been commanded to escort wizards seeking an audience with him to his chambers. I believe the king may already know we're here,'' said Bregit in a hopeful tone.

The king's guard led the pair past the homes of the striped wizards and west of the Depth Mountain. Bregit knew too well where they were going and hoped beyond hope his journey wasn't going to be in vain.

''The mountain it's gone. I can't see it anymore,'' squealed Galli making Bregit jump with fright.

''Must I explain every single detail to you,'' snapped Bregit impatiently.

Galli looked taken back by Bregit's ignorance and refused to be made feel victimised for his insolence. ''I got a fright, is that against your code now, if I get scared or if I decide to change my mood in any way I have to check with the master of ceremony before I allow my change in feeling to control my body,'' shouted Galli her face infuriated.

Galli's aggressive reaction wasn't what Bregit had expected, he held Galli's gaze not daring to blink. After a few drops just staring at her, he smiled and turned away leaving Galli looking blank.

"The reason the mountain is barely visible is because we are walking further up. The Golden Kingdom isn't just a small patch of cloud held together by a few different coloured homes and a mountain," said Bregit firmly. "The king's temple is many miles from the Depth Mountain. If you look closely to the west, you'll see a cloud cave consumed by a swarm of Gliders. And if you look closely, you will see the perimeter wall guarding the Drop Tree Orchard."

"The king has a Glider army?' asked Galli, who was finding it difficult to digest what she was seeing.

There was no doubt, the hoovering creatures with blank soulless expressions huddled close around one another were indeed Gliders. They didn't pay the three wizards any notice when they came within eye shot but Galli and Bregit felt the dark aura flow through the Gliders. It was so intense Galli and Bregit rushed themselves to get away from their mist.

"You don't like them? On my journey to your tower, I stumbled upon the Flower Covered Mountain and was met by a Pixie, it told me you banished the Gliders from Larmont," Galli said to Bregit flatly.

"It was all I could do to stop the killings; those creatures were beyond taming so I inflicted a more punishable trait upon them. Fear!" Breathed Bregit. "The only substance creatures who lure in darkness fear above all."

"What branch of magic would be powerful enough to drive away a swarm of murderous Gliders?" she asked trying not to appear eager.

'It doesn't matter. The point of the matter is there gone from Larmont and with hope far away to infest other lands," said Bregit his voice deepening.

"Maybe they'll pass by Treforledge and erase Lano and his council from the Blue Islands," said Galli, in a hateful tone.

"I doubt even the combined strength of the Gliders could erase such evil. I daresay it will not be long before the Gliders of the Golden Kingdom break free from their services to the king and join with Lano," said Bregit positively.

"What makes you say that?" Galli asked scorning at the Gliders.

"Lano can offer better usages of their powers," answered Bregit. "And I dread to think what chaos would be dealt if they were allowed loose on the Lands of Light," said Bregit gravely.

"Then why does the king keep them if it is known they will turn allegiance to a higher power?" asked Galli.

"Many have asked the same question, but the king refused to share his reasons for having the Gliders under his services," said Bregit.

"If the Golden Kingdom should fall, I would wager it would be the king's own doing. His blindness to see beyond his own doorstep will play a huge part in his dethroning," said Galli bitterly.

Bregit's eyebrows raised. "Would the dismissal of the king satisfy you?" he asked keenly.

''Treforledge lays in ruin and under the control of Lano and not one single thing has been done to avenge the lives of my fallen kin,'' said Galli bitterly.

''We are yet to know if the king has knowledge of Treforledge's demise. Be patient Galli you will see your fallen kin avenged,'' Bregit assured her with a warm smile.

Galli didn't respond, she felt annoyed that Bregit was defending the king. 'How could the ruler of the Lands of Light not know by now that several Kingdoms have been attacked?' Galli thought, her gut feeling telling her the king knew more than his actions were letting on.

''Stand back!'' bellowed Bregit his voice frightening.

Bregit's staff was raised high as was the king's guards, both wizards blocked Galli's view to what they were fretting over. When she moved to Bregit's left, she got to see what all the fuss was about. It was a wizard with red hair and eyes coming toward them.

''I expected a more welcoming party, not a pair of anxious wizards,'' said the Red Wizard in a cheerful voice.

The kings guard lowered his staff at once and knelt on one knee bowing its head. Galli could now see the wizard up close. He was wearing pitch black robes streaked with sizzling lines of blood red and had long straight red hair that was waxed and combed neatly down by his shoulder blades. It had a pretty face and wore a warm smile that seemed to never falter. The staff held within the Red Wizard's hand was like Bregit's, oaken and streaked in veins of red with three scarlet red petals at its top that were latched together to conceal the ruby within. He seemed to blossom like a beacon of flames as he stood looking upon Galli and Bregit with a satisfied grin.

''Who is that?'' asked Galli.

Bregit who hadn't lowered his guard pierced the Red Wizard with a look of dislike his tension showing in the lines under his eyes.

''I have left my chambers to speak with you both in private if I may,'' said the Red Wizard his voice soft as the ground he stood on.

''How did you know we were coming; I wasn't under the impression the king shared his appointments with mere-coloured wizards?'' said Bregit his tone sour.

The Red Wizard's eyes narrowed slightly but his grin widened making him appear menacing and cunning. ''In my father's absence, I am protector of the Golden Kingdom. In response to your presumed facts Lord Bregit. I will speak with you and your companion when we are alone and in private.''

It was a rare sight seeing Bregit frozen tongued. He stood eyes wide with shock staring into the face of the Red Wizard who dismissed the kings guard with a wave of his hand. Without a word he rose from his position, bowed to the Red Wizard, and walked the path he'd previously led Galli and Bregit along. Galli looked at the golden figure sink beneath the clouds until Bregit's voice turned her attention away.

''Lucifer?'' said Bregit after a moment's inspection.

The red wizards smile broadened. ''Finally, you've pieced that together, now can we get a move on before the ears of this kingdom hear that I've left my chambers to welcome two stragglers into my father's kingdom,'' said Lucifer clapping his hands together and moving quickly down the trail.

"Where is the king?" asked Bregit lowering his staff.

"My chambers are a short walk from here, a place for you both to get needed rest and food," said Lucifer.

"A humble wizard among the clouds," jested Bregit who wasn't convinced by Lucifer's caring approach.

"I sense a distrust in you Lord Bregit, I cannot say we have met before, due to me been a Ripeling when you left this kingdom, but I'd have thought been my father's best friend you'd recognise his own son," said Lucifer.

"Wizards are known to change in colour when they are released of their teachings, during my shades as a streaked wizard I had many friends who would barely acknowledge me now, when you reach the age, I have young Lucifer you'll see my point first-hand," said Bregit his words slow and slightly dragged.

"Maybe if your still with us Lord Bregit we could share our experiences on the matter," joked Lucifer grinning.

Galli laughed even Bregit's lips twitched.

"I received word my father travels from the Pin-Fars mist and should be here before the turn of shade. When he returns, he will need council on what has occurred in his absence, meaning he will visit my chambers before retiring. You both are welcome to wait for him there," offered Lucifer.

"We would be glad of some needed refreshments. But we will linger for a short spell only, we have pressing matters to attend to," said Bregit trying not to sound ungrateful.

"Good, now follow me ye two before others become aware of your presence," said Lucifer leading the way.

Chapter 16

The Wall of Illusion

The trees had strengthened during Lanos shades in exile, the once feeble and narrowed twigs now stood sentinel strong with roots stretched so deep beneath the earth even a Slither would find it difficult reaching their cores. The Drop Trees basil-coloured leaves had extended enormously, making them capable of holding intense amounts of weight without bending under pressure. Lano discovered the strength of the Drop Tree leaves shortly after his coming to Dulgerdeen and demanded to see the full extent of their strength by proving their intake of damage.

Kcor and Jaed applied their fiercest techniques in their attempts to break the leaves resilience, but for all their efforts the leaves merely resumed their natural form, given Lano much to consider in what uses their strength may benefit him in the future. Wasting no drops, Lano instructed Kcor to strip every Drop Tree of their leaves and bark and gave the Viledirks the task of forging armour from the tree's outer layers. But this didn't fare well with the Kurlezzias who watched with anger as their sacred trees were ripped apart. But Gazzel and his herd kept their voices held which was a joyful sight that brought a satisfied grin to the Lava Keepers scarred face.

Lano knew sharing wasn't in the Kurlezzias' culture but knowing they were powerless to act made it a happy return for Lano as his dominance was clear for all to see. Now two shades into his stay in Dulgerdeen, Lano kept to himself and shortened his meetings by rudely excusing himself. Never did he stay in the one spot for too long due to the growing dread ever present in his mind that the cloud could make an unscheduled appearance and ruin his plan. Lano put his aggravated behaviour down to his hate of been locked within the boundaries of Dulgerdeen and increased this by reminding his council that he once swore he would burn the forest to its core if he ever got free of the waste lands, or so that was the story he fed his council to hide his anxiety.

The stripping of the sacred trees was a harsh reminder to Gazzel that Lanos leniency had shrunk in his exile. The Kurlezzias were proud creatures and gifted with tactical skills in battle that were unmatched by any army Lano had ever seen. Their awareness and love of the hunt gave the Kurlezzia's great admirers and respect among the forest creatures, so much, they crowned Gazzel king of the forest. But Lano knew the key component to shatter the Kurlezzia's tactical advantages, 'fire', he remembered his old mentor Elan explaining to him when the flamed phoenix sought to claim the forest and use it as a base before attacking the Swans Sanctuary.

''Trees are strong under the ground because their roots are concealed deep beneath the surface. Their strength decreases when uprooted and left to stand alone making them vulnerable. How? You may ask, well water can bend them if applied with enough force, air can lift them and twist them, but fire can slither through its bark and destroy every barrier in its way and erase them for good, remember my disciple it takes more than force to shatter a wall,'' Lano recalled Elan instructing him.

The council had pleaded with Lano to charge into Dulgerdeen and show his full power, but he refused, knowing only one thing would frighten the Kurlezzias, and that was setting a blaze to the weaker parts of the forest. Which would cause the Kurlezzias enough concern to charge with their full strength to the scene. And they did just that, charging through the trees with their hooves whistling in the air and their bamboos held tight within their thin lips. Gazzel quickly realised he had fallen into a trap. When Lano revealed himself, he knew his reappearance was enough to sustain any further conflict. Respectively Lano offered the Mythical King the choice of joining him or death.

Unyielding but unwilling, Gazzel offered no assurances to Lanos offer but requested a pardon of leave to allow his council of Kurlezzias a shade to think over the terms of his offer. "The stubbornness of a leader," was Lanos first thought, a trait even he could not argue with. Knowing he could have forced Gazzel with threats of fire or death, Lano decided to act with his logic, as angered out bursts were no longer his style.

Patience was Lano's new weapon of choice when he considered the matter. He dismissed Gazzel but warned him he would wait no longer than the shade he had granted. Brute force would have gained him the recruitments he wanted. However, leaning too heavily would gain him little trust among his supporters and would leave a seed of doubt in his mind, that his followers only supported him through fear instead of loyalty. It was an impulse Lano did not want among his camp, especially if he were to succeed where last he had failed. Distrust had been his misguide during his first attempt at recruiting an army and leading with similar qualities and was why his followers disbanded and fled when the war turned in the wizard's favour. For no creature was going to die for a leader who inflicts fear upon those he wishes to command. The bitter taste of defeat combined with the looks of so many empty, lost, and defeated faces blurred his thoughts. Lano's experience in defeat hit him hardest at that moment and even now would cease his breath when the look of failure consumed his thinking. But through the losses a lesson had been learned one Lano felt he needed to feel in his quest to once again rise and rule Nocktar.

Lano stood still as a tree while listening to the sounds of the rain lashing from the dark clouds surrounding the forest. He watched as the raindrops trickled down the broken and shattered rocks that lay scattered opposite the stream. Which was once a cave beneath a waterfall that had belonged to the exile wizard, Carka the Static. The wizard who had escaped Dulgerdeen thanks to Dreaquirlas lapse. Been honest with himself, Lano had never expected Dreaquirla to capture nor defeat Carka. It was painfully obvious Carka was in a league of his own when it came down to knowledge and power. But Dreaquirla did force the ageing wizard to flee Dulgerdeen and that was enough to quench Lanos desire. He knew with Carka out of the picture Dulgerdeen was vulnerable. The wizards Dreaquirla had scorched to death had wiped away every magical enchantment casted over the shades by Carka giving him a free pass into the wizard's cave.

Standing in silence Lano felt he should be glad but the thoughts of Carka and Bregit roaming free, caused him stress. Two wizards turned rogue abiding to laws of their own were dangerous and unpredictable. Bregit had already shown his skills first-hand, exposing his army and escaping his clutches. Thanks to his alliance with Tip-Karp, Lano now had a measure of Bregit's plan. It confirmed Bregit was going to the tail of the Cloud Stair to warn the king of his resurrection. But like all who have seen all, Lano knew the king was no fool. However, he was confident of the king's ignorance, especially in the matters of war. The king had proven in the wars fighting against the Aqua Guardians that his mind wasn't so easily turned by persuasion. That same war was what crippled a sizeable part of the Seven Coloured Army. Many lords of lands even cut their ties with the crown over the peace treaty the king signed to end the indifference between the sea creatures and the wizards. For the treaty pardoned Tarlbok the Aqua Chief and his allies for countless murders of innocent wizards and unrepairable damage to many lands. It was Tip-Karp who interfered when the king had the opportunity to wipe the Aqua Guardians out but refused and instead allowed the sphinx to lay out peace terms that concluded the war. The terms of the treaty were never shared only Tip-Karp, the king and Tarlbok know the true extent of the agreed terms but whatever they were ended the great war and ignited a peace between the Aqua Guardians and the Wizards. But the lords of lands didn't approve with this treaty and many loyal supporters to the crown refused to be a part of the king's new regime. For many believed the treaty made the wizards appear weak, a trait never shown by any wizard king.

Now the king's mistake would become his ultimate failure. The lack of allies loyal to the crown was the crack Lano had been waiting for and with his reinstated army and the addition of the Kurlezzias and Rear Clars, Lano was able to slip right through those cracks and obliterate the fist the wizards used to squash and force the mystical creatures down to their knees. But with Carka's escape Lanos hand was forced, his intended strike would need to come quicker than he'd wanted, much to the delight of his vengeance fuelled generals. Their lust for revenge grew deep, to prolong their desires further would no doubt lead to a break of command. A thread Lano knew was slipping from his grasp.

The forest didn't agree with half of his army especially the Varwels. With no space to stretch their wings they grew restless sitting among bare trees. Ockrupver who was dependant on sea water became dehydrated with the growing temperatures and needed to travel far and wide to reach the nearest sea for assurances. Tricklet was growing bored that he had stopped making Jaed chase him over dulling his senses whenever he tried falling asleep.

Deep in thought Lano slowly opened his eyes the weight of his brows growing with the lack of sleep he was forcing himself not to indulge, with his meditated trance broken. Lano paced Carka's shattered cave ignoring the ridiculous decoration the wizard had stamped along the cave's rocks. For two shades Lano had hidden himself within the comforts of Dulgerdeen only deciding to visit the wizards cave in hope of finding a laid-out plan as to where Carka may have gone. But all he found were firefly stones and a strong stench of seaweed. Seemed Carka meant it when he detached himself from the company of wizards, even Gazzel had no idea where the ageing wizard may have scurried to. Lano recalled his questioning of the Mythical King shortly after their welcome, a welcome under a false reservation that cringed Lanos ears to hear. Knowing too well his presence among the forest brought fear especially to the creatures who despised him.

"What of it?" thought Lano, with no care to the feelings of the creatures who hid instead of aiding them in their perils. When the war is won, all mystical creatures who fought for him will be rewarded beyond their wildest dreams. Breathing in a long breath reassured a calmness Lano had forced himself to learn while forging a living roasting under the heat waves of the Wastelands. Such dreams would have to become a reality before granting rewards. Without the Lands of Light under his control he would only be known as a failure.

The sound of heavy footsteps approaching caught the Lava Keepers attention, giving him an excuse to leave the stench of Cakra's cave to see who was the latest to bring him another blow. The rain continued to lash fiercely from the dark clouds surrounding Dulgerdeen. The heavy footsteps belonged to Kcor, the rain poured down his thick bronze skin and dripped down his furred face and bronze mane. He walked with a strut, his giant paws clenched making his muscles visible and his expression sour.

"My lord, Alacoma and Dirren have arrived in Larmont and are setting up a base just outside the borders of Bregit's tower," said Kcor halting his stride inches from where Lano stood.

A slight shock raised his brows. "Unexpected," he hissed. "They arrived quicker than I anticipated," Lano hissed.

"Perhaps the drive that fuels you has infected the rest of the council," said Kcor his voice injected with a low growl.

The rain and wind pelted from the clouds. Though he was a creature of fire Lano valued the effects of rain because it guaranteed conversations were unlikely to be overheard and having spent three cycles of shade in blistering heat rain to Lano wasn't so bad.

"Larmont has many passageways in and out, Bregit had his Slither friends dig routes that would lead him directly into his tower. A tower which is layered in the melted coats of every Pin-Far he killed might make it impossible to enter," Lano sighed deeply rubbing the drops of icy rain from his mouth.

"One tower compared to an entire land which stretches beyond sight seems a great stab against the wizards if I must speak openly, my lord," said Kcor.

"I know you wanted to be the one to reclaim Larmont, but you are needed here, rest assured Kcor it will be reinstated to you once the Lands of Light are back under my control," hissed Lano.

"I understand my lord, my kin will be pleased to know they will be returning home once we rid Nocktar of the wizards," said Kcor in a low growl.

"Are the armies ready for march?" asked Lano.

"Yes. My lord, we have measured our armies and have trained tirelessly. The Seven-Coloured Army will not easily breach our defences. My only concerns are the ariel attacks from the clouds above. If I may be honest the Varwels will not hold out long enough for us to generate.......,''

"Enough," hissed Lano warningly. "The plan goes as instructed and as my leading general you will obey my orders."

Kcors eyes fell to the ground, not wanting to upset Lano further he stood still while the lashing rain beat against him fiercely, but the proud and loyal Viledirk remained quiet as an ounce of regret crawled up Lanos conscience.

"My apologies Kcor," said Lano his hiss less intense by his gratitude. "Take yourself to base and refresh, our march will begin soon, and I want my armies well prepped before march!''

Kcor accepted his dismissal with no argument, his broad figure walked into the darkness of the forest until he was swallowed completely leaving Lano alone in the lashing rain. Moments after Kcor left a large shadow flashed across the moon as a winged creature landed in front of the dismantled cave the pouring rain silencing the large creatures landing.

"Tip-Karp, how pleasant of you to answer my summons I must admit I would have chosen suitable accommodations for our meeting, but I sense a distrust in the air of Dulgerdeen and one cannot be too careful when conveying messages in private wouldn't you agree,'' hissed Lano his forked tongue licking his cheeks.

The sphinx's sharp silver gaze stared at Lano as he folded his wings by his side. "That would depend on the company engaging in that conversation," answered Tip-Karp delicately.

"I am thankful for your coming, I will not linger on niceties we have much to discuss and little drops to do it,'' hissed Lano.

Tip-Karp kept silent, but Lano could tell even with his back turned his head was being turned to the entrance of Carka's cave.

"Good, as you already know I plan to strike the Bay of Bones within the turn of next shade, but I cannot hope to claim victory without your assistance," hissed Lano.

"I plan to fight alongside you there was never any hesitant on my part, you have my sworn word I will fight and die alongside you if needs be,'' Tip-Karp said with assurance.

"No! You will play a greater role in my plan, having reflected on your argument about the wizard's home advantage. I cannot guarantee victory if the wizards have a stronghold to retreat to especially if I cannot penetrate its defences," Lano said firmly.

"I don't quite understand my lord, are you implying we destroy the Golden Kingdom?'' asked Tip-Karp frowning.

"That is exactly what I am implying. And you are the only creature who can do it, destiny has brought you to my side for this particular course of action.''

"You are asking me to abandon the laws of my kin and use their design for a cause of destruction. The foundation which it was built was to use it for the benefit of honourable deeds and not for the basis of war,'' said Tip-Karp firmly.

"All I'm seeing is a scared creature unwilling to do his masters bidding, which indicates your still on the side of the wizards,'' hissed Lano coldly. "The Wall of Illusion can only be passed through by a sphinx without you to function it my plan cannot be fulfilled. I understand the laws you follow and what it means but think about what could happen if it succeeds?'' pleaded Lano.

''You are asking me to disregard all my beliefs and be forever a traitor to my kind, I am uncertain that this course of action is worth that. We sphinxes are honourable and proud, to do what you ask will stain me forever,'' said Tip-Karp.

''This great war may be the last in Nocktars history and the end to the wizards hold over our lands, if breaking one law to achieve this peace isn't worth the risk then why have you joined when knowing full well the laws, I have broken to get us to this position,'' Lano hissed angrily.

Tip-Karp stood in the pouring rain looking up at the white moon deep in thought. When he spoke, he did it with a sigh in each word. ''Such a journey will mean I must leave at once; the wall was built beyond the horizon and out to sea I may not get there by the shade you reach the Cloud Stair,'' Tip-Karp said unsure.

''Gather the Gliders and before you leave Tip-Karp I wish to be consulted on what you have planned, now go before I lose my patience,'' Lano hissed in frustration as he watched the great sphinx take to the sky.

Chapter 17

The Red Prince

Lucifer had brought Galli and Bregit to a tower which was small in comparison to Bregit's and was made of stone that had a wooden door with no handle. Lucifer waved his staff at the door making it magically opened and led the wizards inside. Marching them up a flight of stairs that had a wide circular room at the top. When Bregit and Galli entered the room, they caught the fragrance of roses right away. The walls were decorated in different coloured roses that were enchanted to give off the same fragrance as real roses.

"It's not much but to keep your arrival private this is the best I can offer under the circumstances," said Lucifer with a tight-lipped smile.

"It's fine," said Bregit, "but how long will the king be absent? We haven't travelled here to be treated as prisoners," said Bregit.

"Should I remind you Bregit the circumstances on which you left your duties to your king, because if you prefer, we can walk to his temple and see what the coven has to make of your return," said Lucifer.

Bregit pierced Lucifer with a cold look that heightened Lucifers morale as both wizards stared at the other with exchanged looks of joy and hate.

"Bregit's right, we must meet with the king, and we haven't a drop to waste. Surely, you have guessed we didn't come here for a holiday," said Galli.

Lucifer looked away from Bregit to stare at Galli with a charming gaze that made her feel uncomfortable. "I will see what I can do, but you must know my father doesn't like to be rushed, I will return momentarily," Lucifer said as he made his way to the stairway.

Both wizards gave him a nod as Lucifer left the room and when he reached the bottom, they heard him shutting the doors once he was outside. Then a clicking sound confirmed Lucifer had recanted the spell that he used to prevent outsiders entering his tower.

"I don't trust that Lucifer," Galli admitted. "There's a sly look hiding behind that charming smile of his," she said shooting Bregit a look of annoyance by how relaxed he appeared.

"Your concerns may prove correct, but for now young Galli allow yourself some valuable space to recollect some strength. We have both travelled a long distance and the road indeed wasn't kind," said Bregit his voice exhausted.

Galli's eyes narrowed with frustration toward Bregit's ignorance, as if she could forget the journey here but even their escape from Duxpice wasn't going to sway her concerns.

"If the king has left Lucifer in charge, he has full control over the Golden Kingdom," said Galli. "He could if he wished, keep us locked in here for shades and I'd bet Water Dancer, that door won't open unless it's that two faced sprite's voice giving the order," said Galli her voice flared with a sharp tone.

"If the king is away," he said with a firm calmness to his tone. "Then I am confident it has some bearing to Lano or one of his council members," said Bregit stiffly.

"I don't feel safe here," said Galli honestly, keeping her eyes firmly on the staircase.

"You have nothing to fear while inside this tower, I assure you," said Bregit in a weary tone.

"How can you be so relaxed; Lucifer could be plotting our demise right now while he has us trapped here?" protested Galli.

Bregit sighed a deep exhausted sigh before sitting down on a chair that lay against the tower wall. He looked at Galli with a serious gaze. "Lucifer the Red is the king's son, which means he is forced to obey the laws of his father's kingdom. Laws, that prevent Lucifer murdering two innocent wizards without a fair trial, and ....", Bregit stopped to inhale, "ensuring that if Lucifer did attempt to kill us, it would cause a break in line that keeps peace between wizards," stated Bregit.

Galli tried to swallow what Bregit told her with a grain of hope that it would soothe her paranoia, but it only added more questions to her theories. "And what would happen if we were murdered in this room, I doubt any wizard among the clouds would say a word against their king's son?"

"If that line is ever broken, war won't be long replacing those broken threads," said Bregit in a matter-of-fact tone before laying back on his chair.

Galli looked at him seriously, his eyes were closed but his voice was stern. The forever ageing face was non-expressive as Bregit sat snugly on the wooden chair, his arms folded, and eyes firmly shut.

"When I last ignored my gut instincts, I watched my home and kin be destroyed and I have that same feeling now," Galli confessed. "Lorneid ignored me then and you are doing the same, but you slip off to sleep, I will wait even if it means waiting all shade," she said stubbornly.

"As you must," yawned Bregit falling into a welcoming sleep.

Feeling the straining aches rush up her spine, Galli allowed her body to sit on a wooden chair on the opposite side of Bregit. The moment Galli's backside touched the back of the chair she felt a hot radiation shoot through her like a loosed arrow, warming her insides instantly. 'Seems comfort is hidden everywhere among the Golden Kingdom,' Galli thought feeling a twinge of jealously as her sores and tiredness were replaced by blissed comfort.

The thoughts of Lucifer plotting to deceive her and Bregit now felt ludicrous. Even imagining herself been taken from her comfort zone and locked in a dungeon made her giggle which surprised Galli, because she couldn't remember any moment in her life that she had allowed herself to giggle, but right now in this moment of bliss, feeling embarrassed for acting silly just made Galli laugh out like a clueless Ripeling. This rare feeling didn't last long, because the feeling of loss cannot be so easily laughed aside and with little to distract her, Galli sat back on her chair with the daunting memories of all those she would never see again consumed her thoughts.

Dwelling on what her remaining kin were up to now living inside Tip-Karps Mountain. The last she spoke to them they seemed fine and were distracting themselves by forging weapons from the mountain's rocks. This was the reason Galli instructed Kikitil to live within the mountain for it was a strong fortress incapable of been breached. But the loss of so many lives had shaken the Blue Wizards and with everything they held close now either dead or destroyed it was a miracle trauma wasn't their escape from the pain.

So deep in thought, Galli didn't notice she'd dug her nails deep into her hands, "Anger shields pain," she remembered Lorneid telling her on many occasions after he would disarm her and knock her off her feet during their private lessons. Lorneid as usual was right but even pain could not cure what froze her insides and swelled her throat. Because this kind of pain couldn't be erased by antidotes or kind words. But would only cease when the bringer of death to her kin pays for its crimes. A vow Galli intended on upholding until fulfilled. Focusing her powers of concentrating to remain awake until Lucifer returned. Galli had now convinced herself Lucifer wasn't trustworthy, and knew no matter what Bregit said, there was something sly in Lucifer's charming smirk.

Listening to Bregit's tame snores tickle against her ear drums, she knew each vibration meant she was still awake. Keeping her mind occupied she rotated her eyes side to side up and down, examining Lucifer's room. There were no windows, only see-through curtains hanging over a large bed laying on the other side of the room. The stone floor was filled with furry skins that were lined and stitched to appear as a carpet. Jars made of green glass sat on oaken shelves that contained thick strawberry blonde candles.

Every wall of the chamber had two shelves with a jar a piece sitting on the shelves centre. What interested Galli about them was every candle lasted a lifetime because for as long as she could remember the candle was lit when they had entered the room but strangely it didn't decrease in size. Apart from the two chairs the wizards occupied Galli found the room to be quite bare. The candle's scents and the enchanted roses filled the chamber with the smell of damp that reminded Galli of the saltwater smell back home, each swift line of grey smoke that passed by her stuffy nose filled her mind with refreshing thoughts of waves crashing against rocks.

"The sound of the sea," she whispered softly to herself feeling drowsy.

The twinkling flames dancing on top of the candles kept Galli's eyes alive and steady as sleep's tight claws began plunging through her tired mind, desperately trying to anchor its position. Drops passed slowly, each one that passed making Galli more willing to sleep. Even though she was strong willed and hard reared. Galli was no match against the extreme powers of sleep. And she unknowingly dropped her guard and sunk into a dream state too extreme to withdraw. The fumes consuming her mind, awakening memories of her beloved home as visions of Treforledge whole and undamaged were the last clear images to fill Galli's drowsy mind before she slipped into a heavy sleep.

The sound of thousands of voices stampeded through Galli's ears as she felt herself been lifted by many hands to the roar of thunderous applause that shook the ground beneath her. Water Dancer was held aloft in her right hand and Mirror in the other, she lifted them above her head a feeling of triumph filling her with radiant pride. An arena had formed, surrounding Galli and the admiring wizards carrying her. It was full of multi-coloured wizards who waved and cheered to her victory as they looked admirably at her, chanting her name, and making Galli feel like she was the greatest wizard alive. But then the sound of hissing echoed through the arena silencing the chants, each drop that passed the echo of Galli's name died faintly and were replaced by low gasps of fear. All those cheerful eyes had sunken, becoming wide and fearful as they stared at the round entrance of the arena waiting in anguish for what lurked behind to reveal itself.

Shadows crawled out behind the veil licking against the walls of the arena while spreading its poisonous spores along everything it touched. Its appearance caused the wizards holding Galli to drop her and scatter like a pixie to flame, leaving her alone to face this growing shadow. Puffs of black smoke spit through the veil at the opposite end of the arena filling the nostrils of Galli who hid her nose with the sleeves of her cloak to shield herself from the stench of death. A pair of scarlet eyes beamed brightly through the veil of wispy smoke, and before Galli could react it had formed into the cloud who killed Lorneid.

Cold chills radiated from the cloud as Galli stood transfixed by what she was seeing, as a mouth surfaced inches under the blood red eyes of the cloud. It barred its spiked teeth while hissing viciously at Galli as it moved slowly into the arena not once taking its evil glare away from its prey.

Alone but not afraid, Galli about to react surprisingly found she couldn't lift her arms, they had become numb along with the rest of her body due to been exposed to the clouds freezing aura. Paralyzed! Galli knew it was done and that there was no escape, because without the means to defend herself death would be her only prize in this duel. Every drop that passed the cloud got closer, and with it the realism of her faith. The hammering in her chest convinced Galli she was frightened, but she refused to look away, if she was going to die then she owed it to herself to stare her killer in the face. When the cloud was inches from her skin, Galli felt a burning feeling pulling her mind from one place to the other. For a moment Galli could see herself in an arena and in a blink of an eye she was in a room made of stone which made no sense because she didn't have the power to be in two places at once. The hissing laugh grew louder in her ears but the burning sensation spreading through her arms and legs were too great to overcome and with a great heave Galli felt a throbbing pain erupt inside her head so fast, she could feel the blood in her head beat against her rapid skull. Darkness filled her clouded sight as her lungs swelled and her insides felt like a Viledirk was gripping them in their firm grasp. The only feeling besides suffocating and her insides been strangled was a chilling feeling growing throughout her arms and legs.

Heaving like she'd just been sucked through a vortex, Galli's eyes bulged open; her mouth gasping in lungsful of warm air as she wretched and spat most of her insides onto a stone floor. Breathing fast, Galli looked around and found herself no longer in an arena about to be killed by a cloud but in an inferior situation than the one she had just left. Shackles made of thick steel were painfully cuffed around her wrists and ankles pinning Galli against a stone-cold wall.

Which explained the cold chills running along her arms and legs, but not the dream Galli had just awoken from and how frighteningly real it had felt. Her first instinct was to look for Bregit. And she didn't have to look far because he was pinned against the same stonewall, she was and cuffed in shackles. Except there was one difference. Bregit hung loosely above the stone lined floor with black lines of drool trickling down his heaving mouth as low rasps of cloggy breath told Galli he was having difficulty breathing. Confused, Galli moved her eyes from the hanging drool sliding from Bregit's mouth to his lower body, to her horror deep gashes were slit down his arms and legs, which had traces of magic left upon them, meaning wizards had tortured Bregit but the mystery was why?

Tugging at her own cuffs Galli found them unmoveable and whined when she felt a hot burning sensation singe her skin whenever she put any pressure on the shackles. In that moment Galli realised the trap she had foolishly allowed herself to fall into, what stung her worse was the annoyance she felt toward herself for foolishly dropping her guard and listening to restraining words especially after what had happened in Treforledge. Annoyed and frustrated, Galli in a panicked state cried out to Bregit.

''Bregit, Bregit, Bregit!'' she called in a tremulous voice, which echoed along the walls of the gloomy room.

Feeling useless was becoming a common occurrence for Galli in near death situations. Because yet again she was forced to watch while another wizard suffered and what was worse, she was unable to help. Drawing her eyes away from Bregit's state, Galli looked around in search for any means of escape. Observing the room more keenly she noticed brackets spraying weak rays of red flame that gave off a glim view of the room she was imprisoned. Round and wide with a curved ceiling that blended perfectly together formed in an oval shape room that was filled with rows of wooden chairs barely visible due to Galli's blurred vision. Brackets were nailed along the walls holding thick logs that were alight with weak flames that sprayed waves of red light, giving the room a gloomy aura. Oaken seats with thick arms and comfortable white cushions patched along their front were lined in rows and held in line by thin chains. The chairs had symbols carved into their frames, but Galli was unable to name them having never seen them before. Another row of chairs sat on the stone floor cocooned within the swirling rows of wooden chairs that excelled to the very top of the room. The silver chairs were made of gray stones and had swirling lines chiselled along its narrow arms and legs. The silver chairs looped around a golden throne which nested perfectly in the centre of the silver and wooden chairs, making it visible for every chair holder to see. The throne was made of pure gold and was wide enough to sit a sphinx. Galli had never seen a throne before and wondered was it of the king's own design. Sharp golden spikes longer than Galli's fingers stuck out through the throne's arms and frame with silver thorns sprouted from its pillars while golden leaves sprinkled along the floor, forming a round carpet that kept the throne a fair distance away from the silver chairs.

A sudden unexpected vibration erupted throughout the room snapping Galli to her senses. The walls to her left suddenly split apart revealing a thin line of yellow light that lit up the room instantly. The departed walls slid into hidden slots. Causing vibrations to frequently shudder through Galli's body and caused her shackles to press hard against her wrists and singe her skin so deep she could smell her burning flesh trail through her nostrils. When the walls were fully detached and hidden the room came into full view thanks to the glistening rays of light coming from behind the detached walls. The sound of approaching footsteps filled Galli's ears. With no Water Dancer or means to prepare herself, all she could do was hang there and wait nervously for what was about to enter the room.

Red was the colour that filled Galli's blue eyes when the beat of drumming footsteps entered the stone room. A dozen Red Wizards lined in a row broke through the mystifying wall of yellow haze surrounding the gap between the divided walls. They wore heavy knitted cloaks with long sleeves that had lines of sunset yellow trailing along the sides of their cloaks and sleeves with a hint of charcoal grey stained along the ends of their sleeves and neck space. Their hair was scarlet red, combed, and laid down to waist length with not a crease or split end in sight making Galli's own hair look horribly out of sorts. Their staffs were made of oaken wood and tanned in brown with streaks of blood red swiped along the top, middle, and bottom. At the tip of each staff were three reddish pink leaves and a scarlet ruby placed neatly in the staff's centre top.

None of the Red Wizards looked nor glanced in Galli or Bregit's direction, instead they simply walked through the rows of chairs and settled themselves in the far row at the back. Sitting with their backs not touching the ends of their chair and waiting in silence.

Then came the Orange Wizards who slowly appeared through the detached wall. They were thin with crooked backs and all of them wearing grumpy expressions. Galli watched them; they were smaller than an average wizard and with them came a powerful fragrance of moss scented perfume that seemed to linger at their footsteps. Bright and colourful was the trademark of the Orange Wizards of Tindisinge. Galli remembered their manner very well having endured Corlock the Orange's taunting during her army's battle in last cycle of shades Ultimate Colour. They wore light silk apricot garments covering their bodies head to foot with tight carrot orange neck and waistbands; they walked in a thin line following Corlock into the stone chamber and took their seats in the row in front of the Red Wizards.

Unlike their red counter parts, the Orange Wizards all looked at Galli with deep loathing, their sharp eyes piercing her like daggers as they passed by her and Bregit. Galli wasn't surprised by this reaction; she did publicly embarrass the entire orange army by reducing their most powerful technique the Exploding Lantern to dust and forced Corlock to submit in front of the watching Golden Kingdom because she had decided against killing him. What the Orange Wizards didn't understand was Galli's true intentions were to save as many wizards she could from dying, this tactic didn't however go down well with her opponents who felt Galli did what she did to embarrass her opposition. Even though she did save more than she killed during her rise to the Ultimate Colour triumph. The shame of been defeated by a foreign army and so easily out witted by simple tactics created a deep hatred between the wizards of Tindisinge and Treforledge.

Drops passed with nothing but silence filling the atmosphere. Then without warning a haze of yellow swept along the stone floor as tapping footsteps echoed along the chamber's walls filling every ear drum with their annoying sound. Through the shadowy mist came the bright and beautiful Yellow Wizards. Everything about them was fascinating, their wavy thin blonde hair that was braided and rumoured to be strong enough to withstand any climate without getting damaged. They wore skin-tight garments that stuck to their skin making them appear thinner. The blue stain splashed along the ends of their clothes was to stand for water, pure, and untouched, the centre was a lime green that signified ground unburned and free to grow and the bright rays of yellow light that shone brighter than the yellow wizards face signalled a new permanent colour that the Yellow Wizards strongly believed will consume them all and shed light on everything. They moved into the room quietly with such agility Galli barely seen them enter, their pace was remarkable as all twelve wizards had moved through the dungeon past the rows of red- and orange-coloured wizards with ease. When they were seated in their chairs all yellow eyes looked at Galli and Bregit with a curious stare before resuming their passive unnerved expressions.

The temperature in the room had suddenly intensified, the arrival of the Yellow Wizards spreading a powerful aura throughout the stone room that made the air refreshing. Their depth head bowed to its lieutenants before joining the other silver chair holders in the seven-seated circle.

"Court," thought Galli. That's where she was, in a court room. And sure, enough these were the high ranked wizards of the Golden Kingdom and the coven silver chair holders. And judging from her own perspective her and Bregit were no doubt the ones on trial.

The Blue Wizards were next to enter the courtroom, they wore heavy and shabby midnight blue robes with small glowing white stars decorating their cloaks which stood for the Blue Wizard's beliefs in the stars and their purposes. They wore triangular sea blue coloured paintings on both sides of their faces which matched their gentle eyes. They strutted through the courtroom with their silver staffs glossed in streaks of sky blue with blueberry-coloured leaves attached to one another at the staffs top that had a star shaped stone concealed within the leaves. They took turns looking from Galli to Bregit, showing no sign of concerns and they followed in the same manner as the others and took their seats in front of the Orange Wizards. And like the others the blue depth head general broke away and seated herself beside the yellow depth head general and Corlock in the circle of silver chairs.

Galli didn't have to wait to know what-coloured wizards would be next to enter the courtroom, it was obvious. Their stomps could be heard through the echoes of the room. It was the same sound that drummed through Galli's brain when she and her army patiently awaited Leon and his army. Galli had learned from Lorneid that Leon was an expert in mind games and always delayed his arrival to raise the pressure on his opponents. The fumes fabricated throughout the courtroom were wiped away by the cold temperatures coming from the arrival of Leon and his sour faced Black Wizards, who were muscular and broad with torn garments of buckled black cloaks with the sleeves cut and used to strap the bottoms of their cloaks to their ankles. Their hair was waxed together with blended spits of Woltondox and Tweedly plants juices that when fused creates a permanent sticky gel that can make soft objects rock solid which is how the Black Wizards made their hair hard and shiny. Their combined presence gave off a radiant flow throughout the courtroom, which created a tense atmosphere. The Black Wizard's cold eyes were filled with dislike. Leon stared at many of his fellow wizards wondering the same thing they were and that was why were they here. Leon nodded to his lieutenants to sit while he moved slowly toward Galli a satisfied smirk creasing his perfect features.

"Well, well, seems the little rodent got herself arrested," mocked Leon his voice cold. "Tut, tut," he jested, while relishing in Bregit's state. "I'm all for torture but to embarrass my victims is displeasing and not a style I would use to incriminate my victims, but my brother must have his reasons, I dare say we'll find out soon enough," Leon laughed, turning his back to Galli, and moving toward the circle of silver chairs.

Leon sat beside Corlock. Both wizards wearing satisfied grins as they gawked at Galli, relishing at her position, and watching as she absorbed the sinking feeling of humiliation. A feeling both generals endured by her hand, and because Leon and Corlock were proud warriors and defeat was hard for them to accept especially to a foreigner with next to no skills in the arts of war.

When every wizard was seated a sudden burst of flames erupted beneath the golden throne. Within drops smoke darker than Leon's waxed hair formed within the circle of crimson flames and in a breath the flames vanished. The smoke remained hoovering above the leaves shifting and growing in length until a figure tall and thin materialized. When the smoke cleared a wizard decorated in red robes walked out of the smoke. Every detail about this wizard made Galli's insides bubble with a murderous rage that made her bones shake in anger. Lucifer snapped his thin fingers. The sound echoed throughout the courtroom as the smug face bearing a sweet smile took his place in the centre of the courtroom sitting upon the golden throne. Lucifer's eyes found Galli, but he didn't stare for long, but turned his scarlet eyes to Bregit whose condition satisfied the Red Wizard. Lucifer cleared his throat and looked around the chamber with a quick count and was pleased his summons had been answered.

"My coven chair holders and depth heads, I thank you for coming. You have been summoned to court to bear witness to what happens to deserters who enter our sacred kingdom expecting us to simply forgive and forget their treasonous crimes," said Lucifer, his sweet voice replaced by a strident tone. "Laws were enforced by our elders to secure the safety and survival of our race and without order we are no better than the savages living beneath our feet!"

"As you can see under his long damp hair, hangs Bregit the Yellow the false Lord of Larmont and banisher of Gliders. False titles claimed by a traitor to my father and all who sit here. For those who don't know his companion to his right is Galli the Blue, general of the blue army of Treforledge and victor of last cycle of shades Ultimate Colour," announced Lucifer his firm voice carrying along the courtroom.

A ringing sound of booing echoed through the courtroom and Galli noticed Lucifer give off a slight smirk before half heartily raising his hand to silence the jeering wizards.

"She is innocent and untouched, but I felt as a companion of a traitor she too shall be put on trial and punished accordingly. But first let us deal with the matter of treason and the penalty its bearing has on those who are foolish enough to indulge in its temptation. In our ancient tradition I will offer my silver chair holders the floor to give their individual opinions on the matter and when all holders have spoken, I will as the judge put all arguments into consideration before giving my final decision," declared Lucifer.

Lucifer opened his hands and welcomed the depth heads to speak openly. The Yellow Wizard of the silver chair circle stood up first, slowly rising to her full height the wizard's bright eyes stared motionlessly at Lucifers gesture and spoke in a raspy voice.

"Bregit the Yellow has to my knowledge been lord of Larmont for several cycles of shades. Now if I knew this surely my superiors were aware of Bregit's position? Larmont is one of many lands governed under the king's watch. My point being, if we brand Bregit a traitor then why has it taken so long for his arrest, everyone knew where he ruled," she said it slowly deliberately intending to drag her words. "Adding to my argument, Bregit has no army and poses no threat to this kingdom. I say declare him innocent of these absurd allegations and allow us to get back to work," she finished receiving many dirty looks by the other silver chair holders as she resumed her seat.

"Thank you Pally, your statement will be taken into consideration," said Lucifer who didn't appear to have listened to a single word she'd said.

The blue depth head was next to rise from its chair; it took a placid look toward Bregit which showed Galli that this wizard was indeed a believer in principle. Before speaking the Blue Wizard cleared its throat.

"Two wars have come and gone since I was mature enough to understand. Old my body has become yet my mind still is as young as ever and if my memory serves me correctly. Bregit the Yellow orchestrated the defence of many lands during those wars and risked his own life on many occasions to protect the Golden Kingdom. I strongly believe he must have had a concrete reason for leaving his duties and I will as a member of the coven and as the king's personal advisor plead that Bregit be allowed the chance to speak instead of this ludicrous tactic to belittle a wizard who's reward for his services is to be treated like a common criminal," said the blue depth in a firm ringing voice.

"Your council is much appreciated Meriyoi, your request will be brought forward once every coven member has had its say," said Lucifer his eyes twitching as he gawked at Meriyoi resuming her seat.

Corlock stood up next and spoke proudly to Lucifer in the same pleasant tone he would use in the presence of the king. "Traitors should by law be treated as the law written by our ancestors intended. If one traitor can escape justice, then what is to stop me or any other wizard in this room from simply abandoning our duties? I ask the coven to renounce the laws of our forbearers and use this traitor as a prime example to all, that oaths are sacred, and life bound and not so easily tossed to the wind to live a life in solitude,'' said Corlock in an orotund voice.

Corlock's tone was appeasing, and his statement satisfied Lucifer along with many smiling orange and black wizards sitting in the crowd.

''Your statement will be put forward once the last of the depth heads have spoken,'' said Lucifer giving Corlock a look of agreement.

Leon rose from his chair looking at Galli with his black eyes unmoved and filled with darkness. ''If we as law enforcers allow traitors to escape justice, I fear the stability of our foundations will stand for nothing and show cracks in a system that has held together our specie since the shade of our elders. My father the king once compared us wizards to the unbreakable rocks of Malas! And why would he compare us to such formidable objects? After all Malas belongs to our strongest enemies beneath the Red Sea, but I waited for my father's response and was glad I did. Because he told me wizards were meant to rule. And the key to ruling was that you must be strong and fearless when it comes to decision making, even if everyone else is against it, do it, not because its right but because you believe it to be right and live with the consequences regardless the outcome of your sole decision,'' said Leon bluntly to the crowd.

Leon looked at his brother, bowed his head and resumed his seat, folding his arms and like Galli they all waited for Lucifer's decision. Lucifer sat his face in the comfort of his laid-out palms. When he lifted his perfect face, creases had smudged lines of deep thought along his brow. But Galli wasn't fooled, this was play acting at its finest and regardless of what the coven had said in Bregit's defence. Lucifer had already made his decision and seemed to joy in delaying the verdict.

Sighing deeply Lucifer's scarlet eyes looked along the circle of silver chairs. ''It would appear the Coven has a divided opinion and since it's two favours over two. The decision falls upon me, as I am in fact Depth Head General of the Red Wizards,'' said Lucifer trying to sound aggrieved to be in this situation.

Galli could feel her anger rising, it was all just a sick game to him. A plaything to entertain himself. Lucifer had known all along who would object and agree with his prosecution and used his position as Depth Head to his advantage.

''As the holder of the throne while my father resides in the west, I feel as his son he would share my views and agree that justice must be served. I strongly believe past triumphs do not shield you from breaking the law....,'' Lucifer looked at Galli with a false look of pity, before looking at Bregit who remained silent and unmoving. ''Bregit the Yellow, you are charged with oath breaking and false claiming lands that were not yours to claim. In the condition you were found in before your trial you are unable to provide the coven with any defence that may sustain my final decision......,''

''Lano the Lava keeper has returned!'' cried Galli her voice echoing throughout the courtroom.

The courtroom fell silent every wizard looked at her with worried and confused looks, as Galli looked to the blue and yellow silver chair holders with an appealing look, her heart beating rapidly in her chest. ''He's back, he destroyed

Treforledge and killed the Blue Striped Army along with Lorneid. That is why I am here….,'' but before she could finish her mouth was sealed shut by Lucifer's jinx.

Lucifer appeared out raged that Galli had interrupted his final decision, but she didn't care she had done what needed to be done.

''Before I was rudely interrupted…''

''Forget your speech,'' snapped Pally her voice fierce. ''We all heard what the young wizard said,'' and without caring what the watching wizard's thought, Pally got up from her silver chair and using her ability to move quickly she was instantly beside Galli.

Pally looked ancient from up close, her hair was shiny but through its glow Galli could see the grey lines breaking through the strands. Her face was wrinkled with ageing lines everywhere, but she wore a kindness along each line that made Galli feel assured to allow her to lift Lucifer's jinx from her lips.

''Tell us, what has happened to Lorneid?'' Pally asked kindly, her eyes looking into Galli's untrusting ones.

Galli looked around but found warm hands along her cheeks. ''Me young one just me,'' said Pally sweetly, her face splitting into a toothless grin.

''We were ambushed, a cloud darker than the pits of the sea rose from the mountains and swallowed the Blue Islands whole killing everything in its path. Lorneid and I were on the mountainside when it happened, we rushed to help but were too late. The few we managed to save now hide in the sphinx's mountain,'' she said quickly in case another jinx was cast to shut her up.

Pally looked a little shocked but her ancient eyes found no lie in Galli; she moved her warm hands from Galli's face and swiftly turned to Lucifer. ''Why wasn't this vital piece of information not shared with the Coven?''

Lucifer's eyes soured, he stared at Pally as red and yellow stared un-yielding at each other both wizards unwilling to draw away from the others gaze.

''Lano is banished from the Lands of Light, he cannot return unless my father lifts the enchantment, he cast to keep him out. He has not returned and will never again, to believe such fantasies from the mouth of a traitor and a foreigner who would have us draw out our armies to fight a battle they probably started would risk all that we have built,'' stated Lucifer.

''That is your response then, so Bregit the Yellow came here for nothing? This Blue Wizard of Treforledge who has just accounted her version of what attacked her lands and killed her lord means nothing to you?'' questioned Pally.

''I agreed with your father when he left you holder to the throne when he decided to leave his kingdom because I believed you weren't as power blind as your brother. Now I can see the roots may grow away but they still come from the same tree,'' said Pally in disgust as she walked back to her silver chair receiving a nod of approval from Meriyoi.

The ring of silence only increased the tension. Was Pally's voice powerful enough to sway the other generals to Bregit's defence or were they selfish enough to allow him to be executed?

''By law you are allowed address the king when court is in session, however when I make a decision that decision is final,'' thundered Lucifer.

"And what is your final decision?" called Leon.

"Death by execution!" Lucifer announced to the wizards in the chamber. "Guards take the prisoner to his cell where he will wait until his execution," ordered Lucifer his voice vicious.

"No!" bellowed Galli.

"Silence!" shouted Lucifer his eyes fierce. "While you have twice obstructed me while I was speaking it isn't enough to charge you, and you haven't committed any crimes to my knowledge so Galli the Blue you are free to go," announced Lucifer before storming out of the chamber without another word to anyone.

Chapter 18

The Cloud Cell

Alone in the corner of a chilly cell sat Bregit huddled dwelling on his past experiences within the confinements of his cloud cell. Sitting alone had become a custom trait for Bregit who had spent many shades alone in his youth learning banned magic that was believed unbeneficial by the king. He practiced advanced magic because he felt he owed it to his late father to enhance his magical skills. It was his father who seeded the determined desire consuming him to escape the Golden Kingdom and live a free life away from corruption. But before that realism came to surface, Bregit in his youth had been reckless and naïve, only caring about his personal agenda and elevating his position. But blocking his route to greatness was Nette, Bregit's father who always reminded his son that wizards were equal and deserved the right to live equally among each other. But Bregit pushed his father's speeches aside, unknowing, and uncaring toward the sufferings of others. But like all blind fools, Bregit had to suffer to realise it was an illusion he was living in and how fragile he had been to have allowed the system he served to hoodwink him.

Bregit recalled during his father's ceremony just how right he had been. When the upcoming Ultimate Colour came around, he was by laws of grievance excused from the competition. While watching each battle unfold, Bregit felt sickened to the core at the joy the cheering wizards expressed by watching their fellow wizards kill one another.

''Killing wizards is wrong and by the laws of nature evil,'' his father would drum into his head when they were safe within the confinements of their chambers.

When the tournament concluded Bregit seen clearly that he was the fool and his father the unsighted. Watching the fallen wizards of the Ultimate Colour been cremated and tossed to the wind, pulled the curtain from his brow, and opened his eyes to the dangerous truth. Knowing he couldn't confide the truth with anyone, he instead began researching the origins of the first wizards hoping he could find the reasons behind the creation of the Ultimate Colour. Using his position as Depth Head General to gain access to the archive of scrolls kept within the king's temple. Bregit found what he expected to find and left it at that, knowing in his mind that if there were secrets among the coven, they wouldn't be left lying around for wizards to see. So Bregit sought ways to escape safely from the Golden Kingdom and it wasn't until the following cycle of shade that the opportunity presented itself and as the beaten down wizard sat against the cells chilling wall Bregit recalled clearly how he gained his freedom from servitude.

It was the shade Meriyoi the Blue was stripped of her colour and power by Dirm the Bronze in front of the silver chair holders. Only the prince Nzer the Purple defended Meriyoi during her public humiliation. But the young prince's attempts to spare Meriyoi further torment were folly. Because every wizard present knew Dirm would never forgive Meriyoi especially when her crime was defilement. It had been discovered and proven that Meriyoi had been mating with an Aqua Guardian. A crime forbidden by both species and one they condemned unnatural. Many that shade witnessed degrading in the cruellest of forms as Meriyoi suffered greatly at the hands of Dirm.

What was worse, Bregit, Nzer and all the silver chair holders, were forced to watch as proof to what becomes of any wizard who break the laws of wizards. After finishing inflicting his punishment, Dirm sentenced Meriyoi to death on the dawn of the coming shade. Nzer been the prince was allowed special privileges and got to visit Meriyoi in her cell. It was that shade Bregit's life changed forever. For he too had abandoned his king's rule and gone to visit Meriyoi, having grown up with Meriyoi he found her an intelligent wizard and a good friend, Bregit decided it best to say farewell in private and not before been blasted into dust. But little did he know what he was about to hear on his visit to Meriyoi's cell would change his life forever.

''Nzer my dear friend, I need you now more than ever,'' cried Meriyoi, her voice reaching Bregit's ears as he stood at the end of the cell block concealed by the shadows of the night.

''Hush!'' breathed Nzer softly trying to keep Meriyoi calm. ''I cannot sway my father's mind; he will kill me if he finds out I have been to see you,'' he whispered.

''He can have my life if that is what he wants. Because I no longer value it, but it is not my life I crave to save this shade,'' sobbed Meriyoi.

''Why do you surrender so easily if you clearly have hope of saving others?'' asked Nzer.

''I care for another now,'' cried Meriyoi. ''A life flowers within me so sweetly that I can feel its thoughts filling my mind,'' Meriyoi confessed through her sobs.

Bregit couldn't imagine Nzers expression but felt it was nothing short of astonished.

''What do you speak of?'' whispered Nzer.

''A seed grows in my belly so rapidly that I can feel it clawing at my insides, constantly reminding me that it wants to live. Feel if you don't believe me?'' offered Meriyoi.

Weather Nzer felt Meriyoi's seed growing inside her bosom Bregit couldn't tell, but what he did know was Nzer had committed treason with his next foolish statement.

''I can help you, just say the word you know I will do it,'' vowed Nzer in a voice spoken like he was compassionate toward Meriyoi. Thus, convincing Bregit why Nzer had come to Meriyoi's defence even against his own father.

''I know you cannot free me, but you can free my seed and allow it to grow up with the other developing drops. You can see to it that it grows up right and not a fool like its mother,'' wept Meriyoi.

''Any Ripeling would be proud to call you its mother,'' praised Nzer.

"You are kind. Too kind, especially after what I have done to you," sobbed Meriyoi her voice below a whisper. "I do not deserve your affection Nzer, but I am grateful none the less."

Bregit had heard enough, he stepped out from the shadows and pushed open the bars of Meriyoi's cell with the tip of his staff. Meriyoi screamed while Nzer jumped from his crouched position raising his staff at his best friend.

"Bregit, what brings you here?" asked Nzer his face flushing.

Bregit threw Nzer a look of disgust and looked at Meriyoi's tear-filled sky-blue eyes. Her flesh was pink with black whip marks lashed across her arms legs and face. She was barely recognisable. In a desperate attempt to save what little dignity she had left Meriyoi covered her head with a light garment that was stained in dust and filth, but it did nothing to shield the bald patches along the sides of her head. One glance at her showered Bregit's mind with how Dirm repeatedly tore chunks from her scalp using the blade of his golden sword while Meriyoi screamed in pain.

"I heard everything, and I will give you this one chance to surrender your drop willingly or I will take it by force. The decision is yours and yours alone to make Meriyoi," said Bregit with a force behind his words.

"Get out!" spat Nzer squaring up to Bregit who did not back away. Nzer was a head taller than Bregit but in comparison to power and skill both wizards knew they were equal.

"You risk the lives of us all by offering to be its care giver, have you any idea the abomination it could become? A creature with the cells of an Aqua Guardian and a wizard fused into one!" bellowed Bregit.

"It could learn to be like us, live among us. I will not destroy something innocent just because you think it will turn out evil, it deserves the chance to be judged," argued Nzer.

Bregit's eyes soured but lost none of their composure. "Then you leave me no choice."

Bregit aimed his staff at a defenceless Meriyoi who used her shaking arms to shield her stomach. Nzer attempted to block Bregit, but he was pushed back by his tame stunning jinx that hit his chest and slammed him against the cells wall.

"Bregit, please I beg you," pleaded Meriyoi her eyes wide with fear and wearing a look of desperation. "Take my life but spare my seed it has done nothing to warrant the death penalty."

She was right, but to allow it to live was treason and Bregit couldn't take that risk, but before he had decided what to do, he was blasted through the bars of Meriyoi's cell. Landing hard on the stone floor, Bregit glimpsed Nzer struggling to get to his feet as he tried with sheer determination to shake off the effects of his jinx.

"Nzer stop this," pleaded Meriyoi who had left her cell to stand in front of Bregit with her lashed arms outstretched in attempt to shield him from Nzers next attack.

The effects of Nzers spell had crippled Bregit's insides, but like Nzer his pride refused to be bested as he forced himself to rise from the ground.

"He wishes to kill your unborn seed and yet you defend him?" barked Nzer as he stared at Bregit with hate. "If we do not silence him now, he will tell my father, is that what you want?" Nzer asked Meriyoi.

Alike to Bregit's situation, Meriyoi never got a drop to weigh her options, because at that moment Dirm the Bronze revealed himself from the shadows of the cell block. Dirm, it seemed had been lurking beyond sight throughout their entire conversation and judging by the cold look he bored onto his son, it was obvious the king had heard enough to feel betrayed.

"Betrayed by my own son," Dirm said coldly, his bronze eyes ablaze with fury.

"The blame is mine," protested Meriyoi at once, but her voice was drowned by Dirm's screams and the blinding flash of red light that struck her hard, causing Meriyoi to spiral in mid-air and crash against the cloud wall.

Nzer stood frozen to the spot, his grip on his staff tightening. He looked at Meriyoi's unmoving body which caused his own to shake with anger. Wearing a look of fury, Nzer slashed the air with his staff, shooting multi coloured streaks of lights at his shocked father, who parried his sons attacks aside with the ease.

"You were always easily strayed, to believe lower class like her would choose to mother your seeds," spat Dirm, stomping the ground so fiercely with his staff that it unleashed vicious fissures, that shook the cell blocks foundations like an avalanche, forcing both Nzer and Bregit to conjure energy shields that did just enough to withstand the king's powerful wrath.

Nzer raised his staff shooting streaks of white beams all over the cell block causing the king to laugh aloud. "Is that what I taught you, how to shoot fireworks?" cackled Dirm as he advanced on his son.

Nzer whirled his hands shooting beams of energy at Dirm who looked disappointed at his son's tame spell casting. Before the beams could even touch the king, whips sprung from the depths of his flowing cloak. As a dozen slithering threads smashed through Nzers soaring beams and hit the defenceless prince so hard he was knocked off his feet. Before Nzer could recover, Dirm fluidly controlled his threads to coil Nzer in its thick cloths and pin him to the bars of the nearest cell. With no more distractions Dirm moved toward Meriyoi. As he stood over the unconscious wizard he had defiled and humiliated, Dirm looked down upon her with no sign of mercy.

Bregit watched the king rotate his claw like hands inches above Meriyoi's waist, summoning a blue glowing beam that rose through his palm and extracted the seed from Meriyoi's stomach. Dirm watched the seed swirl over his palm, appearing no bigger than a berry. Looking at it with not an ounce of pity Dirm pointed his index fingers at the drop. It was in that moment that Bregit made his decision, and with a swirl of his arm he summoned the drop to him just a mili drop before the Dirms spell made contact. He waved his hand over the seed the moment it nested in his palm muttering a spell that covered it in a protective shell. Bregit then had to leap across the cell block floor to avoid a green jet of light hitting him. Breathless, he got to his feet, his staff at the ready as he and the king circled the other their eyes locked in a fierce gaze.

"I feel robbed for believing you were as dim as my son, at least he fell for love, what reason have you to betray me?" asked Dirm.

"I see through the lies of the Golden Kingdom and the wizards in charge, and as long as the same wizards remain in their positions I will not," said Bregit,

"You speak as if you will survive against me, but I am here alone and with no witnesses I can easily dispose of you all and no one would care to blink an eye to your disappearance," taunted Dirm, his smirk as wicked as his tongue.

And just as Dirm and Bregit were about to begin their duel a flash of gold streaked the cell block, using his elbow to shield his eyes, Bregit almost lost the ability to speak at what he had just seen. Meriyoi, bald, broken and beaten stood over a crouching Dirm, who was choking on his own gushing blood that spurted from his mouth. Bregit stared with wonder and then noticed a golden sword held loosely in Meriyoi's hand making it clear that while the king was about to curse Bregit, Meriyoi seized on the opportunity to disarm him and stab him in the back.

While looking down upon Dirm, Meriyoi pulled back the king's head and without hesitation slit his throat. As Dirm gulped his last breaths, Meriyoi ran to Nzer and cut him loose of his father's threads with the blood-stained sword. Now free of his father's bondage, Nzer kissed Meriyoi with an embrace that sent warm air gushing from both wizards. After they let each other go and Dirm had bled out, Nzer came to Bregit and asked him what would keep his silence.

"Freedom," was Bregit's reply.

Nzer gave him a hard look before replying, "Granted, on the condition that you never come back. Traitors will never be welcome among the clouds under my regime," said Nzer, adding a tone of gratitude to his voice.

Bregit left the Golden Kingdom that shade and never told a soul about Meriyoi's drop, Dirms demise and the breaking of sealed agreements. Because he knew if he concealed the truth the longer, he would get to live in peace. From what he gathered on his travels the story was Dirm had died at the hands of his son and Meriyoi was reinstated of all her privileges and cleared of her betrayal, the drop Bregit presumed was hidden and now lives unknowing of its true heritage.

Bregit leaned his head back against the cloud wall that radiated soft heat waves which caused his senses to dull. The effects didn't bother him, he'd prefer to die sleeping, that way he wouldn't have to see Lucifer's gloating smile before he died. Nothing was ever going to stop him returning, he knew the moment he recollected his lost memories in Tip-Karps cave. That he was going to alert the Golden Kingdom of Treforledge's faith and Lano's resurrection fully aware of the consequences. Carka and Tip-Karp may have disagreed with his intentions, yet he followed what he thought to be right for the safety of his fellow wizards. Then out of nowhere the sinking feeling washed over Bregit like a cold shower. "What if Lano wins?" he thought.

Lano knew about the Drop Trees and their properties, which Bregit had no doubt would be destroyed if the Lava Keeper regained his old power back. Bregit dreaded the thought but found this life-threatening uprising sparking an old energy he had thought old age had drained from him. Perhaps when he is dead some may renounce his brave efforts. He laughed at the thought. Shaking his head side to side, Bregit rubbed his tired eyes with his raw knuckles that still bore the lash marks Lucifer had repeatedly struck him with each drop he refused to speak. The stinging would heal eventually, he knew the toxins weren't decisive because they were squeezed from the petals of the Woltondox flowers that grew along every pathway leading to the king's temple.

The still silence made Bregit realise there were no Lutizs patrolling the corridors, not even one wizard had come to check was he trying a breakout. Which only meant defences had been strengthened in ways Bregit had no desires of testing. For the sake of having something to do other than dwell on his mistakes, Bregit got to his feet and walked stiffly toward the thick steel bars of his cell door. Sticking his sagged nose through the cold bars, he inhaled the clear air that stung his nostrils, causing his nose to wrinkle. With nothing to stare at but darkness he left the sight of the lonely corridor and sat back on the tore off fabric he was kindly given before his cell was sealed. Sitting opposite the spot he had preserved just to feel the radiant warmth flow through his body again a speck of magical activity tickled his senses. Lifting his head Bregit looked at the only corner of the room that was consumed by darkness. Peering clearly Bregit could make out a presence that had somehow entered his cell. Observing this figure that lurked in the shadow of his cell, totally eclipsed in darkness. Its heavy breath whistling throughout the cell as Bregit scoffed shaking his head in disbelief.

''What do I owe the pleasure of your company...... my old friend?'' said Bregit his voice rasp and hoarse.

The figure moved into the dim light provided by the white clouds. Its face was calm with lines of ageing weighing down one side of its cursed face that had worsened since Bregit had seen it last.

''You kept your height, unlike me,'' laughed Bregit a dry cough added to his sarcasm. ''My back decided to curve through the shades, perhaps sitting on the throne has done you better than good,'' he added smirking.

''I come from a line of straight backs, still the shades punish us all in the end old friend I grant you,'' said the king in a kind manner.

Bregit straightened himself, folding his legs and loosening his arms so he could look more clearly at the king. His hair had grown in length, but it had lost most of its natural colour. The purple which was the anchor of his position was being beaten back by clear white strands that shone brightly off the clouds glistening beams. The king's taste in wear had soured. The handmade garments which over layered him during his shades as prince had died, replaced by patched cloaks of black, webbed in silver lining stitching that did nothing to represent the colour he was branded.

''You've changed,'' said Bregit inspecting the king's appearance through squinted eyes.

''In style yes, but in mind I have advanced further. I have grown wiser since our last discussion,'' said the king in a silvery voice.

''Why all the secrecy?'' asked Bregit, his eyes becoming sharp.

''Disloyalty, corruption, secret alliances formed behind my back,'' answered the king, his voice still having a fierce sting even when it was lowered beyond a whisper.

"Disloyalty, among the clouds. Goodness, who would dare believe such a thing, possible?" said Bregit in a mocking distasteful tone.

The king's expression tensed. "They think I cannot see what plots they're devising behind my back, which is why I have veiled my identity and watched from afar, waiting for the shadows to rise while the beacon is no longer present to push the darkness back," said the king pointing his index finger to his temple.

Bregit had gotten to his feet, he was shorter than the king, but not short enough to notice the fade in his purple eyes. Even his undamaged skin looked pus yellow. "Are you unwell, should I be worried?" Bregit asked, concerned for his own well-being rather than the kings who didn't miss his act of selfishness.

"I am as well as well can be," said the king with a smile. "I have temporarily abandoned my duties, to discover that one of my own kin plans to rally his forces and overthrow me," he said bitterly.

"Still doesn't explain your change in appearance," said Bregit.

'I have come to you during this shade old friend because I have patiently waited every shade since I was cursed with that hideous crown and forced to wheedle around while another power ruled above my head, to tell someone, anyone, that my life is in danger," said the king his voice below a whisper.

"There is no higher power than the position of king, who would dare try hurt you?" argued Bregit.

"In the eyes of no one other than the king yes, in my position no. The shade quickly approaches when my position will be in jeopardy and I will need all the allies I can trust," said the king looking at Bregit who did not return the same curtsey.

"You lock me away like some common criminal for a crime I committed to shield you only to return and be treated like this," howled Bregit showing the king the lash marks on his arms. "Why in the eight shades would I side with you?" he shouted his nostrils flaring.

"Shush...," whispered the king. "You of all wizards should know how easily it is to be heard down here. As for your punishment, the agreed terms for your freedom were that you would never return," the king bit back keeping his voice at a low peak.

Bregit huffed, even though his anger had gotten the best of him, he knew the king was right. The secret pact he had made the shade he left the Golden Kingdom was to never return.

"I will announce my return, but you must know that not even I have the power to overrule your charges," whispered the king heatedly.

"That's probably the reason you let your son do your dirty work, instead of looking like a heartless ruler, you got your least liked son to follow your instructions seeing it as a way to get rid of me and what I know," snarled Bregit his voice sour.

The king smiled making him look even uglier, as cracks had risen from beneath the dead skin trailing along has face making him appear like a cracked egg repeatedly been tipped by a sharp object.

"Crude as fire when melting flesh," jeered the king. "Allow me to prove to you which of my sons have stayed loyal to their father." The king snapped his fingers sharply the ringing noise echoed throughout the cloud cell and into the hallway. "Now you will see, old friend exactly how wrong you are about who rules even if I haven't got my rear end on the throne,'' said the king his drop-in tone making it obvious he was becoming annoyed with Bregit's jesting.

Flames red as the sea, erupted in the small space separating Bregit and the king. A figure long and thin moulded and formed from the blazing flames. Walking through them undamaged was Lucifer his crimson eyes finding the king. ''Father,'' breathed Lucifer. ''Why have you chosen to reveal yourself....?'' but he was silenced by his father's hand gesture.

''Because you have failed to secure the lands we rule,'' replied the king firmly. ''And if a king cannot defend his lands judgement will be pressed upon me!'' said the king.

Lucifer opened his mouth to argue but was stalled by his father's firm voice. ''There is no argument to be had upon the matter. We must deal with this uprising if what Bregit's companion says is true then we have lost the Blue Islands and Dulgerdeen.''

Lucifer nodded his head giving his father the dreaded answer. ''The coven voted not to investigate the matter further,'' said Lucifer his eyes staring at his feet.

''As expected, they would never send forth the Seven Coloured Army so far from the Golden Kingdom. I daresay if Lano decided to reveal himself the coven would still stall until it was their own lives under threat,'' said the king, his voice filled with contempt.

Before either Lucifer or the king could say another word a shocked Bregit had finally found his voice which had abandoned him since Lucifer had appeared from the flames.

''You're quite the performer young Lucifer, so good I am wondering is this another play act to lure me into one of your sickening games,'' said Bregit coldly.

He walked straight into Lucifer's face, both wizards locked eyes, but Lucifer did not return the cold look Bregit was piercing him with. The king dug his long arm between his sons and Bregit's chest parrying them apart. Bregit backed away while Lucifer walked to the cell's bars.

''Lucifer has been my only trusted advisor. The ill-treatment you received was nothing to what the coven would have unleashed if you were given into their custody. Had Lucifer not found you and Galli when he did, we would not be having this conversation!'' the king explained.

''And where is Galli, not dead is she?'' asked Bregit coldly, throwing Lucifer a distasteful look.

''She was escorted back down the Cloud Stair and was last seen attacking my scout before heading west of the plate pathway,'' answered Lucifer.

''Tip-Karps Mountain,'' breathed Bregit.

''What has the sphinx got to do with Galli?'' asked the king, his sharp eye appearing suspicious.

''The last of her kin reside within his mountain, that's where they fled to after Lano's attack she will no doubt be travelling back there,'' Bregit said confidently.

''Then I fear your friend is in grave danger,'' the king said sadly.

"Why do you say that?" asked Bregit, his neck cricking from turning it so quickly.

"My advisors spying within the sphinx's mountain have told me Tip-Karp has joined with Lano and opened his mountain to the Viledirks," the king explained.

"Lies," breathed Bregit, his eyes narrowing. "Tip-Karp swore to protect the innocents of Nocktar he would never join with Lano."

"My spies were forced to retreat before Kcor, and his army entered Tip-Karps Mountain. They are now travelling on foot to Dulgerdeen and with luck be able to gather some information on Lano's next move," said Lucifer he unlike his father kept his voice below a whisper.

The king paid no attention to Bregit, instead he looked to his son. "Lucifer as of now I am reinstated as king which makes you free of burden. Will you as my son leave the protection of this kingdom and find Galli before she falls into the same trap of trust my dear friend Bregit has?"

Lucifer didn't even consider he simply smiled. "I'll find her and bring her back here," he vowed bowing his head curtly.

"No," said Bregit sharply. "I still have my doubts about you Lucifer, but I know Galli enough to know her spirit is true and pure. When you find her go to Larmont and defend it?"

"Two wizards against the might of the Council of Shadows, you would send my son to his death?" barked the king.

"If Larmont falls, Lano will gain access to my magical chains of communications. Chains I threaded together using knowledge I got from Tricklet."

The king and Lucifer shared looks of surprise by Bregit's sudden confession.

"One whiff into Tricklets senses and he will unhinge its barriers and use it to communicate with every creature that dwells in all lands of Nocktar," said Bregit urgently.

The realism sank into the king's mind. Bregit could tell by his deep concentrated look, his memory had gone back to the creatures of the abyss and beyond the depths of Dulgerdeen. Places Lano was clever enough not to venture, but if the Lava Keeper managed to gain access to his threads of communication, he could expand the threads to every corner of Nocktar.

"Channel of communications eh, what else have you brewed up in exile?" asked the king suspiciously.

Bregit expected this and was prepared for his response. "My threads only surround Treforledge as a defence mechanism for all creatures to communicate with me and me only!" he said firmly.

"A likely story," scoffed the king. "Seems to me you created a weapon. One that if laid in the wrong hands could cause an irreversible catastrophe, and let's not forget it's not granted a licence by the king, who I am may I add. Which means by law these threads are illegal!" said the king his good eye and nostrils flaring with anger.

Bregit sighed deeply. "Whatever laws I have broken, I will deal with the consequences. Right now, a serious matter is at hand one far greater than what laws I have broken, if Lano takes Larmont then we all lose understand," pleaded Bregit.

"Lano will be dealt with, what I haven't got is shades. When I announce my return, the coven will demand a feast in honour of my safe return," moaned the king.

"I'd forgotten about those absurd events, we'd three in one cycle when the Aqua Guardians invaded Selavroc," said Lucifer. He walked to the door of the cloud cell grasping the iron bars with his thin fingers. "I'll defend Larmont," he said after a moments silence. "But I have a feeling Galli won't be so easily persuaded, any recommendations on how to get her to believe I was and still am my father's double agent without her lashing out at me?"

The honest answer was no which tweaked a smile on Bregit's face when he uttered the words. "No," a swell of joy filling his damaged pride at Lucifer's saddened expression.

"Always a pleasure serving the honour of my family," breathed Lucifer softly. With a slick flick of his head, Lucifer was swallowed by a crimson gold flame that shrunk in a wisp of clear grey smoke until it and Lucifer were gone leaving Bregit alone with a fuming king.

The tension was hard not to feel, as the king's mind juggled between friendship and loyalty all while trying to support a hardened expression. "How can I see to releasing you after what you have shared with me and my son?"

"A war is coming, one that may challenge our very existence. Lano has out done himself and proved it by reducing Treforledge to ash. Dulgerdeen has allied to his cause and if you are right about Tip-Karp then you will need every wizard available to you for this fight," Bregit reminded him.

"My army is trained in all styles of combat they will crush any charge Lano makes. He knows if he doesn't make a stand soon his allies will rally back to their holes," snarled the king. "All I must do, is simply wait for him to come to me. Then when he is out in the open field with his army behind him, I will bury him and every single traitor in the exact location his first rebellion failed," said the king his tone filled with relish.

"Lano could have easily lay hidden, he didn't. If he is one thing it isn't reckless there is a reason, he revealed his return! What his play is, I cannot tell but with Lano there is always a hidden agenda," warned Bregit.

"You place too much value on a worn-out creature with little to none left of his life expectancy, perhaps he's doing me a favour by gathering all the mystical creatures. Because now when I destroy them their lands can used for higher more beneficial purposes," laughed the king in a hysterical cackle.

"Lano will not lose this war in battle, his numbers may shrink in comparison to yours, but he laid waste to thousands of highly trained wizards with one stroke. I have been to Treforledge and seen the chaos he is capable of unleashing," Bregit said tensely.

The king scoffed shaking his head in disbelief, still in denial that Lano was capable of defeating thousands of wizards in one strike.

"I have witnessed the bodies buried beneath the decaying ash that now resides above the rocks and lands of Treforledge."

"You seen this onslaught with your own eyes?" the king asked mockingly.

"No." Bregit replied.

''Had an envoy brought this message I would have strung him from his feet and left it to rot at my gates. However, you are an honourable wizard and a trusted friend to me. I have no doubt what you have shared is true especially if you risked your freedom and life to come all the way here to warn me.''

Bregit could sense by the slight pause in the king's response that he was about to stamp his own authority on the matter.

''Yet, I cannot shake off this secret weapon you have developed and casted upon Larmont, maybe you did it for good use or personal gain it is hard to know. What I do know from this conversation is we have both grown miles apart from the pair of foolish wizards who dreamed of becoming Depth Head Generals.''

''Yes, we have,'' Bregit agreed. ''Because If you saw what I have you would be as frightened as I am about what is coming,'' said Bregit seriously.

''Please continue to keep me in suspense,'' said the king sarcastically.

''Lano has recruited a being I have never seen the likes of before, but I tell you whole heartily that its power is nothing short of frightening. When I witnessed it stand firm to Tip-Karps power I knew then that this being is why Lano returned.''

The king mirrored Bregit's expression. ''A being, capable of withstanding the force of a sphinx. Unbelievable,'' said the king shaking his head in disbelief.

''It's the truth,'' said Bregit.

''Lano will be dealt with in the coming shades you have my word. I will allow you an appeal. As king I cannot pick sides your appeal will be ruled on evidence.''

Bregit laughed aloud not caring who heard him. ''Fair trial surrounded by corrupted wizards who plot to dethrone their king, leave me to my thoughts old friend. I daresay you have many celebrations requiring your attendance,'' said Bregit, his tone ill and uncaring.

''Jest all you like Bregit. The coven will overrule any judgement I pass in your favour, however there may be a solution one that may secure your survival.''

Bregit considered what the king was hinting toward, it came before he even had to think. ''Challenge a Depth Head with nothing but my wits to defend me. That law was created to thrill your sick minded father who relished in seeing innocent wizards tortured to feed his ever-hungry appetite of inflicting death,'' Bregit threw back.

Bregit's insult toward the king's father soured his expression. ''It maybe a mad king's appetite throwing you a rope to pull yourself out of this mess,'' retorted the king. ''Make your decision and be quick about it, I dear say you'll linger here much longer once my return has been announced.''

''Wouldn't want a traitor stinking out your cells,'' said Bregit his words fuelled with hate.

The king looked more menacing than Bregit had ever seen as he looked down upon him with heated anger fuelling him. ''An attitude like that won't help anyone, use that brain of yours. I'd have thought Bregit the Yellow wouldn't need any more requirements to see himself out of this mess,'' the king said, reminding him that it takes more than power and skill to win a duel.

The king said nothing more as the cloud wall behind him swallowed his body whole leaving Bregit alone again but with much more thoughts to dwell on and consider.

Chapter 19

The Sphinxes Departure

"My Lord," came the soft voice of Tricklet. "A Viledirk is requesting a word with you in private, will I allow him through?"

"No doubt another one of Kcors lieutenants seeking knowledge of their absentee Lord," thought Lano, the daunting feeling of explaining Kcors whereabouts again causing his mind to feel like mush.

"Let him through," hissed Lano in a bored voice.

Straightening himself, the Lava Keeper flexed his body with a wide stretch, the warmth of his cloak leaving him instantly as it fell from his shoulders. Watching from the corner of his dark eyes, Lano glimpsed a Viledirk strutting proudly into the cave, its mane was hanging loosely and filthy, with black streaks trickling down its front. From its ragged appearance and eager expression, Lano sensed something was wrong.

"My lord," grunted the Viledirk, who didn't bow or show any respect to the Lava Keeper but instead stood afar wearing a sour expression. "I have come with speed to your quarters for I fear Kcor has been apprehended."

"What?" hissed Lano realizing his worst fears had come true. "Explain!" he commanded, waving his rod at the stern faced Viledirk.

"We killed all the Harpies as instructed, when we clipped their wings and burned the bodies, Kcor sent us ahead to see was the path to Dulgerdeen clear. We did as our lord commanded and when we found that there were no dangers ahead, we returned to find the fires had died out and Kcor was gone," said the Viledirk.

A sinking feeling had temporarily crippled Lanos speech, he peered into the flames of the dying fire, refusing to allow the Viledirk to see his static state. Lano dwelled on possibilities, but they all came to the same conclusion. Kcor had never failed him, and it was his unyielding loyalty that made Lano realize that his best lieutenant had indeed fallen.

"My lord, with Kcor unresponsive, I feel the other Viledirks will disband and seek out other methods of claiming back the southern lands," said the Viledirk a titter in his speech.

"You reckon?" hissed Lano with a sense of calm in his voice. "Without proof of Kcors whereabouts or situation, you will instruct the Viledirks to go through with Kcors orders and those orders are to fight against the wizards to insure mine, yours and every other creature's survival," hissed Lano viciously.

The Viledirk did not argue or interrupt Lano, but stood upright and proud as was his stature, resenting looking into the Lava Keepers mysterious gaze.

"Let's say you abandon me, and I fail, how long until the wizards root out the Viledirks and kill every last one of you?" asked Lano. His question hung in the air giving the Viledirk something to consider, but not with Lano. The Viledirk knew this was a matter to be discussed with its superiors, and the Viledirk took it as such.

"I will leave it to you to explain what the outcome of your abandonment to my cause will result. Go and I want to be consulted on your decision," hissed Lano, holding up a warning finger to show they had one shade to decide and no more.

The ragged Viledirk left at once as Lano leaned over the dying fire his mind racing. Kcor was missing, he was sure of it. There was no denying he was either dead or in the hands of the wizards. Dead meant Kcor was unable to tell anyone about his plans if he were a captive however his mind could be manipulated into telling his captor everything!

Disciplined in mind and body Kcor maybe but wizards had ways of making their strongest foe turn to a puppet on dangling strings if they saw fit. If Kcor spilled out Lano's plans, then the wizards could be flying here right now to sabotage his army and end the war before it began.

"No!" thought Lano clenching his dry fists in frustration. He had come too far to be thwarted now; and would not allow himself to be defeated in this matter. War was coming from one foot to the other and he was the games main target, the pieces were already set-in motion. If the wizards leave their stronghold above the clouds more the better for Lano, who had the numbers to match the Seven Coloured Army three to one. But through his eagerness a soothing calm came over Lano. The king had yet to move against him. Bregit and his companion were sure to have reached the Golden Kingdom by now, and with them the news of his destruction of Treforledge. Yet no counter strike. Carka was last seen going west to the Grass lands and nothing dwelled there since the Krics. What concerned Lano know was what if his assumption about the king were true and he was planning to rally the entire Seven Coloured Army within the confinements of the Golden Kingdom. If the king used this tactic, it would simply be a waiting game, one that Lano knew the king would win. Breaking through the enchantments preventing anyone but a wizard entering the Golden Kingdoms boundaries were all that stopped him laying siege to the wizard's fortress. "Maybe the cloud could break through?" thought Lano considering the possibility.

Having seen the clouds powers with his own eyes Lano was certain it could achieve the impossible task. Tempting as it was, he refused to give further life to the thought, he wasn't going to risk the life of his most powerful ally until it was fully restored to full strength. The clouds duel with Bregit had moved its healing process back a few stages and had forced the cloud to dwell alone somewhere deep in the forest to restore some of its lost strength. Lano was thankful for the clouds respite period; for now, he could take charge without the chill of the cloud's presence lurking in his wake.

"Tricklet come here," hissed Lano, his voice echoing along the caves closed in walls.

A puff of sky-blue smoke appeared on the wooden rocking chair Lano had sat on momentarily. Tricklets tiny body burst through the smoke a look of wonder expressed on his smug face.

"Don't look so happy, we have a problem that will require your skills in solving," hissed Lano.

Tricklets red swirling eyes glowed in the brightness of Lano's fire, he didn't retort to his master's requirement of his skills but instead waited for his master to do something for which he wasn't favoured.

Desperation was why Lano decided to take this path and with no other choice left to him, the Lava Keeper now had to lay his faith in Tricklet. Scheming and devious the little trickster maybe, he was still a trusted ally with skills even the wizards feared.

''Kcor has been captured. I am not certain of his faith, but I will bet my rod that he has been seized by the wizards and if he has, they may already know of our whereabouts,'' said Lano slowly, making every word sound sincere.

Lano swallowed before continuing, allowing the situation to dawn on Tricklet, so he would realize what dangers they are in. ''Dreaquirla will be upon us by the end of this shade with requirements from the southern isles, word has reached me that she has convinced the Rear Clars into joining us. If my calculations are correct, she is journeying with fifteen hundred strong beasts by her side.''

Tricklet smiled. ''She always had her ways of persuasion I daresay the Rear Clars will benefit our cause they fight in ways the Viledirks could only hope to achieve yet I doubt I have been called from my watch to share growth in numbers,'' squeaked Tricklet.

'Straight to the point as usual,' thought Lano, a flare of anger rising in his body by Tricklet's ignorance. ''I have summoned you here Tricklet because I want you to locate Kcor, find him but nothing more, do you understand!'' hissed Lano raising a finger in warning. ''If the wizards do have him and haven't killed him, we can use the situation to our advantage,'' hissed Lano.

By Tricklet's reaction even the little trickster was shocked by the deviousness of Lanos request, yet he returned the same cunning smile Lano now wore on his skinless face.

''It may take a few drops to bind, the further the distance the harder it becomes to grasp the victims mind, but I'll find him my lord be assured of that. I must surround myself in silence and peaceful air where I cannot be disturbed,'' Tricklet squeaked in rushed excitement.

''I have the upmost faith that you will Tricklet, I taught you well now you must hurry the sooner we know where Kcor is the sooner I can determine our next move.''

''I'll get right to it,'' squeaked Tricklet vanishing with a loud crackling snap of his fingers leaving glittering mist in his wake.

Lano sat back on the rocking chair using the point of his feet to prevent been rocked back and forth. His plan may cost him a commanding general but if Kcor were in the wizard's custody he is already dead; so, he might as well make use of what good was left of a dire situation. War, Lano knew had its prices, and this was one he knew he had to pay to gain the lead over his opponents. Victory was all that mattered now, and how it was achieved was no longer relevant. If Kcor were here and another council member was in the same situation he would urge the same tactic without pause, sacrifices were essential in war and knowing the Viledirkening lord as well as he did Lano knew he would understand.

With Tricklet gone Lano had no guard outside his cave to alert him of anyone approaching and that was why he was alarmed to be face to face with Tip-Karp as his shining silver eyes and large body had without his knowledge entered his cave.

''You summoned me my Lord,'' said Tip-Karp in his usual monotonous tone.

''Ah, yes,'' hissed Lano, trying to appear like he knew Tip-Karp was there all along. ''I hope you have gathered the essentials you need for your journey?''

"Yes," answered Tip-Karp delicately. "The Glider's and I will depart at the start of the next shade if we are not spotted, we may reach our destination by the turn of orange shade."

"Then it would be vital for us to march at once, I cannot have one half of my plan done with the other half trailing behind. It would be a catastrophe on both our parts if the two halves are not positioned in the right place before I give the order to strike, wouldn't you agree?" hissed Lano.

"I do, except we are blind to the wizard's movements. If you march you will meet many bands of outlaws and the yellow army if they haven't surrendered their strongholds and fled to the Golden Kingdom," stated Tip-Karp warningly.

"Outlaws do not concern me, nor does one army. Treforledge had twice the numbers Pally the Yellow has, and a stronger base and I reduced both to ash. Do not question the seriousness I have for my follower's sphinx," hissed Lano seriously.

"The Bay of Bones is two leagues south. The Varwels are west, the Viledirks grow restless and Dreaquirla comes to us with an army of Rear Clars. Why not wait until they have both returned before leaving the forest?" urged Tip-Karp.

"Drops are short, my army will be intact before I reach the Bay of Bones. Your concerns lay deeper than a few missing pieces of my puzzle. The shade will come when your loyalties may decide the outcome of this war. Can I count on you to deliver on the oath you swore to me or will your affection for the wizards cloud your judgement like it did when the Aqua Guardians had the wizards at their mercy?" asked Lano peering Tip-Karp with a searching glare.

Tip-Karp didn't take his eyes away from Lano as the Lava Keeper waited for his reply.

"My loyalty is to you; sphinxes are no oath breakers we serve who we believe worthy to rule and you are Nocktar's rightful ruler and the one creature who can restore peace to the Lands of Light. My part in the war between wizards and Aqua Guardians made peace between both species after all isn't that what we are fighting to achieve? My lord," said Tip-Karp soothingly.

"Clever statement," admitted Lano hating that the sphinx always had an accurate answer for everything. "Still, I will not linger on the beliefs that you have fully turned against the wizards until I see some results and I cannot see results if you are still in my presence, can I?" snapped Lano.

Tip-Karp scoffed. A hint of a smile creasing his golden face. "No, you cannot. When next we meet you will rule the Lands of Light and Nocktar will be restored to its rightful state, until then I wish you good luck, my lord."

Tip-Karp left the cave without further discussion. Lano could feel it in his bones that the sphinx wasn't fully trustworthy, but he did supply steel to his ranks. Rocking back and forth on his rocking chair, Lano felt the air slide against his brow as a raw pulsing feeling flowed through him. For the plan was now in motion, there was no changing it and now was the moment that Lano grasped the realistic outcome and that was in acceptance that by the end of this cycle of shade, all his efforts will be decided in victory or in death.

Chapter 20

A Change of Heart

The plate pathway seemed to drag on forever with not the slightest sign of land. What Galli was sure of, it wasn't the Bay of Bones Leon had rudely escorted her to after Bregit's trial concluded. Having been half dragged and half forced down a slope of rough-edged rocks and dark clouds that numbed her skin, Galli was tossed from the outskirts of the Golden Kingdom. Landing hard on her side Galli was insulted further by been caught around the face by her trailing staff. Wherever she had been shoved regardless of the location, was a relief, because it meant she was alive and not a subject to Lucifer's entertainment, but the only downside to her relief was leaving Bregit behind.

Though her feelings toward Bregit weren't the same as the ones she harboured for Lorneid, he was at this moment the closest thing Galli had to a friend right now. Water Dancer was her only companion now and with no destination to decide on Galli decided she might as well follow the plates until some form of land came into view. The location Galli was walking along was silent and too quiet for her liking. The Red Sea was calm but something in the air didn't feel right. Because her gut kept nudging at her insides, but she decided to disregard her instincts, telling herself they were down to hunger pains and not a signal that danger was near. The Tweedily plants Carka recommended that she pick and bring with her on the journey to the Cloud Stair, were taken from the inside of her robes along with Mirror. Lucifer had not only publicly humiliated her, but the prince had also deprived Galli of the one thing that proved Treforledge were triumphed in the Ultimate Colour.

The Red Sea remained timid and unconcerned as Galli walked for miles. She imagined Bregit rotting in some cold cell alone and getting further taunted by Lucifer. The serpent, who had expertly lured them under his false lies. It maddened Galli to think of Lucifer's smirk expression, wishing she had just one chance to kill the smug prince. But Galli's one hope for vengeance had relied on Bregit, her dependence on him to recruit the Seven-Coloured Army had given her a spark of hope to think on, but with Bregit in custody and Tip-Karp and Carka thousands of miles away she was again alone in that pursuit. Continuing her stroll, Galli became aware of the change in the green shaded sky, it had been a moss green colour last she checked but now it was a ripe green meaning the stuffy air was becoming clearer which swept aside the stench flowing from Galli's robes. The odours flowing from her garments were a mixture of her own body and the dampness from her roll down the cliffside. While Galli dwelled on her personal hygiene, she was given a huge fright by the sudden appearance of a glowing ball of red flame that sat blazing in the centre of a plate not too far from where she stood. When she was a few plates away from the flames they disintegrated, leaving light grey ash in their wake. But it wasn't the sitting ash that stunned Galli it was......, "You!" she cried.

Lucifer took a step forward with his hands raised in protest, but Galli wasn't going to be fooled by his tricks again. With a swerve of her arm threads of gushing water shot from Water Dancer and hit Lucifer square in the chest. The impact causing him to fall hard on his back and wretch with pain. But through the pain the red prince tried with sheer nerve to get up, but the effects of Galli's stun spored ordure spell had taken effect. Taking one step after the other Galli approached the stunned Lucifer and sank the point of Water Dancer deep into his grinded cheek.

Even though he was in agonizing pain Lucifer's expression remained calm which surprised Galli. The princes lowered guard caused Galli to question why he would come here unprotected and unwilling to defend himself, surely, he was expecting Galli to attack him after what he had put her and Bregit through? This uncertainty caused Galli to question Lucifer's motives for been here at all but in return halted her desires to kill him.

"Why are you here?" asked Galli. "Answer me with an ounce of a lie and I'll bury you in the sea," she threatened.

Lucifer heaved as his calm posture was beginning to lose its mystique. Galli looked down on him with satisfaction, her stunning spell inflicting unbearable pain to the wizard who had shamed her. With his body immobilised, Lucifer was forced to lay straight with his arms locked by his side, the only movement he could perform was the movement of his eyes. Which he darted at his bright red robes that whistled along the oceans breeze.

"I was instructed to find you," groaned Lucifer fighting through the pain of Galli's spell.

"Instructed by whom?" questioned Galli not daring to lift her guard.

"Lift...your... hold... over... me... and... I.... ll t.e.l.l yo...u," begged Lucifer, each word piercing his insides with agony.

"So, you can spring another trap on me," snarled Galli, her teeth barred as she leaned heavier on Water Dancer.

"I could've came here swarmed with generals and struck you down where you stood, instead I'm here alone because we both are needed to undergo a mission for Bregit!" screeched Lucifer his eyes bulging with the effort it had cost him to call out the words.

Begrudgingly Galli lifted Water Dancer from Lucifer's cheek, its sharp tip leaving a tiny peep hole in the centre of Lucifer's reddened cheek. Rotating her spare hand over Lucifer's shaking body Galli lifted the effects of her spell. Stepping back still fearful of Lucifer's deceit, Galli's instincts begged her to kill him now before he could manipulate her again. But what Lucifer said did make a solid point. If he did want her dead, he could have brought reinforcements with him and ambushed her, these actions alone made Galli's mind instantly want to know why Lucifer had travelled alone to treat with her?

"One false move and I swear on my honour I will not hesitate to kill you," Galli warned Lucifer as she directed Water Dancer at his chest.

Lucifer sat up shaking himself and retched aloud. Combing back his loose hair with his thin sharp nailed fingers he sighed with relief when he looked upon his reflection in the Red Sea and was satisfied his hair was undamaged. He then looked at Galli showing her no look of hate which surprised her since she had just put him through excruciating pain.

"Bregit said you would take convincing; I wasn't sure what way to approach the matter but now that we have that awkward moment of distrust out of the way perhaps you are now ready to talk? Because what I must ask of you won't be kind, but if we are going to work alongside each other this must be said....,"

"Work alongside you," repeated Galli coldly her eyes narrowed. "There isn't a spell in Nocktar that would persuade me to team up with a snake like you!" she roared at Lucifer.

Lucifer's expression soured; giving off the impression he didn't take to kindly to been referred to as a serpent who was unforgiving and cold blooded.

"I have come because my father and Bregit have agreed it would be wise for us both to lead the defence of Larmont. Bregit is as you know unable to go back there and with Lano marching on the Cloud Stair we must halt his charge as best we can," Lucifer said calmly.

"Lies," said Galli coldly. "If it wasn't for you Bregit would be here with us, you were the one who sentenced him to death and now you expect me to believe the same wizard you put to death sent you to find me," laughed Galli purposely to annoy Lucifer.

"Pretty much sums it up," answered Lucifer, his tone remaining calm despite Galli's taunting. "Had my father left my brother Leon in charge instead of me, Bregit would be dead instead of sitting in a cloud cell. I gave him a sentence with a clause attached to it, if Bregit is smart enough and accepts the clause, he will be allowed to duel for his life and fight a Depth Head General by choice of the king."

"I wouldn't trust a word from your serpent's mouth!" shouted Galli. "Bregit committed no wrongs and yet you humiliated him, what kind of ruler inflicts misery upon wizards who bring them warnings in great peril?" asked Galli her voice brittle.

"I was instructed by my father to safe keep the Golden Kingdom. I am not saying my actions were unjust, but I had an image to uphold and jeopardising that image to save two wizards I knew little about was not going to cripple my hard work! But now that my father has returned, I am free to help you defeat Lano," said Lucifer showing a hint of impatience in his voice.

"You believe Lano has returned?" said Galli frowning, the feeling her heart thump quicker than normal.

"Yes, as does my father. It was he who held a private meeting with Bregit before he commanded me to find you and bring you to Larmont. Bregit says it cannot fall into the hands of Lano. So, if you are willing can you drop your ill will towards me so we can both travel to Larmont as companions?"

"I'll never trust you, but I do trust Bregit, so I'll say this if you're planning to ambush me or lure me into one of your false sense of securities, I promise I won't hesitate to cleave that head from your serpent's neck. Understood!"

Lucifer scoffed his cunning smile increasing his good looks as he began rooting through the insides of his robes, before withdrawing a bright shield that was all too familiar to Galli.

''Mirror,'' gasped Galli.

''I decided before leaving that this was a reward for your triumph and not a stolen artifact as my brother would have all wizards believe. It is yours by right,'' said Lucifer in a respectable manner as he released Mirror from his grasp and allowed it to flow straight into Galli's open hand.

The moment Galli caught the shield a warm embrace spiralled through her arm giving her a boost of energy that she dearly needed. Embracing the refreshing feeling, Galli allowed it to consume her and banish all negativity that she had stored inside herself since the destruction of Treforledge.

''That shield has many hidden qualities, I recall my father telling me and Leon how it can sustain any branch of magic and element and absorb that power to enhance the capabilities of its wielder. The shield was why we fought so hard in last cycle of shades Ultimate Colour; my father shared with us in secret his intentions to reward the malas shield to the triumphant. Leon was beyond control when you forced him to submit and after the armies left the arena and departed, he lashed each of his lieutenants until they bore the marks of their failure,'' said lucifer.

''Failure isn't a punishment it's a lesson that should be embraced. Fear of failure only increases tension which is unnecessary in battle,'' instructed Galli, remembering the lessons she had with her own army and the increase in power she felt just by getting her comrades to commune better.

Leon's approach was one Galli admired because it was unique and showed how hard the Black Wizards trained to use different tactics in every battle. But Leon's leadership skills were beneficial in terms of results but still he was veracious in his approach and inflicted fear upon his rivals and that was what gained him triumphs. It was an illusion that Galli was proud of shattering, because even though the Black Striped Armies tactics were ruthless, Galli couldn't help pitying them as she watched Leon demolish many wizards with words of disrespect and curses of extreme power that enhanced his reputation as the most merciless wizard alive.

''A wise feat maybe, if we survive this uprising, you can share your tactical approaches but for now, we must move quickly. Because the Varwels are flying to Larmont as we speak,'' voiced Lucifer tugging at the inside of his robes.

''Larmont is a hundred leagues from here it would take us two shades to get there flying and 6 on foot, the Varwels will have come and gone by then,'' said Galli, remembering how long it took her to reach Larmont.

Lucifer's smirk stretched wider, lifting his cheek bones, and broadening his glowing features. ''Well, been a prince of the Golden Kingdom does have its privileges,'' he said with a confident smile.

Lucifer rotated his fingers in a triangular formation and after the third attempt he'd managed to conjure a spinning vortex with a night shade sky aura rotating around it.

''What kind of privileges do you call this?'' Galli asked gaping frozen tongued at the swirling vortex.

"One that breaks all the rules I stand for, yet it has its benefits for this portal will bring us both directly to Larmont," said Lucifer.

The thought of Larmont on fire or worse covered in shadow like Treforledge troubled Galli. Flashes of the Flowered Covered Mountain whose beauty had taken her breath away at first glance destroyed and tarnished fuelled Galli's impulses to jump through the portal and rush to aid the defenceless Pixie's. But something held her back, it was Galli's distrust of Lucifer. Going through the portal meant giving Lucifer another chance to ensnare her again! Hadn't he proven he wasn't trustworthy?

"What are you waiting for? The longer we stand here the more of a chance we give the Varwels to capture Larmont," called Lucifer his voice demanding.

Galli remained rooted to the plate she stood on, her eyes staring at the portal her insides hammering. Knowing if she remained on the Plate Pathway, she would be safe and free of Lucifer. But by going with him she may end up on some isolated island where he could have swarms of wizards waiting to kill her, Lucifer may have wheedled his way out of her not killing him, but she wasn't falling for his tricks again.

"Go without me, I'll take no part in the defence of Larmont or any other perils you deem fit of my services," Galli said keeping her firm composure.

Lucifer closed his eyes shaking his head with disappointment, he looked at Galli with disgust souring his expression.

"I would have thought a warrior bent on vengeance would thrive for battle but instead you have allowed your pride to cloud the better judgement you were instructed to follow. I will go to Larmont and defend it not because I want to but because I swore an oath to protect all Lands of Light with my power and my life. Stay here and dwell on what I did to keep my position as ruler intact and maybe when the war is over, you'll realise I had the best interest of everyone," said Lucifer his tone addled with aggression.

Galli watched him dive headfirst into the swirling portal and looked in wonder as it shrunk to nothing until it puffed away in the blink of an eye leaving her alone again. She passed by the plate the portal had levitated over and walked along feeling pleased with herself that she had at last followed her instincts. Lucifer may have given Mirror back, which she was thankful for regardless, but it still didn't erase what the prince had done to her and Bregit, no matter how honourable the gesture. But Lucifer's rogue mission did sway Galli's thinking.

'Why didn't he not have his lieutenants alongside him? He was the general of a powerful army if he were rushing to defend Larmont wouldn't a legion of experienced wizards be a lot more useful than recruiting a single wizard?' thought Galli, as she watched the bright lime lit sky begin to darken into a moss-coloured green.

The more the thought lingered in Galli's mind the less of a possibility that Larmont was under siege became a reality. Galli put it down to another lie from the mouth of a serpent whose every word was diluted with poison. With the darkened shade of green came a frigid wind that instantly began to quicken making Galli clutch her ragged cloak closer to her cold skin.

Back in Treforledge green shade was nicknamed the Long Sleep, usually because the temperatures were so cold it was impossible for the Crafters to mine and forge, so the entire shade was spent huddled in the Blue Wizards quarters and caves as they waited for cold shade to pass. How Galli longed to be under her silk blanket and feathered pillows listening to the silence green shade brought to Treforledge. The water below the plates had begun to ripple but Galli took no notice, her mind was too far away from the situation now to care. But her carelessness proved decisive in the moments to come as the Red Sea rose above the plates and before Galli had a drop to react, she was met by a jet of sea water that hit her in the face, blinding her from seeing who the squirter was as waves of sea water rose and lashed aggressively. Wave after wave smacked Galli from both sides of the plates at such intensity, she was knocked sideways and off balance causing her grip to loosen on Water Dancer, Galli barely clung to the leathered grip and had it not been for her sharp toenails digging deep into the plates she would certainly have fallen into the plinths of the Red Sea.

"What a disappointment, I locate a sample of the wizard I expected to find," came a swift voice that Galli recognised at once.

"Duxpice," cried Galli her voice rattling due to been drenched by the explosive waves of the sea water.

"At ease!" came Duxpice's commanding voice through the sound of lashing waves.

When the waves retreated to the sea Galli whipped around, pointing Water Dancer in the direction of where Duxpice's voice had come from last.

"You can't kill what you cannot see Ripeling, has your companion deserted you or was my first assault enough to finish the wretched fool," sizzled Duxpice's voice his anger causing the Red Sea to splash at her feet.

Soaked and out of her depth Galli knew she was trapped, holding the high ground wasn't an advantage in this circumstance since Duxpice patrolled the sea beneath, with no defence Galli's only hope was to strike Duxpice when he would reveal himself, but getting him to do that was something Galli had to figure out, and fast if she were to get out of this situation alive.

"There is no fear to be got Ripeling you are miles from land with no companion to save you from what I have in store, but instead of me dawdling on let me show you," laughed Duxpice with a deep chill to his sizzled words.

The Red Sea rose taller than a mountain formed in the shape of an eight-legged creature cocooned in a watery mass that shielded it from Galli's attacks. As she quickly found out as her Balasto curse rebounded off the water and struck a plate not too far behind from where she stood.

"Pitiful," laughed Duxpice, his voice echoing from the eight-legged shape that was inches from collapsing on top of her.

Before Galli could counter a calling voice caused her to twist her neck, what she seen was disbelieving because she thought he'd gone but how when he was a plate away offering her his thin claw shaped hand that was outstretched urging Galli to grasp it. As Duxpice's mass waves collapsed upon her Galli knew there was no choice in the matter, life, or death, preferring the painless of the two she grasped the outstretched hand. "The saving hand," thought Galli, as it pulled her entire body into complete darkness and momentarily to safety.

All thoughts of Duxpice the Red Sea and Treforledge abandoned Galli's senses which were now consumed with staying intact as her body shrunk and twisted in mid-air, all she could do was hold on hoping it would end before her lungs exploded. After what seemed a shade being twisted in the air she landed on a soft surface. Opening her eyes Galli found herself laying in a pit of bronze coloured sand that latched to every inch of her cloak and loosened hair. Her stomach was doing cartwheels due to the impact of entering and exiting the vortex. When she mustered enough strength to lift her head from the sand she vomited not once but twice, a mixture of Tweedly roots and sea water gushed out of her mouth like a stampede causing her eyes to leak hot tears from her eyes. Rubbing the tears and sand from her face, Galli found it only made it worse as the sand caused her to blink furiously as the sound of rough footsteps drew near.

''Evaparatio,'' said a calm voice.

A radiant feeling brushed against Galli's body, she blinked delightfully acknowledging her abilities of sight had returned. Standing up she shook the sand from her cloak and magically removed the itchy grains from her hair with a wave of her palm. Water Dancer to her relief lay undamaged in front of a pair of short, veined peach feet with short spear shaped nails. As Galli reached out to retrieve Water Dancer, it was snatched away, zipped up and held firmly in the hand of Lucifer whose narrowed eyes pierced Galli's with a look of fury.

''Had I not decided to rethink my approach and try to persuade you again your body would now be ripped layer by layer until Duxpice found what he liked before roasting your bits while what is left of your senses is forced to watch as part of yourself is crushed and eaten by that murderous serpent and the last thing you'll see is the juice of your insides dripping down his grim face!'' bellowed Lucifer, his breathing fast and rushed as his red eyes glowed like a beacon in the night.

Galli stayed silent, the impact of Lucifer's words hitting her deeply. Too ashamed to look at him, Galli instead kept her head down and faced the bronze glittered sand, feeling a fool for her stubborn actions. What pride Galli had left abandoned her and scuttered back to the pits of her foolish mind. Her shame fuelling a burning appreciation toward Lucifer whose actions had saved her life. Swallowing her pride Galli raised her head and looked Lucifer in the eye.

''I owe you my life and even though bitterness stands between us ever having a bond of friendship…,'' Galli swallowed hard, ''I will go with you to Larmont as payment for saving my life,'' she said with earnest.

Lucifer's head tilted back looking at Galli as if he was shocked by an invisible charge or somehow, he'd been hoodwinked as he concluded that Galli's change in attitude toward him was indeed real.

''There is no need for travelling,'' Lucifer said smiling at Galli.

''Why?'' asked Galli, raising an eyebrow.

''Because we're already here,'' answered Lucifer. ''And it would appear half a shade before the Varwels, let us get moving we have a battle to prepare for,'' said Lucifer, throwing Water Dancer back to her.

Catching it in her hand, Galli examined every particle of Water Dancer and was relieved no damage had been caused. Both wizards began the walk up a thin slip way carved in the centre of a mountain. Following the trail all the way to the top with her eyes, she found a familiar sight looking back at her. The black tower Galli knew belonged to Bregit.

Chapter 21

The Den of the Pin-Fars

Pain pulsed against Bregit's wrists, while a stinging pain streamed up his arms, both barring him from using his reflexes. Blindfolded and chained in thick iron cuffs, he was dragged from his cell, pulled down the corridor, and yanked viciously out into the open. The scabs on his face had fallen off and was the reason fresh blood now trickled down his cheeks and lips. The taste was distasteful, but it did quench his lips that had gone dry in his imprisonment.

When word reached Leon that Bregit had agreed to fight for his freedom the prince spent little drops reminding Bregit who the principal of discipline was among the clouds. Still, it was Bregit laughing loudest during his torture and even paid the young prince an enthusiastic respect by rewarding his attempts with gratitude.

Leon proved none the wiser to Bregit's smart remarks and unleashed cruel torment upon him and had to use every ounce of restraint he had from showing the prince any sign of weakness. Through every whip lashed against his back, legs, and wrists. Bregit remained hardened and refused to bend and allow Leon to break his spirit. Frustrated by his strong will Leon ordered his Lutizs to bind Bregit and drag his body from the cell block and all the way to the Pin-Fars den. The ancient fortress among the clouds that gives homage to the king's loyal Pin-Fars. Them were mystical creatures that swore their allegiances to the first age of wizards during Lano's attempts to rid Nocktar of the wizards. In return for their services the first wizards built the Pin-Fars a stronghold among the clouds to show their gratitude and protect them from the wrath of Lano who had passed several acts that forbid any mystical and mythical creature siding with the wizards.

After the king's departure from his cell, Bregit began to dwell on the possibility of accepting the clause act that entitled him to fight for his life. A clause Bregit remembered voting to instate when he was a silver chair holder of the covenant. The reason he agreed to the clause was because it helps a wizard if there is no proof to determine that the accused wizard is guilty but has been sentenced to death in the magical bonds of the court. In Bregit's own situation Lucifer didn't have a shred of proof to sentence him to death. The prince's case was solely based on rumour. Which was why Bregit was entitled to choose the clause in his sentence which allowed him to fight a one-on-one duel against a wizard of the kings choosing.

If Bregit won the duel he would be set free, the snag of the clause however forbids him to use any object that channelled magic. Dirm the Bronze the most despised king to ever sit on the throne of the Golden Kingdom saw it fit to lower the accused wizard's chances of victory by disarming them of their most dependent weapon against a foe equipped with its own weapon of choice.

''Where was the honour in this?'' Bregit questioned when the act was added to the clause.

Dirm's act proved brutal and effective it gave the king many moments of satisfaction as he watched from his throne while hundreds of wizards got slaughtered for his twisted appetite and broke many ancient bonds between lords and their king. Shades passed after the act was instated with no food supplies from Tindisinge. The Orange Wizards refused to trade with the Golden Kingdom due to their beloved Talli the Orange been executed for theft on the king's grounds. The Orange Wizards act of defiance sent a message to all lords of the lands to stand against the king and refuse to deploy any further services to his cause. This shade in wizard's history would be known as the Halt of Supplies.

But Dirm wasn't the revered king of his age for nothing. Even without the aid of the lords of lands he was still a powerful force to be reckoned with. Dirm gathered his Pin-Fars and Gliders and his own army of highly trained wizards and flew to Tindisinge. With the might of the Golden Kingdom behind him he attacked the orange lands with no mercy, destroying their fresh trees and contaminated all clear pools linked to the mountain stronghold the Orange Wizards resided in when they had heard of the king's coming.

Knowing they would either starve to death or come out Dirm waited with steel patience for three shades until the Orange Wizards finally gave in and charged from their mountain and fought the king's army. Bregit watched Dirm slash aside every wizard standing in his way from his prime target and that was the lord of Tindisinge, Delilock the Orange, who happened to be Carlock's father.

Delilock put up a proud fight against Dirm who would go on to show respect for his duelling skills by appointing his son a coven chair holder. But Delilock was slain and roasted alive in front of his watching army as Dirm looked on with glee at the fall of his enemy. The victory and the matter of it spread fear throughout the Lands of Light and ended the Halt of Supplies. And it was the same fear that kept the other lords in check as Dirm implanted strict laws over the lords of lands. Bregit remembered looking on with annoyance at the lords bowing to the king and pleading for forgiveness for their treachery. Their resistance was for naught, and their pleas for mercy only worsened the king who felt the need to kill one wizard of each land as a sign of loyalty. Dirm enhanced his cruelty by forcing the lords of each land to hand pick the wizard they thought worthy to sacrifice for the king's mercy. Dirm forced all to watch while he tortured each handpicked victim into sheer madness under the influence of pain. Every trial after the Halt of Supplies was a fiasco, wizards with concrete proof of the accused wizard's innocence were shut out by the king and his loyal coven subjects. "Madness!" Bregit recalled Carka tutting after a trail that saw a Pin-Far rider ripped into pieces by a Glider because his Pin-Far had bitten a Ripeling.

It was only after Dirm met his end at the hands of Meriyoi and Nzer was crowned king did he instate that all trails be judged by the coven chair holders so it would last two shades to allow an investigation into the accused crimes. Nzers addition did gain him favour with the lords of lands and his Depth Heads. It was the reason his son's foolish judgement angered Nzer because Bregit wasn't trailed fairly. But because his sentence was finalised in the court of the Golden Kingdom under the magical seals there wasn't a power in Nocktar that could revoke its ancient seal. The magic written and sealed by the first age of wizard's states that if the sentence is not carried out then the powerful enchantments casted and bonded by the elder wizards would reverse and the Golden Kingdom would cease to exist.

But Nzer learned through cycles of shades of research that there were cracks in the elder's law, and he used branches of his own unique abilities to revoke the death sentence and allow wizards a slight change of evading death. Accepting the clause in his sentence meant Bregit would have to swallow his pride and admit to the charges against him. But he was cornered, been left with one single choice didn't guarantee his life but extended it for a brief spell. But his will to live eventually got the better of him and he sent his submissive reply with a heavy heart. The moment Bregit's reply was given to the king he didn't have to be a prophet to know what would follow once his request was heard.

Bregit understood the reason Leon was torturing him. It was to ensure the reputation of his father's kingdom wouldn't be tarnished by an accused criminal escaping justice. Leon was a proud warrior who was descended from lines of kings who were regarded unique in their capabilities, each one had their immortal status to uphold, and Leon been the heir to the throne was burdened to uphold his own name and stature. And if a convicted traitor managed to walk away with his life, Leon would see that as a lapse in power that would spread hope to foreign wizards like a virus that they too could break the law and escape the king's justice and unstable the balance of power they upheld.

If Bregit did manage to win the duel without the use of his staff, he would by law be allowed leave with the stain of traitor cleansed from his titles. Losing to his opponent would grant them the reward of claiming his life, a feat Bregit would be granted if their faiths were reversed. 'The knack in his prize,' thought Bregit.

There was no gain to be got by killing a wizard following orders. Bregit remembered the last Ultimate Colour, he watched before the events unfolded down in the cloud cells. Observing how the king commanded his Lutizs to kill the wizards beyond healing. ''A deserved faith!'' he remembered Dirm announcing to the foreign crowd that stood watching from the stands powerless to act while their kin were ripped in half by the Lutiz's spears. The begging and pleading from the crowds had no effect on the Lutiz's, who were wizards trained to have no reason or doubt, fearing nothing only their master's lash. Killing was their nature due to been hardened by brutality and suffering they endured as Ripelings. Lutizs relished in the suffering of others and rarely killed instantly for they would always savour a kill, once they knew their victim had nothing left to offer. The king's assassin's, Orakil the Silver nick named them when it was passed that Lutizs would be the new kings guard after the lords of lands abandoned the throne. And it was they Bregit feared facing, because if the king picked one of his Lutizs to stand for the crown Bregit had no doubt even his skills would be on par level against such emotionless wizards. A Lutizs' spear was Malas made and able to penetrate anything it met, which became useful when crushing the skulls of their enemies, but they could also absorb magical energies which rendered Bregit's plan of attack useless.

The air had become thick and claustrophobic. Hard ground no longer ripped the skin from his dragged feet, it was now soft and delicate sand he felt brush against his ripped legs. It didn't last long; no luxury ever did in the Golden Kingdom as echoes of booing and hard objects been thrown from the crowd told Bregit he'd entered the den of the Pin-Fars. The cries of loud jeering voices beat against the drums in his ears, deafening him slightly. Traitor and filth were some of the kinder words fired at Bregit from the mouths of wizards he was intending to save.

''Hear them,'' came Leon's gleeful voice. ''No matter what you've done in the past you will die knowing it was for nothing,'' came the faint voice of Leon from behind Bregit's ears.

Their insults didn't bother Bregit, he was too old to allow cruel jibes to affect him. But the restraint he was forcing himself to bare was becoming difficult to maintain. He dreaded seeing his legs, he could feel his skin peeling from the knee down. The dry hard ground had caught hold of his feeble skin and peeled away most part of his legs and covered the patches with dry dirt that pained him terribly.

"My father was a fool to return, this isn't justice but a pathic rouse, and a sad attempt to save his traitor friend. Under my reign no clause will defy a death sentence," vowed Leon.

Bregit couldn't help smiling to himself at how powerless Leon was to overrule his father. The young prince was fuelled by pride and vanity, qualities Bregit knew would one shade be the ruin of him.

"Then scum like you will no longer use cracks in systems to slither from true justice," snarled Leon, just loud enough for Bregit to hear.

The encounters he had faced since leaving Larmont should have killed him yet here he was beaten, bruised, and cut. His dignity tarnished having been the subject to Leon's cruelty. Yet he was alive and as he numbed himself from the physical and mental pain Bregit sat feeling so alone that he wished only for all this to end. His only route to survival was to be killed or kill his handpicked opponent, something Bregit wasn't freely willing to do. But if one life is what's required to save countless others then he had to win no matter the guilt he'd feel after wards.

Firm hands dug its nails in his shoulder piercing his bones and forcing a low grunt to escape his dry mouth. "Sit filth," spat an unfamiliar voice that Bregit had no doubt belonged to one of Leon's Lutizs. Feeling his spine bending by the force of the wizard's strength his rear end was firmly slammed down on the hardened surface. Thunderous applause erupted from the four corners of the den cringing both his ears as his blind fold was pulled unknotted from his face ripping a layer of flesh from under his eyes leaving Bregit with a mild burnt mark that caused his eyes to water. The sun shone bright blinding him, with his hands tied behind his back Bregit closed his eyes and dwelled in darkness until his eyes could adjust to the suns blinding rays.

"It will be a just sight, watching your head spiral in mid-air and your look of complete failure appeasing my joy," jeered Leon, the sound of his footsteps growing fainter in his ears telling Bregit his tormenter had left the den.

Chancing his luck, he slowly opened his eye lids. The sun rays creeped past his eye lashes; however, the bright beams were no longer powerful enough to sting his sight. Regaining his vision, Bregit could make out the stone arena built to shelter the Pin-Fars. It had lost its aura of fear, the once powerful fortress now stood broken and tattered and rotting under the heated sun. Nzer had neglected his duties and had allowed the den to wallow unattended. The surface was bone dry and no longer grew the green grass that fed the Pin-Fars, the pool of clear water which used to sit in the centre of the den was completely gone and covered in a bronze ring that looked like a duelling arena.

Then it hit Bregit, the den was no longer the home of the Pin-Fars but had been built into a duelling arena and a training dome for the Ripelings to practice their unbalanced powers without causing damage to the Depth Mountain.

Now the dreaded wait dawned on Bregit, with each passing drop seemed an eternity. But he remained composed as the prospect of fighting a wizard equipped with their staff caused his heart to beat rapidly. The king appeared on a balcony made of drop tree wood with smoothed railings stained in light brown paint. It was positioned on the peak of a ridge that was held firmly against the stone wall by thick silver chains. Chairs made of silver were placed behind the king's replica golden throne giving the higher ranked wizards a perfect view of the entire den. Nzer wore a light purple garment with black leather straps fitted tightly around his waist and collar. The cursed side of his face remained hung as the beaming yellow sun did everything in its power to show every scar wreaked upon his face. The king's undamaged side appeared deep in frustration as he watched Bregit kneeling in the centre of the arena.

The coven wore their usual sour grape expression, draped in grey sleeveless robes their eyes showing little affection to Bregit's unofficial presentation, it seemed preferable to them that he should have been executed in his cell and be done with this charade.

Thumping stomps reverberated throughout the arena lifting the dry dirt from the ground and made Bregit's body rattle. A muscular wizard with straps of lace black cords tied around his arms and legs grabbed his collar and pulled him to his feet. With a swipe of its hand Bregit was free of his bonds. Steady footed he waited eye bawling the four corners of the den. To his horror four wizards coloured in red riding on the backs of a Pin-far stood in front of every entrance. What little hope Bregit had of victory drained from his face, the Pin-Fars blood red eyes locked onto him. Their pincers snapped viciously while they slow walked toward him taunting him. Counting their long thick legs Bregit's final count came to thirty-two. Thirty-two against a single pair, even if he could channel his powers, he was powerless against the impenetrable skin of the Pin-Fars. Taking down one was tough, four was impossible. The beat down, lack of food and water, along with the unnerving taunts from Leon, was a simple but tactical stroke of genius. Wearing him down until he was near breaking point then shatter what little hope he had by sitting him in the centre of a ruined fortress and present him with little to non-opportunity of survival made Bregit finally realise why the prince looked so pleased with himself as he sat among the coven silver chair holders.

Leon no doubt had inherited the genes of his grandfather there was no denying that and it was surely this method that gained him so many supporters among the clouds.

The king raised his hand drawing all wizard's attention to him. ''My fellow wizards, and coven chair holders. We are gathered this shade in the ruin of one of many fortresses built by our ancestors which has stood for thousands of shades and refuged our greatest assets. This shade however will decide the guilt of a former general who served among my father's ranks and aided the defence of our existence twice against the mystical creatures...,''

Echoes of boos and shouts of treason came out from all angles of the den, the crowd's outburst didn't bother the king who disregarded the comments by using the power of his thundering voice to silence the taunts and jeers of the crowd.

''Had I sat on the throne when Bregit and his companion walked into my kingdom seeking my aid this punishment would not have been charged, but under the magical laws and the penalty if those laws aren't abided my hands are tied!'' declared the king in a high-pitched tone.

''By the covens or wizard laws?'' thought Bregit.

''The ruling passed by my son was elected and bonded in the court under the oaths of magical bindings and while I rule as king magical laws will be upheld!'' declared the king firmly to the applause of the crowd.

When the clapping stopped the king looked down upon Bregit wearing a stern look that didn't give Bregit any indication to what he was going to say next.

"Bregit the Yellow you are guilty of treason to the crown for claiming false titles of lands that were not yours to claim. The sentence has been passed with a clause that you willingly accepted. Part of that clause states you must duel an opponent of my choosing as the law states and if you are the victorious you will on my oath walk out of my kingdom a free wizard cleansed of all charges."

The king's sparkling purple eyes remained on as he concluded his announcement. "Lose and death will be your final act, will my guard clear the den for Bregit's opponent to enter," commanded the king in a final tone as he sat back on his throne.

The crowd did as they were bid, the Pin-Far riders retreated into their dark holes. Bregit didn't pay them much notice because a commotion amongst the balcony had caught his attention. The coven was huddled around the king's throne deep in whispering conversation, whatever they were consulting didn't appear part of Leon's plan because he seemed outraged enough to disband from the balcony and disappear down the wooden steps. The king waved the coven members away and reclaimed his standing position.

"Another law burdened on the shoulders of the king is deciding the opponent of the clause act of the death penalty," he said firmly. "The opponent I have chosen is a wizard we all know; one whose record speaks for itself. Wizards of the Golden Kingdom may I introduce, Leon the Black."

Bregit's eyes widened with shock. Leon, he was going to dual Leon the king's son and heir. Why?

Leon walked out from the left-hand side tunnel, throwing his heavy black cloak aside revealing his muscular arms and broad body. He wore black snakeskin straps along his arms and legs that were laced in a bark made breast plate stained in black paint. Leon walked slow praising the crowd with waves of praise for his admirers. When he made it to the dens centre his eyes narrowed making his nose and cheeks tense. He twirled his staff spinning it wildly in both hands which pleased the crowd. His jet-black hair lay combed and gelled behind his shoulders his bright thin cheeks curling into an evil grin.

"My father wanted you to die by the hand of a noble honourable wizard instead of feeding your witless body to the Pin-Fars. Had you cooperated during your shades in my cells I would've granted you mercy and ended you in a heartbeat but now I'll relish in taking you apart limb by limb," taunted Leon his change in attitude spreading a powerful vibe throughout the den.

Bregit stared down his opponent dwelling on his thoughts. The circumstances had changed dramatically, if he killed Leon would the king allow him to leave a free wizard or was this his old friends plan to rid himself of the burden of killing his own son and ending his plot to overthrow him?

It was too much a coincidence to deny, but Bregit had to leave his emotions aside and find a way to defeat Leon. He clenched his fists and focused his fullest attention on the prince who was his last obstacle to overcome to get out of the Golden Kingdom alive.

"Let duel begin," declared the king, to the roar of the watching crowd.

Leon spun his staff aiming his black diamond to the clouds in the sky summoning bolts of red lightning to its centre core when crimson he looked at Bregit.

"Shall we begin?"

Chapter 22

The Black Tower

Lucifer led Galli to the oaken door of Bregit's tower which she knew was impenetrable because it was protected by a curtain of enchanted water that flowed smoothly over the tower's door and effectively prevented outsiders from entering. Repeatedly warning Lucifer during their climb up the cliffs that the water curtain was unmovable, all he did was give Galli one of his charming smiles, which made him look jaw droppingly gorgeous. It required all of Galli's strong will to draw herself away from Lucifer's seductive gaze, his no response to her caution about the tower's defences making her wonder did Lucifer already know how to unlock the towers defences.

It didn't take long for Galli to get her answer. When they had made it to the doorstep of Bregit's tower, the red prince stood unfazed in front of the water curtain, casually waving his staff fluently and muttering incantations that sounded like he was talking with his mouth full of water, making it difficult for Galli to understand what he was saying. Looking from Lucifer to the water curtain, Galli heard a sizzling noise that sparked at the tip of Lucifer's staff and instantly produced a thin thread of scarlet red that spun and soared from the prince's staff and licked against the flowing water. Galli watched with a gloating grin as Lucifer's spell seemed to dissolve under the pressure of the flowing water. But just as Galli was about to tell Lucifer that she told him so, the water changed colour. It was no longer clear and see through, but diluted in thick blood, which froze the flowing water curtain and immobilised its enchanted mechanism.

"You did it," Galli breathed in awe.

"Polluting water was how my grandfather defeated the Orange Wizards of Tindisinge during the Halt of Supplies, my father taught me and my brother everything there is to know about unhinging stubborn enchantments," said Lucifer in a positive manner. "Now let us get inside before the Varwels arrive, we have a lot of planning and little drops to do it," he said pushing the oaken door open.

Lucifer walked without fear through the door frame, Galli followed him, and was embraced by a warm aura that coursed through her body as she entered a brightened hallway glowing in sunshine yellow.

"Wow," said Galli who stared up with wonder at the long rows of staircases.

The walls were stained golden yellow as were the stairs. Galli took hold of the handles and walked up the thin flight of steps careful not to catch her feet on her damp robes. Each flight of stairs had eighteen steps and at the top of each stair was a long thin corridor. Lucifer passed the first-floor corridor with no interest whatsoever but when it came to the second-floor corridor, he took a left and led Galli into a hallway with three solid wooden doors. The walls were unlike anything Galli had ever seen before. It was like an ocean was trapped within the foundations; clear water flowed swiftly along the corridor's walls.

"This is amazing," gasped Galli who couldn't believe what she was seeing.

"Fascinating, isn't it?" said Lucifer smiling at Galli's stunned reaction. "It would explain the towers defences been so strong, Bregit protects creatures who are unable to fend for themselves and locks them in his tower to keep them away from the cruel world they are forced to live in. My father would consider this kind of treatment soft."

"Sea creatures?" Thought Galli who investigated the watery wall with a keener inspection.

There were serpents long and thin swimming freely along the walls but when their green hazel eyes seen that she nor Lucifer were Bregit they disappeared into the endless depths of Lucifer's enchanted sea. When Lucifer placed his palm on the wall and took it away his hand was dripping of drops that made him laugh that made Galli's legs turn to jelly at how good looking, he appeared when his face wasn't showing any signs of strain.

Galli watched him wipe his hands dry using the sleeves of his robe before walking toward the door at the bottom of the hall. Tapping on it twice with the point of his staff the door creaked and opened by itself. Lucifer tipped the door open wider with his pointed finger giving Galli a glimpse to what was been contained within the room. Shelves made of pinewood and stained in golden bronze paint hung on every wall of the oval shaped room. Strong black chains held thick leathered books on all shelves, the bindings had writing inked in gold, but it was written in a language Galli didn't know so she couldn't tell what names the books were given?

''Why have you brought me in here?'' Galli asked Lucifer, watching him walk through the room scanning each section of books carefully.

''Bregit has knowledge leading back to the shades of the first age of wizards, before he left the Golden Kingdom, he was a silver chair holder and a keeper of scrolls, though he would never steal the scrolls, I bet my staff he memorized each one and wrote them out exactly as they are in the vaults of the Golden Kingdom,'' replied Lucifer with his back to Galli.

''Is that the reason you agreed to defend Larmont, to see what Bregit keeps hidden in his library?'' Galli asked, feeling her hand tighten around the grip on her staff.

''For cycles of shades I begged my father to let me learn about the age of our elders just so I could study their brands of magic and push my powers beyond what I felt to be average,'' answered Lucifer. ''Wanting to advance my knowledge isn't treason or seeking personal glory, I just wanted to learn how a group of wizards with little knowledge of their powers established themselves as one of the dominate creatures of Nocktar. If that is a crime, then we are being punished and deprived of our development because of ruling wizards afraid to lose their power,'' said Lucifer plainly.

''I used to think the same,'' admitted Galli bitterly. ''When I asked Lorneid about the lack of learning facilities in Nocktar he reminded me to keep my mouth shut and my eyes open but when he appointed me his Second, he taught me all he knew. But during my lessons I questioned why weren't all wizards my age been taught these abilities?''

''It seems to have paid off; you planted a big seed of doubt in the lords of lands minds when you accomplished something everyone considered preposterous,'' said Lucifer.

''My Ultimate Colour victory is a memory soon to fade; yes, it brought honour to Treforledge and gave the Blue Wizards some recognition among the other lords. Still, it matters not now, even if Lano is defeated I doubt Treforledge will ever be the same again,'' said Galli with scorn.

''It is a great loss, Treforledge was a great kingdom that served loyally throughout many wars. But what is broken can be fixed. Lano may have wiped out your population, but he didn't destroy you all and as long as there are those who remember Treforledge, its grace will never fade,'' said Lucifer kindly.

Galli smiled as she began feeling her cheeks burn slightly, thankfully Lucifer was walking further down the room to stare at more books on their shelves to notice her blushing.

"What are you doing?" Galli asked herself. "He's a prince, in his mind you are beneath him and lords would never find a Second in anyway attractive so stop your Ripeling behaviour and focus on what you are here for!" said a strong voice in Galli's mind.

"I'm sure if I made any attempt to lift a single book from its shelf, I would endure unimaginable pain, after all why would a stranger from a distant land rummage through a stack of newly furbished books written in the old language of the wizards?" said Lucifer looking at each bookshelf in wonder.

"How do you know they're written in old wizard speech?" asked Galli.

"I've seen enough of markings carved along the hallways of the Golden Kingdoms corridors to know wizard speech when I see it," answered Lucifer.

Galli looked at each book in turn, Lucifer was right the markings on the side of every book were engraved with letters and smeared with golden ink. The letters looked rearranged with odd lines and shapes cutting across each letter.

"What do you think they mean?" asked Galli.

"The only word I can translate is this," answered Lucifer pointing his finger at a dusted book in front of him and showing Galli a symbol of two v's joining together. "It means Sage," said Lucifer noticing the confusion on Galli's face.

"I came across the word when I was a Ripeling because my grandfather had summoned the last line of Sages to the Golden Kingdom to negotiate terms of peace, but it turned out to be a trap and when they were all together in the one room my grandfather executed them one by one until only one was left standing. Before my grandfather finished him, the Sage ripped off its armour revealing this exact symbol carved into its flesh. After the Sages were killed, I asked my father what that sign on the wizard's chest referred to? He told me it was an ancient wizard symbol that meant Sage and that all Sages were branded with the mark…,"

"But why brand themselves, if they were smart, they'd hide their marks and try blend in with the other wizards, it surely would've saved their specie," said Galli.

"The Sages were strong believers of living beyond themselves, that when they die their life force is given to another wizard with a link to their line. My Grandfather feared the Sages and their powers so much he did everything in his power to snuff them out, he fulfilled his quest, but many say there are Sages still out there living beyond the Lands of Light, my father disagrees and claims they went extinct," said Lucifer.

"Sages were peaceful protectors of the Grass Lands; they had no desire for power or riches. I heard the tale of the king's snuffing of the Sages; he lured them into a gathering, making them believe he wanted to negotiate a peace treaty that would grant the Sages a stronghold but when the king got them inside the Golden Kingdom, he arrested them and burnt their leaders," said Galli remembering Lorneids description of the fall of the Sages.

"True, he did," agreed Lucifer. "My grandfather was merciless when it came to a threat, his reign was the worst of any kings in wizard history. I had hoped my father would be different, but he still is as ignorant as his father and far less noticeable of threats. He may say he knows Lano is back, but he has yet to counter him, he didn't even allow me any drops to gather my army to hold Larmont which is why I don't feel he understands the seriousness of what is happening beneath his feet," said Lucifer.

"Bregit thought the same, but he still inclined to travel to the Golden Kingdom to alert the king, it was only his misfortune that it was you and not your father sitting on the throne at that shade of our arrival," said Galli coldly.

Lucifer shook his head in disbelief. "My father was beyond himself when he heard of Bregit's arrest, my brother Leon the wizard who guided you both up the Cloud Stair was planning to execute Bregit and have you stripped of your colour for your kind gesture during your rise in the Ultimate Colour tournament. Had my informants not alerted me of Leon's plot you and Bregit would be dead!" Lucifer explained firmly. "I had to act as a king without giving the slightest sign I cared. Why do you think I got my kings guard to bring you to me and not the golden temple, I had no idea my brother had Corlock on his side? The moment I left you he enchanted my candles to dull you and Bregit into a comatose sleep and bring you before the coven, leaving me with no choice but to trail uses as criminals," Lucifer took a deep breath and cleared his throat. "Bregit will be ok I'm sure of it, with my father back on the throne I am certain he will convince Bregit to take the clause in his sentence which allows him to fight a wizard of my father's choosing. If Bregit wins he will be allowed leave a free wizard cleared of all charges."

"And if he loses?" asked Galli, feeling she already knew the answer.

"He will be killed," answered Lucifer his voice tense.

Galli held her tongue but left the room in disgust, walking up the hallway and back out to the yellow stairway that had two floors above the one Galli occupied. She took the stairs leading to the upper floors trying to understand where Lucifer was coming from but her negligence to understand the ways of the Golden Kingdom kept her anger visible toward Leon. What happens if Bregit dies? And for what, because Lucifer had to play the role of a fool to fool the fool, it angered Galli that even in the Golden Kingdom wizards were play acting with lives just to keep themselves in a position of power.

The third-floor corridor had a wider hallway than the earlier two Galli had passed. There were no doors along the walls but there was a window frame that opened to an outside lookout with thick black stained bannisters that Galli presumed Bregit used to lean on whenever he wanted to stop and stare at the horizon. The stairs creaked every step Galli took, she could feel the weight of her feet press hard into the wood making her cautious not to lean too heavy in case she fell through the floor. The high corridor caught her attention the moment she glimpsed the flower decorated walls that were veined over both walls, every flower trailed along the vines linked to the other and not breaking a thread. The background was coated in a lime-coloured grass that made Galli envious of Bregit's artistic designs. An oaken door lay at the end of the high corridor that had a tree painted around it in the same stained brown as the door. Its leaf less branches stretched out linking to the last flower, it looked from Galli's point of view that the trees were catching the flowers from blowing away.

"The shield in the storm," whispered Galli.

"I beg to differ, it seems to me that the wind is the unstoppable force, and the tree is the immovable object, both forces that can never seem to agree," said Lucifer.

Galli didn't react to Lucifer's unexpected arrival, there was still a doubt lingering inside her about trusting him. Perhaps if Bregit survived she could in shades find it within herself to forgive the prince because he did risk his own life to save hers. And if there was one thing Galli hated, it was owing a debt. Lucifer overtook Galli and opened the oaken door.

The room was scented in organic fragrances that gave the whiff of wild fields. 'Seems Bregit likes the feeling of been outside even when indoors,' thought Galli walking into the room.

When the two wizards stood in the centre of the wide framed room, they got a full view of its inhabitants. A table sat under the square window and was filled with scrolls which were laid out neatly and in line alongside the other. Two wooden chairs with thick solid wooden arms that were laced in green knitted cushions sat in a corner each facing each other. The walls were sunset orange and radiated low waves of heat giving Galli the source of where the fragrances were coming from. A large bed with patched pillows and duvets lay alone on the other side of the room. It appeared unattended for a long spell making Galli wonder would Bregit ever again find the comforts of his own bed.

"The Varwels will be here within the shade, my scouts informed me they have crossed the Grass Lands a shade passed, meaning they will refuge in the sphinx's mountain before laying siege on Larmont."

"Tip-Karp is loyal to wizards he would never allow an army of Varwels to shelter beneath his mountain," said Galli convincingly.

"Tip-Karp has joined with Lano and opened his mountain to the Council of Shadows. The sphinx was always a creature unbended to our laws, it was only a matter of drops before he chose to serve another. My father always said Tip-Karp resented wizards and the sphinx's actions have proven me false and my father right," said Lucifer.

Galli pulled out one of the table chairs and dragged it away from the table. Lucifer looked at her in wonder as to why she didn't just magically summon the chair to her. Galli sat down with her back to Lucifer and her head in her hands. Tip-Karp saved Bregit and allowed her kin to stay in his keeps but if Lucifer were right then, no, Galli would not allow herself to believe it until she seen it with her own eyes. Without thinking she leaped from her chair and ran for the oaken door but before she placed her hand on the handle a firm hand gripped her wrist. Lucifer's red mystified eyes investigated her dejected blue eyes, Galli could sense his concern through the concentrated look he was giving her.

"It's too late," said Lucifer in a firm tone. "Tip-Karp will have killed the survivors of Treforledge. I know it may feel your fault but believe me it isn't the only one responsible for the death of your kin is Tip-Karp."

"Let me go, or I'll make you!" cried Galli, feeling the hot tears slide down her cheeks as she wrestled her arm out of Lucifer's slackened grip.

But as Galli went to open the door it dawned on her like a cold chill creeping up her spine that they were gone and deep down she knew it. The smiling faces of Selpay and Leiva crushed Galli's insides as the thought of them dead made her fall onto her knees and burst into tears.

"It was Lorneid's final wish for me to lead them to Tip-Karps Mountain and me the fool followed a dying wizard's advice," sobbed Galli.

Galli couldn't remember how long she sat huddled dwelling on her dead kin, but it was only when Lucifer sat a clay made mug beside her with white steam smoking from its top did, she finally detached herself from the warm embrace of her limbs.

"Seemed the opportunity to make a hot cup of my famous cherry tea, trust me if that doesn't cheer you up nothing will," said Lucifer his attempt at been sentimental making Galli's skin crawl.

It wasn't because of Lucifer that she felt this way it was because kindness was a rare trait among the islands of Treforledge. Galli despised sympathy and strongly believed it had no place in her life and as the commander of an army it was her duty to shrug off such feelings to be the complete warrior. The cup Lucifer had laid in front of Galli was warm to hold and the fumes flowing from the purplish liquid was refreshing to inhale. Galli sipped the purple liquid with her lips and the moment it streamed down her throat it inflamed her body with such flare she could feel her skin begin to radiate actual heat.

"The secret ingredient is the oil extracted from the Woltondox Flower, when I became Lord of Sun Stroke, I used the flowers to create healing spores and kept their juices to mix with some of wizards favoured beverages. I call the mixture I gave you Quick Spark, because once it hits the pit of your stomach it explodes like a grenade and only ceases when all sense of doubt has been erased," Lucifer explained with a smile.

"Your concoction is a success," said Galli her voice hoarse as she wiped her chin having downed the cherry tea in one swallow.

The feeling flowing through Galli's body was not one of happiness or relief. Lucifer's drink had turned her senses to mush but through the dizziness she did feel a growth in her powers and a reassured confidence she remembered having as a Ripeling.

"I understand slightly what you are going through," said Lucifer. "When the Aqua Guardians rose from the Red Sea, they killed my mother. The grief I suffered led me to do terrible things and the funny thing is I regretted none of it, want to know why? Because it felt good to see their blue coats turn black and smoke while I watched and smiled at their screams of pain, I took my grief so far, I fed them alive to the Harpies which gained me an everlasting alliance with the winged beasts," said Lucifer with contempt in his voice.

Galli didn't know what to say it was probably the influence of the Quick Spark and having regrettably downed in one mouthful, but her idea of vengeance was to kill Lano and no one else, that compared to Lucifer's idea of revenge was deeper than she could ever believe imaginable.

"Is that why you brew remedies, to make your mind forget what kind of monster lurks inside?" Galli asked flatly.

Lucifer looked at Galli with a half grin on his clear features. "You really are smart, I thought you went with the flow when you battled in the Ultimate Colour, that your sole purpose was to embarrass your superiors in some act of revenge," said Lucifer.

"I never wanted to kill anyone, there are other ways of winning without having to murder fellow wizards. Valuing life is not discriminating and something in me always told me to do the right thing even if it meant disappointing everyone else," Galli admitted.

"Maybe if there were more wizards like you, we would indeed have peace, but unfortunately power corrupts and with corruption comes madness and chaos, the ingredients that come freely to those in power," Lucifer said light heartily.

Galli noticed he was reading the scrolls laid out on Bregit's table. "I thought you couldn't read wizard speech?"

"I can't but these scrolls have letters I can translate, you see it's like our language except Bregit has scrambled the words making them appear a poem," Lucifer replied.

"Encrypted, he's put symbols over every letter that begins with a creatures first name," Galli contradicted, pointing her finger at the title which read Sage.

'That word again,' she thought. Reading further down the paper Galli was fascinated about how descriptive and detailed the information about the Sage's appearances, their hair, and marble skin that reflected even the suns beams, having never met a Sage Galli thought they looked like normal wizard's.

''Why would Bregit have these spread out for anyone to see?''

''Maybe he fancied some light reading,'' said Galli not understanding why Lucifer was taking Bregit's laid out scrolls serious.

Galli found that Lucifer was a quick reader because after a few drops of his eyes moving up and down he turned away from the table and looked out into the courtyard. Galli peered over the table looking at the scrolls and read about the power and wisdom the Sages owned above other powers.

''I have a feeling Bregit didn't just send us here to defend his lands,'' said Lucifer seriously. ''I think what he is genuinely wanting saved is what rests in his tower.''

''Like what?'' asked Galli.

''I can't put my finger on it, but something is telling me Bregit is the only one seeing the bigger picture in all of this. He knew those scrolls were left out before he told me to go to Larmont,'' said Lucifer feeling annoyed with himself.

''Are you saying Bregit is withholding information?''

''A wizard who just one shade packs up and leaves his position as Depth Head General and takes lordship over a stronghold without any reason is sure to be withholding something,'' said Lucifer flatly.

Galli considered Lucifer's claims about Bregit but from what he was saying if Bregit had planned for these scrolls to be read by her or Lucifer he was playing a dangerous game, because either one of them could have died before reaching Larmont.

'No!' thought Galli shaking her head in frustration. Lucifer was just being paranoid maybe the battle ahead was making him uneasy, whatever was causing his paranoia Galli didn't know and didn't care, she had her own worries and paranoid beliefs weren't a good mixture before a battle. Not wanting further debate, she held her tongue, nodding and agreeing whenever Lucifer would go on a rant about Bregit playing them like puppets.

''Shouldn't we be preparing for the Varwels?'' Galli said in attempt to change the subject.

''I have sent messages to all creatures among Larmont, none have responded. Bregit has many secret passages in and out of this tower they may be refuging somewhere nearby.''

''If they were to survive, wouldn't it be wiser for them to fight instead of hiding?'' asked Galli.

''Cave keepers and Pixies do not fare well in battle. The trees may withstand an aerial attack, but forest creatures don't it's just you and me Galli against a swarm of Varwels.''

''Two wizards against an army how did I get myself into this,'' Galli sighed.

''We will defend Larmont to the best of our abilities, if it is beyond our skills we will flee. I will not die defending a foreign land and I won't allow you to do the same. This battle doesn't matter in my opinion, saving Larmont won't stop Lano, but if we can decrease his army then I say we should at least try for the benefit of the wizards preparing themselves for the approaching battle,'' said Lucifer.

Galli couldn't argue with his intent, he was right they had the opportunity to cut a chunk off Lano's forces here and now, and if it helped win the war, she would be honoured to play her part.

''Where are you going?'' said Lucifer only noticing Galli was at the door about to leave the room.

''To prepare, if the Varwels are coming I want to be in position before they arrive,'' Galli replied her cunning smile making Lucifer beam with excitement as he followed her lead down the tower's stairs.

Chapter 23

A Viledirks Tale

The clouds were warm to walk among, the shades effects not altering their temperature in the slightest. White beams glazed from the blankets of clouds laid out in front of Carka. Low moans found their way to his ever-active ears, the sound of his captive in pain giving the elderly wizard something to be cheerful for. Kcor tossed and turned in his tight bonds that rendered the mighty Viledirk powerless and unable to throw off Carka's freezing spell.

The Golden Kingdom's bright glow was less than a mile's walk. It's tame beams brightening Carka's features. With every step he put in front forward he could feel the knot tightening around his chest as the very thoughts of returning to that corrupt kingdom made Carka nervous. It was a place he never believed he would lay eyes upon again, but here he was drawing closer to the golden gates unknowing to what kind of welcome he was going to receive. Carka couldn't help feeling slightly on edge at this prospect, especially since his return didn't intend on him returning to the king's service but to instead show him up for the blind fool he had become since his coronation.

His dwelling on thoughts seemed to quicken his pace, for the golden gate was straight ahead, its radiant glows beaming with warmth heightened Carka's morale. But through the glows no gatekeeper appeared which frustrated Carka because he wasn't one to be kept waiting especially when drops were precious in his attempt to countering Lano and his schemes. Waiting, Carka thought about the Varwels, who were on the move to the eastern lands. Carka was unsure about their destination, but with only two bases to attack, Larmont or Tip-Karps Mountain. Carka's bet was Larmont as their preferred target. With Bregit away Larmont was open to assault now that the Gliders were banished and the Cave Keepers were given full reign over Larmont's mountains, Carka dreaded been the one to tell Bregit that his home would no doubt be in ruin by the shade he returned.

Having narrowly avoided the Varwel army on his journey from the lair of the Twig Collectors. Carka was convinced Lano was nesting somewhere beyond the reach of wizards with a powerful force behind him. This idea of dividing his forces was neat because it meant Lano was announcing his return and planting a seed of doubt into the minds of those who claim to know the Lava Keepers ways of thinking. Because without Lano leading the charge into battle who was to say he'd returned, only Bregit witnessed the Lava Keeper since he was banished and the word of one wizard wasn't convincing no matter how high ranked you were, but that was all about to change.

Absorbing the warmth of the golden gates, Carka studied its design with interest. The bars were iron made and sprayed in golden-brown with sharp pointy spears at the top of each thick bar. The golden gate had no handle because only the gate keeper knew the spell to unhinge the enchantment holding the gate tightly shut. Having spent many shades as a Ripeling walking the clouds Carka remembered his many conversations with the gate keeper about why the Golden Kingdom needed two entry points.

Not a wizard to be communicated with due to his long cycles of shades spent in isolation, the gate keeper rudely told Carka that there were many routes into the Golden Kingdom, and it was his job to seal and reseal those routes so that the Golden Kingdom could not be infiltrated by the mystical creatures. Unnerved about the gate keeper recognising him, Carka's change in colour and appearance was his mask and should be sufficient to getting him inside without drawing further inspection.

Stern and narrow were the gate keeper's expression when commoners came seeking an audience with the king. Carka's slight experience of having learned what the gate keeper's attitude was like in his cycles among the clouds was the perfect skill to possess when been greeted by the gate keeper's ignorance. Feeling that he had wasted enough drops standing reminiscing Carka raised his hand and gripped the bar of the golden gate. The moment his hand grasped the shiny bars a whoosh of purple smoke swirled behind the gate forming into a tall figure. The gatekeeper appeared, wearing a thick light-coloured purple cloak with streaks of silver lines trailing up its sleeves. A golden badge lay perfectly straight at his collar pinning each side of the cloak together. Frowning at Carka, the gatekeeper looked at him with his hawk eyes examining him head to toe through the golden bars. Carka stared sternly back giving the gatekeeper a curt nod that narrowed his eyes with suspicion.

"Who goes there? Speak your purpose for entering the Golden Kingdom," said the gate keeper in a demanding tone.

"I have travelled from the grass lands with great heed and demand an audience with your king, at once!" said Carka with urgency in his voice.

The gate keeper's sharp purple eyes moved slightly glancing at the hoovering figure above Carka's head. He then fixed his eyes again on Carka who remained still faced. Carka returned the same examining look back at the gate keeper, who was tall with a dent in both cheeks, his nose was crooked meaning it had been broken more than once, his hair was sun ray purple that was braided and hung neatly along his spine but through his appearance Carka knew just by his stature this was going to fair badly for one of them.

"The king has other matters to attend to this shade, he doesn't have drops to spare for beggars at his gate who presume I will grant passage to any wizard offering gifts. Be gone before I call the Gliders to dispose of what's left of you," said the gate keeper in an unforgiving voice.

The gate keeper's words rose an impatient nerve already throbbing inside Carka from his encounter with the cloud and been forced to flee. He raised his arm stretching his fingers as wide as he could. "Lootaveou," he called, causing the malas stone implanted in the midpoint of his palm to glow a bright silver.

The gate keeper's body froze on the spot, when Carka wrenched his arm the gate keeper's hands came out from under his heavy sleeves. Smiling at how easy it was to control his mind Carka forced him to unseal the enchantments protecting the golden gate. Still clutching the bar of the gate, Carka pushed it open with ease and strolled by the entranced gate keeper whose eyes were sliding in and out of focus under the pressure of Carka's falsification curse.

"Don't worry you'll be back to yourself the moment I leave this wretched place, so if there's any part of that feeble mind able to understand what I am saying it would be in your best interest to not try and stop me leaving," said Carka delicately walking by the gate keeper.

When he entered the boundaries of the Golden Kingdom something felt wrong due to the atmosphere being tense, the golden path leading to the entrance of the king's temple was as bare as a dead tree. The life of the kingdom seemed drained. The Lutizs who would normally patrol the paths and safe keep the city of golden temples were nowhere to be seen. ''Perhaps he should've questioned the gate keeper before taking control of his mind,'' thought Carka feeling foolish for his lapse.

Then it came, a whisper in the wind that tickled the drum of his ears, it was the voice of the king only Carka couldn't figure out exactly what he was saying but he was certain it wasn't far away. Carka looked in the direction the king's voice was coming from, he made out a tarnished broken-down fortress with chunks of rock rotted from its walls even it's great gate of bronze stood bent and broken.

''Seems the Pin-Fars are little concern of the king if he's unwilling to attend to their ancient sanctuary,'' Carka muttered to himself.

'A poor repayment for cycles of shades of loyalty,' thought Carka turning his body left and heading in the direction of the den his levitating victim trailing behind.

The roars of wizards screaming drummed through the skies while flashing lights glowed through the cracks of the weakened rocks of the Pin-Fars Den. There was no denying a duel was taking place within the den the question was why? Carka was aware the Ultimate Colour was a shade away so why were wizards ruining their chances of participating in the tournament by squabbling for the praise of a dozen wizards? There were no defences shielding the den. And that was because no wizard was dumb enough to enter without a Pin-far rider or tamer alongside them, with a duel taking place inside, the Pin-Fars would no doubt be patrolling the outer rears of the den, meaning Carka could sneak in unseen. The entrance was an open round gap suitable enough for two Pin-Fars to walk in and out side by side. Carka pulled his rough shabby hood over his head covering his dim features with a snap of his thin fingers Kcor was cloaked in a concealment spell making him invisible to the naked eye.

Darkness covered the tunnel. On his few visits to the Pin-Fars den he remembered the wide tunnels filled with beacons of golden light that shone from the torches of the wizard tamers who looked after the Pin-Fars and tamed their instincts for killing. A trait Carka valued highly, because taming fierce beasts like Pin-Fars was dangerous especially when they were new-born. Because that was when their killer instincts were at its peak. Pin-Fars thirst for flesh is needed for their coats to harden so they can withstand the shades effects, because without their coats Pin-Fars were as weak as pixies against flame. Through his cycles living in the Golden Kingdom, he saw many wizards become arrogant when they believed their Pin-Fars were under their control only to fall prey to their lust for flesh. It was a fool's mistake but a beneficial one which proved Pin-Fars were not the mindless beasts many portray them to be. After many deaths Dirm the Bronze gave permission to perform more brutal ways of taming the beasts and those measures of cruelty had exceeding results.

Walking cautiously down the tunnel Carka became aware of four tunnels each one leading to a different corner of the den. Twice Carka heard the crackling of the Pin-Fars sharp pincers snapping as the battle in the den seemed to be getting heated. What was worse wizards in red sat on the back of each Pin-Far, meaning they were watching the duel inside the tunnels. Luckily, their attentions were on the duel outside and not what lurked inside the tunnel. Still, this didn't get Carka any closer to entering the arena undetected. 'Great idea Carka go into the den and not consider that every entrance would be covered by Pin-Far riders,' he said to himself feeling irritated.

Leaning against the tunnel's dry wall Carka watched the back of the Pin-Far through the corner of his eye making sure his presence didn't stir its senses. He should've brought along a few Pixies, their powers of allowing others to see through their eyes would be the exact set of skills Carka required at this precise moment. The thought did give him a hilarious idea, one Carka and his friend Orakil attempted when they were training to be generals of the Depth Mountain. Except back then it went horribly wrong and got him whipped severely by the king's guard. Though it was laughable now Carka remembered spending two shades lying on his stomach due to the skin on his back being lashed and he still bore the scars on his back as a reminder to what his foolish ploy as a young ripe almost cost him.

Standing to his fullest height, knowing exactly what he had to do to rid himself of his Pin-Far problem. Carka rubbed his hands together, creating clear white smoke that flowed through his fingers and sailed to the ceiling of the tunnel. Crackling sounds like the snaps the Pin-Fars pincher made, crackled, and popped in Carka's face making bright red sparks sizzle in the air. With a low blow of air from his whistling mouth the sparks merged and formed into tiny fireflies coated in yellow and red flame their wings flappy and dabbed with glittering specks of red-hot sparks.

''Lamco,'' breathed Carka softly to his fireflies.

At the sound of his voice, the fireflies magically soared like a shooting star right up the Pin-Fars back side. Its hissing screams echoed throughout the tunnel, but it wasn't loud enough to draw any outside attention as the Pin-far rider was tossed from his saddle while his Pin-far hissed in agony as the fireflies' burning sensation was too hot for the eight-legged creature to handle.

Smiling while he snapped his fingers, Carka's firefly wreaked havoc inside the Pin-Far exploding at the sound of his snap which sent off powerful waves of energy that caused the great beasts impenetrable coat to shatter and fall into a thousand pieces to the shock of his watching rider. Acting fast Carka immobilized the stunned Pin-Far rider with a neat numbing spell that froze his insides. Approaching him Carka looked down upon him their eyes met as the wonder of what just happened grew in the rider's mind.

''My apologies for my rude coming but I can't risk been seen yet and I know you would've caused a scene if I had in anyway attempted to smooth you over, so no hard feelings you'll be walking in due course until then I'm afraid you'll have to simply wait here and inhale the fumes of your fallen friend,'' said Carka patting the wizards shoulder before leaving him laying immobilised within the tunnel.

Walking into the rays of sunshine that beat away the darkness of the tunnel Carka got a clear view of the sand arena. The ageing walls had parts sliced from their tops and were left on the cracked surface of the den. One stand was visible, and it hung over a ridge high above the battlements with enough space to fit six silver chairs and a golden throne. Which were all occupied by wizards Carka had no trouble recognising.

They were undeniably the coven silver chair holders and there was no mistaking the king whose face was half cursed from his encounter in battle. Apart from the deranged features Nzer appeared strong and stern faced, as the battle below didn't seem to have any interest to him at all. Turning his own attentions to the battle been fought in the den, he couldn't make out who they were from his point of view. The sun was blocking so much of the arena that the shadows of the fighters were clearer to see than their bodies.

Just then the two duellists came under the shadow of the ridge. A wizard wearing a bark made breast plate with black snakeskin straps along his arms and legs was mocking a ragged wizard who'd just withstood a blow to the head and countered with using his elbow to parry the black wizard aside. The drop the ragged wizard blew his hair aside Carka's mouth hung open with shock, because the wizard was in fact Bregit.

Carka watched sceptical while Bregit struggled to repel his opponent's powerful attacks, the speed of this Black Wizard was nothing Carka had ever seen before. Bregit was out of his depth and without his staff to channel his full power he was indeed going to lose this duel and worse his life. But the showing of Bregit and his determination to continue fighting on even when victory was beyond reach filled Carka with pride. As Bregit again managed to shield himself by summoning the fallen rocks of the arena to build a shield around his body. Though a strategic move because the manoeuvre halted his opponents stride momentarily. The Black Wizard was laughing while he twirled his staff along his fingers before brandishing his staff fiercely unleashing magical threads layered in black toxins that smothered Bregit's rock shield and forcing it to melt until nothing was left only an exhausted looking Bregit who was a light breeze away from falling face first into the dirt.

Again, the Black Wizard taunted Bregit shouting to the watching wizards hoovering above the den on floating white patches of cloud. Flexing his muscles, Carka watched the Black Wizard move so fast all Bregit could do was accept the deep blow he received to his mid-section and yell in pain as he fell to his knees. Buckled and unable to get up Bregit's run was up, his smug looking opponent was now in complete control and demonstrated it by not finishing Bregit there and then but turned around to the watching wizards to explain how he was going to end the life of this worthless criminal and use his death as an example to show all defying wizards who dare oppose the king what faith awaits them.

Having heard and seen enough Carka vanished on the spot as the Black Wizard raised his long staff and sent a dark purple beam at Bregit, Carka appeared in front of the defenceless Bregit. Raising his right arm, he blocked the purple jet of light with a well summoned energy shield that parried the curse and deflected it right back at its caster. Knowing the Black Wizard would swerve, Carka used his left hand to summon binding straps of bark that latched to the wizard's breastplate which allowed Carka to control the straps laced around his arms and legs giving him the perfect restraint. Hung and bound by his own lace work Carka slammed the Black Wizard against the wall of the den the impact of the collision forcing his staff to slip from his grasp and fall onto the sand.

''Carka,'' breathed Bregit in astonishment.

''Can't leave you alone for one shade and you get yourself into another mess,'' said Carka with sarcasm but he refused to look at Bregit, because even though the Black Wizard was unable to fight the coven along with the king were entering the den meaning he had to keep his shield intact.

''Carka the Silver, last living descendent of the silver line of wizards and former highchair holder of the covenant, victor of five Ultimate Colour tournaments and traitor to the crown,'' announced the king as he stopped his stride inches from Carka's mirror wall.

''Your curtsey has lost its value as has your honour. What wizard stands by as his friend gets embarrassed and insulted?'' Carka spat savagely at the king and coven members.

The king and his coven silver chair holders stayed in the centre of the den a fair distance from Carka's mirror wall. Many of them looked at him with disgust others seemed pleased to see him, the king however looked furious to have Carka so close. His expression soured probably because of how easily Carka handled his executioner so easily.

"What brings the deserter back from the pits of Dulgerdeen?" the king asked bitterly.

Carka laughed. "I have come unlike to my foolish friend behind me with proof of what Bregit has told you to be true," Carka replied loud enough for all wizards to hear. "Allow Bregit his lordship and colour reinstated, and I will share with you and the coven my proof," demanded Carka.

The king's expression turned into a look of outrage even the dead skin on his face cracked, but Carka could tell he was curious and understood too well that Carka would never have entered the Golden Kingdom without a shred of proof to back up his demands.

"Reveal this proof you claim to possess, and I may consider your terms," said the king loud enough for all to hear.

Carka sucked at the insides of his dry lips, knowing he had the king right where he wanted him. With a wink of his right eye his non-seeing enchantment concealing Kcor was lifted and Kcors body dropped roughly at the king's feet. Shooting tame sparks of lightning at the cords Kcor was released of his bondage. The king didn't appear surprised or scared by the body covered in petals, but when Carka's arm twisted forcing the petals to break loose their hold and open, revealing the broad muscular frame of Kcor the Viledirk the king's mouth gaped open with shock.

"Here lays a creature you banished from the Lands of Light to rot and die in the outer wastelands beyond the Red Sea. Yet I found him rallying up the Harpies and executing them at will in Wivirid. As I recall powerful spells prevented the Council of Shadows ever leaving the waste lands yet, I found one roaming freely throughout our lands, would you care to explain how such a thing happened under your watch?" Carka addressed the king and his coven making sure his voice echoed throughout the den.

Pally the Yellow passed by the king and knelt by Kcors side looking at the fearsome beast with wonder. "This can no longer be ignored," she said with seriousness. "If the lord of the Viledirks has returned then his master has as well, we as a united council must summon our fullest strength and find Lano," voiced Pally to the king.

The rest of the coven remained tight lipped allowing Pally's suggestion to wash over them. The king seemed out of sorts as he knew Pally was right but still, he refused to speak.

"We will continue this conversation in my council chamber, Bregit, Carka you will both attend as will my coven chair holders. Carka bring Kcor with you I want to hear what he has to say. He turned to the confused crowd watching from the stands.

"Wizards of the Golden Kingdom certain problems have come to my attention that need addressing I beg your pardons, but it cannot wait. Bregit the Yellow's crimes will be answered but not until more concerning matters are dealt with now return to your stations, at once!" ordered the king.

The crowd obeyed with no argument, one by one they drifted from the den leaving Carka and a weakened Bregit alone with the king and his coven.

"Carka, Bregit lets go, we cannot afford to waste drops. If what you say is true, then we need to discuss a plan of action," said the king.

"I will not be tricked or lured into your chambers to be woken up chained to your walls, forgive me your highness but Bregit maybe a loyalist and oath holder, but I am not, we will speak here or not at all," said Carka with a coldness to his tone. "Drops are precious to me also, as we speak a Varwel army flies east in numbers that eclipse the sky in golden beams that blind all who stare upon them, so pardon my rudeness, but I haven't come here to quench your thirsts for thrills."

"You will do as your king commands or face the death penalty!" threatened the king his look of frustration not fazing Carka.

"You are a shadow of the king I served and a lesser son of greater wizards," said Carka coldly.

These words stung the king deeply, he stepped within an inch of Carka's mirror wall and stared at Carka with pure hate in his damaged and undamaged eyes. Carka returned the same look while joying in how he'd stung the king with his comparison.

"Conflicts of superiority will not change the matter at hand," came Bregit's tired voice. "Carka has shown you proof of what I've been trying to tell you since my arrival, and it is now the shade that you swallow your pride and listen to sense," Bregit said in a guttural voice.

The king looked at Bregit and how weak he appeared from his battle with Leon and the torment he had suffered at his son's hands. Retreating a few steps from Carka's mirror wall he gestured his hands openly inviting both wizards the floor. "Speak Carka," came the king's tamed voice.

Carka's eyes beamed white the glow shining from his beams erased his mirror wall from the den, he turned to Bregit and with a swish of his fingers Bregit's filthy torn robes began knitting themselves together, with his free hand Carka gave another whooshing flick that conjured Bregit's staff back into his shaking hands. Now clean and presentable the arrival of his staff numbed the unsteadiness in Bregit's arms for he no longer shook like a shaking leaf, but his appearance was something Carka decided not to magically heal, for some wounds were beyond those skills.

"Now that we are all presentable in the eyes of the king let this meeting begin. I will start with my own experiences since I was forced to leave my home under the falls in Dulgerdeen," Carka took a deep breath before continuing.

He explained the warnings from Hinkelthorn to been trapped by the Gliders and Dreaquirla who forced him to flee the forest and seek out Bregit. Carka went on to talk about his encounter with Galli and her encounter with the Council of Shadows. To the meeting in the Sphinx's cave to travelling west to try gain the alliances of the Harpies but was too late because Kcor had gotten there before him and slaughtered a substantial amount of their population. Carka finished by explaining how Kcor tried to kill him but was overpowered and captured. He had deliberately left out the Twig Collectors and the cloud because he didn't want the coven nor the king adding deluded to his titles. Without proof of both things existing, he would only be opening doors for more questions that he did not have the answers to.

"Your version of events is alike to Bregit's and seen as both of you are deserters to the crown how can we believe you? Yes, you have brought Kcor with you but for all I know you could have plucked him from the waste lands yourself, you have yet to present proof to convince me Lano has returned," said the king who appeared disappointed by Carka's presentation.

Carka shook his head in frustration. ''Taorease,'' he said waving his hand over the sleeping Kcor.

The Viledirks' eyes shot open instantly, Kcor got to his feet and stared at Carka with a blank expression, now under the influence of Carka's spell he forced the Viledirk to turn and face the king.

''Here is the proof you require,'' Carka said coldly, snapping his fingers. At the sound of his snap Kcor began to speak in a sleepy dozing voice.

''After me and my kin were banished, we lived under the rocks of the wastelands. Lano and my council counterparts built what bases we could with what little necessities we could find. We accepted our fates and waited to perish, all except Lano who forced us to survive under the extreme climate. Then after two cycles of shade Lano went in search of an escape and returned after a short absence assuring us our return to the Lands of Light would be a reality and no longer a dream to dwell on. We gathered our fullest strength and walked through the king's enchantments unharmed and made our way to the Blue Islands of Treforledge where we distanced ourselves for a shade preparing our assault. Lano used Tricklets illusion powers to make the Blue Wizards believe the tides were approaching and that they had to evacuate. When Lano gave the order to strike we charged at Treforledge and swept through the Blue Striped Army with ease.

Their screams filled the air as thousands fell under our assault until they foolishly tried fleeing which Lano anticipated so he burned the bridges, killing all who tried crossing and awakening the wrath of the Red Sea. Which cleansed the islands of blue of what wizards stayed behind to repel us thus ending the battle and claiming us the victors. After we were found out by Bregit the Yellow, Lano moved us out of fear of the Seven Coloured Army reforming and raining upon us. I led the march to Dulgerdeen where Dreaquirla had taking over until Lano arrived. Upon arrival Gazzel welcomed us and pronounced his undying loyalty to our cause. Dreaquirla gave us the news of her failings to kill the ancient wizard Carka who had escaped the forest. Then Lano became aware by news from Duxpice that Bregit travelled the Plate Pathway with an accomplice, this news opened the door for Lano to reclaim Larmont. Lano sent Alacoma and Dirren along with their full army to attack the fortress and kill all loyal creatures to Bregit. Once the Varwels took flight I was ordered to take the best of my warriors and take out the Harpies nests among the Hills of Wivirid. We caught them unawares and plucked their wings and ate them while they burned on stakes while keeping Grith alive knowing he would lead us to more Harpy lairs.

Before we could move on I sent my many of my warriors to scout ahead while I waited for instructions from my master, but my wait was short because me and the remaining Viledirks were attacked by the wizard Carka, who was too skilled to be overpowered by strength or force and when I tried to strike from out of the shadows, he bounded me then numbed me before putting me to sleep,'' finished Kcor.

After he finished his version of events Kcor lay on his back and returned to sleep all the while the king and the coven stood with awkward expressions.

''That proof enough for you or are you going to try convincing me that I somehow latched that tale inside Kcor's head or are you finally going to admit you were wrong and take some responsibility for the lives your ignorance has cost?'' Carka shouted directly at the king.

They all stood waiting for the king to answer but he didn't, he instead kept his eyes closed and his body tensed, appearing to all that he was fighting a battle with his own thoughts. Ignoring the king's refusal to answer Pally the Yellow and Meriyoi the Blue broke from the covens ranks and walked by their king to stand beside Carka.

"If you are to lead the fight against Lano then myself and Dry Scales are behind you," said Pally with pride.

"As will I," said Meriyoi the Blue a little less strong toned voice than Pally.

"I will side with you as well," said Bregit with pride in his voice.

The rest of the coven looked lost, appearing uncertain without the guidance of the king about who to give their loyalty's to so they remained unsurely by the king's side.

"Seems we are not alike mind to the coming war, if we do not unite our existence will be at risk. If we survive there will be uprisings for your head for abandoning your lands. If Lano succeeds then you will not have the strength in numbers to defeat him, so I will ask you again will you join us?" asked Carka.

The king raised his head, opened his eyes, and looked at each wizard in turn before drawing out his golden staff that had golden brown leaves at its centre top with a purple Malas ruby seeded between the shiny leaves.

"War is upon us again and with war comes death, pain, and misery. Outcomes I thought would no longer exist under my reign, yet here we are. Darkness spreads and with it monsters more fouler than anything imaginable, so I will give you your answer Carka. The Seven Coloured Army will fight but not alongside you…. they will fight for their king!" he replied in a thunderous voice.

The king shot a streak of silver without even looking at his target from the tip of his purple mala's ruby, it struck Leon releasing him from his bonds.

"I have no doubt you were listening, so I will save the explaining, as my son and heir you will return to the Cloud Stair and send word to Reterask to gather your forces. Pally, Meriyoi and Corlock send word back to your homelands explain the situation and command your armies to travel here immediately!"

"Why are we to stay here while our armies gather themselves. Our instructions would be better delivered by us not our commanding lieutenants?" questioned Meriyoi.

"I will not risk the lives of my generals and coven chair holders, you will send word by methods of your own communication, but you are forbidden to leave this kingdom," said the king impatiently. "If Lano has destroyed Treforledge and taking rule over Dulgerdeen then none of your armies are safe in their strongholds. The Golden Kingdom is the only safe fortress left and that is where we will gather and plan our next move, it is not a request it is an order," he finished, in a final tone.

The king turned and stared into Carka's eyes, his cursed eye still had a burning desire in its depths, his lips were thinner and drained of fluid, but Kcor's return and the realism of what Lano had done since his return had awoken the sleeping restraint inside him. It was this precise look that convinced Carka he had succeeded in gaining the king's favour to joining his cause. Sparking a hope inside Carka that the Twig Collector's prophecy might turn out to be false and that there was some hope for the wizard's survival.

"My son is on his way to Larmont, I will need you and Bregit to get there at once if there is any hope of saving it from falling," the king said to Carka.

"Lucifer is gone to Larmont?" cried Leon in disbelief.

"Yes, on my orders he was instructed to safeguard Larmont until Bregit's trail was finished. He may have arrived there I cannot be sure but if the Varwels are launching an attack he will not last long against them….,"

"He would have lasted a lot longer had he me by his side, if you knew Larmont was in danger then why send him alone?" asked Leon in a demanded tone.

The king didn't respond with words instead he answered with action, swinging his arm Leon was hit hard across the face with the full force of the king's staff. Leon took the blow to the face well but didn't retaliate or make any move to counter, he smirked as he regained his balance as a red bruise began emerging from under his swelling cheek. Leon's stare had venom in its depths that convinced Carka, Leon shared the same killer genes his grandfather possessed.

"Who are you to question my decisions eh? You do as I say without hesitation or question, or I will kill you so quick you'll enter the afterlife before your foolish head leaves your shoulders is that understood!" bellowed the king so fiercely Leon stepped a few paces back by the sheer force of his father's voice.

Leon made no argument and dropped his evil glare the moment he regained sense before dropping to one knee and bowing his head under his father's waist. "Father forgive my rudeness my concerns for Lucifer overshadowed my sense it will not happen again," begged Leon, his tone of voice deliberately sprinkled with kindness.

The king's hand waved over his son's head gesturing him to rise to his feet. Breathing heavily, he spoke in gulfs of heated anger.

"I give the task to my father's oldest friends to return to Larmont and save my son and all who still fight for us. If you are lucky, you may save the land itself, but your main priority is to secure your own safety, Larmont can be won back if lost your lives cannot."

Carka and Bregit exchanged looks of shock as they were not used to having others worrying about their wellbeing.

"I want no heroism from any of you get there save what you can and get out again the real fight hasn't started yet, and I would be grateful to have two experienced generals by my side when Lano arrives," said the king.

Carka nodded in agreement so did Bregit a sigh of relief extinguishing their anguished faces. "It's a rare thing agreeing with the words of a king. It's a feeling I never thought I'd come to like," said Carka smiling.

The king returned the smile in kind before looking at the other generals. "The rest of you go and gather your armies and what means needed and I will do the same," he said, sweeping his cloak across the dirt as he moved toward the exit of the den the coven trailing in his rejuvenated aura.

Chapter 24

The March

Lano inhaled the cleansing air, allowing it to clear his dulled senses. The drumming sound of the beating hearts beneath him was overwhelming. For his senses told him the creatures below him were feeling on edge about the coming battle, the one he knew would decide the outcome of their existence.

Dulgerdeen was now many leagues behind. Having made it through miles of swamps and marshes Lano and his army were now on level footing among sand filled lands. Lano secretly was glad to be away from the forest and out in the open, having spent two cycles of shades squeezed in the heat and a contained within a marginal area the opportunity to stretch his legs and feel the aura of his surroundings was more beneficial to his army than prolonging their stay in the stuffy aired Dulgerdeen any further.

On the eve before their departure from Dulgerdeen, Rac, Kcor's advisor paid Lano a visit and assured him he would on Kcors honour fight alongside him. Pledging if he falls in battle his next in line would follow and serve and so on until there are no more Viledirks left to serve. Touched as Lano was by Rac's loyalty, he had seen with his own eyes the levels of crazy Rac could reach over the simplest of misunderstandings and regarded the Viledirk, a loose cannon, which was Lano's main reason for not offering Rac the same privileges he had offered Kcor.

Lano knew Rac only gave his allegiance because he wanted a seat on his council. By not mentioning it during their conversation, Rac intended to be given the position there and then, but Lano cleverly put the strain of war down to been unable to decide and told Rac he will give him his answer once the war was over. But the thought of Rac among his high ranks gave Lano displeasing images as to what a deranged creature such as Rac would do when in possession of power. Lano's only hope to avoid such a catastrophe was to hope Rac died in battle before the conclusion of the war, otherwise he would be hard pressed to deny him his request after risking his and his army's lives fighting for his cause.

Lano felt that by giving Rac a position of power it would end in disaster because Rac would only want more than he deserved for his efforts, unlike his other council members who choose what they wanted and stood by their wants instead of extending them. Lano allowed Rac believe he was in contention for the vacant seat in his council, when honestly, he had no idea whom to offer it to. Tip-Karp would be the ideal candidate, but his loyalty was still iffy and with the pressures of war and keeping his numbers intact, the last thing on Lano's mind right now was filling another gap among his ranks, and yet here he was sat on his own dwelling on things that may never happen.

The sound of whooshing wings caught Lano's attention as Dreaquirla appeared by his side the flapping of her wings decreasing in propelling as her midnight blue eyes looked at Lano with seriousness. Lano smiled at her coming. Dreaquirla had returned when he'd led his forces out of the forest's perimeter and was joined by Rizz and his army of two thousand strong Rear Clars. Their intimidating size and presence gave Lano much joy. Rizz was the high general of the Rear Clars Clan and stood ten-feet tall with grizzling grey fur that resembled the colour of his eyes and the great Clar wore a bark made breastplate that weighed the same amount as a boulder. Rizz happened to be the son of Zab who Rizz confirmed died three shades past due to mountain sickness. This news warmed Lano because it was Zab who refused to send his army forth to aid his cause. Rizz joining his army meant the rift between the Rear Clars and himself were extinguished. Rizz proved by deploying his forces to his cause that he was unlike his father who was stubborn and unmoved by concerns of the outside world. Rizz looked to strengthen the position of his kind instead of labouring in caves until they died. Which was why he accepted Dreaquirlas invitation to join with Lano.

Lano filled Rizz in on his plans to attack the Bay of Bones which excited the Rear Clar who thirsted for battle, a trait he had injected into his army because they revelled in the prospect of open battle. Lano thanked Rizz for his services and left him to regain his strength having journeyed from the misty mountains.

''This is it, my lord, one league stands between us facing the wizards who banished us. One league away from avenging our fallen,'' said Dreaquirla, her eyes focused on the path ahead.

''We will honour them by restoring Nocktar to its original state and ridding our lands of those filthy wizards, because that is what they died fighting for and it is what we are all willing to do,'' hissed Lano delicately.

''Come off it,'' scoffed Dreaquirla not buying Lanos change in approach. ''Surely some form of vengeance still burns inside you?''

''If we are to be different to our opposers then vengeance cannot be the monument we fight for,'' said Lano his voice sounding tired.

''We won't have a monument if we fail,'' countered Dreaquirla.

''Keep your negative opinions to yourself,'' hissed Lano warningly.

''Cautious,'' Dreaquirla retorted. ''A quality we lacked in our failure; you can't deny returning to face them in open battle isn't stressing.''

''I haven't come this close to have your negative downpour spread through my ranks like a virus,'' hissed Lano a venomous sting added to his tone.

''Understood,'' said Dreaquirla a little too out of tone to be believed serious before leaving with a dive from the mountain top.

Lano watched her fly away as he did, he looked down at the creatures who stayed loyal to him. They rested under the shade of a mountain side by the sea. Choosing this location, Lano knew that if anything dared to ambush them from the side or back deserved to beat them. If they were to be attacked, it would be from the front, and they had five miles of clear land to prepare for anything willing to sabotage them. Lano back down on the cold mountain he looked at the orange shaded sky. The colour that will shine over the Bay of Bones, the location that will decide who rules the Lands of Light.

Taking his eyes away from the sky he closed them and dwelled on the failed attempt to channel Tricklets mind into Kcors. It confirmed the dreaded feeling he felt the moment the news of Kcors disappearance had reached him. Tricklets failure confirming his most trusted ally was dead. An unnecessary loss for a creature of Kcors mantle. Kcor had stayed loyal to him through every struggle and every battle. Until the very end, he was loyal and will be honoured Lano vowed in secret.

''My lord!'' heaved Dreaquirla the sound of her wings pelting annoyingly against Lano's ear drums. ''Scouts have returned claiming Dry Scales, Reterask, Tindisinge, and Sun Stroke have deserted the eastern lands. To where I am uncertain,'' said the rasping voice of Dreaquirla.

Lano smiled menacingly ''My theory was correct,'' he scoffed in delight. ''The king has called all his forces to the Golden Kingdom and left the entire Lands of Light wide open,'' he hissed, feeling satisfied with this information.

''So now we can reclaim the Lands of Light without having to battle the wizards straight up, we can do exactly what we did to Treforledge,'' piped Dreaquirla.

''The plan is in motion; it cannot be changed even if I wanted,'' hissed Lano. ''We will fight the wizards on their own doorstep as planned, if the thought scares you then by all means leave! Otherwise leave me to my thoughts and cast away your ill feelings, they have no bearings on a battlefield,'' Lano hissed with annoyance.

Dreaquirla shrouded her feelings, but Lano knew his words had a deep impact on her, she was a sensitive creature who buried her feelings deep and wasn't short on expressing them in torturous ways.

''I followed you into battle without question or doubt but with Kcor gone, the realism of all this has shrunken my confidence a bit,'' she confided with Lano.

''Really?'' hissed Lano, tilting his head in consideration.

''Yes. Kcor's capture has opened my eyes that attacking the Bay of Bones isn't the best idea. We have an army larger than any in Nocktars history, we can wait the wizards out or let them rot in their kingdom, we have the Lands of Light within our grasp, isn't that what we're fighting for?''

''Hmm……,'' hummed Lano. ''So, you would see us gladly go about our ways living under the shadow of our enemies, wise move. Dividing our forces to secure those lands while the wizards grow in strength and numbers. Have you forgotten orchards of Drop Trees grow in the Golden Kingdom and last I counted drop season begins next cycle of shade, two shades away to be exact, which means more wizards and more problems,'' hissed Lano showing a hint of impatience in his voice?

Dreaquirla did not argue, she clearly hadn't giving full thought to her beliefs of what would happen if they swayed from their cause.

''How many wizards will be ripe and matured by the shades we have the Lands of Light secure and ready for a wizard siege?'' Lano asked with anger.

''I don't know,'' answered Dreaquirla in a small voice.

''Thousands by my last count and trust me Dreaquirla I have counted. Shades I have sat and thought of every obstacle that stands in our way. Don't you see? It isn't a matter of numbers; we have to strike now before the wizards expand,'' he hissed.

''That just builds more pressure on our shoulders. If, the wizards don't buy the bait, then we'll lose everything we've gained,'' argued Dreaquirla.

''This is war and in war drastic actions and decisions must be made to ensure victory, haven't I taught you that? Nothing will be changed from here on out. Is that clear? I have come too far to settle for second place!'' hissed Lano.

''You've gambled with our lives on the belief that the wizards will play into your hands, a plan that could backfire and end us all. Why?'' asked Dreaquirla, careful not to add her anger to her light tone.

Lano got to his feet and crossed the mountain side, staring at the sky but not seeing it. His thoughts carrying him far from the reality he lived in. Dreaquirla was not wrong about him, still it angered him that she objected to his methods.

"Life is a gamble," sighed Lano. "I was handed a choice, rot in the wastelands and die with failure crawling through my bones or gather all our hopes into one idea and force our way to a noble death or a legendary triumph."

"I don't want my death to be in failure," said Dreaquirla, the tension in her face increasing.

"It won't if you play your part right," Lano assured her.

"You cannot guarantee my life we both know it so don't feed me hope when you've none to offer!" cried Dreaquirla her voice turning brittle.

"You'll just have to trust me, believe in what drives me every drop of every shade to achieve my goals," hissed Lano.

"What drive do you possess now that is different to the one you had from the previous battle?"

"You dare question me?" hissed Lano, venom spitting through his clenched teeth.

He approached Dreaquirla who did not back away. Lano peered into her purple beady eyes and in that moment, he seen clearly the doubt clouding her mind and the fear of failure beginning to consume her spirit.

"I presumed to know you and in moments even persuaded myself you may even consider me your closest ally," said Dreaquirla, with acceptance in her tone.

"You are allowing your doubt to cloud your judgement. The journey back has been daunting. I value all my council members loyalty the same, what has happened since our first step back into the Lands of Light hasn't swayed those beliefs," he hissed.

"I was wrong to think like that, to cling onto things that are not real. Just to feel closure, when in fact our attractions to each other are our ambitions not friendship," heaved Dreaquirla, inhaling a lungful of air.

"War has ways of weighing imperceptible pressure, do not allow yours to say something you may later regret," Lano warned his tone calm. "I will fight alongside you," Dreaquirla assured him. "But if we defeat the wizards, I want my island back for me and no other, with no alliance to you," said Dreaquirla.

'You are a principal creature among my council and a master commander are you willing to walk away from your duties just to live in solitude?" asked Lano.

"Rac can have my council seat and position if he likes or give it to the next creature who fulfils your needed requirements," Dreaquirla said not caring anymore about titles and devotions.

"Done!" hissed Lano firmly. "But be warned, in your exile you will be under the ruling of no one and will be branded an outlaw under my regime. And if you leave your island in pursuit of power or endangering my ruling, I will be forced to act accordingly and by that, I will rain down on you so hard, I'll erase any trace of your existence, is that understood?" he hissed.

"Crystal!" said Dreaquirla, with no sound of regret to her response.

"Then we have no more to discuss," Lano hissed, dismissing Dreaquirla from his presence. He watched her silently float down the trail which would lead her down the mountains slope and out of his sight. 'Another member gone,' he thought.

But he felt he had to be honest with Dreaquirla, she was his most trusted advisor who followed his orders to perfection. He couldn't hold it against her been in a panicked state of mind, he knew many who lay under his gaze were feeling the same. His hopes now lay in the paws of Tip-Karp. If the sphinx was successful, his plan will be complete. With his trusted Gliders among the sphinx's company, he was confident Tip-Karp would see out his mission. But uncertainty lingered like a dry cough in Lano's chest. His greatest concern on the eve of battle was the whereabouts of the cloud. It hadn't revealed itself since he'd left Treforledge. The aura of its presence was nowhere within the camp or the perimeter he'd set before pausing for a rest. With no way of communing with the cloud or summoning it to his side Lano was left to dwindle on the hope that it will return before the battle begins.

The walk down the mountain seemed longer, his absentee council members had left a hole in his forces. He'd sent word using Tricklets power to call the Varwels back. Deciding earlier on that Larmont was no longer a land worth claiming. It so happened that Tricklet was hoovering outside his campsite when Lano returned to his tent. Which was a high red and black laced curtain with black metal poles on each end to keep it high and wide. He walked by Tricklet who took his ignorance with a smirked grin.

"I have waited many drops for your return, my lord," squeaked Tricklet while floating into the tent and watched Lano ignite flames from his fingertips and nesting them on the pile of dry logs in the centre of his tent.

"I haven't the patience for small talk, so get to the point of why you are here," hissed Lano, his voice rasp from his drops upon the mountains peak.

"My lord, Alacoma has reached Larmont and has pursued in his quest to claim Larmont," said Tricklet, abandoning his squeaky voice to use a firm serious one.

The dread slid down Lanos forehead, wrinkling the scars on both sides of his cracked face. Dread quickly formed into hot prickling anger that pulsed through him, forcing heated words through his head. But his shades in exile had helped sooth his desires to lash out and remain composed when his anger came up for air.

"Alacoma has abandoned our cause then?" asked Lano, looking at Tricklet. The glow of his flames giving him a clear view of the little trickster.

"There was no mention of returning nor of abandonment, my lord," said Tricklet, careful to not squeak his words.

"There will be no need for further conversation with the winged beasts. Larmont is defenceless, their conquest will not last long," Lano hissed delicately.

Tricklets eyes narrowed with an annoyed look tightening his facial skin. "I presumed they would be punished for not returning when their lord commanded," he asked.

"Let me decide the faiths of the winged beasts when the shade is right, for now we must focus our attentions to what lies ahead and not what is behind us," hissed Lano looking into the fire with a tired expression.

"I agree my lord. I will not lie nor deny that Kcor's death has not shook many of our members. Loyal and unwilling to speak unless necessary was my problem disliking Kcor, but his presence brought a calmness among us," admitted Tricklet, his sentiment for Kcor hitting Lano like a dagger into the heart.

"Kcor will be missed," said Lano. "But I will not allow his passing to disrupt my army's objectives. Can I count on you to restore our lost grit?" Lano asked, eyeing Tricklet for a sign of uncertainty.

"I will do my upmost to fill the void left by Kcor," piped Tricklet with a gratified grin on his smug face.

"I'm afraid even your best will not suffice in this requirement," Lano whispered, while watching Tricklet vanished in a whiff of smoke.

The gloom of his feelings spread throughout the confinement of his tent, on the upside no more of his council came to forfeit their services, so Lano sat straight with his arms flexed on a throne formed of smoke rising from the fire beneath him.

"Alacoma no doubt was behind the Varwels refusing his summons, he will indeed answer for his disloyalty. Again, he pressed the sole blame on himself, so eager he was to crush Larmont and get inside Bregit's tower, and for what?' thought Lano. 'To end a line many believed extinct. There was no evidence to support his suspicion only his gut feeling that one still lingered unseen in the Lands of Light. Waiting for the opportunity to rise when he least expected. Carelessness had cost the last battle against his foes. He'd already lost two vital pieces of his puzzle. To remain in line, he would now have to abandon all other desires he craved and set his sights on the primary target. The wizards,' Lano said to himself.

Lano's eyes glowed a scarlet red summoning red swirling flames throughout the tent that ignited the heavy curtain and the blackened poles. When the smoke of the burnt items swirled on the tip of his finger, he rose high in the air now wreathed in crimson fire, his glow shone over his army as one by one they knelt and looked up to him as their beacon of hope.

"Creatures of Nocktar, through the cycles we have had our quarrels and misunderstandings. Yet! here we stand as one, one force, willing to stand against superior power to rectify our failings. Orange Shade will be the colour in the sky when we stand and fight, not for ourselves, not for glory, but for every creature forced into the bonds of slavery, for every creature who died fighting alongside us and for every drop and shade we were laughed and jeered and left to rot in the waste lands!!" cried Lano through the sizzling flames.

The roars of his army intensified. As such that the sand beneath their feet lifted from its resting place and splashed across their feet, but it didn't seem to faze them one bit. Their roars of defiance echoed through the heated breeze flowing from their master.

"I say to you all now, under the mountain of Iraz. Win! Win for all who shelter in holes praying for the shade when creatures such as yourselves will rise and end their sufferings!"

Cheers followed by loud howling roars filled the mountainside, as fists were thrown into the air and the chants of Lanos name echoed in the distance.

"Win!" he cried over the cheers. "And show our enemies that we are not to be tossed aside and forgotten! Win! So, we will never have to again!" roared Lano, raising his rod of multi flames and shooting streaks of flames to the sky.

Relishing in the cheers and stomps of the Rear Clars and the roars of the Viledirks while his flames exploded into tens of smaller threads that filled the night sky. Lano pointed his rod forward. The realism hitting against his chest, it's beating sound like drums in his ears. Still, he refused to yield his fret. Instead, the Lava Keeper swallowed his fear. Allowing it to sink to the bowels of his stomach and in its place, rose a surging voice

"TO WAR!!!!"

Chapter 25

The Golden Sky

The courtyard was silent as nothing stirred. Galli and Lucifer stood in front of Bregit's fountain their breathing shallow as they watched a golden cloud approaching.

"They will swoop down in packs to distract us, while the watchers will swipe talons from afar. Be on your guard, Varwels are rapid when in flight, our best way of fighting is to….,"

"Clip their wings," finished Galli coldly.

The Varwels had passed over the mountains and would be within the perimeter of Bregit's tower in mere drops. Looking at Lucifer, Galli could see the fear beginning to consume him as his breathing became heavy and his eyes were now inclined as the prospect of death filled his mind.

"They are watching us, pay close attention to the trees. Varwels have a connection along their legs that allows them to channel their feelings into the tree's roots," said Galli, accepting that if she was going to survive, she was going to have to work with Lucifer to ensure that outcome.

The treetops around the courtyard rustled and shook; gales of high-speed winds swished through the skies as one by one, golden winged beasts broke through the trees, soaring at Galli and Lucifer with eyes as red as the sea and wearing a look of mad desire that bulged the Varwels pupils.

Galli fluidity swung her staff around her head, magically levitating the sand around the courtyard to rise and incircle her and Lucifer. Lucifer in turn ignited his red ruby to glow scarlet red.

"DOKADA MORB!!!" he roared.

The power of Lucifer's spell forced the sand to immobilise and solidify into a thick wall that stood twice the size of Galli and Lucifer. Their combination stood firm against the charging Varwels who were too late to avoid colliding with their protective sand wall. Hundreds of Varwels smashed into the magical moulded sand shield due to the intense impact of their collision. Waving her arm, Galli forced the sand wall to disintegrate. In its wake lay the feathered bodies of the charging Varwels who lay crushed and broken on Bregit's courtyard. Their golden glow had diminished from their bodies, meaning they were dead.

"Keep yourself on the alert Galli! They were just the pawns to see what counter measures we would use; the next wave will not be the same. Eyes open and head on our surroundings," called Lucifer, keeping his eyes fixed on the golden cloud.

Bitterly Galli accepted that Lucifer was right because momentarily the next wave came directly from the golden cloud. Threads of sparkling beams wove and circled from the golden cloud, sprinkling the sky with grey flowers that had been drained of their beauty as they drifted lifeless onto the bodies of the dead Varwels. Galli magically summoned one of the dead flowers to her hand, but the pressure of her spell crushed the stems and petals to specks of ash that vanished in the wind. A burst of yellow light forced the wizards to raise their elbows to shield their eyes from the blinding rays now streaming from the golden cloud. When the light dimmed to a narrow, a thread circled the golden cloud giving off waves of electrical currents that gave it a radiant defensive shield.

''Copycats,'' said Lucifer.

Galli looked at Lucifer and then at the shining cloud. Lorneid was right again! The Varwels were reprising the same defensive manoeuvre they themselves had just used to protect themselves from attack. The pace of the rotating ring circling the golden cloud was gathering momentum. This behaviour looked familiar to Gall as the answer seemed to dawdle on her tongue, then it came in the form of a memory that made Galli's eyes widen with fear.

''There not mimicking us!'' Galli cried. ''There preparing….,''

''For what?'' asked Lucifer looking at Galli in deep wonder.

''Comets,'' Galli replied. ''It's one of their formation techniques, Comets Launch, Varwels use it to destroy surroundings and clear the landscape with a shower of razor-sharp talons,'' she cried.

When Galli last encountered this manoeuvre, she was surrounded by her elite lieutenants, now she was alongside a wizard with different methods of fighting. There were no drops to re-enact the spell Galli and her army used to destroy Pally's Comets Launch and with just drops to act she stood in disappointment for allowing herself to fall blindly into this situation.

''It's almost ready,'' she muttered, as the glow airing around the golden cloud tightened. ''And when it strikes, Larmont will be a distant memory,'' said Galli bitterly, annoyed with herself.

Lucifer remained quiet, he stared at the golden cloud with a curious stare. Galli however didn't need to look because she knew what was coming and felt a fool for not preparing for the Varwels. It wasn't like she didn't know they were coming. She had an entire shade to prepare but no, she had allowed Lucifer's charming ways to sway her mind from her intentions.

''Fall back if that's their plan we'll be destroyed by the impact. Move back to the tower we will be safe behind its defences!'' shouted Lucifer signalling with his hand for Galli to follow him to Bregit's tower.

Galli didn't move, because she was a warrior and warriors did not flee, they rose to the challenge and if she were going to die then she would do it upright and proud and not by hiding behind enchantments to prolong the inevitable. Raising her staff in acceptance of defeat, Galli pointed it at the radiant cloud that launched a powerful blast of shiny golden beams down upon Bregit's courtyard. The beams split into miniature circular threads, each thread holding a pack of Varwels in the formation of a boulder that had the capabilities of reducing Larmont to rubble.

''TALTRO!'' bellowed Galli in a desperate attempt to divert the comets toward the Red Sea.

Swipes of aqua air waves burst from the point of Water Dancer and hit at least five comets, but they were ineffective, as Galli's waves merely bounced off the comets and ricocheted out of sight.

''No way!'' breathed Galli in disbelief.

''My turn,'' came Lucifers stern voice, who no longer wished to flee.

The prince stepped in front of Galli and held his staff up in the air. Pointing it at the nearest comet, Lucifer swirled his staff conjuring crimson flames that covered his entire body, concealing his appearance in a molten mass of controlled flames. Swinging his staff like a lasso Lucifer absorbed the flames and hurled them at the incoming comets. The flames spread and multiplied and entangled a handful of comets, halting their momentum. Tightening his hold on his staff Lucifer tried redirecting the comets direction but found it too difficult a task under the pressure of holding such immense power. Judging by Lucifer's agonizing expression, Galli could tell he was struggling with the efforts required to hold the comets within his grasp. But he held firm just long enough to divert the comets away from the courtyard.

As Lucifer's screams of pain filled the courtyard his grip relinquished due to the intense shaking of his staff, it twisted and turned before flying out of his grasp and soared through the air and out of sight. But Lucifer had succeeded in his purpose as the comets spun uncontrollably and crashed into one another causing a cascade of explosions that filled the sky in flashes of golden light.

''You did it,'' cried Galli in a tone of surprise that made her smile with relief.

But Galli's joy was quickly turned to ash. Completely defenceless, Lucifer was struck hard in the chest by a golden thread that the Varwels shot down on him from the golden cloud without warning.

''No!'' cried Galli who watched in horror as Lucifer was lifted off his feet and forced to collide with the base of Bregit's tower due to the impact of the Varwels strike.

Lucifer hit the towers outer wall headfirst and fell from a high drop. He smacked down on the sand causing the golden grains around the towers perimeter to lift from the ground due to the impact of Lucifer's collision with the ground.

Galli's instinct took control of her legs and without even knowing, she was running full belt towards Lucifer. But she only made it a few feet when she was blown back by powerful gusts of wind that lifted her off her feet and caused her to land painfully on the courtyard floor. Galli tried moving but the gusts raining down on her prevented her from moving an inch. Twisting her head, Galli knew it was up. Lucifer was out cold, and another wave of comets were beginning to take aim on Larmont.

Focusing her remaining energy on embracing her defeat Galli accepted the thumping sound beating against her chest was assurance and not fear, a trait she would not show in the face of death. Having expected pain, Galli was surprised the wind restraining her had suddenly stopped. Quickly she lifted herself to her feet. The golden cloud was still hovering above Bregit's courtyard but what surprised Galli was the ring of gold circling the cloud and the comets had retreated. Looking around the wrecked courtyard Galli caught sight of two bodies standing side by side a few yards from where she stood, when Galli got closer, she was stunned to see that the two bodies belonged to Bregit and Carka.

''Let's make little work of this,'' Carka said, piercing the cloud with a look of pleasure as he swung both his arms, conjuring white streaks of light from his palms.

Carka then placed both hands in the air summoning bolts of white lightning from the incoming clouds now circling the Varwels golden sanctuary. Bregit in turn rotated his staff causing his yellow ruby to vibrate and shake variously. Taking aim Bregit threw his staff straight into the belly of the golden cloud.

'What is he doing it will be crushed before it even touches the cloud?' thought Galli, remembering how ineffective her wind waves were against the cloud's defences.

Bregit's intentions came clear when Carka again twirled his fingers and shot lightning bolts from his fingertips at the glowing malas stone. The lightning struck the glowing yellow ruby causing a blinding flash to eclipse the sky just as it struck the golden cloud. The force of their joint attack caused an eruption so intense the golden cloud split and shattered. Forcing the Varwels to abandon their sanctuary and flee, their cries of agony a sweet tune to hear, as one by one they shrunk in the distance until nothing was left of them but the stench of their deceased kin.

Galli rushed to Lucifer's side, stomping on the bodies of dead Varwels in her pursuit, when she was standing over his still body, Galli turned him over with a swipe of her arm. Examining his neck and wrists for a pulse Galli was thankful to feel a beat in Lucifer's wrists. But when she drew her hand away it was covered in blood, that was spilling from the side of his head which was drenched and covered in black sticky pus that trailed down his face and under his collar. About to perform a healing spell Galli was distracted by Carka's sudden appearance.

''Move aside,'' he growled roughly as he shoved Galli aside with his elbow that caught her round the chin.

Carka placed his palm above Lucifer's chest and whispered an incantation under his breath. Galli watched in admiration as Lucifer's body flailed and twisted until he jumped up with his eyes wide and fearful.

''Relax,'' said Carka seeing the confusion on Lucifer's face.

Carka did not speak any more to Lucifer he simply moved a few paces away and stood in silence with his arms folded. Calming his breathing Lucifer lay back on the cracked surface studying Carka in wonder to who had just resuscitated him?

''How did you come to meet with Bregit, last shade I seen you was in Tip-Karps Mountain?'' Galli asked Carka.

''It's a long story and I haven't the drops to tell you,'' he said in a stiff tone. ''I will no doubt be forced to tell you one shade because It would be either telling you or killing you due to your annoying methods to get on a creature's nerves,'' answered Carka.

''What spell did you use to heal him?'' asked Galli, looking at Lucifer's body and noticing his face was no longer covered in black pus.

''I would have thought a knowledge eager wizard such as yourself would've noticed a simple leer maw spell.''

''I never seen one performed before'' countered Galli.

''I wouldn't have expected you to, the spell is complex and hard to master and Treforledge isn't famed for overstretching the imagination,'' said Carka making sure his tone wasn't disrespectful.

Bregit joined them when he was satisfied his courtyard resembled the way he had last seen it. He nodded his head to Galli with a pleased expression on his thin face.

"Galli it is a joyous sight to see you alive and well. Lucifer did as he promised for that I am grateful, but I must insist on leaving these lands and return quickly to the Golden kingdom."

"What?" said Galli hoping she had misheard Bregit.

"Before you go on a long rant allow me to explain the facts," pleaded Bregit.

"No! I listened to you before. And last, I recall it got me hung against a wall in chains. I swore when I left that place, I would never return not for you or anyone," said Galli in disapproval.

In her frustration Galli turned to Carka feeling he at least would agree with her, but the white-haired wizard merely leaned against Bregit's tower with his arms folded and eyes diverted to the sky.

"Galli, the king has come to reason and has gathered the Seven Coloured Army and is as we speak preparing for Lano's assault. Isn't that what you wanted and why you travelled with me to the Golden Kingdom?" asked Bregit.

"I no longer want war; all my kin are dead. Tip-Karp has joined with Lano, I don't need to be a genius to know what his treachery meant for the Blue Wizards he sheltered," Galli said hiding her grief behind a hardened tone.

Bregit sighed heavily appearing like he was carrying the weight of all Galli's troubles on his shoulders. "Tip-Karp will pay for his disloyalty," Bregit said reassuringly. "But now is the shade we fight, and we need every wizard if we are to overcome Lano. You have seen with your own eyes the destruction he can inflict, just imagine what he will do if he triumphs. Wouldn't you like to look back one shade and tell the Ripelings you teach how you fought so they could live, or will you wallow in self-pity?"

Galli wanted to tell Bregit that he didn't understand, none of them did. It wasn't a matter of joining the wizards it was again her instinct telling her not to go and the last shade, she didn't follow her instincts she nearly died and no matter what Bregit said in attempt to convince her, she wasn't going back to the Golden Kingdom.

"I'm not going," Galli said firmly.

"I think she's ripe enough to make her own decisions, and if there's one thing, I've learned is the stubbornness of Blue Wizards," said Carka in a gravelly tone.

Bregit looked from Carka to Galli and finally admitting defeat he shrugged his shoulders and walked to the entrance of his tower. Carka nodded his head in the direction of the tower indicating that Galli and Lucifer should follow. Carka walked in front of them and was second to enter Bregit's tower. Galli helped a light-headed Lucifer whose legs went wayward when he tried to walk, leaning his weight on her shoulder they both entered the tower.

"Don't consider this a kindness once my debt is paid you and I are even," Galli told Lucifer, half with annoyance and half with regret.

Lucifer chuckled on her arm, but Galli felt she needed to put it out in the open that she was only helping him because he saved her life. Reaching the top of Bregit's stair was a struggle with near many misses once Galli even considered tossing Lucifer's body down the stairs and shouting to get up off his backside and walk. But her restraints paid her well in those moments of anger as she lay Lucifer on the armchair in the corner before throwing herself on the wooden chair nearest the open window the feel of the cool air a refreshing welcome to an out of breath Galli. Breathing fast and waving her hood continuously at her face Galli only noticed Bregit sitting on his bedside reading a long chart that flowed along the floor. Carka stood over him watching and waiting for Bregit to finish.

"Those scrolls give any directions to defeating Lano or are you going to finally reveal the real reason you sent me here?" asked Lucifer.

"Be silent!" growled Carka throwing Lucifer a sharp look of annoyance. "If it were up to me, I'd have you strung up by your legs and pealed layer by layer so we can see does the ruler of Sun Stroke have a spine, you insolent little ripe!" spat Carka his eyes furious.

Lucifer forced himself up from Bregit's chair, walking toward Carka with a slight limp to his stride, the prince showed no sign of fear as he stared into the sharp silver eyes of Carka.

"I'd give my lands and titles to see you try," Lucifer said coldly pressing his face against Carka's.

Carka made a move but was grabbed around the wrist by Bregit who was on his feet still clutching the chart he was reading.

"Be seated Lucifer and excuse Carka's ill manner he is one of few with zero tolerance for wizards of the Golden kingdom. Now you have asked me a question as to why I have brought you here, I thought my reason was clear, to recruit Galli and defend my homeland as a repayment for sentencing me to death," Bregit said plainly.

"We both know what the outcome would have been if I didn't play my part so spare me your lecture Bregit. Those scrolls on your table were deliberately left out for me and Galli to find," Lucifer said hotly.

Bregit looked at the table with no flicker or sign of been caught out he simply smiled at Lucifer. "Before Arb enlightened me of Treforledge's siege I was writing down old records of what I had learned about the Sages…"

"And why would a wizard of yellow be so interested in the Sages?" asked Carka who eye balled Bregit with suspicion.

Taken back by Carka's cold attitude toward his interests Bregit looked at Carka with surprise. "As a wizard who desired further knowledge than the pieces offered by the wizards of the Golden Kingdom, I did a lot of research into the origins of the Sages and decided to write their short lifespan to teach the next generation of wizards about those who walked rule free among the Lands of Light. But in my rush to get to Treforledge I was left with little drops to put away my scrolls. If they offend you, I can put them away?" said Bregit.

"It seemed too good to be true that's all I thought you left those as a clue," said Lucifer his cheeks shining a bit brighter than usual.

"Clue to what?" laughed Bregit shrugging his arms in question. "The Sages are gone! Your grandfather saw to that, even against the opinions of his advisors my father among them. But there's no point dabbling on about what cannot be altered," Bregit said calmly as he lazily wove his hand enchanting the scrolls to fold and levitate under his bed.

"Before you interrupted me, I was looking through a chart I designed from the map you would recognize from your father's throne room. It tells us the paths wizards discovered before they built the Golden Kingdom and if what Carka has told me we both feel Lano is using his battle at the Bay of Bones as a diversion, so a pack of his trusted advisors can sneak into a vulnerable Golden Kingdom and destroy it."

Lucifer laughed at the foolishness of that ever becoming a reality, Galli read the seriousness on both wizard's faces and sensed they believed their theory was more than a fantasy.

"Can it be done?" asked Galli.

"There is only one creature with the skill to pass through such enchantments, only one, and unfortunately for us that creature now resides with the enemy," sighed Bregit.

"Tip-Karp?" breathed Galli.

"Yes," said Bregit nodding his head. "We learned from Tip-Karp that the sphinx's designed a portal of cosmic energy with the capabilities of transporting any sphinx wherever they chose by simply picturing the destination in their head, but this portal's location is unknown," Bregit said turning his attentions back to his map.

"Then we must stop Tip-Karp at all costs, if he gets inside the Golden Kingdom while the battle is commencing it will be entirely defenceless," suggested Galli.

Lucifer scoffed and looked at the three wizards for a reaction signalling any sense been shown, when none was revealed, Lucifer spoke. "Pardon me but there is no proof to back up your claim, forgive me but if this portal were real, then how come my father, the king is none the wiser to its existence?" he asked the trio.

"The prince believes us deluded," sneered Carka.

"A bit yes, our main priority should be the safety of wizards and defending the stronghold of our elders and not spending pointless drops searching for something that does not exist!"

"No one is asking you," spat Carka. "If I had my way, I would toss you in an arena half dead and see how long the royal prince would last when all he has is his wits for a weapon," growled Carka.

Lucifer whipped his staff from his side and aimed it at a laughing Carka. It was probably the laughing, or the lack of respect shown by Carka either way when Lucifer unleashed strings of red flames from his staff they instantly shot at Carka who was no longer sniggering.

"Not so overconfident now!" Lucifer laughed watching his strings form a ring around Carka.

The princes joy however was short lived, as a smirking Carka raised his two index fingers and summoned Lucifer's fire strings to sit calmly on the tips of his thin fingers, where they remotely coiled and vanished with a whistling blow from the ageing wizards' mouth. And just when it seemed Carka was going to use words to further insult Lucifer he surprised them all when his eyes flashed blood red, causing Lucifer to shriek in pain as he was lifted into the air wrenching in agony.

"You don't sit on a throne now Ripeling, here in the real world you fight or die," growled Carka advancing on a helpless Lucifer who hung in the air while Carkas spell bound his body, as Lucifer's resistance decreased with every passing drop.

"Stop it, you'll kill him if you keep this up," cried Galli.

"His life is no loss to anyone," said Carka menacingly, "he would stand in our presence and play our helper and then when his own power is questioned, he'll run back to his father like a good little brat," said Carka who relished in the slow torture he was causing the prince as Lucifer's eyes began rolling in back of his head.

It wasn't courage or bravery that made Galli do it, but one drop, she was pleading the next she was jinxing Carka with a neat swelling jinx that caused his hands and fingers to swell and bubble which forced him to release Lucifer from his binding curse. Yelping in discomfort, Carka fell to his knees growling from the agony of his hands swelling. Bregit gaped, amazed by Galli's actions, and looked at her like he'd never done before. Lucifer regained himself, though hurt the prince remained on his feet, flexing his hand his staff returned to him, he aimed it at Carka but the thought of attacking him seemed to stall his instincts. Galli stood in front of Carka shielding him from Lucifer's aim.

''As much as I would like to kill you, I have an army to gather,'' Before he left, he turned to Bregit. ''Larmont is safe I hope this makes us even and you Galli…,'' he looked at her with affection, ''consider your dept paid in full,'' he said firmly as he stormed out of the room without a second glance.

''Vanishio,'' breathed Bregit waving his hand over Carka.

''That worked well old friend, I must admit I would've preferred it was you getting jinxed all the same we got the result intended,'' laughed Carka relieved to have Galli's jinx lifted.

''Indeed, we did,'' said Bregit smiling whilst helping Carka back to his feet.

''You used me to get rid of Lucifer?'' asked Galli.

''Galli, we had no intentions of returning to the Golden Kingdom. We believe Tip-Karp is going to use the Wall of Illusion to destroy the Golden Kingdom. But you saw Lucifer's reaction when I told him, he was in denial of such a thing even existing,'' said Bregit.

''What you have to understand is the wizards of the clouds have never seen our world they live and die among the clouds only leaving their sanctuary when troubles arise, so it would be difficult for any of them to accept something they've never seen or heard of before,'' stated Carka.

''I believe, and I've never heard of this wall,'' Galli said reminding them both she was on their side.

''Your belief comes from your past trauma; you want what we say to be true because it will set in motion a purpose for you to feel wanted again,'' said Carka.

''That was a bit harsh Carka,'' said Bregit who seen the little colour in Galli's face drain.

''If the ripe wants soft tales and comforting lies, I'll bring back that worthless prince, the world is ugly and if you had one ounce of sense you'd stop looking like a lost little ripe and realize life isn't fair. How many wizards must die before you see the picture!'' barked Carka his eyes inflamed with rage at Galli's wimpy actions.

Galli felt like Carka had striped her bare and exposed her to a crowd of laughing jeering creatures, yet his raged outburst did hit her inner judgement, because there was no purpose for her besides vengeance, which made her think, ''what would she do with herself if the wizards were triumphant?''

''Galli, you were the only one between us who could have completed our plan we depended too much on your honour, so yes in a less honourable way we used you, but our intentions were not to wrong you only to rid us of the burden of Lucifer,'' said Bregit.

''It's done, I hold no bitterness for your actions,'' Galli said, frankly.

''Good then we can leave and stop that wretched sphinx,'' said Carka.

"Easier said than done, do any of you know the location of this wall?" Galli asked her question intended for Bregit.

"No, the sphinxes were secretive about their designs, but we can follow Tip-Karps traces which may lead us straight to it," answered Bregit.

"Unless he leaves false trails that could lead us astray, listen to yourself Bregit. Tip-Karp will be flying not walking to the wall with a pack of strong hosts to protect him. Lano will not have let him travel alone, so you should be asking what breed of creature would assist him on his journey?" interjected Carka.

"I know what you are suggesting, and I will not let them drive me on a rampage quest, no we will go to the mountain maybe there are clues to where the wall maybe," Bregit contradicted.

"Then you will be alone, drops are wasting debating. Lano marches to the Bay of Bones and the Varwels will be joining him as we speak, and Tip-Karp is nearing his destination. Rooting around deserted caves will only gain Lano the advantage," said Carka.

With no idea where Tip-Karp was the three wizards sat in silence each wizard dwelling on their own thoughts. Bregit continued examining his map hoping the answer was there somewhere. Carka sat on the edge of Bregit's bed with his eyes shut and wearing a look of impatience, while Galli sat on the window ledge looking down on the courtyard praising Bregit's skills of repairing, because from where she was sitting no one would ever believe it was swarmed in a blanket of dead Varwels. Galli had to admit without Bregit and Carka's interception her and Lucifer's attempts to defend Larmont were a certainty to fail. Never had she seen two wizards combine their skills to repel an army of Varwels. Their comets launch technique was supposed to be impenetrable, yet Bregit and Carka shattered right through it with ease. Even watching Carka taunt Lucifer was immense and still he wasn't using much of his power. Bregit was nicknamed the Banisher of Gliders now Carka was the banisher of Varwels two legendary feats that Galli could only hope to achieve.

"I may have found the walls location," came Bregit's voice that unsettled the silence.

Carka was off the bed and on Bregit in an instant, he leaned over him and almost touched the paper with his pointed nose. Galli stood on the opposite side looking at the dot of black Bregit had magically imprinted.

"Selavroc, you think the walls in Selavroc? Did that duel with Leon addle your brain or have you finally lost it?" asked Carka disappointedly.

"Not in Selavroc but above it, listen why did Tip-Karp stay when all other sphinxes left, why is there a fog that never weavers surrounding the entire island? When Orakil came to the Golden Kingdom he gave a brief of what the fogs were doing to him, I tell you Carka the Wall of Illusion lives within that fog," Bregit said in a confident manner.

"Selavroc is a far distance from here it would take us a shade to get there," Galli said flatly.

Bregit rolled up his map and tossed it on his table. "Will you journey with me old friend?"

"I hope you know Bregit that if the wall isn't in Selavroc we will be too late to save the Golden Kingdom unless you've figured a way for us to be in two places at the exact same moment?"

"Unfortunately, I haven't, but trust me blindly on this and I swear you will not regret it," Bregit said seriously.

Carka smiled and offered out his hand to Bregit. "Then what are we waiting for?" said Carka to Bregit who graced his offering and grasped his hand.

Both wizards turned to Galli who was clueless to what was happening.

"Take my arm Galli and you will experience magic beyond the boundaries of forging crafts," offered Carka showing her his vacant arm.

Galli looked at Bregit who gave her a weak smile that eased her doubt. Galli grasped Carka's wrist and in that moment his eyes flashed white. Galli screamed as a bolt if white lightning smashed through the towers ceiling and struck the three wizards, making them vanish in a flash of blinding light.

Chapter 26

The Morphing Fog

''There was no need to use that much force,'' Bregit complained while rubbing his right arm.

''Stop your whining Bregit, it was Galli's first experience and I wanted her to feel the full effects of fast travel,'' Carka laughed joying in Bregit's annoyance.

Carka had gotten his wish, though the pain was bearable, the unease Galli was feeling in her stomach combined with her inability to stand, forced her to remain in the position she had appeared. Crouched down on all fours and clutching her mid-section the discomfort forcing her to remain as still as possible to allow the effects of her first fast travel to wear off.

''Ah, this is living, you smell that Ripeling? Inhale the fresh cleansing air,'' breathed Carka embracing the wide-open space with open arms as the ageing wizard twirled on the spot.

''Much to your joy Carka, we are here for more concerning matters,'' Bregit reminded him. ''Come Galli walking will help ease your queasiness,'' he said tapping her back.

Galli did as Bregit bid and was glad to find his advice to be a comfort, because after a few steps the unsettlement in her bowels began to unsettle which allowed her some breathing space.

''I thought you said Selavroc was contaminated in fog?'' said Galli, now satisfied whatever was threatening to erupt from her stomach had decided to remain dormant.

''It is,'' answered Bregit. ''Carka has transported us to the outskirts and away from the fog. Bregit turned on Galli so fast that she almost fell backwards, ''I implore you to be on your guard here Galli, creatures moulded and shaped by darkness can be feisty beasts especially under the influence of the fog,'' Bregit warned with a sternness to his tone.

''The trees, there all dead,'' whispered Carka in disbelief.

''Like all living things that once lived here,'' said Bregit flatly still looking at Galli seriously.

When they reached the fog, they found the ground sheeted in soft gray sand, any sign of life was either hidden or consumed by the thick fog that drew nearer with every foot the three wizards put forward.

''Is the fog immovable?'' Galli asked feeling the vibrant vapour pass through her hands.

''Our elders wrote many cycles of shades ago that the fog of Selavroc would not pass under the influence of persuasion, magic, or force. The only known creature to dwell here without falling into madness is Lano,'' Carka replied tensely.

''Which was the reason he was allowed the shades he needed to orchestrate his battle plans, because wizards do not fare well against the fog because of their inability to know its effects. Lano an ancient creature knows every land and its weaknesses all except….,''

''The Golden Kingdom,'' said Galli finishing Bregit's sentence for him.

''We're here,'' said Carka. ''Whatever counter curse or spell you may think of Galli remember the fog can anticipate it, your only defence against its powers are warmth and light,'' he advised.

'Warmth and light,' Galli repeated in her head. The two essences she had little knowledge of. It wasn't down to her lack of skill but more to the fact that in Treforledge the basis were water spells and manoeuvring objects. Lorneid explained fire spells but only in theory, she had never learned the practical essentials to summoning powerful beams or fire-based spells.

When the trio were inside the thick fog it became difficult to move, it was if the gravity had increased. Bregit who was holding his staff aloft had conjured flames that gave them enough light to make each other out as the flames radiated warmth throughout the trio.

''I can't sense any heat signatures anywhere; it seems probable that the entire land is consumed by this fog,'' said Bregit.

''Probable, but what you can't sense is what I can see,'' said Carka tugging Galli in the right direction. ''Shush,'' breathed Carka and before they could stop him, he was absorbed into the fog's thick layers. Galli made a move to follow him, but it was Bregit's hand on her shoulder that stopped her.

''Easy Galli, Carka knows what he is doing,'' Bregit whispered in her ear.

''Disligwa,'' came Carka's firm voice from the depths of the fog.

A bright light of crimson gold pushed back the fog and covered their surroundings in an air bubble. Carka walked through the bubble with ease, but he wasn't alone something curled and ragged was getting pulled magically along by Carka.

''What is that?'' asked Galli, looking at Carka and then to the wretched figure floating immobilised by his side.

Carka grabbed the wretched creature roughly around the neck and tossed it across the hard ground, the creature rolled in anguish before raising its dirt-stained face. The state of the creature's face caused a squeal to burst from Galli's mouth as the face staring at her was revolting. The creature's eyes were soggy grey which matched its frail skin that seemed dead, it wore rags that scarcely covered its lower body, but Galli couldn't help noticing the deep claw marks dug deep into its ribs and back that could be mistaken for white veins.

''This creature has been following us since we arrived, I thought it was a loose Slither but once it got close enough, I knew who and what lurked in our shadows,'' panted Carka who seemed to be having trouble catching his breath.

''You know this creature?'' Bregit asked Carka still looking at the filthy creature with a look of pity.

''Did,'' heaved Carka. ''He was once a wizard now I am afraid to concede resides with our enemies.''

''Orakil?'' said Bregit moving past Galli and near enough to look closely at the gaunt figure in front of him.

''Don't stand too close Bregit, we do not know who may be watching through his eyes,'' cautioned Carka.

''Bregit?'' gasped the creature in a deep hallowing voice.

''What has become of him?'' Bregit asked Carka looking at him in wonder.

''The fog has destroyed the wizard inside of him and formed him into a creature of darkness and a watcher for the Gliders,'' answered Carka.

''Orakil, have any Gliders passed through here?'' Bregit asked in a soft caring voice.

Orakils head tilted from one side to the other, his eyes a fraction of a drop slow to follow, but he looked at Bregit who was showing signs of sympathy toward his old friend.

''I am tired old friend,'' he said sadly. ''For cycles of shades have passed and still I cannot summon the will to leave this foul place. Darkness has woken from its slumber and showers us with deceit while cunningly blinding us to the real threat. For they move among us, spying on us with one eye while using the other to pray on our weaknesses until the shade comes when they are ready to strike,'' said Orakil sounding exhausted.

''The threat is already awake old friend that is why we have come here to end it; we need to know did a sphinx travel through here not long before we arrived?'' Bregit asked in a compassionate tone.

''Yes, but not alone,'' heaved Orakil deeply. ''The sphinx travels with those who watch and wait.''

''We can't trust him, you know that'' said Carka in a firm voice. ''If Tip-Karp has passed through here, he may have told him to point us in a different direction.''

''Perhaps, but it's the only lead we've got Carka,'' said Bregit.

''Don't allow your feelings for your former friend cloud your judgement Bregit, I will not risk our lives because you haven't the mindset to see beyond who someone used to be,'' snarled Carka.

''What will we do with him, we can't just leave him here?'' said Galli, looking at a wizard who appeared defeated in every aspect of life.

''I have no meaning anymore,'' Orakil sighed heavily. ''The powers I once possessed have vaporized, what you see now is a shell clinging to a soul, a soul ready to soar beyond the veil of the living.''

Orakil wasn't seeking sympathy, but the trio could tell from the sadness in his voice that all the empty wizard wanted was to leave the sad existence he'd become accustomed to. And judging by Orakils appearance that if one of them didn't grant his wish, starvation or madness would claim him eventually. Galli put herself in Orakils position and knew if it were her, she would want to be put out of her misery instead of having to spend another drop just existing. And just as Galli had grasped the responsibility of stepping up and doing what needed to be done Carka had walked around the defeated wizard and raised his hand over the back of Orakils head and whispered, ''Kildurmar.''

A flash of blue light shot from Carka's hand and sank into the back of Orakils skull. Orakil gave a low relieved sigh before welcoming the killing blow and allowed it to soar through him without restraint. The sound of Orakils head hitting the sand confirmed Carka's curse had done what he had intended. The trio stood staring at the lifeless body of Orakil for a brief spell. Carka gave his hand a wave, sprinkling Orakils body with sparks that ignited his body and burnt it to ash. Carka walked away first with no show of remorse and soon Bregit and Galli followed. The sudden death of Orakil the Silver no doubt playing a part in their silence.

"Vanishio," said Carka aiming his hand at the bubble, the force of his vanishing spell wiping it away.

"Can you feel the drop-in temperature? We must be getting close," ushered Bregit.

"Wait!" screeched Galli.

Carka tutted in frustration, but Bregit stalled.

"What is it?"

"When last the drop-in degrees occurred Treforledge was attacked!" cried Galli.

Carka nodded his head in frustration even Bregit rolled his eyes, but Galli remained persistent.

"I know I sound mad but listen the cold you are feeling right now is the same one I felt moments before Treforledge was attacked," pleaded Galli in an appealing voice.

"Galli listen the fog has ways of showing us our deepest fears and using those fears as weapons to startle our minds, this is your first experience within its confinements you.........,"

Bregit's voice muted as Galli's prediction came to pass. The fog had begun to morph so fast the three wizards were absorbed into a fascinated trance and watched in horror as a darkened gray cloud with red sparkling eyes took form, its curved mouth split into a menacing smile as it stared menacingly at the three stunned wizards.

"It's here!" Galli cried, raising Water Dancer as the beating in her chest intensified.

Carka wove his hands and unleashed powerful gusts of swirling wind from his palms. The cloud cackled a mad laugh showing its forked teeth at Carka's approaching attack. With a glow of its red eyes the surging wind stopped in mid-air and vanished in an instant.

"Impossible," breathed Carka, who stood baffled by the clouds short use of power to halt one of his most veracious attacks.

"I have battled this cloud before, we are no match against its powers, we must flee now!" shouted Bregit.

The cloud glided toward Carka its sneer mocking them as its scarlet eyes planted a seed of doubt into their minds. Carka relished in the prospect of the clouds challenge and used both his hands to conjure surging lightning storms from the clouds above the fog. With a howl of anger, Carka unleashed such a force the ground shook violently as Carka's lightning storm collided with the welcoming cloud who hadn't moved or made any attempt to dodge the surging bolts.

Bregit and Galli looked from Carka to the smoke rising from where his attack had struck. Carka had surely made contact, the three wizards were sure the cloud couldn't defend against a nature-based attack. But as the smoke faded the cloud was still in the exact spot, undamaged by Carkas attack.

"What is this monstrosity?" panted an exhausted Carka, who couldn't believe his attack was ineffective after he'd channelled all his strength into it.

Bregit swung his staff summoning green flames that flew from his staff's tip. Waving his arms, Bregit created a sizzling line of fire in a desperate hope that it would prevent the cloud advancing further. Galli watched on finding her body paralyzed, the clouds scarlet eyes mirroring the ones she had dreamt about while hanging against the walls of the covenant chamber. Bregit's fire wall was extinguished by the cloud who was advancing slowly upon the tree wizards. Showing no sign of fear only a mad desire to torment before adding the three wizards to its kill list. Galli couldn't find it within herself to fight, the clouds aura was enough to tame her impulses. Carka and Bregit were forced to use the maximum of their skills to keep themselves level with the cloud. But both wizards crumbled under the pressure the cloud was applying. With every deflected and misaimed spell Bregit and Carkas strength decreased while the cloud wasted little by merely using a shadow wall to block their attacks. Demonstrating how futile their attempts were, the cloud unleashed an energy wave so powerful it shot right through Bregit and Carka's enchanted barriers. The impact causing both wizards to spiral away from the fray and deep into the depths of the smouldering fog, leaving Galli alone with this unstoppable being.

With no sign of Carka or Bregit returning Galli was forced to accept her faith and it for reasons unknown she raised Water Dancer and prepared herself not for a fight but for a noble death.

''I know I cannot beat you whoever you are, but it won't stop me trying,'' said Galli, making her voice sound unafraid.

But all Galli's brave stance did was heighten the clouds moral as it levitated slowly toward her. Just when Galli was about to unseal her lips, a stab of pain shot through her palms causing her to cry out in pain. An ear cringing crackling sound drew Galli's attention away from the blackened stain splashed across her hands as she seen Water Dancer coiled within tentacles sprouted from the cloud.

Flexing its tentacles, the cloud remorsefully snapped Water Dancer into pieces and brushed aside its remains. The blue star shaped ruby lay in the gray sand, its glow dimming until it slowly faded before cracking down the middle and dissolving into nothing. Defenceless the cloud took delight in sensing Galli's fear as she scrambled back, but an invisible force kept her rooted to the spot. It was the fog, somehow the cloud was controlling it to do its bidding. Black shadowy tentacles licked against Galli's face and limbs as she was lifted into the air and was like her staff moments before coiled within the clouds chilling tentacles. And it was in that moment that Galli felt her powers numb, and it hit her. ''It can stun the powers of creatures,'' said a voice in Galli's head.

''Alcutom!'' echoed a rasping voice through the fog.

The voice reverberated throughout the fog confusing the cloud and Galli. Using its spare tentacles, the cloud swiped at the locations to where the voice was coming from only for it to change position. Then, out of the shadows came a streak of brightest green, which struck the cloud with such force it was hurled into the fog and out of sight. Still clutched to Galli she was hurled in the cloud's direction. But before she was lost in the fog's plinth, she felt a warm embrace grab her arm which was enough to break the thread attaching her to the cloud. Falling onto the sand, Galli twirled on the spot in search of her rescuer and was filled with delight to find it was Carka, who was standing breathless behind her.

''I thought you were finished,'' breathed Galli as an electric surge coursed through her that filled her with hope that she was safe.

''Not quite,'' heaved Carka. ''Get behind me, I have a hunch the fog has been manipulated by this cloud and if I am right then we are as open as a tree in the desert,'' panted Carka.

Galli could sense the anxiousness in his voice. Behind his stern expression, fear lingered. ''Keep behind me Galli and eyes and ears on the alert we cannot afford a moment lapse in concentration,'' cautioned Carka in an ushered tone.

Galli understood and was grateful for Carka's awareness, because without Water Dancer to wield her powers she was the weak link of the party. Judging by Carka's protective instructions he too was thinking along the same lines.

"Where are you going?" whispered Galli.

"We still have a mission and if Lanos new weapon is present then I'll bet my malas stones the cloud is protecting the trail to the wall. And if I know Bregit, he will have used his leave from the battle to find the wall while the cloud was busy elsewhere."

"Really?" said Galli.

"Bregit sees a larger picture than me and you, take no offence to his methods, while we see the enemy in front of us Bregit sees a window of opportunity from every aspect."

"For the benefit of everyone except himself?" said Galli, trying to find ease in Bregit's way of selflessness.

"Precisely."

Galli was about to argue Carka's point of Bregit's views when she felt a chilling spine bending cold creep under her skin. Carka must have felt it too, because he whirled around instantly shielding Galli from the bright red beams projecting through the cloud's eyes. It floated in mid-air, its eyes narrowed and nostrils flaring the cloud appeared enraged with Carka for catching it off guard. Carka raised his hand, the malas stone dug into his palm shone white as he spoke in a commanding voice.

"Be gone, shadow of darkness! Your presence is an abomination to these lands. BE GONE I SAY !!!" he bellowed, casting surging waves of glistening white beams that stayed the clouds advance.

Carka pushed his spell hard against at the cloud who conjured a shadow wall that slowly marched toward both wizards absorbing everything it touched. It was a battle of wits and determination now. Carka was using the extreme of his abilities which frustrated the cloud who wasn't having it all its own way against an opponent it believed unworthy. Feeling fearful for Carka Galli reluctantly raised her hands. Focusing hard she felt a warm surge flow through her. Feeling the force of Carka's spell she transferred her own energy to enhance the stance of Carkas radiant wave of light.

"Whatever fuels your power now is the shade to use it Galli we may not get another chance," called Carka through gritted teeth while stamping his feet firmly into the sand.

Galli remembered what the cloud had done and who it had done it to, the very thought of Lorneid and all her kin sparked a strength inside her that was fuelled by hatred for the creature yards away. "Anger shields pain," she recalled as Lorneids kind voice filled her mind and the flow of her power pushed out from her palms.

"Don't congratulate yourself so soon, our foe is not defeated yet!" said Carka.

Carka was right. Even though their combined efforts were equal to the clouds shadow wall, they weren't gaining any ground which meant one slip could be vital. Carka's beams stopped radiating light much to Galli's confusion, then to her horror Carka was lifted from his feet by a piercing shadow dagger that had cut straight through his stomach. Hooked in the air, with splashes of black blood squirting from his mouth Carka wriggled and tried with all his strength to unhook himself but the clouds hold was too strong. Unable to hold against the clouds shadow wall, Galli dived away before the clouds wall broke through her holding spell.

The cloud rose to face Carka as the ageing wizard was white as a ghost by the amount of blood he had lost, his fading eyes met the scarlet still wearing a deep look of hatred toward his opponent. Cackling, the cloud flung Carka to the sand where he rolled right at Galli's feet. Dying. Carka rolled onto his back, his shaking hand clutching where the cloud had pierced him. Galli leaned over him. It was DeJa'Vu all over again except it was Carka not Lorneid clinging on to his fading life. Carka raised his free hand, gurgling words through gushing spits of black that foamed from his mouth. Instantly Galli gripped her fingers around Carkas palms, his malas stones were stone cold. Forcing herself not to pull away, Galli channelled the warmth of her fingers to Carkas shaking hands.

"I …. should…. ve…tol…d yo…u," gasped Carka fighting to stay conscious.

Galli could tell he was struggling to stay among the living. The pain in his voice making it obvious for her to understand what he was trying to say. Observing the area, she found no scent or trace of the cloud's presence. Trying to shush him, Carka shook and twisted, he was reluctant to say what he had to say. All Galli could do was hold him for the wound was festering at a rapid pace. Then as if Carka had returned to full health he spoke plain and softly.

"You will do what I could not young Galli. War is coming from all regions of Nocktar. You will be the beacon of light, to swallow the darkness and cleanse our planet," said Carka his last three words sounding like they were an echo.

Before Galli could ask what Carka was referring to his hands glowed white, except unlike his previous spells this beam was rising and circling Galli's wrist. Slithering like a serpent, the beam coiled and dug its way beneath the skin on her palms. Galli was unable to retract the beam as it forced back her restraints and when she tried pushing her hand away, she was stung with an electrical charge. Carka's wrist had slipped from Galli's grasp. When she tried retrieving his fallen arm it broke into specks of ash at her slightest touch. Slowly Carka's skin began to crack as dark purple lines fissured along his face slithering down his neck and beneath his overalls.

"No," she cried as Carka's body broke, detaching into specks of ash.

Carka's head fell back, leaning against her lap. When Galli looked for a sign of life in his faded eyes, all she found staring back at her were blank eyes staring at the sky but not seeing anything. Death had changed Carkas stern expression into a blank motionless posture. Looking at him like this swelled Galli's insides as hot tears found their way out from the sides of her eyes and streamed down her cheeks as she held onto what remained of Carka. Drops passed in silence. Galli held the fading Carka whose body had become stiff, due to his organs no longer functioning. The pace of Carkas decentration had gathered momentum, looking below Carkas waist Galli noticed his legs had gone and soon the rest of him would be nothing more than specks of ash. Galli didn't know why she kept hold of Carka. It wasn't down to compassion or any mutual feelings for him. But she knew that if it were her, she would want someone around to comfort her, even if she wasn't alive to embrace their good will.

Sitting alone and friendless all Galli wanted to do was call out for Bregit, but he had abandoned her and in this fog she hadn't a hope of finding him. When Carka's body finally disintegrated, all that remained of him were his ragged cloak, as his ashes flowed motionlessly into the fog which mystified Galli because instead of flowing up and drifting beyond the wind Carka's ashes were unexplainably absorbed by the fogs mystifying inhabitants. Knowing there was no point dwelling, Galli scooped up Carka's cloak and threw it over her own.

Feeling the warmth give life to her numb limbs Galli pulled the hood over her head and drifted slowly through the fog with no idea where she was going, or what dangers lay ahead.

Chapter 27

Carka's Legacy

When Galli imagined Selavroc, an image of sea and rocks always came to her mind, comparing her imagination to what she was seeing now shattered that vivid illusion to pieces. Selavroc seemed from Galli's perspective a land contaminated in a thick fog, making it extremely difficult to know where anything was. Out of the three wizards who had entered the fog it was Carka who knew what route to take without the aid of magical requirement. Galli wondered what other qualities the elderly wizard had stored in that ancient mind of his.

It felt shameful for Galli that she couldn't honour Carka with a decent passing but whatever the cloud had stabbed him with had erased that possibility. Every step she took brought her back to that moment when Carkas body cracked and turned to ash. It was a passing unheard of, because when wizards normally die from wounds their bodies are lifeless and become stiff not slowly fade in nothingness. The clouds use of powers against Galli and Carka were effortless it even seemed disappointed by their combined attempts to defeat it, if memory served Galli correctly the only indication the cloud gave of showing its real strength was when Carka wounded it. But what annoyed Galli was the fact that Bregit had fled when the cloud had parried his efforts to shield himself from its advances. Carka had explained Bregit intended to sacrifice them so he could pursue the location of the Wall of Illusion. But Carka could have fled and left Galli to die but instead chose to return and fight against an unstoppable being that Carka knew he could not defeat.

"Why though?" Galli asked herself. Carka didn't have any bearings to her, it was the Lorneid situation all over again, and it was that same niggling feeling Galli felt during her walk through the gorge that gnawed at her again as she slowly crept deeper into the fogs of Selavroc.

A chilly wind crept past Galli's face, meaning someone or something magical was getting closer to her location. Even without Water Dancer, Galli could smell a magical trace which she found strange because she had never learned the ways to detect magic through airwaves, but for some reason the ability just felt natural to her. But inheriting this new skill didn't help Galli when it came to defending herself. With nowhere to hide Galli lay on her front with her face pressed into the soft sand, quickly she waved her hands causing the sand to splash repeatedly over her body in hope that it would conceal her.

"The risk is too grave; you must go and go now!" came a whistling voice through the air.

"You ask much, too much! The circumstances of our agreement have changed drastically since we last communed," said a different voice with a delicateness to its low tone.

"You agreed, now begone before we are both found," said the same delicate voice.

The wind turned cold again gusting past Galli and out of range, when she felt safe to lift herself back to her feet, she noticed a dark figure coming toward her. Was this the owner of the voice Galli had overheard? Whoever it was knew she was there, why else would it walk directly to her? Closing her hands into fists Galli felt the tips of her fingers press against a solid object. Reacting surprised, Galli opened her hands and to her dismay found a stone, round and glowing engraved into the centre of her palms. Mirroring the malas stones Carka used to wield his magic, but how did these stones get into her hands without Galli knowing? Looking at her other hand it was identical, two stones white as the moon and bright as day were resting within her palms.

''Galli,'' came a quiet voice.

Jumping with fright Galli let out a squeal that echoed through the fog for miles. It was Bregit, tall and wearing his patched cloak. He looked drained and white with worry.

''I would have thought you would use that brain of yours to get as far away from here as possible. This is no place to want to redeem yourself,'' said Bregit who sounded furious.

''I'm not redeeming anything; I came to find you,'' lied Galli quickly.

''Find me you have, now what is the plan?'' asked Bregit, mocking her lack of thought.

''I...I... I hadn't thought that far ahead,'' Galli admitted with a stutter.

''This is no tournament, this is reality. You don't get to analyse your opponents and talk among friends before the big event. Out here it's the smartest and strong who out last the rest,'' said Bregit sounding disappointed at Galli's misuse of her senses.

''Really!'' snapped Galli an unknown flush of anger caused her eyes and nostrils to flare as she stared angrily at a shocked Bregit. ''Is that why you left us to fend off the cloud while you hid in the shadows? Carka is dead and my staff got shattered, while you ran to play the hero!'' bellowed Galli.

Bregit wasn't a wizard to be talked back to or contradicted about his opinions and Galli expected him to argue or shadow her argument with his reasons for withdrawing from the fight. Shockingly all Bregit did was stare at the gray sand beneath his toes.

''I was sure Carka could delay the cloud long enough for me to find the Wall of Illusion and return before my absence was noticed. I got side-tracked following two creatures I thought were Gliders in disguise but when I sensed your energy, I believed it to be you and Carka,'' said Bregit in a defeated tone that disarmed Galli.

''He died in my arms, when the cloud cut through him it thought me of little worth and left in pursuit of you,'' said Galli sadly.

Before Bregit could pay any sacrament for Carka whooshes could be heard close to where he and Galli stood.

''It would seem the hunters have become the hunted,'' called a voice behind the fog.

Bregit grabbed Galli and forced her behind him, he raised his staff making his yellow stone shine bright white.

''Come wizard, light will not sway me away,'' jeered a laughing voice.

''What is that thing?'' Galli asked in wonder, as she watched a serpent like creature emerge from the thick fog.

Estimating its length Galli presumed its entire body was probably the length of Treforledge, she watched as the serpent's coils slithered along the gray sand appearing like it was encasing them within its coils.

"Jaed," said Bregit, "the great lord of the seaweed columns beneath the Red Sea."

"Right, you are Bregit," laughed Jaed. "Last I saw of you was when you were hooked from the sky and tied to a rock," jeered the great serpent.

"Fond memories," said Bregit, "last I saw of you my effortless stun spell had knocked you out cold, I daresay the trauma of that is still fresh in that unforgettable mind you posse?"

Jaed slithered up until his yellow eyes sparkled in the moonlight. With a roar of pain, he spread his dark wings wide, eclipsing the sky.

"Bregit the Yellow, Lord of Larmont, and friend to sphinxes," said the monotonous voice of Tip-Karp, who had appeared like Jaed unnoticed and fully aware of what was going on.

"Tip-Karp, I daresay your appearance isn't an unwelcome one," said Bregit bitterly.

Jaed lowered himself back to ground level his shadowing of the light to ensure Tip-Karp entered the scene undetected having worked a treat. Jaed's head now hoovered inches above the gray sand as Galli noticed a bright glint of orange linger in the depths of the serpent's eyes.

"I see Lano has given you your own guard to accompany you on your travels. A generous gesture, who would have known him to be so loyal to his devoted subjects?" jeered Bregit.

"Wars are not won on battle fields old friend. They are won through actions. Wizards have spent cycles above the clouds living on what they believe to be their rightful stature. I am a keeper of peace; my allegiances are to the cause who wants what I want and sadly wizards do not want peace," said Tip-Karp his voice calm. "Your race only craves power and position, while uses sit in comfort, creatures are slaughtered and used for the befitting of cruel wizard's sport. My ancestors left so they wouldn't have to watch while creatures are made to serve and fight to claim what should be theirs by free will not by the decision of those who believe power gives them the right to rule," said Tip-Karp, the added force behind his words leaving a long silence in their absence.

"That was quite a speech, I'd like to see you describe such emotions with no tongue," said Bregit coldly.

Unprepared Tip-Karp was hurled into the air by the force of Bregit's outraged attack. Stepping forward he wove his hands rapidly casting spells from a bright enchanted beam shaped like a square with creatures of green, gray, blue and red swirling along its edges.

"What kind of magic was this?" Galli asked herself as she stood transfixed by Bregit's skills. Having studied many ways of performing spells not one text or scroll in Treforledge ever mentioned solar beams manually casting spells without a caster's command. Galli watched amazed by the magic been put on display in front of her.

Jaed was the one who caught Tip-Karp and prevented him falling into the bowels of the fog. Flapping his wings, the great serpent whirled a powerful hurricane that caused many of Bregit's spells to swerve away from their intended target. Before Galli could think of a defence a gale force wind met Jaeds whirlwind head on. Looking round, she saw that the square shaped beam swirling around Bregit's outstretched knuckles had a winged beast crested in the squares centre. The winds hurled and spurned fiercely at the other creating a wind shield on both sides. Bregit's stand against Jaed looked the perfect diversion for Tip-Karp to slip away, he may have done so had Galli not glimpsed the shine from his bright wings slip behind the darkness of the fog.

Without knowing or thinking Galli found her legs had acted without her acknowledgement. It wasn't bravery that kept her pursuing Tip-Karp it was desperation, with Bregit fighting Jaed she was the only wizard left who could still save the Golden Kingdom. The sound of Tip-Karp's sprints weren't hard to miss but his speed was difficult for Galli to keep up with. Sand splashed off her ankles and lashed up against her thighs sticking to her skin causing irritations Galli had no use for.

"You are brave to travel alone and without your staff. I suppose it will fare better for me that your lack of requirement will benefit me more than it will you," said Tip-Karp who had stopped running to confront his pursuer.

"TRAITOR!" yelled Galli at the top of her voice, hoping her scream reached Bregit and alerted him to her position.

Galli understood it would be foolish to convince herself she was a match against Tip-Karp, even if she had her staff in her possession it would take extraordinary skill to kill a sphinx in battle.

"A cherished title, but I will not cherish hurting you, so I will offer a sublime gift. If you stand as still and frightened as you are now while I make haste with my purpose, I swear your life will be spared," offered Tip-Karp.

"Interesting offer. But why not kill me and move onwards anyway? It shouldn't take you long, it's like what you said I have no staff and my magic without it is less likely to cause you concern," said Galli holding her arms wide, hoping by allowing Tip-Karp to attack it would be enough to keep him here until Bregit arrived.

"You are quite in tune with words even when under the mercy of a superior. I have seen and counselled creatures with your nerve cycles of shades ago, however they are all dead now. Still the resemblance is uncanny, Treforledge may have kept more than rocks in their stores," said Tip-Karp eyeing Galli suspiciously.

"He was an odd creature, even now when his last obstacle was there to be destroyed, he disbands from priority to speak in riddles," thought Galli,

It was a distraction, one that may have worked had Galli's body not acted of its own accord and fluidly moved with agility Galli never knew she owned. Her reflexes were so quick Tip-Karp missed his target and landed roughly in the sand. Swerving around, spitting sand from his vicious mouth. Tip-Karp pounced into the air, spreading his powerful wings wide before diving at Galli. Again, she was ready. Somehow her instincts were able to read Tip-Karps intentions and prepare her with a counterstrike of her own. Threads, thick and glowing in a sea blue aura flowed through her fingertips. The threads moved freely through the air sweeping past the sphinx's every attempt to destroy them until they caught Tip-Karp around his four ankles. A surging pull forced Galli to grasp the threads flowing from her fingertips and twist them tightly within her grasp. Stunned to see the sphinx coiled in the threads she had unknowingly conjured Galli was unsure what to do?

"Now what?" thought Galli, forcing herself to remain focused as Tip-Karp fought against his restraints.

As Galli weighed her options in what to do next Tip-Karp's bonds were cut and sliced by the reappearance of the cloud. Gliding, the cloud circled Galli before positioning itself above the sand.

Tip-Karp didn't wait for an introduction instead he stretched his enormous wings and flew into the heart of the fog and out of her sight. Galli knew It was suicide even considering chasing after him. The cloud would just intervene and strike her down with her killer shadow weapons the moment she attempted to chase Tip-Karp. Staring at the cloud Galli felt no fear or eagerness to flee, what she felt aroused suspicion in herself because never had she felt this notion before. It was tingling her brain to attack the cloud. Her mind was even telling her what incantation to perform.

"Was this the cloud?" thought Galli in wonder, "had it somehow a brand of magic capable of convincing creatures to perform a spell that may harm her or worse kill her?"

"What are you and why did you destroy my home?" Galli asked the cloud.

The cloud's eyes flashed brighter red, its mouth curling as thin whiffs of light smoke flowed from its slits for nostrils. The sand levitated from beneath Galli's feet, flowing swiftly toward the cloud whose gaze never left the bright blue of her eyes. The sand spun and twirled in the air forming into multiple sand twisters. Like serpents the sand twisters dived at Galli their eyes widening in attempt to swallow her whole. Again, Galli's instincts proved divine, unknowing her arms automatically swished and flowed freely conjuring a circular shaped shield that glowed seven distinct colours. What was more the shield she had summoned was Mirror and it withstood the sand twisters attack and repelled them back at the cloud, who easily made them disintegrate.

Slamming her palm hard against Mirror it shattered into sharp shards of wind diluted in bright colours. "My turn," said Galli in a confident tone that she had never used before.

Pulling back her right arm she felt the warmth of the malas stone nesting in her palms radiate warmth that flowed through her arm and shoulder. Powered to its maximum Galli swiped the air in a ferocious swerve that she released waves of energy that gave the shards of her shattered shield enough fuel to charge at the cloud. Gurgling the cloud spat black liquified acid from its mouth, countering Galli's attack and dissolving her charging shards of glass to nothing. But the dread Galli predicted never chilled her senses, not one bit. Instead, her mind relished in the cloud's demonstration like a quenching thirst not satisfied with its requirements, but instead desired more. This newfound confidence changed the stance of the cloud, it no longer seemed so sure of itself but cautious of its next move. It was a stare down with tension increasing every passing drop. The situation wasn't one Galli was accustomed to, but strangely her senses were assuring her she was the one in command.

The cloud's eyes flashed as Galli's followed suit; red beams shot from the clouds as white radiant beams shot from Galli's. They met in mid-air. The combination of their attacks causing the ground to shake. Then it happened, unexpectedly and without purpose. Flashes clouded Galli's vision, and, in that moment, she felt her body leave the duel and soar at lightning speed to a deserted wasted land. Unfamiliar to her surroundings Galli watched as a creature, green skinned and black of hair lay on the banks of a river a short distance from the Red Sea. It lay heaving and clinging to life as the effects of green shade took its toll over the creature's body. Finding she could walk; Galli cautiously approached the dying creature. Its eyes were in the back of its head, its body shook and wretched in agony, she tried helping but found her touch was useless. Her hand simply went through the agonizing creatures head when she tried to soothe its pain with a caring touch.

The realisation of what was occurring pulled Galli away from the creature, her breaths came in heavy lungful's that increased her fear of her surroundings as someone nearby was panting hard, she looked around to see a skeletal figure rushing to the dying creature's side.

"Lano," squealed Galli raising her hand.

Shockingly the Lava Keeper didn't react to Galli in anyway. Instead, he knelt beside the dying creature who seemed unaware of Galli's presence.

"Balasto!" cried Galli aiming her hand at Lano's head.

But no surging blast shot out of her hand nor was there any retch or cry of pain from Lano who was waving his skinless hands over the green skinned creature. Smoke, gray, and see through flowed gently from Lano's fingertips and latched onto the dying creature. The thin clouds widened into threads, spreading a numbing aura around the deserted bay. Twirling the creature around using his dark threads of smoke Lano concealed the dying creature in wispy smoke. The creature's body coiled and moulded until it was consumed entirely.

"Rest now, your body has been weakened by the shade's effects. What you find yourself inside is a cocoon that prevents the shade's effects crippling your limbs," hissed Lano gently to the fully formed cloud.

Rays of scarlet red began breaking through the cloud's eyelids but when the cloud tried to open its eyes fully it couldn't. Lano moved aside wanting a clearer picture of his creation, the cloud floated in mid-air a cold intimidating aura radiating from the clouds flowing wisps as Galli looked on in horror to what she had just seen. Then when Galli had convinced herself, she was safe because of Lanos unresponsive behaviour toward her presence, the clouds beaming eyes locked onto her making her back away with fear of exposure. But before the cloud could react Galli felt herself been pulled backwards until she was back within her body. Feeling the sand against her shaking arms Galli found she was laying sideways under a blanket of soft green grass. Feeling numb with a pounding headache she tried getting up but found her body unable to react to her summons.

"Galli you're awake," said a relieved Bregit, who had appeared out of nowhere with his staff alight in a radiant white glow.

"What happened, why can't I move?" Galli asked finding her voice was croaked.

"You don't remember?" asked Bregit who was looking at Galli with a searching expression.

"Remember what?" she asked her croaks layering over her inpatient tone.

"You banished the cloud. The ritual you cried when your beams faded struck the cloud and forced it to flee. I think the complexity of summoning such a force drained you of what strength you had left."

Images flashed across her waking eyes, still she couldn't remember anything Bregit had described to her. The last thing she remembered was a pair of red murderous eyes staring at her.

"Since your awake and able to speak, I would like to know what happened once we parted. I have a strong hunch you failed to stop Tip-Karp?"

"He got away," Galli admitted with a sting to her pride.

"That much I gathered," Bregit said a little too hasty.

"I had him bound and strapped. but then the cloud appeared and cut my threads releasing him. He fled, using the clouds appearance as a diversion," she answered remembering Tip-Karp turning tail and fleeing.

"Interesting. This cloud can prevent its power levels been sensed. Powerful creatures can only possess that skill. Lano must have known we would be searching for the wall and sent his hidden ally to follow Tip-Karp to prevent him failing," said Bregit.

"Why would he send his most powerful ally based on a what if? There was never a guarantee we would go looking for the wall," said Galli.

"To ensure Tip-Karp reached the wall unscathed. Remember who jumped to his defence the moment Tip-Karp revealed himself," Bregit reminded her.

"Jaed and the cloud," breathed Galli.

"Two powerful allies alongside a sphinx, would confirm Lano marched to the Bay of Bones with his army incomplete," stated Bregit.

"It's a possibility. Still, we don't know if Lano has marched to the Bay of Bones yet, for all we know he's laying low waiting for Tip-Karp to return," said Galli.

"Think Galli. Lano knew me and Carka were gone rogue, meaning this was his plan all along. He kept us away by feeding us a single piece of his plan. Yes, he was intending to destroy the Golden Kingdom and he needed Tip-Karp to do so, but it could've been their secret so why did he give Tip-Karp a personal guard?"

"It doesn't fit, even if Lano did plan to keep you and Carka out of the fold. The Seven Coloured Army would still crush his. Maybe he got desperate and, in his desperation, caused him to make snap decisions under heated pressure," suggested Galli.

"Lano is an expert manipulator in power and mind, he would never disband his army without good reason. This is how he dictates his operations by secret and filled with confusion," said Bregit.

"Then how do you expect us to counter him if we're stranded in Selavroc?" asked Galli.

Bregit looked at her with a friendly chuckle. "We are far from Selavroc, after the cloud retreated, I grabbed you and brought us to the Cliffs of Iraz," said Bregit.

"The Cliffs of Iraz?" said Galli confused.

"Sanctuary of the winged beasts. Well, it was before the roots of the Drop Trees grew strong enough to reclaim their lands. You see before wizards rose from the Red Sea. Drop Trees were used as firewood and their leaves were ripped and torn into bearers of water. Iraz the Gray Falcon tore down every tree from here to the mountains and built nests for his winged beasts. But when Iraz died his cliffs were deserted for hundreds of cycles. In their neglect the roots and steams of the Drop Trees regenerated and rose from beneath the surface. Covering the cliffs and mountain but because of Iraz's honourability and services to Nocktar the cliffs title remained in his name to salute him," explained Bregit.

"I never knew. In Treforledge we never studied the creatures that existed before us," said Galli amazed by Bregit's story.

"Most believe it unnecessary to dwell into the past since it is already written and cannot be altered. Still, it is peaceful to know there was such a thing as peace. Perhaps one shade there maybe again," said Bregit sighing.

"Wishful thinking," thought Galli.

Getting enough feeling back in her arms Galli dug her hands into the soft brown earth and plunged hard enough that she was able to raise her back and sit against a nearby tree. The feeling of hard bark against her sore skin was just bearable enough to not whine.

''I would've used magic to heal you, but your injuries were the only proof I had to show you what your duel with the cloud had taken out of you. I was going to wait until you were healed to ask but I can tell by your refusal to lay down and allow your wounds to heal that patience isn't your virtue, so I'll get to the point....,''

''Wait!'' said Galli hesitantly.

Galli slowly raised her arms revealing the stones pierced into her palms. Wondering would Bregit know how they had come to be there because at this point, she was clueless.

Bregit's look was hard to read as he observed the stones with a keen interest. Galli could tell he was concentrating hard on what she had revealed to him. Bregit moved over and knelt in front of her, gently coiling his fingers round her wrists and studied the stones for many drops without saying a word, which made Galli feel on edge. Bregit released his hold of Galli's wrists and stood up. The shine from his yellow eyes reflected off her blue as a broad smile filled his ageing face with revived hope.

''Carka the Static may have saved us all,'' breathed Bregit.

''Carka, but he's dead,'' said Galli, looking at Bregit with concern for his mind state.

''Dead he maybe, but his legacy lives on.''

''How?''

''Through you.''

Chapter 28

One Step Ahead

The Bay of Bones had lost none of its mystique, every part of the island appeared the same since Lano had last stood upon its sands. The Lava Keeper looked upon the plinth of the bay with a saddened look as the memories of the fallen constantly reminding him of his previous visit. The Seven Coloured Army were lined in their usual formations, behind their king and coven chair holders. The king was centre stage nesting on a golden throne that sat on the back of an enslaved Pin-Far.

"The king I will dethrone by the end of this shade," Lano vowed to himself whilst looking at Nzer with hate. Lano signalled to his followers to stay in their positions while he negotiated terms with the king. Forming a guard of honour Lano passed through his front line and walked without fear into the centre of the battlefield his eyes firmly focused on the king who was applying the same instructions to his coloured generals. Some would assume that Lano and Nzer were about to engage in a duel by the stature of their approach, indeed it would be more practical and less life consuming to do so, but wars weren't won that way so instead both opponents walked with their chief weapons held firmly within their grasp as the they came face to face to give their terms of peace. But peace terms were far from the objective; this was a short negotiation that both creatures knew whatever each one offered in the terms of peace would be disregarded by the other. Still, these were the terms of war, terms that needed to be applied if the victor needed to rely on the support of the other lords. In Lano's situation, he needed to be recognized as a creature who could be trusted to oblige by the rules and not unwilling to uphold the simple procedures because of his hatred for his enemy.

"If ever there were a creature to stun me, I would say your resurrection almost reached the top," said Nzer in a degrading tone.

"Only a fool regards themselves unfamiliar with the full awareness of their senses. Wizards aren't quite as brilliant as they like to boast," Lano hissed politely.

What little joy residing within the king was wiped away, his smile became a snarl as his good eye twitched uncontrollably all the while Lano stayed calm and focused.

"Offer your ludicrous proposals and be done with it. Then I can draw nearer to crushing you. Again!" ordered the king with a hint of impatience in his voice.

"As king and ruler of the Lands of Light it would be selfish of an opposer to defy you the right of offering first, especially since it is your table we have gathered at," hissed Lano, bowing his head in curtsey.

The kings faint smile vanished; he was now inches from touching against Lano, his purple eye narrowed down to a slit, showing Lano the full scale the previous war had done to his face.

"Jests and schemes have gotten you far, too far. Still, I am glad you have made it here. For when I reduce your band of traitors to dust, you Lano and all that you've done will fade so far into history that nothing, even your name will be remembered,'' said the king sourly.

The king's insults washed over Lano like a wave, their ill effect cleansing all doubt niggling at his restraints. Forcing his urging temptations back, Lano forced a smile.

''Lay down your army, leave the Lands of Light and pass every creature on your way and apologize for cycles of shades of murder, blackmail, and theft. Those are my terms,'' hissed Lano, to the crying roar of his army.

The king scorned before turning his back to Lano, who in turn did the same. Smiling, Lano called after the king. ''I guess that concludes negotiations?''

Nzers pace lightened, on the verge of turning around he instead straightened his back and resumed his walk back to his coloured generals. Feeling he got the upper hand in that little spat Lano re-joined his ranks, looking along the front line of his army he caught the sorrow in the Viledirks eyes. Even now they still mourned for Kcor. For each furry face Lano's eyes met looked enraged with vengeance. Lano's however did not, and it wasn't because he didn't respect Kcor but because harsh lessons had awoken him to realizing that vengeance fuelled with desire wasn't an advantage in war but the perfect ingredient towards failure. It was the lust for killing that Lano used to ignite his first rebellion and the proof of his failings lay wasted on the bay he and his army now stood upon. He recalled how easy his army were ripped apart by the strength of one single spell. Wizards that his soldiers towered over were able to castrate his army and succumb him. It was then that Lano accepted that fighting wasn't the only way to win a battle and he now needed all the nerve he possessed to prove that theory right. And just as Lano had the battle plan prepared the coloured lords did something unexpected and climbed on their Pin-Fars and left their Lutizs on the front line in their wake. As the coloured wizards elevated to the safety of the clouds their Lutizs formed a line measuring themselves the width of the bay to show their growth in numbers.

''Cowards!'' growled Rac.

''The pawns are always first to fight Rac,'' hissed Lano calmly unmoved by this tactic. ''It is their shield against the rain, let's see them withstand the downpour I have coming for them,'' he hissed in a confident tone.

Taking three paces right and six steps forward Lano twirled on his heels, finding himself facing the thousands of creatures lined up and sworn to him. Every breath they took could be there last. Yet here they stood willing to die for his cause.

''Loyalty!'' hissed Lano looking at his followers with admiration. ''A trait entrusted among all creatures by our four sacred guardians. I was fortunate to have served under the greatest ruler of them all, Elan the Flamed Phoenix. He too valued truth, loyalty and above all fairness. Three qualities that have kept us bonded since the extinction of our guardians. This shade we renounce the old ways to eclipse the usurpers who claim we are here to serve their ruling!'' hissed Lano to his army.

The mystical creatures stamped their feet against the sand and roared at their enemies across the bay, the words of Lano sparking a fire within them that he prayed would not die out.

''I say not to myself but to you all, for those who have suffered and died to get us here, under the Orange Shaded sky and above the bones of our fallen. That we send these appraisers back from whence they came!'' bellowed Lano to the howling roars of his army.

The roars of the mystical creatures heightened the king's frustration. Not wanting to drag it out any longer Nzer raised his hand to the stunned looks of his generals. The clouds glowed brighter and then suddenly dimmed for a matter of drops until coloured beams hatched open the clouds. Streaming flowing rainbows soared and swerved in the air. As one by one they crashed against the bay, sending fissures throughout the dirt causing the ground to quake as flocks of Pin-Far riders launched from the clouds using the rainbows as their passage to the battlefield.

"They will strike us like lightning, quick and without caution. Picking us off bit by bit," called Gazzel watching on in fear.

"And trample us with the impact of their landing," added Rac in a taut voice.

"A new tactic, they've been busy in my absence," hissed Lano unconcerned. "Let us show them the meaning of the phrase fool me once, take out their eyes," he commanded.

Understanding his intentions both the Viledirks and Kurlezzias charged. Leaping above the Viledirks the Kurlezzia's led by Gazzel allowed the air to catch them and used it to lift their hooves high enough for a direct shot. Unsheathing their bamboos from their back straps, each Kurlezzia spit rapid thorns directly at the centre of the raining Pin-Fars eyes.

"CHARGE!" roared Lano.

The Viledirks leaped on all fours, letting roars of anger rear through their lungs. Their sentiment toward the loss of Kcor enraging their feline abilities making the Viledirks less aware of their natural capabilities and more in tune with their murderous instincts. The Pin-Fars were enraged by the stinging thorns piercing their eyes that they twisted and turned in the air, causing their rider to unbalance and fall a hundred feet to the welcoming arms of the Viledirks. Broken and outnumbered the fallen wizards were no match against such hated purpose, against the matched strength of the Kurlezzias and Viledirks the Pin-Far riders were ripped limb from limb until the bay was stained in their blood, but to Lanos shock the Lutiz's remained in line.

"Tricklet, you're up," hissed Lano not daring to waste a single drop.

The little trickster floated above the battlements with a cheeky grin etched along his face. Moving his fingers Tricklet soothed the blinded Pin-Fars with sprinkles of silver mist. Tricklets mist restored the Pin-Fars sight and bent their will to his commands. Smiling Lano looked to the clouds wanting to see clearly what effect his disposal of the Pin-Far riders had on the king and his generals. Their grim expressions satisfied him, but Lano remained cool and calm. Fully aware this was only phase one of many obstacles, soon the real battle will take fold and when that moment came, he needed to be strong willed to overcome the wizard's unpredictable manoeuvres. No cheers filled the bay, the previous encounter among the bay had injected realism not false dreams into Lano's army of creatures. Resuming their positions, the Kurlezzia's and Viledirks stood again by Lano's side. Tricklet now sole ruler of the Pin-Fars set a strong wall using the Pin-Fars impenetrable bodies as their shield and still the Lutiz's didn't stir, their non-involvement beginning to irritate Lano.

"Now let us see them rain their spells from the clouds," thought Lano smiling as he allowed himself a moment of respite.

The rainbows slithered back to their clouds, what replaced them were whirlwinds, tame but for a purpose. When the wind cleared, ranks of coloured wizards were left in its wake, thousands armed with staffs standing still awaiting their kings' command.

"Unexpected, they must want to finish this battle quick," said Gazzel.

"Like all who cannot see an opening, they try to force one with rash decisions and over whelming numbers. Be ready, they will be swift with their strikes," warned Lano.

"Then we shall be swifter," came Dreaquirlas voice.

Lano knew what Nzer was planning, an all-out assault, the one tactic they both knew would end in the wizard's victory. Commands to press forward were given by the coloured generals who pushed the Lutizs to charge, which indicated they were being controlled. They advanced quickly, their Malas spears in front.

"Dreaquirla, use your shock waves, shatter their spears," Lano commanded urgently.

Stretching her tiny wings, Dreaquirla let out a caterwauling scream unleashing powerful waves from her glowing chest. The appearance of Dreaquirlas attack did nothing to faulter the wizard's stance, quite the opposite. They embraced the electrical waves charging at them with calm as the Lutiz's fell to their knees and held their spears firmly into the cracked bay. Lano anticipated this, which gave him a single drops warning. Panicking, he sprinted with haste from the front line of his army, trying to put enough distance between his army and the wizards as bright beams rose from the tips of the Lutiz's spears, uniting them into a bright rainbow shield that withstood Dreaquirlas shock waves, their electrical current losing its effects due to the shields absorbing capabilities. Not only was the rainbow shield there to protect it was also in place to be offensive. Glowing brighter its reflective powers pushed Dreaquirlas shockwaves away rebounding them right back at their caster. Panicking Dreaquirla flapped her wings rapidly, trying to whirl her reflected waves away from her comrades. But her attempts were worthless against the now magically charged waves.

Lano knew the moment the rebounded waves collided with the wizards shield it would enhance the waves power, so that no power the mystical creatures had would block the rebounded shock waves slicing them to pieces.

"Underestimating us again," hissed Lano smiling with joy as he stood alone in the centre of the bay watching with a grin as Dreaquirlas rebounded waves charged at him.

Raising his rod of multi flames, he faced the rebounded waves. The emerald engraved in the rods centre shone brightest green, with a surging wave of his arm he let loose his rod that was now coated in a sizzling green flamed aura. Lano watched as his beloved weapon collided with the rebounded waves. The impact of both forces colliding sent fissures throughout the bay splitting the island into three separate lands.

Lanos attack had succeeded in destroying the incoming shock waves and shattering the wizards rainbow shield. Now with the wizards dazed and unsighted due to the dust surrounding the bay Lano knew this was the moment to strike. "Attack!" he shouted, not daring to miss this opportunity.

Pouncing, the Viledirks raged into the dust-filled bay with the Kurlezzias by their side. As the Rear Clars followed closely behind their grizzly appetite for flesh enhancing their urgency to get to the battlefield. Dazed and unaware the wizards struggled to overthrow the effects of the explosion. Streaks of light whizzed through the smoke due to the wizards blindly casting curses in a desperate attempt to stall the mystical creatures charge. The sheer might of the Viledirks hardened skin repelled the flowing curses, the Kurlezzias weren't so fortunate. Even with their speed and agility they were powerless against wizard's spells as each curse that made contact killed them instantly. The Rear Clars tossed their lifeless limbs into the crowd of wizards making use of what remained of them, hoping that the raining bodies of the Kurlezzias would trample the wizards they fell upon. Many fell to their deaths before reaching the disassembled army of wizards. The massacre had begun, heads of wizards spiralled in the air, limbs were cut, and cries of pain sang along his bay.

'Is this your desire Nzer? To watch us act like the animals you believe us to be?' thought Lano watching trios of wizards take down two injured Viledirks with swipes of their staffs.

Dreaquirla swooped in and out of the smoke, but even her skills were no use. Looking at him for instructions, he knew he could no longer hold back. With a curt nod she flew from the detached bay and out to the sea.

''Tricklet you're up,'' hissed Lano giving Tricklet the nod to enter the battle.

Tricklet cried a hoarse cry, charging on his manipulated Pin-Far the others followed. The Pin-Fars charged at speed their eight legs covering the ground like a leaf leaper among trees, crushing through wizards who believed tame shields could halt their charge, it was a brilliant piece of advice from Tip-Karp to take control of the Pin-Fars, Lano had to admit.

The fighting was evening itself out, from Lano's count he still held superior numbers to the wizards. His only misfortune were the many dead bodies of the Kurlezzias, their army were down to a handful. But then when the battle appeared to be tipping its balance in Lano's favour the clouds burst. Jets of light fell upon them like comets, Lano dived under a nearby rock and commanded his army to find shelter. The king had out done himself not only was his approach killing chunks of the mystical creatures, but they were also killing their own kind as wizards fell dead in front of the Lava Keeper who watched his army scatter for shelter and knew he had to take back control but without his rod to control his power he knew that unleashing his full power could kill many of his trusted advisors. But this was war and with war came death and that wasn't going to be Lano's faith. Rising from the rocks he lay beneath, flames appeared from every particle of his body. Casually he walked over the dead wizards' bodies making sure to ignite every cloak he passed. Wizards tried to launch themselves on him not fully understanding the flames surrounding him were no mere flames. They were the flames of his master Elan and trained to anticipate and shield him from harm. Rising above the bay, taking the air with him. Lano swirled himself around increasing the strength of his fire coat which heightening the radiant glow of his flames. Spreading his arms wide the flames flowing along them widened forming into crimson gold wings sheeted in flames. The heat radiating from his flames halted the fighting, each eye stalked him in wonder. Through the barking orders of the king the wizards folded and twisted into ash under the waves of his Flaming Nova technique as Lano directed the second wave of his attack to the wizard sitting amongst the clouds.

Many wizards were smart enough to evade his attack by using their staffs as lifts to shoot themselves into the air. ''Fools!'' thought Lano, watching them suspended in the air thinking their quick minds had saved them from death.

Red crimson flames lit the sky and plunged through every cloud in sight thus forcing the king and his generals to flee their sanctuary and reveal themselves. The Viledirks leaped to meet the generals and caught most of them off-guard and pummelled them to the ash covered bay. Feeling the weight of his fire coat leave his body; Lano in the moment wasn't ready to waste his energy maintaining such a draining technique. Knowing he would need his strength to finish what he had started so he landed back on the bay the effects of his Flaming Nova causing him to step back to catch his breath. Rac returned to his side with trickles of wizard's insides drooling down his face and mane. The look of savage there for Lano to see in full.

"My Lord, the Kurlezzia's are almost spent. Where is Ockrupver and Alacoma? We need reinforcements, we alone cannot hold back the next wave of attacks," growled Rac.

"Gather your army and return to the outskirts. Do it now! Lano hissed aggressively before Rac could argue.

Lano watched the clouds in search of the king. With two legions down and a complete onslaught backfiring Lano knew the king's frustration would soon be upon them. He walked around the fighting slashing aggressively at any foolish wizard who thought they would be the one to end the war by killing him. Lano reached the outskirts and sat on the broken rocks of the bay watching the Rear Clars prove why they were no push overs, their sheer strength was enough to parry numerous wizards aside with one mighty swipe of their enormous paws, Gazzel sat over his kin his losses beyond count while Tricklet was relishing in commanding the Pin-Fars to do his bidding. Rac and his Viledirks joined Lano seeing this as a rally the Rear Clars and Kurlezzia's rushed to his side.

"Why have we retreated to the out skirts? We are winning," called Rac spitting out blood from his rasping mouth.

"Be silent. Or our sufferings will have been for naught," hissed Lano still trying to catch his breath.

Comets soared from the points of the coven chair holder's staffs. The king joined by a batch of gliders launched from the clouds flying with pace toward Lano and his army. Tricklet intervened right on que. Using his puppet Pin-Fars to shield them from the raining comets. Lano pushed his way through the crowd of creatures. Manoeuvring his arms, he caused eruptions of molten lava to burst through the cracks of the bay which caused the Gliders to break from their formations and remain high in the sky. Rotating his arms counter clockwise and back again, Lano expertly linked the lava threads to form a barrier to prevent the kings aerial attack impacting him and his army. But a heavy gong sound reverberated through the bay and out to sea. Whatever it was shredded Lanos lava barrier to specks of ash. The coloured wizards had picked themselves up and reformed their ranks and were running at full pelt toward the army of mystical creatures. Watching the king and his band of Gliders draw near it felt like all living things had frozen to this exact moment as Lano watched Tricklet squeal as three wizards blasted him aside, releasing the Pin-Fars of his manipulation. Rac and his band of Viledirks were losing ground, been forced back by the brute strength of the wizard's combination of spells and combat skills. Silver threads slithered like serpents underneath the bay causing eruptions of rocks and stone to rise and fall leaving only the piece of land Lano, and his remaining army held untouched.

"The Bolts of Iraz," breathed Lano.

He could hear Rac's barks but couldn't understand a word he was saying the cries of pain blocking his hearing. The air become still, everywhere he looked were shadows of eager wizards drawing closer. The king led the charge from above while his soldiers led the charge on foot trapping the mystical creatures. There only escape now was death or to dive into the Red Sea. Not taking his gaze away from the approaching king as he drew closer to finishing his nemesis, Nzer retracted his arm behind his head with his long golden staff in clinched within his grasp the king's mouth opened, preparing the incantation that would surely end Lano. Feeling the softness of his cloak, Lano drew his free hand inside feeling round for the object he was gifted the shade he had made his mind up to challenge the wizards and reclaim his lands. Watching the kings mouth move Lano withdrew from inside his robes an oaked trident with three scarlet rubies engraved in its centre. Raising the trident high above his head, he watched the smile flicker from the king's expression. Digging his nails into the oaken strap wrapped around the tridents handle, Lano felt surging power flow through his body and broke free through the points of the trident as waves of swirling water rose from the plinths of the Red Sea to the shock of everyone present. The charging wizards were obliviated by the crashing waves of the Red Sea. Screams of shock flowed through the Bay of Bones as thousands of sky-blue muscular creatures burst through the waves led by the head of their order, Tarlbok the Aqua Chief.

The Viledirks roared in triumph, leaping to aid the Aqua Guardians as did the Rear Clars and Kurlezzias. The wizards who evaded the Aqua Guardians surprise attack were hooked lined and sunk by the accuracy of their pitch forks and tossed into the welcoming arms of Lano's army who savagely ripped them asunder. Feeling a rush of pride Lano walked over the battlements, passing Dreaquirla who was attending to Tricklet who seemed dazed by a wizard's spell. Wizards in all colours of the sky lay mutilated at his feet while the few dozen that were left were being rounded up by the Aqua Guardians. Walking without fear Lano searched the battlements for the fallen king and found him under a pile of collapsed rocks that pinned his legs deep under the cracked ground. Unable to free himself from bondage Lano stood over the injured king. Their eyes met with the same hatred etched along the kings' fading lines. 'Even near death he was unwilling to admit defeat,' thought Lano embracing the warm delight flowing through his body.

"I warned you to kill me when you had the chance, now your failure will be your undoing," hissed Lano smiling.

"You've won nothing," coughed Nzer. "The Golden Kingdom will stand long after my passing and long after yours, wizards will return and you, Lano will perish under the rocks you once called home," Nzer laughed faintly.

"I should thank you. My shades spent in the dry lands prepared me for this precise moment and trust me my old nemesis, tearing your kingdom layer after layer was my main priority and I knew the perfect way to do it," hissed Lano.

"You lie," coughed Nzer who tried pulling himself up, but the rocks weight was too much to overthrow and without his staff the king was powerless to do anything but lay and listen to the cries of his dying kin.

"I'll allow my actions to speak for themselves," said Lano seriously.

Looking past the clouds the perfect picture came into view as an explosion with such impact whooshed through the skies. Pillars, stones, and rubble fell from the sky and crashed landed into the Red Sea. Cheers filled the Bay of Bones as the Viledirks, Rear Clars, and Aqua Guardians raised their fists in victory roaring their fiercest cries to the fall of the Golden Kingdom and the end of the wizards.

"Do you see the depths of your failure now?" hissed Lano leaning over the king with glee.

"Im...poss...ible," cried Nzer, the pain of his wounds reflecting through his agonizing disbelief.

"Impossible towers above you, impossible has defeated you, and impossible will reign far longer than you," Lano hissed with venom.

Clenching the tridents handle firmly, he impaled the king through his chest making sure the sharp spears broke through every bone before cutting through his back. Patiently he watched, waiting for the life to leave the king's eyes. The joy of seeing the end of the one that caused him and his followers so much pain, shredded shades of weight from the Lava Keepers shoulders. Extracting the trident from Nzers chest, he embraced the joy, allowing it to come out of hiding and flow over the articles he had hidden his feelings behind for so many shades. And for the first shade in cycles Lano breathed freely, replenishing lungsful of sea air cleared his mind which allowed him to accept his toughest challenge fulfilled. Walking without caution, he found Tarlbok alongside his chieftains congratulating them with words of praise.

''It is done,'' said Lano greeting Tarlbok with a low bow.

''The battle is won lord Lano. The war is not, many wizards fled before we could round them up,'' said Tarlbok his voice tough.

''The coven will run and hide like the cowards they are their escape does not cause concern. My only dread now is the princes, they were absent during battle. Which means they had business somewhere more important than defending their kingdom,'' Lano hissed sternly.

''Maybe they have abandoned their oaths to protect their own lands, they wouldn't be the first lord of land to sit back from a battle to ensure the safety of their own kingdom,'' argued Tarlbok.

''You know as well as I do what the mantle of king of the Golden Kingdom means. You are also wise to know what that position grants,'' Lano reminded Tarlbok, his crypted words directed only for the Aqua Chief to understand.

''I am. The position has been recited many shades to me, even if what you say is true none among them would hold such a prize. Eventually the remaining wizards would try use their prize as a rally to gather followers,'' said Tarlbok.

''Exposing themselves. Rest assured my friend; I will have them well dealt with before that happens,'' Lano promised.

''How?''

''When I have honoured our fallen, I will return to Saradice, it would be welcome to have you as my honoured guest and whilst you're there we can discuss the precautions needed to ensure that we never again fall under the ruling of wizards,'' Lano gestured.

''Honour your dead, I shall wait for you with a tribe of my best guard along the shores. Be warned lord Lano, you would do well not to keep me waiting,'' warned Tarlbok ending their conversation on a sour note.

''You will be needing this back,'' Lano called, holding out the Aqua chief's trident.

''Ah, yes. The price of our arrangement, use it to signal your return to Saradice where we can conclude our alliance.''

''I'll do that,'' hissed Lano while watching the Aqua Guardians take their leave receiving praise from every creature they passed. The Aqua Guardians left the bay. Reaching the charred outskirts, leaving the same way they came. In a burst of swirling waves.

Dreaquirla, Gazzel, Rac, Rizz, and Tricklet stood in front of him, all weary from battle but wearing looks of pride that gave Lano an overwhelming feeling that he could not explain.

''You all fought valiantly, for that I uphold your oaths fulfilled, the Lands of Light is won, now we must ensure they will never again be taken from us!'' Lano hissed to the nodded agreements of his council.

"Good, now gather your fallen comrades, and march to Saradice. There they will be honoured, I will be with you on the rise of next shade," Lano said delicately.

Lano walked over the bay crossing many sand patches before entering the cold chilly mountain that had remained silent since his banishment. Placing his hand against a rock it glowed red before splitting down the middle, Lano walked casually down a brightened hallway and with a flick of his wrist another door of silver opened revealing a staircase that led deep beneath the surface. Lanos very aura gave new life to the mountains core, and when he reached the end stairs, he looked over the stone bridge delighted to see flowing lava again flourish through his former volcano.

A chilling vibe in the air came to Lanos senses as a creature in jaded colour skin entered the volcano. It walked on two legs its waist covered in long leaves and it wore these thin vines along its body that was barely visible because of the length of its thick black hair. When their eyes met Lanos spine shuddered the creatures usual red glow had been replaced by envy green.

"You recovered your strength, I am glad, I take it the wizards are dead along with Tip-Karp," said Lano.

With a twist of its wrist a head appeared in the creature's hand, it held it by its hair revealing to Lano the head of Tip-Karp whose eyes were rolled back while stains of blood covered his mouth. Lano smiled and lifted his arm and with a flex of his fingers a sphere glowing ball lifted from the lava pit and settled in his grasp. Looking at the stone Lano handed it to the green skinned creature who tossed Tip-Karps head into the lava pit before taking the stone from Lano with glee.

"The power of that stone grants the wielder unlimited power, as a guardian I am unable to access it due to my sealed promise to Elan, but destruction isn't your goal in all of this, no, I sense you seek the other three, if that is your purpose I can no longer help, the wizards took the others many cycles ago and has them hidden I know not where," Lano hissed eyeing the creature for any sign that he was close to knowing its plans.

But once in possession of the fire stone the creature simply walked away from Lano and before it left, Lano called after it, the creature stopped when at the silver door.

"Will you come for me once your mission is complete?" Lano asked not daring to blink.

The green skinned creature smiled revealing its forked teeth as its eyes glowed scarlet red, before vanishing in a burst of black smoke, leaving Lano to feel at loss when he'd just achieved the greatest victory of his life.

Printed in Great Britain
by Amazon